# Sisters of
# Misery

# Sisters of Misery

## Megan Kelley Hall

KENSINGTON PUBLISHING CORP.
http://www.kensingtonbooks.com

KENSINGTON BOOKS are published by

Kensington Publishing Corp.
119 West 40th Street
New York, NY 10018

All Kensington Titles, Imprints, and Distributed Lines are available at special quantity discounts for bulk purchases for sales promotion, premiums, fund-raising, and educational or institutional use.

Special book excerpts or customized printings can also be created to fit specific needs. For details, write or phone the office of the Kensington special sales manager: Kensington Publishing Corp., 119 West 40th Street, New York, NY, 10018, attn: Special Sales Department, Phone: 1-800-221-2647.

Kensington and the K logo Reg. U.S. Pat. & TM Off.

ISBN-13: 978-0-7582-5830-4
ISBN-10: 0-7582-5830-5

First Trade Paperback Printing: August 2008
First Mass Market Printing: August 2010

10  9  8  7  6  5  4  3  2  1

Printed in the United States of America

*To my little ray of sunshine,*
*my creative inspiration,*
*my fairy princess,*
*Piper Elizabeth*

## Acknowledgments

While there are many people to thank, I have to begin by thanking my parents first and foremost. They raised me in a house filled with thousands of books, instilling me with an immense appreciation and love for literature. I could not have written a single word without their love, support, and encouragement to follow my dreams of being a writer. They made me believe that anything was possible and that is a gift that carries me through each day.

To my mother, Gloria Kelley, thank you for your wisdom, your love, your strength, and for being the most giving and self-less person I have ever known. You inspire me to be a better person (and a better mother). I am consistently awed by your abundant supply of caring and generosity, even when times are tough.

To my father, Jim Kelley, I thank you for passing along your creative and artistic genes. Who would have thought that so many readings of *I Packed My Trunk* when I was a toddler would have set my career as a writer in motion? Thank you for carrying the Mickey Mouse cards for all those years. I think that they were indeed lucky.

To my sister, Jocelyn Maeve Kelley, you are my biggest cheerleader, my strongest defender, and my best friend. You fill all of our lives with boundless enthusiasm and happiness. Even though you are my little sister, I look up to you (no short jokes, please) more and more each day. I'm so happy to be working with you and Mom in Kelley & Hall Book Publicity, and I thank you for coming up with the idea of doing something with our love of books and authors. It's definitely been a fun (and sometimes crazy) ride.

To my brother, Connor Patrick Kelley, your knowledge of books and writers and literature is astounding. You put all of us to shame with your powerful and unwavering love of books. You are the dark horse who will one day—quietly and effortlessly—write the Great American Novel.

I would also like to thank my agent, Elisabeth Weed of Weed Literary, and my editor at Kensington, Danielle Chiotti, for making my dreams a reality. You both made Cordelia, Maddie, Kate, and the rest of the Sisters of Misery real for me. Your endless devotion to making every word, every character, and every plot point sing is more than any writer could ever dream for in an agent and editor. Elisabeth, thank you for taking a chance on me and my vision and helping me find a home for my debut novel. Danielle, thank you for taking my story and working tirelessly with me until it was ready to be shared with the world. I am forever indebted to you both.

It is also important to thank the following people: to Professor Steven Millhauser, I feel so fortunate to have taken so many fiction writing classes with you at Skidmore College, and yet I'm still searching for that magical well that you seem to have unlimited access to for your stories. I hope to someday find it and infuse my own work with it. To my friend and client Michael Palmer, thank you for the warning. The words WRITING IS HARD, BE FEARLESS will stay over my computer, as will the ingredients for Rhinoceros Stew. I really appreciated your advice when I was in my first stages of trying to get published, and I'm happy to have had the chance to work with you promoting your novels. I would also like to thank Doug Mendini, who became a friend long before I joined the Kensington family, Kristine Mills-Noble for her amazing cover design, Christiana Sahl for her insightful edits, my in-house publicist Adeola Saul, and, of course, Kelley & Hall Book Publicity for your tireless efforts in promoting my book.

To my husband and best friend, Eddie Hall, thank you for being so supportive of my writing career from the very start. Most men would have been scared off by their twenty-something girlfriend writing about parenting and childcare for magazines long before there was even a proposal in sight. And yet you stood by me, giving me the time and space to write and follow my dream of becoming a published novelist. You have also been an amazing father to the most important person in our lives, Piper Elizabeth. Eddie, you've been there through the most challenging times and have always given me more love and support than I ever thought possible. You and Piper truly are the loves of my life.

And, of course, to Piper, who inspires me every day. Thank you for coming into our world and making us appreciate the little things in life we had all taken for granted. You bring sunshine to our lives and continuously amaze us with your artistic, independent spirit and gentle, inquisitive nature. From the time when you were a 2.5 pound preemie—with your daddy's wedding band fitting over your foot—to today when you are one of the healthiest and most beautiful five-year-olds I've ever known, you make each moment magical and filled with wonder. I write these stories for you, so that one day you'll be as proud of your mommy as I am of my baby girl.

According to the *Illustrated Encyclopedia of Divination* the word "rune" means *hidden, whisper, mystery* or *secret*. Originating as the written language and letters of the Norsemen of northern Europe (dating back to the time of the Vikings in 800 A.D.), rune stones were often associated with magic, divination, and witchcraft. The runes were never the basis of a spoken language, but through their written use, they were believed to be powerful magical symbols, each linked to a god and a specific meaning. As Christianity spread throughout Europe, runes were eventually banned from the Church. Rune casters (typically women) quickly became associated with paganism and ultimately, witchcraft. To speak or write the name of a rune was thought to summon the powers of nature and the universe. Many believed that runes were a way of interacting with both the spirit and the living world.

> *Runes were upon his tongue,*
> *As on the warrior's sword.*
> —*Longfellow*

# Prologue

There are some girls who have everything.

And not just the ones who are born with silver spoons in their mouths.

Some girls are born with an intangible, magnetic aura: something that radiates beneath their flawless skin.

You know who they are: the Cleopatras, the Marilyn Monroes. They are the present day sirens—girls who have the power to transfix any male who comes their way.

Then there are the jealous ones.

Resenting their effortless beauty, the jealous ones—like the Evil Queen who gave Snow White the poisoned apple—will stop at nothing to destroy these special girls—girls like Cordelia.

Yet these are only stories, fairy tales. Sometimes, in real life, there are no happy endings. The glass slipper shatters; the poison spreads quickly.

This is a real story, and Maddie Crane played her part.

She was careless because she was consumed by fear.

Cordelia is gone.

*And Maddie fears she may be next.*

ജ

*The outline of Cordelia's body hangs slack against the tree perched high up on the sand dunes of Misery Island. The clank of the buoys in the distant harbor are part of the dawn's symphony of sounds that spread across the island—the screech of the gulls, the gush of waves, the groaning of boats as they strain against moorings. Cordelia's bloodied and bruised body is barely discernable through the gauze of the early morning mist.*

What have they done to you? *Maddie cries, making her way across the clearing to her cousin's side. The bonfire has died down to embers, occasionally throwing a spark or a hiss. They are trapped together in the eerie halflight between night and day. Everyone else has fled, returning to their houses as if nothing bad has happened.*

*But it has.*

*While the others run off into the mist under the cover of darkness, Maddie secretly remains on the island, tending to the scars, burns, and welts Cordelia had acquired through the night's events. Gingerly, she plucks the sharp blood-soaked reeds from under her cousin's blackened fingernails, brushing away the mud and sticks caked into the singed strands of Cordelia's copper-red hair.*

*The grimy rags that secure Cordelia to the birch tree are taut as tourniquets. Stepping closer to Cordelia, Maddie's almost afraid to untie her, fearful that her cousin will blame her for all that has happened.*

You saved me, *Madeline whispers.* I understand that now.

*Cordelia has taken her place as the Chosen One, saving Maddie from that fate.*

It's all my fault, *Maddie's voice breaks as she sees no flicker of life in Cordelia; her hair rises and falls with each briny gust of wind that sweeps across the shore of the small island of Misery.*

*But Maddie knows the rules—the ones created by the Sisters of Misery long ago—and if Cordelia is released, Maddie's punishment will be far worse. The hair on the back of her neck prickles, and fear tightens across her chest as she senses another presence on the island.*

*Are they watching?*

*Without another thought for the consequences, Maddie begins pulling at the knotted ties, biting at them when her nails start to fail. The bitter taste of dirt mixes with salty sweat and the metallic tang of blood. The makeshift handcuffs aren't giving an inch, no matter how much she shreds and tears at them. Soft as sand, voices travel up from Cat Cove.*

We have to hurry, *Maddie cries.* Cordelia, open your eyes!

*Terrified, Maddie begins to tug and yank at her cousin's arms and legs, prying them away from the tree. But it seems that the more she pulls, the tighter Cordelia sticks to the aged birch, the white papery bark clinging to her pale skin, the thick gnarled roots underfoot wrapping around the girl's legs like snakes. Then incredibly, the tree springs to life and begins devouring Cordelia, pulling her deep into its core. Maddie falls backward, horrified and stunned into silence. In an instant, she hears others coming up along the shoreline, dragging their schooners up the beach.*

We have to go now, *Maddie pleads, trying not to stare directly at the surreal transformation taking place in front of her.*

I think they drugged me. I-I think I'm seeing things. I

can't . . . can't . . . I won't leave you. Not again, *Maddie shouts.*

*Her sobs are drowned out by indifferent gulls overhead.*

*And then, just as quickly as Cordelia had been sucked into the tree that once held her captive, she returns to her original form as a bruised and battered girl barely clinging to life. Maddie inches closer to her, still reeling from what she has just seen, consumed with fear.*

*Bleary-eyed, Maddie watches and waits as the sun begins its ascent into the sky.*

You're too late, *Cordelia says, snapping her head upright, and her eyes, once the loveliest shade of lavender blue, are now hollow and black.*

I'm already dead.

*Maddie screams as sirens slice through the breaking of dawn.*

&

Maddie Crane swung furiously at her alarm clock. And just as swiftly as the morning came upon her, the nightmare mercifully slipped away.

# Chapter 1

## JERA

## YEAR

*Anticipation and Excitement Before a
Major Turning Point in Life*

## AUGUST

"Isn't that girl up yet? Today, of all days, she decides to sleep in. I don't care if it's summer vacation. She needs a good dose of work ethic, or else she's going to be a bum just like her father."

Maddie could hear her mother's muffled words as she ranted and stormed around the kitchen. Her nightmares were getting worse and more detailed; she'd been waking up more exhausted than when she went to sleep the night before. Ever since Madeline Crane learned that her cousin would be moving in with them, Cordelia LeClaire had appeared in her dreams again and again.

After showering and drying her hair, she padded down the uneven staircase to the kitchen. Her grandmother, Tess, was clad in a faded bathrobe, and was in a high state of amusement watching Maddie's mother.

"Good afternoon, Madeline. So glad you could make it up in time for lunch," Abigail Crane scolded without turning to look at her daughter. She continued to swipe the impeccably clean counter even though breakfast had long since been cleaned up. Maddie rolled her eyes, but Tess winked and patted the chair next to her, motioning for Maddie to join her at the kitchen table.

"Mom, it's only ten o'clock, and it's going to be a long day," Maddie said, sighing heavily and trying not to laugh as Tess rubbed her fingers together in a tsk-tsk gesture.

"Well, let's get one thing straight," Abigail continued her tirade. "Breakfast always has been and always will be at eight AM sharp. There are some things that I refuse to let slide around here. If you miss it, then you have to fend for yourself. I don't need to deal with any more aggravation than I already have. Understood?"

Maddie's mother hadn't adjusted well to the news that her flighty older sister Rebecca was moving back to Hawthorne and would be living with them at Ten Mariner's Way. The grand old Victorian belonged to Tess, and Maddie and Abigail were technically guests, though they'd lived there for most of Maddie's life. So when Tess gave word that Rebecca and her daughter, Cordelia, were moving in, Abigail didn't have a say in the matter, something that she apparently wasn't handling very well.

Maddie imagined that this was what it would be like to have Martha Stewart as a mother—living with someone with an unyielding desire for perfection and control.

And with that, Abigail stormed out of the kitchen, leaving Maddie and Tess looking sheepishly at each other like two bad little girls getting scolded by their teacher.

Maddie cringed, knowing that her mother's mood was only going to get worse once Cordelia and Rebecca arrived later that day. While Maddie typically dreaded field hockey practice on the hot, sticky days of August, it was a great excuse to get away from the house and all the last minute preparations for their relatives.

Maddie gathered her things and got ready to head down to the field for practice. She bent over to give her grandmother a kiss on the cheek and whispered, "Are you going to be okay with her today?"

"Humph," Tess snorted, fighting a smile that tugged at the sides of her mouth. "I've tackled bigger battles than this in my day."

∞

Preseason field hockey practices were always tough, but this one seemed especially brutal. Kate Endicott had naturally been chosen team captain of Hawthorne Academy's junior varsity squad, and she was determined to beat the school's varsity team in an upcoming scrimmage. Maddie jogged down to meet the girls and waved excitedly to her best friends Hannah, Darcy, Bridget, and, of course, Kate. Maddie didn't remember actually choosing these girls as friends; they were just part of the fabric that had made up her everyday life for as long as she could remember.

Growing up, Abigail Crane had made certain Maddie's social calendar was filled with every opportunity that she felt she had been denied as a girl. Horseback riding with Darcy Willett, ballet and piano lessons with Bridget Monroe, tennis tournaments with the Endicotts, and golf outings with Hannah Sanders—if there was a lesson to be taken or a social opportunity to attend, Abigail made sure that Maddie was there. But what her mother didn't realize was that there was a darker side to their friendship. Things that they did together that bonded them as "sisters" as well as friends. Bonds that could never be broken without paying the consequences.

"Get out there, Crane," Bronwyn Maxwell called. She was

also a Hawthorne Academy alum and a recent college graduate. Bronwyn was the all-time field hockey champion of Hawthorne Academy, and the school had offered her the chance to lead their teams to victory once again, this time as a coach. Hawthorne Academy always took good care of its own.

Maddie pulled on her cleats, the sweat already dripping down her back. She would be completely spent later on that day when her relatives were scheduled to move in.

*Ugh,* she sighed, exhausted by just thinking about it. After running a couple of warm-up laps, Maddie collapsed onto the fresh-mown grass, feeling the prickles of the blades against her steaming skin.

"Crane, you loser, get up." Kate laughed as she dropped down next to her. She stretched her toned legs out in front of her and arched her back like a cat, allowing her long, honey-blond hair to graze the ground. She looked seductively over her shoulder, knowing she had the boys on the Hawthorne soccer team practicing on the next field as an audience. "Oh, I see, you're checking out the lawn boy. He's pretty cute for a townie."

Maddie looked up to see a dark-haired guy riding a lawn mower on the other side of the field. His shirt was off, revealing a deep tan and sinewy muscles. Maddie hadn't even noticed him, but he seemed to be watching them intently. "Maddie and the lawn boy sittin' in a tree . . ." Kate sang, giggling.

"Not today, Kate," Maddie warned, hoping to fend off Kate's usual bitchy remarks. She'd grown accustomed to Kate's taunts and teasing—even expected them as part of her daily ritual—but for some reason, she knew she couldn't handle them today. Not with the craziness going on in her own house. Today, of all days, she just couldn't deal.

"What's the matter, Maddie? Feeling a little hungover? Didn't you have fun at my party?" Kate asked innocently.

Just then Hannah, Bridget, and Darcy jogged over. "I was just asking Maddie if she liked the party last night. Did you girls have fun?"

They all giggled. Something was up.

The party was just like all the others Kate threw. Drunken guys in baseball caps, girls in overpriced outfits, tons of beer and alcohol, and the inevitable "get thrown into the pool fully dressed." Then everyone would either skinny-dip in the ocean or get more wasted in the hot tub. It was like there was an un-written script that every Endicott party had to adhere to.

"Kate had fun."

"Lots of it."

More giggles and hushed laughter.

Bronwyn saw them sitting down and blew her whistle. "Get up, you lazy bitches. I need to see some hustle out there."

Maddie grabbed hold of Kate's wrist before they headed back down to the field for dribble practices. "What happened last night?"

"Trevor and I finally did it," Kate said, smiling as if she had really expected Maddie to believe that she hadn't lost her virginity long ago. Maddie clearly remembered the night it happened. It was one of those parties at Fort Glover where the older guys ended up preying on the "new blood." Kate got so wasted that she gave it up to her older sister Carly's boyfriend on the dirt floor of the old fort. Maddie remem-bered warning her not to go off with Carly Endicott's boyfriend that night, but Kate hissed that she knew what she was doing and that she could take care of herself. "I guess you can say I'm no longer part of The V Club."

Maddie rolled her eyes. Honestly, the V Club? Kate had always acted as if she was the most worldly and the oldest of the group. Back when they were all first initiated into the Sisters of Misery, a select group of girls from Hawthorne

Academy, Kate was so anxious to please the older "sisters" that she would do anything to be accepted as one of them. There was never a question that Kate would be part of the clique. Her older sister Carly made sure she was inducted into the not-so-secret society of girls who were known to have the best parties, date the cutest boys, and hold secret meetings out on Misery Island. Maddie wasn't sure how far back their group had begun and it wasn't something she would ever question. Like the monstrous Ravenswood Asylum at the center of town, it was something that was always there, bigger and more powerful than any of them. But once inside, you never got out.

Kate, not wanting to be the only girl her age in the group (and the sole target of the older girls' taunts), brought Maddie and her other friends into the mix. This pleased Abigail to no end, but Tess grew more and more concerned every time Maddie took off with her group of friends. Even though she'd had playdates with the girls since grade school, taking ballet lessons, sailing courses, anything and everything that Abigail could sign Maddie up for, she still felt like an outsider. It was as if she didn't really "know" them, and they would never understand her. Maddie just assumed that's how all friendships were—on the surface and for show.

"So Trevor's not with Nicole anymore?" Maddie had heard that Kate's on-again, off-again boyfriend had been hooking up with another girl in their grade recently. Kate obviously felt she needed to get the upper hand and win Trevor back by sleeping with him.

Kate looked out at the field, smirking as Nicole ran up and down the field, going through the rigorous drills. "Like he was ever serious with that fat ass?"

Nicole looked as though she'd been crying, her eyes red and puffy. But it wasn't enough for Kate to take her boyfriend. Nicole's red and puffy eyes had a matching puffy lip by the end of the practice after Kate "accidentally" smashed into her head-on. It was just par for the course for Kate Endicott. No one ever got in her way.

# Chapter 2

## GEBO

## THE GIFT

*Partnerships, Relationships, and Unions Are Reached*
*Through Sacrifice and Balance*

After a particularly grueling field hockey practice, Maddie was dead tired. Her coltish legs felt like rubber, and her long brown hair was sticking to the back of her neck and the sides of her face. The humidity was almost too much to bear as she trudged toward home, but she could always count on the extraordinarily icy Victorian to cool her down once she passed through the front door.

When Tess had informed them a few weeks earlier about her plans for Rebecca and Cordelia's arrival from the West Coast, it didn't seem set in stone. Rebecca was known for planning a return visit to Hawthorne, only to end up in some distant, exotic location. But this time, it seemed like the real deal. They were, without question, moving to Hawthorne, and Abigail was, in Tess's words, *fit to be tied.*

"Mark my words, we are not going to let them spoil everything I have worked for," Abigail hissed when she first learned of their homecoming. From the beginning, she was dead set against the return of her sister.

Maddie, however, was ecstatic. She had grown up hearing

stories—ones that had almost a fairytale-like appeal—about the eccentric and willful Aunt Rebecca who fell in love with Simon LeClaire, an ornithologist (Abigail always referred to him as "the crazy bird guy") who had come through Hawthorne conducting research on the migrating pattern of brown-speckled sandpipers. Abigail always said it was one of the happiest days of her life when her newly pregnant sister and her boyfriend had taken off for the West Coast in search of a warmer climate and the endangered Snowy Plover. Maddie, on the other hand, always wished that Rebecca would return with her daughter Cordelia. It would have been like growing up with a sister, despite her mother's insistence that Sisterhood was highly overrated.

It wasn't until a few months after Uncle Simon's death that they learned of Rebecca's plans to come home. Abigail used every opportunity to show Tess how small the house was, how expensive it would be to have two more people in the house, how difficult it would be for Rebecca to readjust to life in Hawthorne after so many years away. But Tess wouldn't have it. They were as welcome in her home as Maddie and Abigail were, and she never failed to remind Abigail whose house Ten Mariner's Way really was.

Tess had brought Maddie and Abigail in after Malcolm Crane deserted them and they had nowhere else to go. Abigail used to run around behind him, picking up the evidence of his destructive outbursts, formulating excuses for the noise if the neighbors dared to mention the commotion the next day. But no matter how hard she tried, she just couldn't put the broken pieces of the family back together again. Now Malcolm existed only as a drunken, bullish figure in the recesses of Maddie's early childhood memories.

"It's a good thing that he took off when he did," Tess often replied when Maddie asked about her deadbeat dad. "If he ever pulled any of that nonsense with you that he pulled with your mother, he'd be six feet under by now." Maddie loved hearing her frail grandmother talk about how she'd protect Maddie against the big brute of a father who had left them long ago. Abigail, on the other hand, was only concerned about town gossip. She kept their dire financial situation a secret, guarded it like a sore. Coming from a wealthy seaport town on Boston's North Shore and having a prestigious last name like Crane, they had everyone fooled. Abigail made sure of that.

∞

Despite the aloof coolness Maddie tried to maintain around her friends—Kate especially—she could barely contain her excitement about the arrival of Rebecca and Cordelia. As Maddie approached the house, Abigail came outside in a huff, her thin brown hair swept tightly into a severe bun, her long face pulled into its usual grimace. Tess stood next to Abigail her face, in stark contrast, brimming with excitement.

"So, are they here yet?" Maddie asked her mother.

Abigail's body visibly stiffened. The blades of her shoulders twitched beneath her Talbots linen tank dress. She stood erect, spine perfectly straight, head held high.

"Just get inside already," Abigail Crane said in an exasperated tone. "Our *guests* have already arrived." Abigail was obviously hoping their stay wouldn't be permanent, and from the stories Maddie had heard about Rebecca, she didn't seem to stay rooted in one place for too long. But Maddie had a feeling this time would be different, and she hoped her premonitions were true.

Maddie moved past her mother and threw her arms around her grandmother's frail body. "Hi, Grams. So they're really here? Can you believe it? Are you excited?"

"You have no idea," Tess said brightly. The wrinkles in

her face deepened as she smiled widely. She was so tiny, fragile like the porcelain dolls Maddie's mother had given her as a child. Maddie could look at them but was never allowed to touch. "All my girls back together again. It's simply magical!"

"Don't get too comfortable," Abigail warned, ignoring her mother. "Remember, we're going to the Hamilton's for a cookout, and I'd like you to look presentable." She eyed her daughter up and down, silently appraising her appearance, and then added, "Well, the best that you're capable of. Don't worry. We're not bringing *them*."

Maddie followed her mother's gaze up to the guest room window of the old Victorian and caught a glimpse of a pale girl's face peering out the window. The moment they made eye contact, the red-haired girl vanished from the window, leaving the curtains fluttering.

Tess nodded toward the house. "Rebecca is getting ready for the farmer's market since we're going to be fending for ourselves for dinner tonight," she said. "Cordelia's upstairs in the guest room. It will be a nice change for you to get to know some real folk, not just those uppity girls your mother's always forcing on you." Maddie's mother threw her hands up in the air and stormed inside.

Despite Abigail's insistence that they were the "right" friends for Maddie—the type of friends that would open up more social circles to all of them—Tess wasn't fooled. She always seemed to know what nasty tricks they had up their sleeves—even before they did anything. Tess had always encouraged Maddie to be more independent, to stand up for herself more. Maddie tried, but what her grandmother didn't realize was that sometimes, it was just easier to go with the flow than risk Kate's wrath.

"Go on and introduce yourself," Tess said. "You're really going to like her; I can just feel it."

Kissing her grandmother on the cheek, Maddie hoped that she was right.

Then, as Maddie pushed through the expansive front door, Tess whispered, "The cycle is just beginning." Her grandmother's words sent a ticklish feeling up Maddie's spine as she trudged up the narrow staircase.

೪

In the guest room, Maddie found a girl sitting cross-legged on the bed, her long, red hair spilling over her shoulders and trailing down her back. She dangled a crystal necklace from her slender hand, swinging it back and forth in front of her face. Her wide blue eyes fixated on the makeshift pendulum as if in a trance. Cordelia looked as if she didn't belong in this century, let alone this town. She had a haunted, almost unearthly look about her. Solemn yet regal, like the black and white photos of historical royalty. She didn't look like she had ties to Hawthorne, but more like a descendent from the lost Russian princess Anastasia, the one who was never found after the fall of the Romanov dynasty.

Even though they had moved from California, her creamy skin was porcelain pale and flawless, as if she never saw the light of day. Her upturned nose and full lips made her look like a cross between a pixie and a princess. She was shockingly beautiful, something that Maddie hadn't expected. Though she'd seen pictures through the years—Christmas cards and vacation shots—her exquisite beauty somehow had never been translated through the lens.

Maddie watched for several moments as the girl's eyes followed the dangling stone.

"What are you doing?" she finally asked.

"Hypnotizing myself," the girl said flatly.

"Why?"

"Why not?" Cordelia answered without looking away from the crystal. "This will help me harness my psychic powers, give me something to do in this strange little town."

Maddie raised a skeptical eyebrow. How could Cordelia think that *this* was an unusual town? Obviously, she hadn't taken a good look at herself. Maddie turned to leave, suddenly deflated.

"Well," Maddie sighed, disheartened, and said flatly, "Welcome to the neighborhood."

"Thanks. Thrilled to be here." With that, Cordelia dropped her necklace onto the floor and walked into the bathroom, closing the door behind her. Maddie looked at the bathroom door, shook her head, and retreated downstairs, trying to quell her feelings of disappointment. She'd already had to deal with being friends with the most beautiful girls in the school, but now, her model-perfect cousin was just one more person to be overshadowed by. And the worst part was, Cordelia didn't even seem to like her.

ಹಿ

Tess convinced Abigail to allow Maddie to skip the cookout that evening. At first, Abigail objected, but she knew that once the old woman set her mind on something, nothing but an act of God would change it. Maddie was secretly thrilled to be let off the hook. It was just one less social event that she was forced to fake smiles at and endure boring conversations all night. When Rebecca asked if she'd like to join them for a picnic on the beach, Maddie jumped at the chance.

Abigail grabbed Maddie firmly by the arm as she followed her aunt and cousin out the front door. "Don't worry," she whispered. "You won't have to miss out on any upcoming social obligations. Let's just let this one slide to keep your grandmother happy and off my back for a change, okay?"

As they walked down to the water's edge, mixing with the other evening beachgoers, Cordelia and her mother stuck out like wild tiger lilies in a field of plain green shrubs. With their long crimson hair hanging down their backs, their pale, almost translucent skin, and skirts that swirled and gathered as they walked, they drew attention and curiosity from the Patagonia-clad onlookers. This was a town where the men and women didn't dress that differently from each other. Khaki shorts, polo shirts, and boat shoes during the summer; in the fall, Oxford shirts and fleece vests. And when the temperature dropped to single digits, out came the cable knit sweaters and down ski parkas from trunks all around Hawthorne, carrying the sharp, woody scent of cedar.

In contrast, Rebecca and Cordelia looked like they had stepped right out of a fairy tale. Consequently, the women they passed smiled politely, but Maddie knew they were seething behind their tight smiles and steely gray eyes. But Rebecca and Cordelia didn't notice, or if they noticed, they obviously didn't care.

Tess and Maddie paced a few steps behind their new houseguests, who were so caught up in taking in the sights of Hawthorne, chirping and laughing as they toted their picnic basket overflowing with food from the farmer's market, that they hardly noticed the serious discussion taking place behind them.

"Rebecca and Cordelia are starting a new cycle, Maddie," Tess explained solemnly. Everything was cyclical in Tess's mind. The world, time, seasons, everything was just one big circle. "Now that Simon has passed, we have a very important role to play in helping them start over. You must remember that. They need us now. And perhaps one day"—she stopped and placed a hand on Maddie's shoulder—"we will need them."

"My mother doesn't seem to want to help them with their

new *cycle*," Maddie said wryly. Tess waited a beat as Rebecca and Cordelia started unpacking the food on one of the weathered picnic tables on the beach.

"Your mother has her own issues that she needs to resolve, things that shouldn't concern you. You need to listen to your heart and your soul and your dreams. Your mother has always blocked those messages out. You need to learn how to let them in"—she nodded then to Cordelia and Rebecca—"and let your new family in, too."

Maddie couldn't resist a smile. Tess was always making things sound more mysterious—like there were larger forces at work.

It wasn't until much later that Maddie realized how true Tess's words would turn out to be.

# Chapter 3

## RAIDO

**ᚱ**

### THE WHEEL - TIME

*New Beginnings, Promise, Opportunity;*
*A Spiritual Journey or Quest*

Over the next few weeks, Rebecca and Cordelia settled into life in Hawthorne. Abigail kept a sullen distance, but Tess practically floated around the house, happy to have her house brimming with life once again.

Despite Maddie's attempts at conversation, Cordelia remained aloof, making it clear she didn't want any new friends. In sharp contrast, Rebecca was open and warm. It was hard not to love her—with her musical voice and infectious optimism, she seemed to make everything a little bit brighter. She threw herself into work right away, making plans to open a New Age flower shop and setting the town all abuzz.

"Aren't you excited about the store?" Maddie asked her cousin one hot, muggy morning as they sat across from each other at the breakfast table. Tess was humming as she prepared eggs, toast, and coffee for them.

Cordelia gave her a withering look and buried her head in the *New York Times*, obviously more interested in what was going on in the rest of the world than anything happening in Hawthorne.

"Of course she's excited," Rebecca said brightly as she whisked through the room, planting a kiss on all of their cheeks, grabbing a slice of toast and part of Cordelia's paper. "She just doesn't know it yet. It's just the beginning, girls, just the beginning." She rifled through the stack of mail on the table. Cordelia and Maddie looked at each other, and they both fought back smiles, rolling their eyes. At least they could both agree on Rebecca's eccentricity.

"Oh my God! It's here!!" Rebecca yelled. She held a piece of yellow paper aloft like it was an award, shaking it so hard that the beaded bracelets that crowded her lithe arm rattled like a maraca. "It's official!"

The paperwork and lease for the store had arrived. It was really happening. Despite Abigail's insistence that this would only be a temporary stopover for her sister, that she never stayed in one place for too long, this new development proved otherwise. Rebecca embraced each one of them, whooping with delight. "Look out Hawthorne, the LeClaire girls are here to stay!" she called out with a hearty laugh.

Everyone stopped talking abruptly when a loud crash sounded from the next room. Maddie ran into the living room to find her mother furiously cleaning up shards of broken glass from a crystal bowl that had fallen from the mantle. Maddie wasn't sure if it was a deliberate action on Abigail's part or an accident from the shock that the inevitable was happening, something that Abigail didn't want to accept: Rebecca and Cordelia weren't going anywhere.

∞

Later that week, Maddie swung through the heavy leaded-glass door of the store, aptly named Rebecca's Closet, and was met enthusiastically by Rebecca, who was blaring Fleetwood Mac's "Rhiannon" from an old tape deck. They had already done an overwhelming amount of work on the store.

The floors and woodwork gleamed. Every inch was scrubbed. The walls were freshly painted white with the tiniest hint of lavender, giving it an airy feel.

"Well, aren't you a doll for helping us!" she exclaimed, gathering her niece tightly into her arms for a hug. Maddie was overwhelmed by her scent—an exotic, musky mixture of thick perfume and floral oils. It was the sweet smell that flowers exude right before they die. It was a welcome change for Maddie, who was accustomed only to the faint whiff of Chanel No. 5 perfume that her mother had dotted behind her ears and wrists every day for as long as she could remember.

Maddie shrugged. "It's no problem, Aunt Rebecca."

"No, don't call me that. Too formal. Just Rebecca," she said, brushing her long, red hair away from her wide, luminous face. Maddie suddenly understood why people mistook Rebecca and Cordelia for sisters. Rebecca's youthful, vivacious spirit made her seem much younger than Abigail, despite the fact that Rebecca was the older sister. Her beauty was startling and almost unreal. She was movie star beautiful. Maddie had never known anyone in real life who had such ethereal looks. And even without a stitch of makeup, she had a radiant glow. It made Maddie feel special, yet slightly uncomfortable, to be in her presence. "I'm surprised that my sister is even letting you help us."

"She suggested it actually," Maddie offered weakly, blushing at the awkwardness of their living situation.

"Hmmm . . ." Rebecca considered that for a moment; something appeared to be nagging at her. "That's surprising."

Rebecca settled back down onto the worn plank floors, tucking her hair behind her ears as she unpacked a crate. She unwrapped a series of glass bottles, apothecary jars, and vases and then nodded in the direction of the back room.

"Why don't you go help Cordelia in the back while I get

some work done out here? That way you two can start getting better acquainted," she suggested. Maddie nodded glumly and headed toward the stock room.

"I have a feeling you two will get along famously," Rebecca offered in parting. Maddie tried to manage a weak smile for Rebecca's sake before continuing into the back room. While she could understand why Rebecca was encouraging a friendship between them, it just wasn't coming very easily, at least not from Maddie's perspective.

Making her way past all of the boxes stacked precariously in the back room, Maddie heard a muffled sound coming from behind a crate. Cordelia was crouched on the floor with her legs curled underneath her, holding a frame on her lap. Her hair, long and red as a stage curtain, shielded her face as tears dropped onto the glass of the frame. She rocked back and forth, crying softly.

"Are you okay?" Maddie whispered hesitantly.

Cordelia jumped slightly, her body stiffening, and wiped her cheek with the sleeve of her peasant blouse. She stood up, dusted herself off. Her lashes were beaded with tears, but her blank stare lacked emotion.

"Fine," she said, shifting her gaze away from Maddie, unwilling to make even the slightest eye contact.

"Who's that?" Maddie asked, motioning to the frame.

"My dad. He's dead," she said quickly, definitively.

"I know. I'm so sorry."

"Why are *you* sorry? You didn't even know him or anything," she said and quickly turned away and busied herself with unpacking a box.

"Is that why you moved back to Hawthorne?" Maddie asked to make conversation.

Cordelia looked at her dead-on, reluctant to let her guard down.

"My mom couldn't live in that house after he died. Plus,

we couldn't even afford to stay there. All the money went into treatments."

"Treatments?" Maddie asked. "How did he, um . . . pass away?"

"The Big C."

"Cancer?"

Cordelia continued unpacking the box in front of her as if the question was rhetorical.

"So that's why you're here?"

"Bingo."

A long silence stretched between them. Cordelia was obviously not going to elaborate. Maddie had been dismissed. But she wasn't going to let Cordelia off that easily. If they had to live together, at least they would be friends. She settled onto the floor next to her cousin and started unpacking another box.

"I lost my dad to the Big M-S," Maddie offered.

Cordelia waited for a moment and then looked at her quizzically.

"Multiple Sclerosis?"

"No, Mindy Sherman, the cocktail waitress he ran off with," Maddie deadpanned.

A smile slowly spread across Cordelia's face. She nodded at a box, and they both went to work unpacking. They weren't exactly *best* friends by the end of that particular day, but it was definitely a start.

∞

Later that evening, after Rebecca had passed out from sheer exhaustion from all of the work they had done on the shop and Abigail retired to her room for her nightly reading, Maddie heard a soft knock on her door. Cordelia was standing there in a long, white nightgown.

"Tess wants to talk to us," she said hesitantly. Despite

their bonding earlier that day, Cordelia didn't seem like she was one hundred percent sold on their new friendship. The two had barely spoken at dinnertime, and Cordelia had promptly buried herself in a book the minute she was excused from the table. It was as if the hours of telling stories and laughter in the store that afternoon never happened. She was, as Tess was fond of saying, a tough nut to crack.

Maddie hopped off the bed and silently followed Cordelia. Her grandmother's room overlooked the ocean, and Tess often spent her evenings gazing wistfully out to sea. Maddie imagined that was how Tess had looked on the night so many years ago that she discovered her husband, Jack Martin, was lost at sea.

Tess beamed at her granddaughters and patted the bed, motioning for them to join her. Maddie allowed herself to be enveloped in the cozy darkness of the room, relishing the comfort of the old mattress piled high with quilts. She listened to the sounds of the summer night blow in through the open window. Kids were heading down to the beach. Maddie couldn't hear what they were saying, but their voices bounced and echoed through the room. Every now and then, a girl would yelp and then start laughing—carefree, yet haunting in the darkness.

"You know that you girls are special, don't you?" Tess asked once the girls were settled. Cordelia and Maddie looked at each other, trying not to giggle at Tess's serious tone as their grandmother continued. "The women in our family possess a gift, a sort of extrasensory perception that allows us to know things that cannot be explained." Maddie smirked, used to Tess's stories about "special powers and gifts," but Cordelia leaned forward, fascinated.

Maddie had heard this before, of course. Every time Tess spoke of the "family gift," Abigail laughed it off, saying that it was one of Tess's many eccentricities, the result of having too much time on her hands. Maddie wondered if the gene had been passed along to Cordelia and Rebecca, because it certainly hadn't made its way through to Maddie or her mother.

"I discovered my gift when Rebecca was just a baby," Tess began, allowing her gaze to drift back to the window. She explained how she dreamt about the color blue for weeks, her mind crowded with wide expanses of deep blue skies hovering over cool aquamarine waters. She dreamt of blueberries, fat and ripe, rolling across the dining room table, which was formally set with expensive china as delicate and blue as a robin's egg. Cobalt blue water goblets were filled to the rim with grape juice, and the vases were cluttered with hydrangea, cornflowers, and sweet pea. "The images stayed with me long after the dreams dissipated, but I shrugged it off, not knowing what to do with the premonitions."

"So what happened?" Cordelia asked.

Tess sat up a little straighter, her face flushed with excitement at having a new, rapt audience to tell her magical stories to. "It wasn't until I awoke from a late summer afternoon nap and felt compelled to look in on my sleeping baby girl—your mother—that my dreams started to make sense," Tess paused dramatically. "As soon as I walked into the nursery, all the blue images came rushing into my mind when I saw that your mother's face was the color blue that had haunted my dreams."

Cordelia gasped as she learned that the baby had become tangled in her bedclothes and blankets, and the lack of oxygen had caused a blue tinge to stain her cherubic face.

"What did you do?" Cordelia cried. Maddie was surprised at Cordelia's emotional reaction—the tense energy coming from her cousin was palpable. Tess explained how she quickly hoisted the child from its confines, pressed her mouth against the baby's tiny sliver of blue lips, and forced heavy bursts of lifesaving air into the lungs. After several tension-filled minutes, the baby began gasping and wheezing, her returning pink coloring flushing away the deathly blue.

"After that, I knew that my dreams would foretell an important event, but the symbols never gave me a warning," she said ominously. "The symbols were there; the meaning was not. This is why it is so important to be aware of the signs that are always around you. If you look close enough, you can see the patterns of what's to come. You can and you must use the signs to protect yourselves—and each other."

Maddie was suddenly overcome with the feeling of being watched. She rubbed away the goose bumps that appeared on her arms.

Finally, Abigail threw open the door and glared at Tess.

"Is there a reason you're keeping these girls up so late? You know that they have a lot of work ahead of them in the store tomorrow," Abigail scolded. Tess ignored her daughter and simply clasped the girls' hands tightly in her own. Abigail sighed and said as she shut the door, "Fine. Don't blame me if they're the walking dead tomorrow."

"Your mother refuses to see her gift," she said to Maddie. Next, she turned to Cordelia. "And your mother doesn't know what to do with hers. I think she blames herself for not being able to stop your father's death—just as I had no way of stopping your grandfather's." Maddie noticed Cordelia stiffen at the mention of her father, her mouth drawn into a grim line.

Tess continued, "It's important not to share the knowledge of this gift with anyone but each other. You know what Hawthorne is like." Tess said, turning to Maddie.

Maddie nodded solemnly, but she couldn't help feeling left out. For all this talk of "gifts," she didn't seem to share this gift that everyone in her family possessed but her and her mother. Unlike her grandmother, Maddie never had visions or premonitions. She looked over at her cousin, whose eyes were brimming with tears. *What does she see?* Maddie wondered.

Tess and Cordelia stared at each other for a long time. It was like they were sharing a silent conversation. Then Tess started talking about the dreams she'd been having recently. They were mostly typical laid-back summertime dreams: swimming in the ocean, boating to the local islands, dancing around bonfires, sand, and stones—her attempt at easing the tension. Then Tess squeezed each of their hands and said, "All right, that's enough of this for one night. You'd better get to bed before Abigail has a fit."

The girls kissed their grandmother on the cheek and headed for the door. As Cordelia reached for the handle, Tess spoke again, her voice soft but firm. "You two need to stick together. No matter what. *No matter what.*"

Later that night, Maddie rested in the darkness, replaying the conversation in Tess's room. In the moments before the deep, heavy folds of sleep slipped over her, Maddie jerked wide awake, inexplicably unnerved by Tess's dreams of bonfires and swimming, of islands and stones. If her dreams were, in fact, prophetic, what could they possibly mean? Could they have something to do with her own dreams? And why did Maddie have the sinking feeling that something ominous was just around the corner?

೮೦

As soon as Rebecca's Closet was open and ready for business, customers began to pour in. Most were just curious about the newcomers to town. Everyone who wandered into the shop was welcomed by a burst of exotic fragrances and vivid colors. Glass apothecary jars containing dried herbs and spices lined the wooden shelves and bottles of flower tinctures were nestled away from the sun in the heavy oak bookcases.

Cordelia and Rebecca hung jewelry, handmade from dried roses and silk ribbons, on an antique coat rack and draped dried bouquets and wreaths from the wooden rafters that crisscrossed the high ceiling. They pressed flowers between pages of antique books and lined shelves with a jumble of decorative items: antique watering cans, handmade soaps, fat candles, thick stationery, sealing wax and ribbons, calligraphy pens and ink, and porcelain jars. Rebecca made sure to prominently display a wide selection of New Age books, crystals, incense, and various tools of divination—rune stones, tarot, and oracles—in order to capitalize on the store's proximity to Salem, the Witch City.

And the flowers! Brilliant sparks of color shot out from every angle. They filled jars and buckets with blue and lavender hydrangeas entwined with ivy; dewy roses stretched out alongside sprigs of lavender and bright shades of phlox. Demure calla lilies rested against the haughty foxglove. Red salvia and pink petunias were alive with fire. Orange-scented pomanders hung from doorknobs and chair rails, efficiently strung by satin cords. The flowers filled every crevice so that once inside the tiny shop, Maddie felt like she was smack dab in the middle of the Garden of Eden.

Both Rebecca and Cordelia were skilled at making perfume from essential oils and floral extracts. They even claimed that certain aromas could heal almost anything—from the common cold to getting over a broken heart. Although most people came in regularly for the flowers, they were also tempted to try the herbal remedies available.

When elderly Mrs. Elliott complained about not being able to sleep well at night, Rebecca whipped up an ounce of *Night Whispers,* a mixture of crushed yarrow, dried lilac, essential oils of rose and jasmine, and dashes of foreign spices. When gossipy Hattie McGregor came into the store complaining of migraines, Cordelia made up a lavender, sage, and eucalyptus tincture to soothe her aching head. And large numbers of women came in anxious to try the cowslip potion that was rumored to magically erase wrinkles.

Even though the shop had become quite popular since its opening, whisperings of witchcraft, spells, and magic arose with every single mention of the store and its owners. But Rebecca and Cordelia paid no attention to the gossip and rumors swirling around them. They were just thrilled to have a thriving business, one where they could be surrounded by beautiful things and magical items. Maddie was so entranced by them that she didn't care what people said. They were like images from a Botticelli painting come to life, luminous and mysterious. Maddie wanted to soak in everything and be a part of the glittering halo that seemed to surround them.

Unfortunately, Abigail had other plans. She didn't want Maddie to be associated with any of the goings-on at her sister's store. Even Tess knew that the townspeople would only tolerate Rebecca's Closet for so long and that eventually, being associated—even in the slightest, most innocent way—with outsiders would inevitably come back to haunt them. And though Tess was always so quick to hide any association with the supernatural or psychic abilities she believed she'd been granted, she had only one word to say when she saw the store—*Grand!*

Though they had only been in town for a few weeks, Rebecca and Cordelia already felt like a familiar presence in Maddie's life. It was as if they were the missing piece that Maddie had always been seeking, and now that they were finally here, she couldn't imagine life without them.

Luckily, with field hockey camp in full force, Kate, Hannah, Bridget, and Darcy hadn't had the time to come to Rebecca's store. And every time Kate suggested that Maddie meet up with them for end-of-the-summer parties, Maddie found a good excuse not to go. While this angered Abigail, it thrilled Tess. When the girls weren't helping out in the store, Tess whisked them off to the museums in Boston, shopping excursions in Newburyport, and endless sea glass searches along the craggy shores of Rockport.

Maddie and Cordelia had become inseparable over the past few weeks—staying up late into the night talking, sneaking down to the beach for midnight swims, playing cards and backgammon with Tess after dinner. They were becoming more and more like a family. It was something that they all needed at that point in time.

But Maddie knew that the inevitable was right around the corner. School would be starting soon, and she'd have to share Cordelia with the rest of her friends. It would be no easy task, for sure. Maddie could already picture Kate's reaction to her free-spirited cousin. Kate with her Lilly Pulitzer attire, blond hair perfectly highlighted and swept back neatly with a pastel headband. And then there was Cordelia with her long floral skirts, muted tanks layered over her long torso, untamed red hair flowing down her back with tiny braids woven intermittently throughout, arms and neck wrapped with strands of semiprecious stones. The two couldn't be more different, and Maddie went to great lengths to keep them apart for as long as possible.

While Maddie didn't have the expensive wardrobe that matched Kate and the other girls in her group, over the years, she had mastered New England preppy attire in order to fit in. Yet the peasant blouses, crystal necklaces, and colorful skirts that Rebecca and Cordelia had given her just seemed to feel more natural and refreshing than stiff Oxford shirts and khaki pants.

Maddie walked into the store one afternoon wearing a Polo golf shirt with a long patchwork skirt, her wrists adorned with lapis lazuli, aventurine, and rose quartz bracelets. She completed the look with her beat-up Keds, a silk, multi-colored scarf knotted around her head with the ends trailing down her back, and large hoop earrings. The outfit, which Cordelia could have carried off with ease, made Maddie look like she was playing dress-up. Cordelia raised an eyebrow, amused at her cousin's transformation.

"What?" Maddie asked defensively.

Rebecca and Cordelia eyed each other, obviously trying not to laugh.

"You look like Martha Stewart and Bob Dylan's love child," Cordelia said.

Rebecca swatted her daughter and opened her arms, inviting Maddie into a big bear hug. "I think you look beautiful. It's an essential part of growing up to develop your own style."

"I think that you're being generous with the word *style*, Mom," Cordelia said again. Maddie made as if to hit her. "Kidding, kidding! You look very cool."

Rebecca returned to her paperwork, totaling up the vast number of sales that they'd raked in ever since the store opened.

"I hope that this store isn't just a flash in the pan," she said, almost to herself. "If people keep buying like this, we'll be having an excellent Christmas this year." She smiled.

"Mom, let me read your fortune," Cordelia said, spilling rune stones across the old farm table. Maddie rubbed her nail-bitten fingertips over the carved symbols in the stones.

"How 'bout I read yours instead?" Rebecca suggested.

"Nah, I already know mine: Cordelia LeClaire will run off with a handsome prince who shows up on horseback, whisking her off to his castle a million, trillion miles from Hawthorne, Massachusetts. And she'll never look back."

"You're going to leave your favorite person in the world here?" Looking at Maddie, Rebecca mouthed the word *Me* and then pointed to herself. "All by my lonesome?"

"Hey, it was your choice to come back here, not mine. And I don't think that as long as there is a man alive in this world, you can ever say that you're lonely," Cordelia joked. Rebecca pretended to whack her daughter. "No, really, let me read your rune stones."

Listening to their happy banter made Maddie feel like a third wheel. The strength of Cordelia and Rebecca's relationship was so foreign to her, so very different from any other mother-daughter relationships she knew, with her own at the very top of the list. Maddie's friends barely tolerated parents, only giving them the time of day during holidays or some other gift-giving event. And even then, the amount of affection was almost always in direct proportion to the dollar value of the gift.

"Why don't you do Maddie's?" Rebecca smiled at her. "Wouldn't you like to know what the future holds for you?"

"No, that's okay. I really should be getting home to help my mom get dinner started." Maddie desperately wanted to stay and learn more about fortune telling and hear all of the stories of their travels and the interesting people in their lives back in California, but she knew that her mother would be furious if she shirked any more of her chores.

As Maddie started gathering her things, Cordelia squeezed her eyes shut and thrust her hand into the black bag of stones. She pulled her closed fist from the satchel and opened her palm flat toward Rebecca. They both peered at the blank stone. Cordelia flipped it quickly to display the other side.

"Hey, I got a faulty one. There's nothing on this."

Rebecca flipped through the Rune handbook. "No, that's an actual stone. It's called the *Odin* or the *Wyrd* stone," she continued reading. "This is the Fate stone, the unknowable. It is the stone that represents both the beginning and the end. It symbolizes the unknowable, that which cannot be known or controlled. Only Fate will decide the outcome."

Cordelia's eyes widened. "Ooooh, scary," she giggled as she jumped from her perch on the table. "Maddie, did you hear that? My future is *unknowable* and *uncontrollable*."

Maddie felt a sudden wave of nausea as her dream of Cordelia out on Misery Island came back to her. She had mentioned the Sisters of Misery to Cordelia once or twice without going into great detail, but Cordelia had laughed it off, comparing them to the Junior League or a silly sorority.

"I don't need a rock to tell me that you're uncontrollable, my dear," Rebecca joked. She lit an October Harvest incense stick, and the store quickly filled with the scents of autumn—cinnamon, nutmeg, allspice, and apples.

Maddie smiled, wishing that she didn't have to leave the cozy scene behind. Waving a reluctant good-bye, she walked home where surely, her mother waited to pounce on her and start yet another argument.

Abigail was always eagerly waiting to point out all the things Maddie hadn't done recently. Maddie *didn't* go to field hockey camp; she *didn't* secure an invitation to the Endicott's end of the summer party; she *didn't* place high enough in the sail meet for them to attend the awards banquet at the yacht club. All the things that Maddie *didn't* do represented the one big thing that her mother didn't do for her—love her unconditionally.

When she got home, Maddie found her mother furiously cleaning the kitchen. Maddie quelled the urge to run upstairs before her mother caught sight of her, demanding help with the chores, and instead joined her in the kitchen.

"Hey, Mom," Maddie said tentatively, trying to gauge her mother's mood, "How about going out for dinner tonight?"

Abigail turned, and from the look on her face, Maddie was expecting a lecture on not having enough money to go out to restaurants or how Maddie should try cooking a meal once in a while. She was taken aback when her mother said, "Well, that would be nice. What's the occasion?"

Maddie felt a surge of excitement, not quite understanding her mother's change of heart, actually spending money—and time—with her daughter.

"Oh, no occasion, Mom. I just—well, I thought that we could go someplace nice together." She hesitated, adding, "Maybe even bring Tess, Rebecca, and Cordelia?"

"Oh," Abigail said dryly, trying to keep the disappointment out of her voice but not sufficiently hiding it. "I just thought—well, I assumed you had been over to the Endicott's this afternoon, that, well . . . never mind."

"What do you mean, Mom?" Maddie's earlier excitement was crashing and burning, leaving her insides feeling like leaden carnage.

"Well, I haven't been to Crestwood Yacht Club in ages, and I *assumed* that you and I had been invited by the Endicotts for dinner. I mean, that's the only place around town that's worth paying for dinner, and you can't eat there if you're not a member, and it's been such a long time since we've done anything socially with Kate's family. Don't you remember how much I adored Crestwood's Cobb Salad?"

Abigail droned on, touting the merits of Crestwood's menu, but Maddie stopped listening. She felt like one of those cartoon characters that had smoke steaming out of its ears in anger. Maddie couldn't hear anything but the sound of her own fury and disgust. Of course, her mother wouldn't want to waste time going out to dinner with her own daughter. To

Abigail Crane, spending time with Maddie was only worthwhile if it was a social event.

She felt a flash of jealousy toward Cordelia, back in the store, laughing with Rebecca. Rebecca loved her daughter no matter what she did. Cordelia had no idea how lucky she really was.

Maddie quickly excused herself and ran up the stairs to her room to change, so consumed by her feelings that she barely noticed the darkening swell of the ocean that churned outside her bedroom window. If she had looked more closely, she would have noticed that the sea had turned to the color of slate. If she had listened to Tess's advice about paying attention to the signs that were all around them, perhaps Maddie could have glimpsed the future and would have known that the lives of all of the women in her family were in greater peril than any of them realized.

# Chapter 4

ISA

**I**

ICE

*Coldness Between People; Obstacles, Challenges,
and Frustration; Slippery and Unsafe*

## SEPTEMBER

On the first day of school at Hawthorne Academy, Maddie and Cordelia left early, as the sun was barely rising over the ocean. Maddie wanted Cordelia to register for classes, but Cordelia had other, less practical things on her agenda. As they passed the sun-dappled forest, Cordelia gushed, "It's so beautiful here, so surreal! Let's come back later tonight and look for forest elves and nymphs. I'll bet there are fairy trees in there."

Maddie laughed. "There's no such thing as fairies. I stopped believing in that stuff when I was five."

"I'm not surprised," Cordelia sniffed. "Considering where you grew up."

"What's that supposed to mean?"

"Never mind. Let's come back here later, and I'll prove to you that there are fairies. I've seen them. I visited Ireland when I was a little girl, and I came across a real live fairy circle. I watched them as they drank elderberry wine from crystal goblets and wore dresses made of gossamer thread and velvet. They danced until their snapdragon shoes fell apart."

Cordelia danced down the street, doing pirouettes and making silly faces. Cordelia's wild imagination melted Maddie's cynical side, and for a moment, she almost entertained the idea that something magical like fairies could, in fact, exist. Maddie laughed, but then looked past Cordelia into the grove, feeling a chill creep through her skin. Something felt wrong—it felt like they were being watched, studied.

"They're haunted. The woods, I mean."

Cordelia stopped dancing, and her eyes widened. "Then let's go! Why should that stop us?" She spun around once, twirling her floral skirt, and then sprinted into the woods. She wove in between the trees, expertly avoiding fallen branches, as if she'd run through there hundreds of times. Maddie tried desperately to keep up with her, but she kept losing sight of her cousin. The deeper they went into the wood, the more intense Maddie's sense of foreboding became.

"Who are they haunted by?" Cordelia called.

"Cordelia!" Maddie yelled. "Come on! We don't have time for this. You're going to make us late for school."

"Who cares." Her voice sounded miles away, echoing through the trees.

Maddie stopped to catch her breath in a dim clearing. The branches overhead were so thick that no sunlight filtered through. Maddie felt the chill again. The last place she wanted to be was deep inside Potter's Grove searching for Cordelia. With all the creepy stories she'd heard over the years, Maddie had sworn that she'd never enter the place. "Where are you?"

Cordelia's voice came in a whisper from behind her. "Right here. *Boo!*"

Maddie jumped, and Cordelia laughed uncontrollably.

"Don't do that," Maddie snapped. "Not here. Not in these woods."

"So, who are these ghosts you're scared of?" Her eyes twinkled despite the few weak rays of sunlight that made it through the canopy of trees.

"I don't know. This place is supposed to be filled with all sorts of spirits, according to local legends," Maddie whispered, suddenly aware of the growing silence around them. But she liked having Cordelia's undivided attention, so she pushed aside her fears and continued.

"The site of Old Captain Potter's Tavern is somewhere around here. We're probably standing on top of it, for all I know. Anyway, the townspeople hated the tavern. They were sick of all the creeps from neighboring towns coming here, so they decided to burn the place down. To get revenge, Captain Potter had one of his slaves, who also happened to be a voodoo priestess, put some kind of a curse on the woods and the entire town of Hawthorne."

Cordelia's eyes grew wider with every word. "So that's where the rumors of witchcraft came in?"

Shaking her head, Maddie explained that the infamous witchcraft trials took place in the neighboring town of Salem, but that Hawthorne had its own witch scandal of sorts. When the beautiful Pickering sisters—Honor, Constance, and Patience—moved into the small town of Hawthorne, they were quickly accused of practicing witchcraft.

"Back in those days, anything you did could be reason enough to get you called a witch," Maddie explained. "You could cook with a strange spice or wear bright clothes and get called a witch. Some women were even called witches if they were really pretty and the men in town had dreams about them—they were accused of 'bewitching' the men and forcing them to have 'impure thoughts.' "

Cordelia surmised, "So basically, it's the same as being called a slut today, right?"

"Only now, you can't burn sluts at the stake," Maddie said.

The two girls giggled.

As they picked their way along the meandering, overgrown path through the grove, Maddie filled Cordelia in on the legend of the Pickering sisters. As soon as the women had moved into town, they became well-known for their fiery tempers and were often credited with having "fits of hysteria"—something that was a sure sign of a practicing witch. Then people started saying they had "spectral evidence" of the beautiful sisters' powers of witchcraft: curdling milk with a single glance, ruining entire crops with a harsh word, and even luring married men into adulterous situations in their dreams.

Cordelia almost fell over, hysterically laughing when she heard that.

The woods were eerily quiet, and Maddie wanted to finish the story quickly. They were on the verge of being late to school, and Maddie knew Cordelia wouldn't leave Potter's Grove until she heard every detail. Maddie told her how the women ran and hid in that very forest in order to escape their trials, hoping they could stay until the witchcraft rumors ended. What few friends and family they had, used to sneak into the woods, bringing the women supplies and food to help them survive. Many were too afraid to go in after the sisters because of Old Man Potter's curse. Plus, town officials tortured, imprisoned, or killed anyone caught helping the three women. The official town documents contained severe punishments for those they called "The Witches' Brethren."

"Tess told me once that people born within the town lines have the power to hear the cries of the Pickering sisters on certain nights," Maddie said quietly. "The sounds are like low, mournful wails and high-pitched hysterical shrieks. Tess swears that on some nights, she gets woken up by those cries."

"Have you ever heard them?" Cordelia asked excitedly.

"Lucky for me, I was born in Boston," Maddie laughed.

They stopped walking, and Cordelia stared into the depths of the woods. A stiff wind picked up, swirling dead leaves around the forest floor.

"So, then what happened?"

"Well, then the witchcraft hysteria ended, but not for the Pickering sisters," she continued. "They thought it was safe to return to town, but the people of Hawthorne weren't done with them just yet. They were put into the jail at Fort Glover and tortured for days and days. The town officials seized all of their belongings as payment for their incarceration—they basically had to pay for their own torture. And then they were labeled lunatics by the town doctors, so they were put into Ravenswood State Asylum, or at the time, what they called The Witches' Castle."

"The Witches' Castle," Cordelia spoke slowly, a smile tugging at the corners of her mouth. "Did they ever get out?"

Maddie nodded. "Legend has it they escaped. But no one knows how they managed it. Many people thought they would come back seeking revenge for what happened to them. But they never did. There were other rumors that they were sold into slavery and prostitution or that they were murdered. Some people think that they were forced out onto Misery Island and that they died out there, either froze or starved to death. People think that the Pickering sisters haunt both the island and these woods." Maddie hugged herself as a chill came over her.

"Ooooh, spooky," Cordelia said. "Why is it called Misery Island?"

Maddie explained that a shipbuilder named Robert Moulton got stuck out on the island while harvesting timber in the 1620s. He was stranded out in a terrible December storm for three "miserable" days, hence the name Misery Island.

"So does he haunt the island, too?" Cordelia asked, clearly amused.

"I don't know; I never stayed there by myself."

"What's out there besides ghosts and witches?"

Maddie laughed. "We go out there to party sometimes. It's pretty secluded. It used to be this big resort and casino with all these beautiful summer homes back at the turn of the nineteenth century, but a big fire destroyed everything. It's just a bunch of ruins now." Maddie paused for a moment, thinking about all of the nights that the Sisters of Misery had gone out there and what had taken place. "The ruins of the casino look like a castle. It's actually a really beautiful place."

"When you're not being attacked by witches and ghosts, right?" Cordelia asked. "Well, on your next trip out there, bring me along. I'd love to see an old castle. Maybe I can find some fairy circles inside."

They finally emerged from the forest across the street from the ocean. Maddie smiled, nodding in the direction of the island so that Cordelia would follow her gaze.

"Anyway," Maddie continued, "there's also a creepy stone wall on Ravenswood hospital with these faces that keep showing up year after year. Supposedly, they're the faces of the Pickering sisters put there as a reminder that one day, they'll return seeking revenge." Maddie felt like she was now a tour guide for the witch trials. She then added with a smile, "So now you know why nobody here likes outsiders."

"I wish I was a descendant of one of those sisters. Maybe," Cordelia said with a cluck of her tongue, "maybe I am, and I was destined to return here."

Maddie laughed. "Revenge is sweet, right?"

"'And sweet revenge grows harsh,'" Cordelia quoted. "Shakespeare. *Othello*." This was a game that Cordelia and Rebecca played often in the store. They'd spend hours going back and forth with quotes, trying to one up each other.

"Oh, okay. Let me think. Hmm . . . 'Sweet is revenge . . . especially to women.' Lord Byron," Maddie said, loving the feeling of being a part of Rebecca and Cordelia's private game.

Cordelia closed her eyes, the tree branches shifting behind her in the owl-light of the forest. "Mmmm . . . Oh, I've got a good one. 'In revenge and in love, woman is more barbaric than man is.' Nietzsche."

Her eyes fluttered open, startling Maddie. Cordelia glared at her, her brilliant smile fading, her eyes clouding over, and for a moment, Maddie thought her cousin was going to hit her. Then Cordelia peered into the woods, so dark and impenetrable in the early morning light, almost as if she saw someone or something. Maddie's entire body hummed with tension, the hairs on the back of her neck standing at attention.

Then Cordelia's smile returned, her eyes cleared, and she broke the moment that enveloped them by yelling, "Race ya!"

Cordelia squealed with laughter as they ran all the way past Town Hall, Fort Glover, and Old Burial Hill. As they ran, Maddie glanced at Ravenswood and the wall that somehow had become a monument to the Pickering sisters. Headlights often threw gruesome shadows on the towering stone wall of the red Gothic monstrosity of Ravenswood, illuminating the ghostly faces that appeared to come alive in the dark. Don't look directly at them, or you'll catch your death, people would say. Some believed the faces carved into the stone were a reminder of the terrible fate of those three girls.

A warning, a way of making sure that the people of Haw-thorne would never let it happen again.

Not ever again.

When driving past Ravenswood, people averted their eyes from the faces for fear of bad luck, much like children hold-ing their breath while passing graveyards. The aging build-ing had been erected on the site of a fort that once defended Hawthorne Harbor during the Revolutionary War. It was once a prison, a part of the town's history that no one liked to talk about. And nearly a century ago, it had been reborn to accommodate a different cast of inmates, those imprisoned by their own minds. Its formal name was Ravenswood State Asylum, and it was a hospital for the mentally ill.

No one knew how or when the faces were carved into the towering stone wall. They just always remembered them being there.

Again and again, people tried to cover up the faces, squeezing gray plaster and mortar into the gaping grimaces and empty eye sockets. But days later, never longer than a week, the girls' faces rose to the surface once again. For the cement, no matter how thick or strong, just disappeared. The faces stared out defiantly. There for an eternity. There to tell their story, to be a reminder of the past.

Maddie never paid much attention to the faces on the wall or the horrible stories of the torture that the Pickering sisters, wrongly accused of witchcraft and ostracized by an entire community, had to endure. And she didn't want to show Cordelia the wall that immortalized the fate of those three girls. Not yet, not now. Because recently she'd been having terrible dreams.

And in Maddie's recent nightmares, she saw the appear-ance of a fourth face.

The face of another young girl.

The face of Cordelia.

ॐ

"I'm so excited for you to meet everyone," Maddie said as she and Cordelia slowed to a walk, heading up the narrow pathway to the school.

Ever since she and Cordelia had become closer friends, Maddie felt like she was growing out of her awkward, self-conscious behavior and tapping into Cordelia's unwavering confidence. It was hard to believe that they were related. Cordelia just exuded this natural poise and self-assurance, whereas Maddie had pretty much always been a wallflower. Maddie could just imagine her friends falling all over themselves to try to befriend this mysterious, yet very cool girl from California.

"There they are," Maddie said as she waved over to the group of girls. They were gathered in an unapproachable knot, tight as a tourniquet. Kate turned and waved them over, as if they were opening their exclusive doors for a brief moment. Maddie watched as their eyes drifted from Cordelia's espadrilles, which crisscrossed up her legs, to her bright, floral skirt, and then finally up to meet her eyes with arrogant indifference.

"Oh, sweet Jesus, it's the Stepford wives in training," Cordelia said under her breath. "Do they all share the same hair dye or what?"

Maddie glowered at her cousin for a moment. She wanted this to go as smoothly as possible. But then she realized that they *were* all wearing the same uniform of pastel Polo shirts, khaki skirts or shorts, headbands, and Kate Spade purses. They were a J. Crew catalog sprung to life. Maddie wondered why she had never noticed that before, but realized as she looked down at her own clothes that she unknowingly had chosen the same unofficial Hawthorne Academy "uniform."

"Hey girls, this is my cousin, Cordelia LeClaire. She just moved here a few weeks ago from California," Maddie said. None of them smiled. "Cordelia, this is Kate Endicott, Hannah Sanders, Darcy Willett, and Bridget Monroe."

"Oh, the infamous Cordelia. We wondered who had taken our little Maddie captive. It's like you fell off the planet, Maddie," said Kate curtly. "We could have used you in field hockey camp. Most of those fat asses couldn't even do the drills without passing out."

Kate then turned her attention to Cordelia. "California, huh?" Kate sniffed. "Are you an *actress* or something?" The girls laughed in unison.

Cordelia smiled, unaffected by Kate's remark. "Not really."

"Nice skirt," Bridget said, not making it clear if it was a compliment or not. Maddie shifted uneasily from one foot to the other. This wasn't going to be as easy as she had hoped.

"Thanks," Cordelia said tentatively. "I bought it in a village market in the French countryside."

"A *flea* market?" Kate asked. A few of them giggled.

Maddie could feel her face flushing as she looked at the girls. *Why are they being so rude?* Cordelia's expression hadn't changed, which seemed to egg them on even more.

"Come on." Maddie protectively grabbed her arm. "We should get you registered." Maddie pulled her away from the girls before they could say anything else.

"Nice meeting you, Cordelia," Kate called after them.

Cordelia wrangled out of her grasp and turned back to face the group of girls. "No, really, the pleasure was all mine. I hope *everyone* here is as friendly as you." She then whipped around and marched ahead of Maddie up the stairs to the administration building. Maddie quickened pace to keep up, the muffled laughter fading behind them.

"Nice friends," Cordelia said flatly. "Real charmers."

"I honestly don't know what's gotten into them," Maddie said, even though she wasn't completely surprised by the chilly reception her cousin had received.

"Maybe you just can't see it because you're one of them," snapped Cordelia. She raced into the registration office, letting the heavy door slam behind her.

Maddie's heart sank. The bond that had grown between them over the past few weeks was on the verge of being broken.

૭

"What's with you and the hippie chick?" Kate taunted Maddie at her locker at the end of the school day.

Maddie swung around and glared at Kate's perfectly featured face; her heart-shaped face, tiny nose, and freckled cheeks made her the poster child for the all-American girl. Her silken hair fell down her back, sleek and polished as always, and her expression was absent of tolerance.

"I can't believe how rude you guys were," Maddie reprimanded her.

"Well, *I* can't believe that you blew us off for, what, like the entire summer for that—that freak!" Kate laughed. Bridget, Hannah, and Darcy came up behind Kate, nodding their heads in agreement. "Did you forget about us, your friends? Your Sisters!"

"She's not like us, Maddie," Darcy offered. "You know that. She's like, I don't know . . . weird."

"Yeah, she was in my European History class today, and she told Mr. Wilson that his description of one of the cathedrals or something was wrong. She said that she had been there and that she could describe it better," Bridget added. "I mean, who does she think she is?"

"Just give her a chance. She's really very cool." Maddie said halfheartedly, not really wanting to get into it with the girls.

"Madeline, you need to drop the welcome wagon act already. She'll never be one of us, you know that," Kate insisted with a smile. Then the smile faded, a stain of shock spreading over her face as she stared at something behind Maddie.

Maddie turned to see Trevor Campbell and Cordelia strolling down the hallway together, talking and laughing. His eyes were glued to her face, like a lost puppy hungry for whatever Cordelia had to offer him.

As they walked past the girls, neither of them acknowledged the stares from the group. An odd, raspy sound escaped from Kate's mouth as she overheard Trevor offering to give Cordelia an ocean-guided tour of Hawthorne from his new Whaler, the latest gift from his parents. Cordelia flung her hair over her shoulder and agreed halfheartedly, as if her mind was somewhere else entirely.

Kate spun angrily. "Who does that bitch think she is? You'd better tell her to keep her hands off of my Trevor! Do you understand, Madeline?"

Darcy snickered. "*Your* Trevor? Are you sure he knows that?"

Kate turned to Darcy, "Why don't you shut up, you little bitch? You've always wanted him, and I saw you throwing yourself at him the other night. It's pathetic."

Darcy looked uneasy for a moment but wasn't about to let herself become the focus of Kate's wrath. "Pathetic is what I'd call Maddie's cousin. Throwing herself at a guy she barely knows. Jesus, Maddie. She's only been in school for what, a few hours? And she's already gunning for someone else's boyfriend."

Maddie slammed the locker shut. "Listen, I don't know what's gotten into everyone. She *just* moved here. Her dad *just* died. And she doesn't know *anyone*. I don't see why you have to make it so brutal for her!"

"I'm sorry, Maddie dear. I don't do charity work," Kate snapped. "And if I were you, I wouldn't hang with the help unless you want to be treated like them."

With that, she stormed off angrily after Trevor and Cordelia, leaving the others to smirk and roll their eyes.

Darcy looked concerned for a moment and then ran after Kate, obviously trying to make amends.

"Try to get yourself off her shit list, Maddie," Hannah offered, leaning closer to Maddie. Her narrowly set hazel eyes opened wide in warning. "If you don't control your cousin, Kate will make life a living hell—for both of you."

After years of bending to Kate's every wish, Maddie knew that wasn't an exaggeration.

# Chapter 5

## KAUNAZ

## FIRE

*A Period of Darkness and Confusion; A Warning
or Spiritual Omen*

"So what's up with you and Trevor?" Maddie asked her cousin that evening while they sat at the kitchen table, doing homework. The late afternoon sun slanted through the trees and created a barcode of shadows along the wooden table.

"Who?" Cordelia asked earnestly.

Tess was humming a foreign tune in the other room.

"Trevor Campbell. I saw you walking down the hall with him after school."

"Oh yeah, blond hair, blue eyes, kinda cute. Was his name Trevor? Hmm . . . fits his type, I guess. What about him?" Cordelia asked, more interested in their reading assignment—short stories by Edgar Allan Poe—than boy talk.

"Well, he's sort of been dating Kate, like, forever."

"Poor guy."

"Yeah, really," Maddie laughed. "Seriously though, he's cute and all, but I just wouldn't get involved with him. He's bad news."

Cordelia laughed hysterically. "Get involved with him?

Oh, please. I'd never get involved with a guy my own age. I mean, he's okay, I guess, but . . ."

"Oh, I see. I'm sorry. I just thought that . . ."

"Where is this coming from, Maddie?" interrupted Cordelia. "I can take care of myself. Always have."

"Of course. It just looked like—"

"Looked like what? Like I was flirting with him? So what if I was?" Cordelia stopped reading suddenly. A smile spread across her face. "Oh, I see. This is about Kate, right? She freaked when she saw her pretty boy following me down the hall like a puppy dog today, didn't she? And you're her messenger girl, is that how it is?"

"No, I'm not her messenger," Maddie snapped. "But I just don't think it's a good idea for you to piss off Kate. I mean, you just started here, and you don't want to be on her bad side."

"You mean there's a good side to her? Funny, didn't strike me that there was one," Cordelia said, almost to herself. "Like I said before, Maddie, I'm not the one you should be worrying about. I can take care of myself. Always have. You, on the other hand, have to stop worrying so much about what other people think and say."

"I don't!"

"Whatever," Cordelia smiled. "Besides, Trevor Campbell isn't even my type. I need a man with a little more maturity, you know? Now, his older brother, Mr. Campbell, well, he's another story altogether. He's more my type, for sure. I think I could be—how does that Van Halen song go—"Hot for Teacher"? But now that I know that there's a controversy brewing . . ." Her blue eyes flashed wickedly, and she bit her ruddy bottom lip. "This could be kinda fun."

Reed Campbell had forever been known as "the hot teacher," due to the fact that he was barely out of college and his looks hadn't changed much since he was voted Most Popular, Best Looking, and Most Likely to Succeed back when he was a student at Hawthorne Academy. All the girls harbored secret crushes on him, even Maddie. But Cordelia was the only girl who seemed capable of attracting his attention. Maddie wasn't sure if it was her maturity, her picture-perfect looks, or her passion for literature that made Cordelia the quintessential "teacher's pet."

"Did any of you know that we have King Lear's favorite daughter right here in this classroom? And since she's here, I think she should tell us a little bit about herself," Mr. Campbell said one afternoon. He sat on his desk and looked at Cordelia. Maddie could have sworn that she saw a blush creep onto Cordelia's face, something that seemed totally out of character.

Kate whined, "What are you talking about, Reed?"

The smile dropped from Mr. Campbell's face, and he walked over to Kate's desk. He leaned over her and said quietly, but not so quiet that Maddie couldn't hear, "I know that you and my brother are together, but while we are in school, please treat me with a little respect. I am your teacher during the school year, got it?"

"God, I've got it Ree—er, Mr. Campbell, you don't have to smother me." Kate laughed her throaty laugh. "You're going to make people start talking."

He turned when he got back to his desk at the front of the classroom. "I'm going to have the headmaster talking . . . to *you* if you don't cut the crap, Kate."

Hannah and Darcy giggled. Kate turned and gave them the death glare.

"Now, as I was saying . . . King Lear's favorite daughter, for those of you who are not familiar with the words of good, old Will Shakespeare, was the beautiful Cordelia."

He raised his hand to Cordelia and directed her to the front of the classroom.

She smiled, blushing still, and said, "'O thou good Kent! how shall I live and work To match thy goodness? My life will be too short, And every measure fail me . . . These weeds are memories of those worser hours: I prithee, put them off.' "

Mr. Campbell laughed while the rest of the class looked at each other, dumbfounded. "I see that they do a good job of teaching Shakespeare in the California school system." He turned and explained to the class. "She was just quoting something that Cordelia said in *King Lear*." And then he shook his head, looking down at his syllabus, almost at a loss for words. "Very impressive, Ms. LeClaire. Very impressive. How about you tell us about yourself?"

Cordelia flushed at the compliment and then took her place at the front of the class.

"Well, there's not much to say. My mom is from Hawthorne. I was born in California. My dad passed away about six months ago, and now I'm living with my cousin, my aunt, and my grandmother. That's pretty much it." She laughed and held her hands up awkwardly. "Am I done?"

Maddie smiled. Even her cousin's awkward little speech came off as charming and utterly cool. All the guys in the room—including Mr. Campbell—stared at her as she fiddled with the pale pink bra strap that peeked out from her peasant blouse. Kate seethed when she noticed Trevor staring intensely at Cordelia. Maddie observed it all from her seat in the back of the class, knowing that nothing good could come of any of this.

∞

A couple of weeks into the semester, Kate and the girls had made it quite clear that they were not going to give up on making Cordelia's life miserable. Maddie couldn't understand why her cousin had become the brunt of all of Kate's anger, but she assumed it had something to do with the fact that Cordelia was probably the only person in the history of Hawthorne Academy who wasn't completely terrified by Kate Endicott. She wasn't impressed by her money, her family's influence, or her obvious wrath.

During French class one afternoon, Kate kicked a cheat sheet under Cordelia's desk. When Maddie tried to signal to Cordelia, Madame Rousseau noticed the interaction and demanded to know whose cheat sheet it was. Kate giggled, eagerly anticipating Cordelia's punishment.

But Cordelia stood up and said in a loud, clear voice, "Je ne sais pas qui a écrit la note, Madame Rousseau. Peut-être elle appartient à quelqu'un dans la classe qui n'a jamais habité en France ou ne peut pas parler la langue couramment, comme j'évidemment bidon."

Kate turned and looked with great surprise at Darcy, who shrugged her shoulders. Madame Rousseau smiled and said, "Ms. LeClaire has informed me that she doesn't know who wrote the note, but perhaps, it was someone in the class who has never lived in France and cannot speak the language fluently, as she obviously can."

She turned to Cordelia and said, "Two things are obvious, Cordelia. One is that someone is trying to get you into trouble"—she narrowed her eyes at Kate before continuing—"and two, you belong in a higher level of French."

"Merci, Madame," Cordelia said gratefully. "Je suis d'accord complètement avec vous."

∞

After class, Maddie slammed her lunch tray down on the table, exhausted from having to divide her allegiance between the Sisters of Misery and Cordelia. Luckily, Cordelia had been spending her lunch hours with Mr. Campbell. She was excelling in his English class, so he was giving her training to do some tutoring work on the side. As much as she wished she could have lunch with her cousin, it worked out perfectly because Maddie knew that she'd never be accepted at their lunch table.

"Nice job in French class today, Kate. Real nice," Maddie said angrily.

"Je ne comprends pas," Kate said innocently. "I was just trying to help your cousin out. Who knew she was freakin' Celine Dion?"

"Celine Dion isn't from France, you moron; she's from Canada," Darcy said.

"French Canadian! Close enough." Kate retorted. Bridget took her place at the table, and Kate smirked when she saw that Bridget's tray held nothing but wilted lettuce and a fruit cup. Bridget, who used to be a normal, healthy weight, had wasted away to nothing over the summer after Kate had gotten the rest of the girls to call her Bridget Bubble Butt or Triple B. She begged her mother to put her on Weight Watchers and supplemented her diet with a daily cocktail of assorted diet pills. Some were smuggled out of her mother's medicine cabinet, and others—illegal in the U.S.—she bought off the Internet. Her rapid weight loss didn't seem to send up any red flags for her teachers or her parents. So she continued to waste away, the skin around her eyes sunken and hollow, her clavicle too prominent, and her head too large for her slender body. Maddie finally understood why girls who lost weight that dramatically were called The Lollipop Girls.

When Maddie mentioned to Kate how concerned she was about Bridget's health, Kate took great pleasure in singing or humming the "Lollipop" song or simply doing the *plop* sound whenever Bridget walked by. And then, whenever Bridget started looking healthy again or was seen eating normally, Kate was always at the ready; whether it was "innocently" blowing bubbles with bubble soap or bubble gum, anything that reminded Bridget of Kate's taunts from the previous year would send her spiraling back into picking at lettuce or gnawing on carrots, while wistfully looking away from their full lunch trays.

"You're going to need more than that to eat if you're going to be any help to us today in our match against Cross Prep," Kate complained. Bridget pretended that she didn't hear her and pushed food around her plate. "Or maybe you'd like to save your energy to try to hook up with Trevor again. I bet he'd *love* that."

Kate controlled all of the dynamics within the Sisters of Misery, and when she was in a bad mood, she typically took it out on the rest of them. Once, when Trevor and Kate were broken up, he'd hooked up with Bridget after having too much to drink at a party. This had infuriated Kate to no end. If Bridget hadn't been part of the Sisterhood, her life would have been mercilessly destroyed by Kate. Once they got back together, Kate and Trevor started calling Bridget "Fish Sticks," saying that Trevor only did it to see how far she would go with him, but that he stopped when he realized she smelled like fish and her body felt like a bag of sticks. When that scandal faded, they made up another rumor about catching Bridget hooking up with another girl.

But today, Bridget was desperate to deflect Kate's wrath onto someone else. "Where's your cousin, Maddie? Isn't she the one who's been hitting on Trevor these days? Or is she too busy being Mr. Campbell's teacher's pet?"

"I already told you," Maddie sighed, "she's not into Trevor. I don't think she's into any of the guys at Hawthorne," Maddie said, conveniently ignoring the comment about Mr. Campbell. Even though Cordelia stressed that their relationship was purely platonic, strictly student-teacher, she didn't want to give Kate more ammunition.

"Well then, there are plenty of girls for her to choose from," Kate laughed. "Just tell her to stay away from me." She paused and looked over at Bridget. "Hey B, you want a shot at Maddie's cousin?"

Bridget shot Kate a fierce look and then gave her the finger.

Kate laughed louder. "Rrrreowr! She's a tiger. I think Triple B may be too intense for your skanky cousin."

Kate twirled a strand of honey-blond hair around her fingers, staring Bridget down and smiling. "Hey, I know, Maddie, since our game against Cross isn't until later tonight, why don't we check out your aunt's store after school today? I mean, it must be a pretty cool place if you'd rather spend your time there than hang out with us, right? Do they have cauldrons and eye of newt and bat wings and all that jazz?"

Maddie gave Kate a sour look. The last thing she wanted was to have Kate and the rest of the girls there poking fun at Rebecca and Cordelia. She could handle it at school, but she didn't want to deal with it anywhere else. "I don't think it would interest you, Kate. If you want a witch store, go to Salem."

Undeterred, Kate turned to Bridget. "Maybe they have some sort of potion for losing weight. Whaddya think, Bridge?"

"How about a potion to make people stop being such bitches," Bridget cried as she shoved her tray in Kate's direction and took off in tears.

"Why did you do that?" Maddie asked Kate. Hannah and Darcy were giggling like crazy, excited that they had managed to escape Kate's wrath—at least for today.

"Because I can, dear," Kate snapped. "Because I can."

# Chapter 6

## URUZ

ᚢ

## POWER

*A Dark, Unstoppable Force, A Challenge, Unpredictable
Power, Death, and Greed*

Maddie was already at Rebecca's Closet when the girls filed into the shop, one after another, their faces a mixture of curiosity and disgust. She had foolishly hoped that they wouldn't show up. The less interaction between Cordelia, Rebecca, and the Sisters of Misery, the better.

Kate ran her fingertip along the wooden shelving and then brought it up to her face, as if inspecting for dust. Maddie smiled, knowing that Kate Endicott had never dusted in her life, so it was probably something she'd seen in a movie and was doing for the other girls for effect.

Stopping next to the shelf filled with essential oils, Kate picked one up and said, "Ah, Oil of Abramelin, just what I wanted."

Maddie gave her a curious look and was met by one of Kate's signature blinding smiles. "Hey there, shopgirl, I need some help ASAP." She banged her hand on the bell that sat on the counter.

Maddie rolled her eyes. "Kate, why are you here?" Maddie said weakly. She was afraid of what they would say or do.

The girls were eyeing the store ravenously, looking for something to use against Cordelia at school.

"That's no way to treat a paying customer. I think you need a lesson in customer service, young lady."

Darcy squealed as she ran over to inspect a large oak barrel filled to the top with crystals and polished stones. She dug her hand deep into the pile of smooth stones and grabbed a handful, inspecting each one closely. "This is so cool!" she said excitedly. Kate shot her a look, and Darcy, as if on cue, dumped the contents back into the barrel and sheepishly joined the group.

"Welcome to Rebecca's Closet," Rebecca said cheerfully, coming up behind Maddie. "Are you friends of Maddie's and Cordelia's?" she asked innocently.

Kate seemed to be the designated spokesperson for the group. "We're friends of Maddie's," she said pointedly.

"Ah, but soon you'll be the best of friends with my little girl as well. I can tell," Rebecca said brightly as she continued unpacking a box filled with packs of tarot cards.

"How can you tell?" Kate asked with a feigned wide-eyed innocence. "I mean, are you a psychic or something?" Maddie seethed as she heard the other girls choke back their giggles. Rebecca seemed oblivious to Kate's sarcasm, and Maddie was thankful for that.

"Well," Rebecca said, choosing her words as she narrowed her eyes in thought, "we are all a little psychic. It just takes practice to harness those powers. We all have gifts. You just need to know how to use them."

Rebecca's answer was so earnest that it broke Maddie's heart because she knew that the girls were just playing along.

"So can you tell people's future?" Bridget asked excitedly.

Kate gave her a withering look. "Of course she can," Kate said under her breath. "She's a witch."

If Rebecca heard Kate's comment, she didn't show it. Silently, Maddie prayed that the girls would just turn around and leave. She stared at the incense burning on the counter and willed it to set off the fire alarm, forcing everyone out onto the cobblestone street. Anything that would remove them all from this potentially explosive situation.

Rebecca eyed the girls for a moment and then reached underneath the oak counter. "I can't tell things just by looking at you, but if I use tools like these," she said pulling out a pack of tarot cards, a bag of rune stones, and a crystal pendulum, "they help me focus my energies and look into the future."

Kate moved forward inquisitively and looked at the divination instruments laid out in front of her. Just then, Cordelia came bursting into the store, her arms filled with bags.

"Help!" she called over to Maddie cheerfully. Her enthusiasm died down suddenly when she saw Kate and the other girls. "Oh, hey," Cordelia said offhandedly.

Kate beamed. "Your mom is going to tell our future. Isn't that cool?"

Cordelia eyed Maddie and Rebecca as if they were traitors. "Yeah, cool," she said. She turned to her mother. "How much are you charging her for a reading?"

Rebecca looked confused. "Oh, I wouldn't think of charging your friends for a reading."

Cordelia laughed sharply. "Friends?" She shot Kate a look. "Like I said, how much are you going to charge Kate?"

Rebecca flushed, suddenly realizing what Cordelia meant. "Well, I . . . oh . . . I don't mind doing it just this once."

Kate gave one of her phoniest smiles. "I'd love for you to give me a very complete reading. Is this enough?" She handed over a crisp one-hundred dollar bill as offhandedly as if it were a five.

Maddie's stomach flip-flopped. How was it possible that she had never realized how condescending Kate could be?

"Rebecca, you don't have to—" Maddie stammered.

Cordelia interrupted, "No, Maddie. Let her. I'm curious to see what's in store for the infamous Kate Endicott."

Rebecca tentatively took the bill, shifting her gaze from Maddie to Kate to Cordelia. "Come over here," she said to Kate, leading the way to a table covered in black velvet.

The other girls crowded around as Kate took a seat directly across from Rebecca. Kate placed the apothecary bottle down on the table. When Rebecca saw what Kate had chosen, her eyes widened slightly, and she regarded Kate quizzically. Cordelia hopped up onto the oak counter, swinging her legs back and forth. The sound of feet banging on the counter filled the brick store like a hollow metronome.

"Where's your crystal ball?" Kate asked. The other girls giggled, and Rebecca's eyes clouded over as she realized that these girls were not serious about the reading. They were here to make fun of Rebecca, Cordelia, and this store. Maddie gave Rebecca a pleading look, hoping to impart that she had nothing to do with these girls coming to the store that afternoon.

Rebecca's voice lost its friendly tone. "I don't use one. I use other . . . tools."

"Like from Home Depot?" Kate said, again with an innocent tone. The others snickered.

Rebecca raised one eyebrow, sat up very straight, and grabbed Kate's hand suddenly.

"Ow," Kate said, laughing. "Boy, this really is a hands-on reading." Maddie wasn't sure, but she thought she could almost detect hesitation in Kate's voice.

Rebecca placed Kate's manicured hand over a well-worn stack of tarot cards. She grabbed a bag of rune stones and dumped them onto the table, arranging them around Kate's down-turned hand.

"Pick one," Rebecca ordered. Her easygoing demeanor was now replaced with a more serious focus. Rebecca, like Tess, had the ability of seeing through people to their core. She obviously didn't like what she saw when she looked at Kate. Her aunt's beautiful face, typically characterized by a wide smile and relaxed expression, had hardened and drained of color.

Kate tried to look serious as she dug down through the pile and pulled out a card, but then she glanced at it and quickly shoved it to the bottom of the pack. She pulled another card, looked at it, and seemed pleased as she handed it to Rebecca.

Rebecca remained expressionless as she placed the card—the Queen of Pentacles—in the center of the rune stones and looked at each one closely. Then she instructed Kate to select four stones. Kate hesitantly pointed at four onyx stones with different, unusual shapes on them. Rebecca arranged the card in the center of the four stones. She pointed to the card and said, "This is you." Kate reached to turn the card around, but Rebecca stopped her. "Don't move the card," she warned. "Part of the meaning is tied to the direction in which the card is pointing."

Kate seemed pleased. "I'm a queen!" she said, turning to the other girls. "I always knew I was royalty." She laughed as Rebecca regarded her with narrowed eyes. "What does the Queen of Pentacles mean?"

"Well," Rebecca said hesitantly, her eyes fluttering up to meet Cordelia's. Maddie knew that the card was reversed—or upside down—which almost always had a negative meaning. Typically, it would be the opposite of whatever positive fortune was held within the card. But Maddie wasn't sure how much Rebecca would reveal to Kate. Usually, she didn't like to share anything bad with her customers, and despite her obvious dislike of Kate, it appeared that she was going to remain professional. "The Queen loves beautiful things and has an artist's eye. She enjoys material comforts and surrounds herself with people who give her what she wants. Her home is impeccably and lavishly decorated. Everything about her is beautifully and tastefully maintained: her clothes, her appearance, her jewelry. She gets what she wants and ultimately," Rebecca paused, holding Kate's gaze, "she gets what she deserves."

Cordelia laughed. "Now, tell her what the reversed meaning is."

Rebecca shot her daughter an angry look, but continued. "Well, the reverse meaning is that the Queen enjoys being surrounded by people who shield her from criticism. Often, she cannot see beyond her own wealth and material possessions. She uses her good fortune to display grandeur and opulence."

Rebecca took a quick look at the bottom card of the deck before shuffling it back into its velvet pouch. Her face darkened. She moved the four stones around the card as she continued her reading.

"The stones you have selected are Isa, which represents ice; Hagal, hailstorms; Thurisaz, thorns; and Gebo, which means gift."

"What do they mean?"

"Isa represents great strength and independence, but also a coldness which can give rise to conflict and arguments. Hagal means hail and is symbolic of uncontrolled and destructive forces, upheaval, and discord. Thur also represents strength, but it can only be found by observing the past and the future. If not, then it can represent negative change, contemplation, and conflict."

"Well, I like the gift part," Kate muttered, "I'm not too

thrilled about the rest of them. God, that reading pretty much sucked." She allowed herself to look disappointed for only a moment before brushing it away. She smiled, turning to the other girls. "Well, at least I know it said I was a queen and that I have a gift coming my way. That's pretty cool, right?"

Cordelia jumped off the counter and took a closer look at the reading laid out on the table. "Actually, the gift stone is reversed, too."

"Cordelia . . ." Rebecca interrupted. "I don't . . ."

She continued. "It shows you bringing harm to your friendships and intense separation all due to your self-centered behavior. I think that's a pretty accurate reading, Mom. Good job."

Next, Rebecca dangled a crystal pendulum over the card and stones, watching intently which way the crystal swung. Maddie had never witnessed Rebecca doing such an intense reading before. It seemed to go beyond simply what Kate wanted to know. It seemed as though Rebecca was doing it for herself.

Suddenly, she dropped the crystal, and she grabbed Kate's hand again, wrenching it toward her over the table as if she was looking for something hidden in the lines of her palm. She almost seemed confused, even flustered.

"Um, ow?" Kate said again, widening her eyes toward her friends.

Rebecca paid no attention to Kate's remarks, instead furiously studying the lines in her hands. The longer and harder she stared into Kate's upturned palm, the more distraught Rebecca seemed to get. It was as if she was witnessing something horrible unfolding in Kate's future.

"What?" Kate said anxiously. She peered into her own hand as if there was some secret message inscribed there that she could also see if she only looked deep enough. Then, catching herself, she put on a bored expression and said in a haughty tone, "Well, what do you see?"

Rebecca looked up at Kate and released her hand, obviously holding back what she really wanted to say. "It's actually quite close to your card and stone reading. Your palm tells me that you are very fortunate. Just beware that some things that you take for granted—that you feel are your due—can come back to haunt you."

"Oh, wow," Kate said in a mock serious tone. "Thank you so much, Mrs. LeClaire. I feel so enlightened now. This has been so educational."

Rebecca didn't look at Kate or the other girls as she packed up her divination tools. She grabbed the bottle marked *Oil of Abramelin* and held it out to Kate. "Are you sure *this* particular oil is what you want?"

Kate smiled, "Oh, yes. I read about it somewhere, and I just knew that this would be the place to find it."

Rebecca held Kate's gaze for a moment, her beautiful face expressionless. "Then I won't charge you any extra for it. But be careful. These are not things that should be played around with. Maddie, I need Cordelia's help out back. Can you watch the store for me?"

Maddie nodded as Rebecca and Cordelia hurried into the back room.

"Do you think that she could have guessed all of the crap about the Queen and material wealth and good taste and that I get everything I want by my Rolex, my diamond rings, my Kate Spade purse, or was it really all in the cards? Ooooohhh, so mysterious!" Kate said jokingly. "Plus, the only reason she said all that crap about me being a bitch and wreaking havoc or—what did she say?—having uncontrolled and destructive forces is because that's exactly what Cordelia wanted her to say. Just to scare me. Look at me, I'm shaking," she said, holding out her hands. The other girls laughed along with her. "God, what a racket they've got going here. Good thing for them that we've got so many gullible people in this town."

"Kate," Maddie said in an exasperated tone, "what else do you want? I mean, are you finished here?"

"Oh, no, Maddie darling," Kate said. "I'm just getting started." She burst out laughing as the other girls followed her out the door. "Don't be late for the game tonight. Or else, you'll be subjected to my destructive and uncontrollable wrath."

Maddie went into the back room after the girls had left, curious to see what Rebecca really saw in the lines of Kate's hands. Rebecca was speaking in hushed tones to Cordelia, but stopped abruptly when Maddie entered. Rebecca quickly made an excuse to leave, saying something about needing supplies as she hurried past Maddie.

Rebecca then stopped mid-stride, turned to the girls and said, "I don't think you should be spending much time with that Kate girl. Her aura is very bad, very dark. Plus," she hesitated for a moment as if choosing her words carefully, "her purchase this afternoon is disturbing. Anyone buying that particular oil . . ." her voice trailed off. "Have you ever heard of chaos magic?"

Maddie stared at her blankly. "Oh . . . never mind," Rebecca said quickly. "I know that you've been friends with those girls for a long time, but trust me when I tell you that they are up to no good. They are dangerous."

She paused for a moment, as if weighing how much she wanted to tell Maddie.

Maddie recognized the worried look on Rebecca's face—it was the same one that Tess had when it came to the Sisters of Misery. Maddie was always worried that Tess would disapprove if she found out what went on in their meetings, especially the initiation rituals. According to the ritual, each member of the Sisterhood had to spend the night alone on Misery Island. Luckily, up until that point, Maddie had never been chosen to stay the night—Kate had never held her to it because of her family name. Somehow, the Crane name was both a blessing and a curse. She was fortunate that she didn't have to spend the night out on Misery, but it always felt like she had little choice in her friendships.

"The card that Kate originally picked was this one." Rebecca extended the card so Maddie could take a closer look at the grotesque figure on the card and read the word at the bottom: *Devil.* "To make matters worse, it was reversed when she pulled it from the deck."

"What does that mean?" Maddie asked, knowing from Rebecca's expression that it couldn't be good.

Rebecca looked back and forth at the two girls. "It means you need to stay away from that girl—all of those girls—but that one especially." With that, she raced out of the store, claiming that she needed to cleanse herself from all the negative energy.

"What was that all about?" Maddie asked Cordelia, who was putting price tags on various items.

"Mom just got freaked out by your friends," Cordelia said, making air quotes when she said the word friends. "She wants us to stay away from them. She said something about Kate taking 'the left-hand path' and seeing darkness and then when Kate pulled the Devil card, well . . . whatever."

Maddie wouldn't let it go. "What did that card mean? What did Rebecca see?"

Cordelia explained, "Seeing the Devil card in any reading isn't a great thing, which is why Kate probably tried to hide it from my mom. But it's especially bad when it's reversed. It means a lot of things, actually—none of them good. The reversed Devil card signifies true evil, abuse of authority, greed, bondage to a person or situation or thing, emotional blackmail, and even death."

Cordelia's words hung over them for a few moments as they stared at each other.

Finally, she shifted her gaze back to the price tags. "Whatever," she muttered. "Why did they even come here? God, it's bad enough that we have to deal with those snobs at school, but here? That just sucks."

"What did Rebecca mean when she mentioned chaos—er something?" Maddie asked. She'd always thought the little rituals that Kate orchestrated out on Misery Island were just pretend games. But were they?

"Chaos magic. It's a kind of black magic. One where you kind of make stuff up as you go."

"You sell that stuff here?" Maddie asked.

"We sell magic supplies and Wiccan tools. We hope that people use them for good magic. But it depends on the person," Cordelia said flatly. "We have no control over what's done with the stuff once it leaves the store."

"Well," Maddie stated, "no one has ever been able to control *anything* that Kate Endicott does, so it's no big surprise there."

"Here, this is for you," Cordelia said, handing her a silk brocade purse.

Maddie opened the purse and found that it was filled with rocks and herbs.

"What's this for?"

"Protection. It's called a mojo bag. I figure with those girls as your friends, you need all the strength you can get, right? And now that my mom is all freaked out about Kate, you probably need it more than ever," Cordelia said offhandedly, retrieving the small silken purse from Maddie's hands. She opened it and pointed carefully to its contents. "Mandrake for protection, thyme for courage, and tiger's eye stones—they'll help you overcome your fears and give you a little more independence. I figure it can't hurt. See, I even made one up for myself."

Cordelia reached around her neck and pulled the silk bag up from under her shirt. She opened the bag, displaying the herbs and stones that made up her protective charm. "I've put in some nettle—that keeps away petty jealousies," she laughed.

Maddie had never realized how difficult living in Hawthorne would be for her cousin. Kate and the others made no effort to hide their feelings of contempt. But Cordelia didn't seem to care. It was as though she could endure thousands of insults hurled at her like stones without feeling a thing. No one could touch her.

Of course, Cordelia knew about the rumors that swarmed around her like angry insects surrounding their nest, stinging, swelling, but eventually subsiding. She could handle the taunts and insults that would have forced even the thickest-skinned kids at Hawthorne Academy to tears. And this angered Kate more than anyone. The more Cordelia withstood the girls' attacks, the harder they tried to break her down. Even when someone scrawled WITCH in bright red letters down Cordelia's locker door, she simply shrugged it off and proceeded to cover the word up with stickers of flowers, rainbows, and peace sign stickers.

The boys in their class, most of them sweaty-palmed and snickering, gazed at her through half-lidded eyes, making bullish, clumsy advances. But when Cordelia ignored them, she was teased and taunted, called a lesbian or a prude.

"I also added bloodstone to get rid of sadness and rose quartz for healing. Plus, I added a moonstone and an opal because they bring me the ability to commune better with the spirits of the night," she continued.

"What's that one?" Maddie asked, pointing to a reddish flower.

"Oh," Cordelia said, her eyes widening. "That's called dragon's blood."

"Yuck." Maddie made a face, wrinkling her nose. "What's that for?"

"Revenge," Cordelia said in a matter-of-fact tone. "Sweet revenge."

&

Maddie and Cordelia decided to eat their dinner down by the ocean that night. The water was calm, and the sand still held a little warmth from the afternoon sun. As they ate their sandwiches, Maddie opened up a little more about her group of friends and how they were called the Sisters of Misery, the initiation rituals, and some of the milder things they had done. Shop lifting, egging people's houses, toilet papering trees, spray painting mean words on the sidewalk in front of people's houses. As Maddie relayed this information, the expression on Cordelia's face turned from mild annoyance to disgust.

"And you call these people your friends? Why, Maddie?"

Cordelia picked up a flat stone and whipped it toward the water, watching it skip across the calm sea.

Maddie couldn't explain. There was never a time in her life that those girls weren't her friends. They were just always there—for the good times and the bad. She'd never really questioned it before, not until Cordelia came into her life.

"You'll see," Maddie offered. "It's just a lot easier being on their side. They can make life pretty brutal."

Maddie told Cordelia about the first time she was involved in one of Kate's schemes, one that still made her stomach wrench with guilt. When they were ten, Kate had taken a particular dislike to a girl in her class, Emily Patterson. Kate decided one afternoon to lure her into their group. From the look on Emily's face when Kate was kind to her, it was as if the clouds had parted, and she was basking in the warmth of Kate's attentive glow. At only ten years of age, Kate had already taken part in a few Misery Island rituals with her older sister. And she seemed eager to take the dirty tricks she had learned from the older girls out on others. Maddie, Hannah, Bridget, and Darcy were just happy to be on Kate's side. It was much safer than being against her.

"Come on, Em," Kate said cheerfully as she invited the group back to her house after school. Emily trotted along happily beside Kate like a lamb being led to slaughter. As the girls gathered round the granite island in Kate's expansive kitchen, Kate set out some cookies for everyone, watching as they happily sat back and chomped away, gossiping about school, boys, teachers, other girls in the class. Emily devoured her cookie and slugged back some milk. It killed Maddie to sit idly by, forced to watch Emily's humiliation.

Earlier that day, Kate had dipped Emily's cookie in the school toilet, allowing Darcy and Hannah to take turns peeing on it. Maddie watched them, horrified, begging Kate to reconsider. Kate hissed, "If you say one word to that cow before she eats the cookie, plan on having to closely inspect everything you eat around us from now on. Got it, Crane?"

"But, Kate," Maddie pleaded, "she hasn't done anything to you. It's not fair."

"Life isn't fair, Maddie," snapped Kate. "The sooner you figure that out, the better."

So, Maddie watched sadly as Emily happily munched on the cookie, thrilled to be included in the "cool" girls' afternoon plans. It was only after she finished eating that Kate gleefully told Emily what she had just consumed.

Maddie had always thought "turning green" was just an

expression. But that afternoon, Emily Patterson's face turned a mild shade of chartreuse. She abruptly ran for the counter sink, heaving into the stainless steel basin. The girls all laughed, and Kate said something about how she was only trying to help Emily kick start her diet. Maddie felt compelled to run to the girl's side, rub her back, pull her hair from her face, do something, anything to make her feel better, but just as she made a move from her chair, Kate caught her eye.

"Don't do it, Maddie. Never cross your sisters," she said icily. "Never."

When Maddie finished her story, Cordelia was staring at her, almost in disbelief. "Now it makes sense."

"What makes sense?"

"Why you put up with all this crap. You're terrified of them," Cordelia mused. "Keep your friends close and your enemies closer. I get it."

Maddie turned away in anger, but Cordelia appeased her by saying, "No, no. I totally get it. I'd be freaked out by them, too, if those were the only people I'd ever known. But you need to know that the way they act—what they do to you, to other people—is NOT normal."

Maddie nodded. "Kate definitely has a power trip thing going."

"You think?" Cordelia said with a laugh, shaking her head. Maddie silently hoped that her cousin didn't think less of her because she went along with the Sisters.

"So, just stay away from them. Easy enough, right?" Cordelia offered. The air was starting to cool down, and a wind had picked up across the coastline.

"Actually . . ." Maddie admitted to her midnight plans—going night swimming with Kate and the girls. It was a tradition that Kate had started years ago at the beginning of every school year.

Cordelia thought for a moment and then said flatly, "Then I'm coming."

"What? No!" Maddie said quickly. She hated the thought of going by herself, but if Cordelia tagged along, it would be even worse for both of them.

"Why not? After what I've seen and heard, I don't trust them. Plus, my mom warned me about those girls. She saw something . . . something bad."

"Exactly," Maddie insisted. She knew it was a bad idea from the start. "But I'm safer with them than you are."

Cordelia smiled. "I'm a strong girl. I can take it. Besides, maybe I want to join your little sorority."

Maddie looked at her, dumbfounded. She couldn't be serious.

Cordelia broke into hysterical laughter. "I wish you could see your face right now. It's priceless!" She paused for a moment, chewing thoughtfully on her sandwich. "Don't tell Kate I'm coming, though. I don't want to give her time to plan any little surprises for me."

Maddie was surprised at how well Cordelia could anticipate Kate's actions.

Maddie was beginning to feel like a frayed rope in an endless game of tug-of-war between Cordelia and the Sisters of Misery. She only feared what would happen when the rope inevitably snapped.

ജ

A look of shock passed across Kate's face when Maddie showed up with Cordelia high atop the jagged rocks at Fort Glover that cool September evening.

"I didn't realize we were bringing new recruits tonight," Kate said.

"I wanted to see what all the fuss was about your little

group, that's all," Cordelia shot back. "Maybe I want to join."

Kate and the other girls laughed hysterically.

"We're not like the Y. Not just anyone can join," Kate said.

The tide had changed dramatically since their peaceful dinner on the beach, and the water churned angrily below them. Maddie could only see the white caps on top of the black water, moving as if it was a living entity, a monster beneath the surface, waiting to devour its eager and willing prey.

"Isn't there a nepotism clause? I mean, I *am* related to one of your members," Cordelia said, not willing to back down.

Kate looked at the others and then turned back to Cordelia.

"Fine, but you have a few things you need to accomplish before you are officially a Sister."

Cordelia sighed and then crossed her eyes at Maddie, obviously holding back a grin. Maddie tried to avoid eye contact. The last thing they needed was for both of them to start giggling.

"So, if you really want to be a part of the Sisters of Misery," Kate stated as she pointed to the angry squalls below, "dive right in."

Maddie held Cordelia back. "Kate, you can't be serious. We never dive in from here when the waters are this rough. She'll kill herself."

Kate and Cordelia were locked in an intense stare. It was as if whoever looked away first was giving in. Kate had never given in to anyone in her life.

"Who ever said joining our group was easy?" Darcy laughed.

This was getting out of hand. Even though Cordelia and Rebecca refused to say what they saw in Kate's future, Maddie realized it must be pretty bad if Cordelia would actually want to join a clique of girls she so obviously hated.

Maddie longed to grab Cordelia's hand and run in the other direction. She couldn't stand to see them being cruel to Cordelia. And she knew that she couldn't control Kate. That was one of the things that tied her to Kate and the others. She could never leave or go against the group.

Ever.

In order to remain in good standing with the Sisters, each of the members had to have a picture taken of them committing a crime, no matter how small or—in some cases—horrific it might be. Only a select few knew the locations of those pictures, and Kate Endicott was one of them.

"It's kind of like insurance," Kate joked with them once.

"Or blackmail," Hannah muttered, knowing that some of her actions were the most horrendous. Kate took great delight in having Hannah hurt neighborhood pets because she knew how much of an animal lover Hannah was.

"Depends on how you look at it," Kate said lightly. "I like to think of it as something that will keep us bonded together as friends—friends forever."

No one would ever say it out loud, but Maddie knew that they all felt the same way about Kate and the Sisters of Misery. It was like making a deal with the devil. A debutante devil, but a devil nonetheless.

"Hope you can swim, California girl," Kate said.

Cordelia looked down into the churning black water below. "How cold do you think it is?" she asked Maddie.

"Let us know when you get down there," Kate said, shoving Cordelia toward the edge of the cliff.

*Don't do it, don't do it, don't do it,* Maddie inwardly chanted, hoping that Cordelia could somehow hear her pleading.

Cordelia turned and smiled at the girls, "See you in a few." She pulled her sweatshirt over her head, kicked off her shoes, and tied her hair back into a loose bun. The girls all held their breath as she was getting ready to make her dive, not believing that Cordelia wasn't going to shrink down from the challenge.

Then out of nowhere, a siren sounded, *Whoop, whoop, whoop.*

Headlights beamed brightly on the girls, who shielded their eyes from the blinding light. A voice came over the speaker, "Girls, step away from the rocks. I repeat, step away from the edge of the rocks."

"Great," Kate muttered under her breath. "Just when the fun was starting."

A police officer got out of his car and gave them a verbal warning, saying that if he caught them up there again, he'd have to take them all in.

"Guess it's your lucky night," Kate hissed under her breath to Cordelia. "To be continued, girls." Kate stomped past the cop, with the others quickly falling into line behind her. Maddie was silently thanking the gods, the guardian angels, the power of positive thinking, anything and everything that had gotten them out of that potentially lethal situation.

As Cordelia and Maddie made their way back home, Maddie was overcome with relief. "I can't believe how lucky we were. You were so close to jumping! You could have killed yourself. Kate will definitely back off you now that she knows how strong you really are." Maddie rambled on and on all the way back to the house.

Finally, Cordelia turned to her and said, "Maddie, luck had nothing to do with it. I had a friend watching out for us. I told him if things looked shady, to call the cops. And he came through for me. That's all."

Madeline was confused. "Your friend? What friend? Who was following us?"

Cordelia smiled like the Cheshire cat, "You have your secrets, Miss Mysterious Sister of Misery, and I have mine." She gave Maddie a quick hug and ran up the stairs to her bedroom.

# Chapter 7

## TIWAZ REVERSED

## WAR

*Beware Dishonorable Motives, Underhanded
Actions, Leaving You Helpless*

### OCTOBER

One brisk afternoon a few days later, Kate excitedly discussed plans for the upcoming weekend as they changed into their gym uniforms in the locker room.

"Trevor told me that his parents are going away on vacation, and he's planning one of his famous parties! It's going to be amazing!"

Kate chattered on as the Sisters of Misery formed a semicircle around her. Further down the bench, Maddie and Cordelia pulled their clothes from their lockers. Cordelia paid no attention to the Sisters of Misery, humming a Carly Simon song as she changed into her gym clothes.

Cordelia's act of bravery on the cliffs had done nothing to change Kate's opinion of her. If anything, her hostility seemed to have increased. Kate pushed her way out of the circle and ambled over to Maddie, completely ignoring Cordelia.

"Madeline Crane, I would love it if you came with us," pleaded Kate. "You haven't been to one of our parties in so long. I feel like you're blowing us off."

Her presence at the parties never seemed to matter one way or the other. Maddie used to go all the time, but lately, the activities of her friends had become wilder and more destructive. After growing tired of the recreational drugs and alcohol that formerly were staples of their parties, her friends were now experimenting with harsher drugs with names that even *sounded* frightening. "Maybe she has better things to do with her time," Cordelia offered in a bored tone.

"Really, like what? Hanging out with a freak like you?" Kate snapped.

"Oh, I'm sorry. Maybe she *should* hang out with rich bitches who enjoy being playthings for oversexed and underworked future frat boys."

"That really hurts coming from a slut like you." Kate's eyes narrowed, and everyone in the locker room grew silent. Cordelia continued changing her clothes without even a glance at Kate and the others. She almost seemed to be enjoying the growing tension.

*Here we go*, Maddie thought.

"Oh, I'm the slut, huh? Well, that's not what Trevor told me last night," Cordelia said.

What are you doing? Maddie thought, shooting a glance at her cousin. Maddie knew for a fact that Cordelia hadn't spent any time with Trevor, but she must have known that it would put doubt in Kate's mind, and that's all that was needed to get under her skin.

"What did you say?" Kate sputtered.

Cordelia laughed and turned away from Kate. She nonchalantly tied her cleat and murmured, "*Bitch*," under her breath, despite the prickly atmosphere in the locker room.

Kate reached down and grabbed the other cleat from the wooden plank bench and whacked it against Cordelia's bare back, dragging the spikes of the cleat across her skin. Kate then whipped the shoe into the rusted locker, filling the dank room with a loud clang. Then she lunged at Cordelia, clawing at her face and arms and ripping the necklace from around her neck.

Maddie yelled out, "Kate, no!" as Kate ended the attack by spitting at Cordelia.

Cordelia winced slightly, but kept a forced, tight smile on her face despite the assault. Yet Maddie could see the tears forming in Cordelia's eyes as the beads of the necklace scattered across the cool cement floor, skipping and bouncing along the run of lockers.

Shock stained all the girls' faces. Bloody welts quickly rose to the surface of the pale skin on Cordelia's back.

Kate seemed taken aback for a moment by her own actions, but even more surprised by its lack of effect on Cordelia.

Cordelia said evenly, "Now that wasn't a very sisterly thing to do, Kate."

Maddie couldn't take it any longer, suddenly exploding and shoving Kate hard against the lockers.

"I'm so sick of this shit, Kate! What the hell? Cordelia has done nothing to you. Nothing! I'm not going to let you walk all over my cousin the way you walk all over everyone else. If you keep this up, you're . . . you're going to be sorry."

A smile tugged at the corners of Kate's mouth. She seemed to be enjoying Maddie's outburst a little too much. "Well, Maddie. I'm sorry you feel that way."

"Honestly, who the hell do you think you are?" Maddie screamed into Kate's freckled face.

"I'm Kate Endicott," she said, smiling calmly. "No one speaks to an Endicott like that. Especially not a piece of hippie trailer trash!"

The others, in a daze, obediently followed Kate out the door.

Hannah indignantly marched by Cordelia, who was now focusing all of her attention on tying her cleat.

"Witch," Hannah hissed under her breath.

"Right now, you'd better hope to hell I'm not."

Maddie waited until the heavy door swung shut before tending to the scars on Cordelia's back.

"Let me get some cold water," Maddie said, rushing over to the sinks.

"I'm fine," Cordelia muttered.

"It's a power thing with Kate," Maddie whispered, trying to explain the girl's actions, though she didn't really understand them herself. She wadded up some paper towels and ran them under freezing water. She gently pressed the towels onto the swollen scars, and Cordelia winced slightly. "Easy, easy. It will stop the swelling and bleeding."

"I'm fine!" Cordelia snapped.

Maddie recoiled and stepped away quickly. Cordelia pulled on her gym shirt, cringing as it slid along her back.

"Please, just help me pick up my necklace," Cordelia's voice finally cracked, her eyes glossed over with tears. The physical pain didn't seem to bother her. She was more concerned with collecting the remnants of her sea glass and semiprecious stone necklace, a gift from her father right before he died.

"Sure," Maddie whispered and fell silently beside Cordelia on her hands and knees. They worked in silence until every last piece was retrieved.

On the way out to the field, Maddie walked a few steps behind Cordelia, trying to think of something to say that would soften what had just happened. Cordelia marched onto the field, head held high as she swept her hair up into a tight ponytail. Finally, Maddie forced a short, hard laugh, trying to break the tension and at the same time, quell the growing fear in the pit of her stomach, "I've never seen anything like that before. I really can't believe Kate did that."

Cordelia stopped, looked her straight in the eye, and said, "If you honestly think that's all Kate is capable of, Maddie, then you're just as crazy as she is." Then she walked toward the field where the Sisters of Misery were yelling and laughing in the amber glow of the late afternoon sun.

Maddie's smile froze on her face. She wondered just how far Kate's wrath would extend, and deep down, she knew who would inevitably be on the receiving end.

∞

Maddie desperately wanted Cordelia to come with her to the party, but Cordelia had other plans for that evening—ones that definitely did not include hanging out with Hawthorne Academy kids, especially the Sisters of Misery.

"I don't even think you should go," Cordelia warned as she applied a sheer coat of lip gloss on her mouth. Maddie sat on Cordelia's bed, watching her cousin get ready, wondering what it would be like to look into the mirror and have such a perfect image as her reflection. Cordelia was very secretive about where she was going and made Maddie swear that she would tell Rebecca that the two of them were attending the party together.

Maddie was skeptical of her cousin's plan. "You know how she gets," Cordelia pleaded. "She wants me to fit in here, for some reason. And the last thing I want to do is hang out with those rich bitches you call friends. Or, I'm sorry, *Sisters.*"

Maddie spotted Tess standing in the doorway. She wasn't sure how much of the conversation she'd heard. Slowly, Tess walked up behind Cordelia and knowingly placed a hand on Cordelia's back. She didn't seem surprised when Cordelia winced slightly in pain. Tess gently pulled up the shirt, revealing Cordelia's bruised and scarred back. Tess looked back and forth between them, shaking her head sadly.

"What is happening, girls?"

"Er . . . ah . . . nothing, Tess," Cordelia fumbled. Maddie knew that the last person she wanted to involve in this brawl with the Sisters of Misery was Tess. Poor, frail Tess.

Maddie jumped in. "She got hurt in gym class today. Fell into a pricker bush."

"Must have been one angry pricker bush," Tess said calmly. She peered closely at the angry welts on Cordelia's back, then turned and quickly strode from the room. Maddie and Cordelia looked at each other quizzically. *How did she know?* The thought passed silently between them.

Tess returned with a green plant. She broke one of the leaves and squeezed out a thick white paste. "Aloe," she said evenly. "For the 'pricker bush' wounds."

Tess lifted Cordelia's flowing blouse and gently rubbed the aloe onto her back, careful not to make her wince or cry out in pain. When she was done, she looked at her grand-daughters.

"You need to take care of each other. The people in this town . . . the things I've seen . . ." She shook her head. "Be careful. You two need to stick together. It's the only way."

She grasped both girls' hands tightly, squeezing them to-gether. She looked at both of them with pleading eyes before she finally left the room. Maddie and Cordelia eyed each other. If Cordelia wasn't going to mention Kate Endicott's attack, Maddie wouldn't either. She just prayed it was some-thing that they could handle on their own.

≪

The party was just like any other Hawthorne Academy party. This time, it was Maddie who was different. She felt distant—set apart from the rest of the drunken Hawthorne kids. Trevor's barn was the usual party spot when his parents were vacationing. He had set up an ice luge at the door, and everyone who entered had to take a chilled shot at the base of the block of ice. Maddie pressed her mouth up to the freezing luge, and Trevor slid a shot of Raspberry Stoli down to meet her waiting mouth. The icy chill of the vodka burned the back of her throat.

"Ugh," she said, laughing and wiping her mouth with the back of her hand. "Thanks, Trevor."

"Anything to get my girls in the mood tonight," Trevor said.

"Pig," Maddie said under her breath. She continued into the barn, wishing that she had Cordelia by her side. With Cordelia, Maddie felt impervious to everything. It was as if she was the moon and Cordelia was the sun—Maddie simply borrowed the rays from Cordelia in order to shine.

So there Maddie was, hanging out with the Hawthorne Academy kids, still trying to decipher her grandmother's cryptic warning and at the same time, wondering why Cordelia was so adamant about not telling her where she was going. At least she'd be safe from Kate and the Sisters. Maddie's only glimmer of hope of having a good time that night was if Mr. Campbell showed up. Trevor warned everyone that his older brother might make an appearance as the quote unquote chaperone and that they shouldn't freak if they saw one of their teachers while they were totally wasted.

"He's cool," Trevor insisted and then added, "He's cool about anything that has to do with drinking. Just don't get in his way when he heads for the luge."

Kate had obviously put more effort into her appearance on the off chance that their hot teacher would show up, despite the fact that she was dating his younger brother. Her staple Ann Taylor blouse and jeans were replaced by a tight-fitting V-neck shirt and low-slung jeans that showed off her slim hips. Her hair, typically pulled neatly back by a head-band, had a mussed-up, just-rolled-out-of-bed look. With eyes rimmed with smudged kohl eyeliner, Kate definitely seemed like she was on the prowl, but Maddie wasn't sure who was going to be the target that night.

Maddie took another icy shot of vodka to take the edge off and then joined her friends, who were huddled together, giggling about something.

"What's going on?" Maddie asked, wiping her mouth with her sleeve.

"Here, take one," Kate handed Maddie a sticker. It was a tiny, glittery star. Kate licked one and stuck it on her cheek. Maddie noticed that all the other girls had one as well.

Kate's giddy mood seemed to indicate that she'd gotten over the locker room incident and was ready to forgive and forget. Maddie wanted to resist, but without Cordelia by her side, she didn't feel she could stand up to Kate. So she decided to play along rather than have a repeat of the ugly incident in the locker room. "Okay." She licked it and then stuck it to her cheek.

Trevor appraised their stickers and yelled, "Whooeee, these girls are ready to party tonight!"

He grabbed Kate, and they started making out with growing intensity in front of everyone.

Hannah yelled, "Get a room!" but then proceeded to make her way over to a group of the boys on the soccer team, grinding up against them as the music floated up into the rafters of the barn.

"What's going on?" Maddie asked Darcy.

"You'll see," she giggled, then ran off with Bridget to get a drink.

Suddenly, the music pulsed through Maddie's body as if it were a tangible entity. Maddie started dancing in spite of herself, like the music was moving her body on its own.

In the distance, she saw a beautiful face. Mr. Campbell had made his way into the party and was watching the kids solemnly. He was playing the role of chaperone, but he obviously wasn't going to get in the way of his younger brother's good time. Nor did he look like he was happy about watching his students getting drunker by the minute. Maddie suddenly had the urge to go over and sit next to him, to touch him, to feel his face under her fingertips. On her way over to him, Kate grabbed Maddie by the arm.

"I wouldn't do that if I were you," she snapped.

"Do what?" Maddie giggled, feeling giddier by the moment. The vodka seemed to be taking over her body. It felt like liquid sunshine.

"You'll regret it, and we'll all get busted," she said seriously.

"But Trevor said that his brother was cool with us drinking," Maddie said, confused. Bridget, Hannah, and Darcy came out of nowhere and surrounded her.

"Yeah, but he's not cool with Ecstacy," Darcy insisted.

"Who . . . when?" Maddie asked. Then suddenly, it hit her. The sticker. Disgusted, Maddie pulled it off of her face.

"Too late," Kate singsonged.

"How could you do this to me?" she cried, her euphoric mood crumbling into tears.

"We're just having a little fun," Kate said innocently. "Get that stick out of your butt for a change and live a little." Darcy and Hannah laughed and played with each other's hair.

Maddie was furious. Pushing her way out of the group, she dashed past Trevor and his stupid luge, avoided Mr. Campbell, and ran down to the ocean. Lying down on the beach, she decided to wait out the effects of the drug before heading home. She wanted to be able to think clearly if Tess or Rebecca questioned her on Cordelia's whereabouts. Maddie let the Indian summer breeze caress her body as she waited for the high to end.

Suddenly, someone was at her side. Cordelia whispered in a concerned tone, "Are you okay?"

"How d'you find me?" Maddie slurred.

"I don't trust those girls, so I decided to check out the party to see if you were okay. Reed, er, Mr. Campbell said he saw you head down to the beach." Cordelia knelt over Maddie, a look of real concern across her face.

"I'm fine, fine, fine," Maddie said, giggling. Cordelia's face seemed to blur around the edges.

"What did they do to you?" Cordelia asked, her voice tense.

"Just too much to drink," she sighed. "Just lemme relax here for a little while."

"You'll never get sober if you just stay here," Cordelia insisted. "Come on!"

She dragged her cousin down to the water's edge. Cordelia yanked off her clothes and sprinted into the ocean, diving headfirst into the waves. She called back to Maddie to swim out to meet her. Maddie jumped up and splashed clumsily into the water, shedding clothes as she ran.

Despite Maddie's athletic build, Cordelia was a far superior swimmer. She slipped beneath the surface, disappearing for long stretches of time, gliding underwater like a sea creature. A few weeks ago, Tess had told them that Cordelia was an Irish name for "of the sea," and Cordelia was convinced it meant she was some type of mermaid washed ashore. Maddie half-expected her to dive under the waves and head out into the open sea, just like a real mermaid.

They exited the waves, sputtering and giggling. Their underwear and tank tops were plastered to their rail-thin bodies, their hair streaming down their backs like seaweed. Maddie knew something was wrong as soon as they came ashore. Their clothing had been moved, thrown across a few jagged slabs of rock. Cordelia whipped around to see who had witnessed their nighttime swim, but the beach was deserted. If it had been the Sisters of Misery, they would have stolen the clothes, destroyed them, or thrown them into the water. But this was something entirely different. It was almost like someone wanted them to know that they were being watched.

Just as they reached the end of the beach, Maddie looked back and spotted the dark outline of a man watching them. Before she could get a better look, he turned and disappeared over one of the dunes, swallowed up by the night.

# Chapter 8

## HAGALAZ

# ᚺ

## HAILSTORM

*Wrath of Destructive, Uncontrolled Forces; Testing, Trial, and Suffering*

### HALLOWEEN

"**N**o way," Cordelia said firmly as they were getting ready for school. She no longer trusted Maddie to go along with Kate and the girls, especially after Trevor's party. "Why the hell would anyone want to spend the night on some creepy island? Just blow them off, Maddie. You don't have to go through with this. You know that you don't!"

"I kind of have to. You know that I'm part of this—this Sisterhood," Maddie cringed. She could see how ridiculous it sounded by the look in Cordelia's face. "Kate will kill me if I don't go along with them as usual."

"Oh, good Lord," Cordelia sighed. "What's the big deal? Geez, people treat me and my mom like we're witches, and it sounds to me like you're the one who's in a coven," she said, laughing uneasily. "Has Kate ever stayed out on the island?"

Maddie explained that Kate's older sister, Carly, forced her to stay on the island when she was barely nine. Kate, never one to shrink from a challenge, had remained the entire night. The next morning when they all met up to retrieve her, Kate seemed totally unaffected by the night's challenge. While they were congratulating her on making it through the night, Kate's eyes glazed over as if she was willing herself not to cry. That was the only time Maddie had ever seen Kate vulnerable. As they all filed back along the path, Maddie gave Kate a supportive, yet awkward hug, but Kate just shoved her away in disgust, unwilling to show the slightest bit of weakness. Kate Endicott was the youngest girl in the history of the Sisters of Misery to ever stay out on the island, making her somewhat of a local legend.

Cordelia fell back onto Maddie's bed in disgust. She stared at the ceiling for a few minutes and then sat up purposefully. "Then I'm going with you," Cordelia said flatly. "It's suicide for you to go out to Misery Island with those girls, and on Halloween of all nights."

Maddie was nervous about going, but she knew it was a bigger risk for Cordelia. It wasn't just that the Sisters of Misery hated her; they were jealous of her—that much was obvious. Why shouldn't they be? Even Maddie had her moments when Cordelia's confidence and natural beauty were too much to take. Jealousy can make girls do crazy things. Malicious, evil things.

∞

Surprisingly, Kate gave in quickly and easily—almost too easily—when Maddie mentioned at lunch that Cordelia wanted to come along on the Misery Island trip. It worried Maddie that Kate may have been anticipating it all along.

On Halloween night, Kate Endicott marched the Sisters of Misery and Cordelia along the loamy path that wound its way deep into the core of Misery Island. Blindfolded, strands of hair snarled tightly in the knots in the back of their heads, they made their way across the island, all in a line, each clutching the hand of the girl in front of them. No one knew whose turn it would be that night; all of them feared being the Chosen One.

Branches tore at their exposed legs as they trampled through the underbrush toward a stand of trees. Mosquitoes dive-bombed their faces and bare skin, attracted by the pungent scent of bubble gum, soap, and perfume. Maddie shook her long, chestnut-brown ponytail to keep the biting creatures at bay, taking care not to break the chain for even a moment.

"Stop!" Kate ordered. "We've reached the sacred ruins of Misery Island. It is now time to show our strength and to offer up one of the members of the Sisters of Misery to spend the night."

Nervously, they squeezed each other's hands. Cordelia's hand remained limp and cool. This was her first time on the island. She didn't know enough to be afraid.

"For those of you who've been through this before, you know what the rules are. For *others*," Kate paused, and even blindfolded, Maddie could almost see her sneer, "This is your first time to show solidarity with your Sisters and to show that you are truly one of us."

*You two need to stick together*, her grandmother's words rang out clearly in her mind. *It's the only way . . .* Maddie wondered if Tess knew about this night, if she had seen it coming and was warning them. Warning Maddie not to leave Cordelia behind. No matter what. Maddie shook off the chill that crept over her.

"Girls, you know what to do. Once I remove your blindfold, head back to the boat. One of you lucky ladies, however, gets to stay tied to this tree all night—"

"The Sacred Birch," Hannah whispered.

"That's right," Kate continued. "As the Chosen One, you will spend the night on the island tied to the Sacred Birch outside of the island ruins as a way to prove your worthiness to the group. If you're lucky, you'll make it through the night without being visited by the three witches of Misery, the ones who died out here after being exiled from Hawthorne."

"And still remain in spirit . . ." Darcy whispered.

Kate paused. Maddie felt Cordelia bristle for a moment.

"Yes," Kate said, lowering her voice. "They're here, or at least something is still out here." Kate drew in a dramatic breath and continued. "Tomorrow morning, we will all meet back here at sunrise to make sure that the Chosen One spent the night with no help and no attempts to get back to the mainland. Break the rules and face the consequences, ladies."

Cordelia let out an exasperated sigh. Maddie was almost grateful for the blindfold because she knew one look at her cousin's bemused expression would cause them both to break out in hysterical laughter. There'd be no stopping Kate then.

Now, as they waited, each of them anticipating the worst, Kate paced in front of them, her long, hard glares almost palpable to each of their blindfolded faces. The chorus of their breathing was shaky and uneven. Finally, Maddie's blindfold was torn from her face, along with a few tangled strands of hair. Kate nodded her head toward Cat Cove where the boat was waiting to take the rest of them back to the mainland.

Maddie hesitated, Tess's words still ringing clearly in her mind, and then turned for the path, forcing herself not to look and see who had been left behind. Racing down toward the water's edge, Maddie had a sinking feeling that there was only one reason she had escaped spending the night out on Misery. *Cordelia.* Guilt washed over Maddie as she realized what she had done: she had brought her cousin as a sacrificial lamb.

∞

Maddie made her way back to the cove and waited for the other girls under the darkening skies, but no one followed her. She swallowed the lump of fear in her throat. Was this a trick to get her to spend the night alone on the island?

After twenty minutes of waiting, she decided to risk it and returned to the ruins at the center of the island. The girls were all in the same spot, standing in a circle.

"Earth, Water, Wind, and Fire! We call upon each of the elements to hear our voices and receive our offering." Kate's voice rose up above the churning growl of the ocean.

Maddie looked uneasily at the other girls, shifting her gaze from face to face. "What the hell is going on?" she whispered to Darcy, who was pouring red wine into paper cups.

Darcy whispered back with a smile, "Kate wants to try something different tonight. Tonight is going to be special. Just wait."

Kate had become intrigued with witchcraft ever since visiting Rebecca's Closet, and it chilled Maddie to the bone to think of how far Kate would take her new hobby. Cordelia was to the right of Kate, next to the bonfire. She rolled her eyes and smiled, but Maddie could tell there was a little fear behind her brave façade.

"What is Kate going to do?" Maddie whispered to Hannah, who shot her a look of disgust and loudly shushed her. Kate stopped and glared at her.

"Maddie, do you want all of our attention? Because if you do, I'd be happy to oblige."

"Kate, I don't understand . . . what are you doing?" Maddie asked. This was nothing like she'd ever witnessed before. Kate was out of control and drunk with power.

"What I'm doing is offering up a toast." Kate motioned to Darcy, who then provided each of them with a cup of red wine. "Here's to the Sisters of Misery."

Maddie hesitated, looking at each of her friends, but no one would make eye contact with her. "Why did you send me off to the boat?" Maddie asked angrily.

Kate simply shrieked, "DRINK!"

They all finished their wine in long gulps, throwing the cups into the fire. The fire was built with driftwood, so the sea salt turned the flames various shades of blue, lavender, and red. It was magical.

"We have come here tonight to initiate our Sister Cordelia into our sacred group—into the Sisters of Misery. But first, she must prove herself," Kate said, walking over and grabbing Cordelia firmly by the arm. Darcy moved to the other side of Cordelia, seizing her free arm.

"What the hell?" Cordelia looked angrily back and forth at them. Then she turned and looked at her cousin helplessly. "Maddie, what's going on?"

A lump rose in the back of Maddie's throat. What *was* going on?

"Kate, this is crazy. You've gone too far." Maddie tried to push the fear from her voice, but instead, it came out strained and anxious.

"I don't think we've gone far enough," Kate said smugly, staring Cordelia down. "If Cordelia is to become a part of our Sisterhood, we must cleanse her of her sins, make her worthy of the group."

The color drained from Cordelia's face as quickly as the pink and purple sunset had shifted to an ashen gray. Kate let go of her arm and turned toward the rest of them. She pulled something from her back pocket.

"I have something here in this envelope . . . information that could prevent her from becoming a part of our Sisterhood. Information that could hurt all of us if we were to become associated with her."

Maddie turned to Cordelia and looked at her in confusion, but Cordelia fixed a stony gaze on Kate.

"The evidence within the envelope will only be destroyed if each element is appeased by Cordelia. That is, Earth, Wind, Water, and, of course, Fire. And then after Cordelia has appeased the elements, it's our turn." Kate lectured. Maddie had never known anything like this to happen during an initiation ritual. And she had a sinking feeling that her role in this evening would not be an enjoyable one. "Cordelia, what would you like to do? The choice is yours."

Cordelia wrestled out of Darcy's grip and tried to grab the envelope from Kate.

"Don't even try it," Kate snapped, holding up a perfectly manicured hand. "If you don't want to be the Chosen One tonight, we could always choose someone else. Maddie, perhaps? What do you say, Cordelia—would you like Maddie to pay for your sins?"

Bridget rushed over and grasped Maddie roughly by the arm.

Maddie tried to struggle out of Bridget's grasp. "Let go of me, you bitch!" she shouted. Despite Bridget's frail frame, she easily overpowered Maddie. It didn't make sense. Maddie was much stronger than Bridget out on the field hockey playing area.

Cordelia stared at the envelope in Kate's hand. Then she looked over at her cousin sadly. Maddie shook her head, trying to convey to her cousin that she had nothing to do with this.

Cordelia looked from Kate to Maddie, then back again. "What do I have to do?" she asked, her voice resigned, her face pale with fear.

"Appease the elements. Balance out the negative karma that you brought into this town with you. Once you have

cleansed your sins—and we have cleansed your mistakes—
we will be even," Kate said and then quickly added with a
smile, "And Sisters."

∞

"The first element is Earth." Kate folded the envelope in
half and held it out to Cordelia. Just as Cordelia reached for
it, Kate snatched it back.

"Dig," instructed Hannah.

Cordelia looked around. "With what?" The ground was
cold and hard.

"Your hands, of course. They're already all blistered and
rough from all that manual labor you do in your little *witch*
shop. It shouldn't bother you a bit," Kate said. The other
girls laughed.

Cordelia got down on the ground and scratched at the dirt
with her fingertips.

"Faster, or else this will make you famous." Kate waved
the envelope in Cordelia's face.

Cordelia turned back to the ground, her hands digging furiously into the dark, cold earth. Her hands became black,
and sweat pooled at the back of her neck. Long strands of
red hair brushed the dirt.

Many times, she stopped and looked anxiously up at
Kate, but Kate would only shake her head and say, "Deeper."

Finally, after digging for what seemed like forever, blood,
dirt, and saltwater combined to make a mottled paste on
Cordelia's hands and forearms.

"You seem to be enjoying this a little too much." Kate
snapped.

"I'm just pretending that I'm digging your grave, Kate,"
Cordelia said as she stood up. "So, have I *appeased* the
earth?"

"Not yet," Kate said. "Upon such sacrifices, my Cordelia, the gods themselves throw incense."

Maddie recognized the quote from *King Lear*, and that's when it hit her—this had all been planned from the beginning. Once she knew Cordelia was coming, Kate had tailor-made the entire ritual for Cordelia, Kate's guest of honor.

As if on cue, Hannah, Bridget, and Darcy grabbed Cordelia by the arms and shoved her back down to the ground, smashing her face into the hole she'd dug. Cordelia screamed and thrashed as they shoved dirt into her face and mouth. They pulled at her hair and ripped her clothes. Maddie's legs felt rubbery. It was straight out of some crazy horror movie. Kate gleefully presided over the brutality, her arms folded across her chest.

Maddie screamed and ran at Kate, intending to tackle her to the ground, but her legs buckled, and she hit the ground hard. Her vision blurred as she struggled to get to her feet. The wine! Kate must have put something in her wine. The group of girls became a clawing, writhing, tearing, muddy knot on the dark island floor. Kate smiled widely at Maddie's feeble attempts before kicking Cordelia in the side. Maddie crawled forward, attempting to pull Hannah off her cousin, but it was no use. They were out of control.

"I would stop unless you want to be next, Maddie," hissed Kate. Then she stepped toward the group. "Stop!" she ordered. "Cordelia has appeased the element of Earth."

The girls pulled back one by one with ragged, heavy breaths. Cordelia lay crumpled and limp on the ground, her entire body cut and bruised and muddied.

Kate Endicott stepped forward, shaking her long hair out of her triumphant face, her eyes glowing orange in the light from the bonfire. "Are we ready for Fire?"

Kate insisted that they were being kind to Cordelia by doing Fire before Water. The water would have washed off all of the mud, and therefore, the matches that the girls put out on Cordelia's skin would have stung more. Kate was feeding all of them a neverending supply of wine. The drunker the girls got, the more vicious they became, taking every opportunity to ruin Cordelia's beauty and destroy her spirit. Kate instructed the girls to tie Cordelia's delicate arms behind the Sacred Birch—or the Tree of Life, as Kate had begun to call it for some reason—and to force-feed her wine, all the while assuring Maddie that it would help Cordelia numb any pain she might be feeling.

Maddie watched in horror as Cordelia withstood the slow torture of the burns inflicted upon her skin. Her eyes had glazed over, and she no longer showed any signs of pain. Never in her life had Maddie felt so paralyzed with fear . . . and something else. She felt sluggish and heavy, similar to the way she felt that night at Trevor's party. Only, the euphoria she'd felt that night was replaced with a growing anxiety and paranoia. It was just as much of a punishment to sit by helplessly while Cordelia withstood so much agony and degradation.

Maddie desperately wanted to help Cordelia, but felt like she was spiraling down a tunnel. It was as if the world was actually shifting beneath her feet, and the sounds were getting more and more muffled as the ritual went on. Maddie wanted to run, but her body wasn't functioning properly. She felt like she was viewing the scene through a fish eye lens. Grotesque shapes swirled around her as she tried to clear her head and figure out a way to get them both safely off the island.

After the girls made burn marks up and down Cordelia's arms and legs, they decided that the Fire element could only be completely appeased by charring the ends of Cordelia's hair. Luckily, the mud and water caked into her hair prevented her whole head from going up in flames. By the time they were through with fire, Cordelia's hair hung muddied and tangled, with uneven scorched ends trailing down her back and along her scarred back and arms.

For the Air ritual, the girls danced around their bruised and bloodied "sister" and screamed cruel and vicious insults.

*Slut . . . whore . . . bitch . . . trailer trash . . . loser . . .* The insults went on and on.

Maddie was crying as she walked in the circle with the other girls, Cordelia at its center. Through her tears, Maddie became mesmerized by the green and blue bonfire, the flames licking out with pointed tongues.

*Circles, circles, everything in cycles.* Maddie could hear her grandmother's words ringing in her ears, the sounds of the girls' shouts and giddy yelps muffled by Tess's voice in her head, *how could you let this happen to your own flesh and blood? I warned you, Maddie. I told you to be afraid, but you couldn't see. You didn't listen. Now you're one of them. One of* them . . .

Maddie shook her head, barely able to walk, and the world was spinning; the salty night air was heavy. The girls' voices faded in and out as she was carried and shoved forward by the others. Finally, it was time to appease the element of Water. Kate shoved a bucket into Maddie's arms and told her to run down to the ocean and fill it up.

As Maddie turned to go, she caught a glimpse of Cordelia and screamed. It was as if her nightmare had come to life. Cordelia was slumped down against the tree; the blindfold hung around her neck like a noose, her mouth, slack and slightly parted, her chin on her chest. Maddie's head was pounding; her tongue had grown three sizes too large for her mouth. Still, she screamed "How could you do this to her?

You're evil! You're all evil bitches, and you're going to pay for this!"

She heaved the bucket into the stone ruins and ran blindly toward the boat. She would get the motor started somehow and make it back to shore to get help. She had to. The ritual had already gone too far. How much further would Kate take it? She was almost to the boat when something hit her in the back of the head. Maddie stumbled, but regained her footing and heaved herself toward the shore, sobbing uncontrollably. She splashed into the water and fell over the side of the boat. As she chanced a look backward, trying to see who was following her, she was met with another blinding blow, this time to her forehead.

She heard a low chuckle, which was nearly drowned out by the relentless crashing of the ocean.

Everything went black.

# Chapter 9

## LAGUZ REVERSED

## WATER

*Stormy Waters and Emotional Turmoil; A Time of Confusion, Deception, Uncertainty*

### NOVEMBER

"Where is she?" Rebecca screeched, pulling Maddie up by her shoulders into a sitting position in her bed. The Sunday afternoon light poured into Maddie's bedroom, quickly banishing the nightmarish images of Misery Island from her mind. Maddie blinked her eyes furiously, trying to bring the room into focus while at the same time wondering how and when she got home.

Tess stood in the doorframe, looking at Maddie with great disappointment. She knows what happened last night, Maddie thought, even though it was impossible. But if Tess suspected anything, she didn't let on. Instead, she stood silently in the doorway as Rebecca raged over Cordelia's absence.

"I-I don't know what you're talking about," Maddie insisted. Every inch of her body screamed in pain. She finally understood the full meaning of the expression "being put through the ringer." Her head throbbed from the alcohol and the huge bump on her forehead. Someone had hit her, but who? She knew that Cordelia was still out on the island.

They were supposed to retrieve her at dawn, but judging from the bright daylight streaming through the window, obviously Maddie hadn't made the trip back out to Misery Island. "What time is it?"

"What time is it?" Rebecca said in a mocking tone. "What TIME is it? I think it's time that you told me where the hell my daughter is."

Maddie glanced at the clock. It was past noon, and Cordelia should have been home by now. The previous night's events were hazy. Vaguely, she remembered being discovered, sprawled across her front stoop by her mother in the early hours of the morning, dropped off in haste by the other members of the Sisters of Misery. Abigail had dragged her into the house, hissing, "Are we running a brothel here? Are you and Cordelia trying to destroy my reputation?"

What *did* happen last night? She looked down and saw that her hands were cut and bloodied before quickly shoving them under the covers. "Umm . . . I-I don't know. Honestly, I don't. I mean, maybe she just crashed at a friend's house?"

"Friends? What friends?" Rebecca demanded. "Those girls I told you both to stay away from? The ones that I saw that were . . . were nothing but trouble? *Those* friends? You're Cordelia's only friend."

Those words struck Maddie like a thunderbolt. She was all Cordelia had, her only friend. And she brought her out to Misery Island with those girls—those evil, evil girls.

&

After washing the grime and sand and stink of wine off of herself in a scalding shower, Maddie remained hopeful, telling herself that Cordelia would walk through the door at any moment. But when the steam from the shower faded from the bathroom mirror, Maddie noticed the huge bruise on her forehead. She'd have to make something up quickly.

She brushed her long bangs to the side, covering the growing welt. She snuck into her bedroom to call Kate and the
others, but no one was answering. Maddie wondered if they
were all still out on the island and if she should try to get
back out there to see what was going on, yet she knew there
was no chance that Abigail or Rebecca would let her out of
the house. Not until Cordelia came home safely.

When Maddie emerged from her bedroom after unsuc-
cessfully trying to reach any of the Sisters of Misery, she
was met by Rebecca, Abigail, and Tess and another barrage
of questions. She explained the bruise by saying that she'd
been hurt at field hockey practice, but she knew that no one
was buying it. Tess, looking at her as if she was reading her
mind, was shaking her head disappointedly.

Rebecca made Maddie recount the events of the night
again and again. Maddie knew that she couldn't implicate
Kate and the others for fear of repercussions, so she kept her
answers as vague as possible.

"We went swimming down at the cove."

"Who else was there?"

"Just us . . . at first . . ."

"Were those girls involved? Did they do something to my
Cordelia?"

"Yes . . . I mean, no. Yes, they were there, but we were
just swimming and drinking and, um . . . I don't know what
the other girls were doing."

"Did they drug her?"

"No."

"Are you lying?"

"No."

"Did they drown my baby girl?" Rebecca cried.

"No!" Maddie said vehemently. The questions from Rebecca, Abigail, and Tess swirled around her, and soon she
didn't know where one question ended and the other began.

Rebecca's voice was accusatory at first, then despondent. The women whispered amongst themselves and watched Maddie for signs, clues as to what might have happened.

Maddie was torn. If she told them about the Sisters of Misery or what had gone on at Misery Island, who knew what Kate would do to her? She now knew that Kate was capable of anything. Maybe even murder. Maddie shivered and pushed the thought from her mind.

Rebecca raced around the house, checking every closet, peeking under every bed, leaving nothing unturned, while Maddie and Tess stood by helplessly. After the house had been thoroughly searched, Rebecca began calling everyone in town. She went through the phone book, name by name, number by number. Then, when the four walls of the house could no longer contain her, Rebecca and Maddie walked the entire town by foot, searching every path, knocking on every door, asking everyone they came into contact with. "My daughter?" Rebecca would plead, extending a picture to whoever she passed. The more they searched, the more withdrawn Rebecca became. It got to the point where Maddie had to do all of the talking and Rebecca just stood by her side, a look of anguish painted across her face.

As the daylight hours waned and the evening sank heavily onto all of them, Maddie had to face what her instincts had been telling her all day: something that happened out on Misery Island was preventing Cordelia from coming home. An investigation into Cordelia's disappearance began later that evening, though it was much too early to officially declare her missing. It was midnight—almost twenty-four hours since Maddie had last seen Cordelia—when Officer Garrett Sullivan came to their house.

They all gathered in the living room as Officer Sullivan asked Maddie again and again about the last time she'd seen her cousin. Maddie, trying to think of a way to lead the police in the right direction without giving up too many details about the night out on Misery, gave him the same short, noncommittal answers she'd given her family. She knew that she wasn't helping the investigation, but a part of her felt the need to hold back. Wasn't she just as responsible as the others? Hadn't she gone along with it? Maddie tried to think of a way to word the events of the night, but each time she sank deeper and deeper, as if Cordelia's blood were on her own hands as much as anyone else's.

Kate may have done all the dirty work, but Maddie had brought Cordelia out there. Didn't that make her just as guilty? She was so ashamed, that she couldn't bring herself to say anything to her family. How could they ever look at her the same way again?

"Is she dating anyone? Does she have any enemies? When was the last time you spoke with her? Has she seemed nervous lately? Is she in the habit of just taking off? Who are her friends? Do you know if anyone held a grudge against her?" Sullivan shot questions at Maddie as though she were the target on a firing range.

Gulping breaths of air down between her answers and sobs, Maddie tried to give a clear picture of Cordelia to the small-town cop, a guy barely out of school himself who she remembered as a big drinker and partier not so very long ago. Who's to say that he wasn't involved in Cordelia's disappearance? she thought. Cordelia was beautiful, unattainable, free-spirited, and rebellious. That made just about everyone in town a suspect—even Maddie.

∞

The next day at school, Cordelia's empty desk served as a reminder that nobody was safe. Flowers were heaped upon

Cordelia's homeroom desk in a makeshift memorial. Maddie almost started to think warmly of her classmates until Kate and Bridget started weaving them into each other's hair.

Lunch that afternoon was the first time the Sisters of Misery had a chance to discuss the events of Halloween. Maddie suggested that the girls go to the police with their version of the night's events leading up to Cordelia's vanishing.

"Are you insane, Maddie? Maybe you want to go to jail for being an accomplice to a crime, but I certainly don't," snapped Kate.

"What do you think could have happened to her?" Maddie asked.

"Don't pull that innocent crap with me, Maddie. You were right there with us all night. You know *exactly* what happened," Kate hissed and then lowered her voice. "And if any of you want to find out firsthand how it felt to go through Cordelia's *special* initiation, feel free to go to the police. Tell the world, I don't care. Just prepare yourself for an even more exciting night on Misery Island."

Maddie shuddered at Kate's threat. She ran the events of that night through her mind again and again, but they just weren't coming together logically. She didn't have any memories between running to the boat and being dumped on her front porch, then waking up to Rebecca's screams the next morning. Could she have helped Cordelia off the island and just blocked it out? The girls said that when they returned the next morning to retrieve Cordelia, she was already gone. Somewhere between Misery and Mariner's Way, Cordelia had simply disappeared.

"I don't see how we had anything to do with her actual disappearance," Darcy insisted, almost as if she was trying to convince herself as well as the others. "I mean, just 'cause we brought her out there doesn't mean we're responsible for her. Maybe she was kidnapped or something?"

"How do we even know something bad happened?" Kate demanded. "For all we know, she could be hiding somewhere just to get us all in trouble for what happened out on Misery. Maybe she wants us to sweat it out for a while. You know, payback for what we did to her."

Kate's idea seemed plausible enough for the other girls, but Maddie wasn't convinced. It seemed insane to Maddie that the world kept moving on, indifferent as air, when Cordelia was undoubtedly out there somewhere, feeling hurt, scared, and alone. Classes went on as usual. Students followed their daily routine. It was as if Cordelia LeClaire had never existed. And no one seemed to care.

At the end of the school day, all the girls gathered at Maddie's locker. "Come on, let's go see what news stations are in town. I'll bet they even have national news cameras here," Kate said excitedly, as if this were her shot at stardom.

Maddie was following the girls glumly down the corridor when she again had that sticky feeling of being watched. She glanced behind her and thought she saw a figure move quickly out of sight, like a shadow disappearing into thin air. Maddie turned to see if any of the other girls had noticed, but they were chatting away, trying to plan a way to get in front of the cameras.

"Come on, Crane," Darcy yelled back to her. "We don't want you to disappear on us, too!" The girls snickered at the cruel joke.

*How can this be funny to them? Do they even understand how serious this is?* Maddie thought. A lump formed in her throat as she realized that none of them really cared about what happened to Cordelia. As long as they didn't get in trouble, it didn't matter to them. Not one bit.

Any time a pretty girl goes missing, it becomes the top news story of the day. News of Cordelia's disappearance eventually spread beyond the local media, for a little while at least. News vans crowded the narrow streets. Reporters knocked on doors. Policemen and the K-9 units scoured the wooded areas.

It was the hot story of the moment, and everyone put on a great show, especially the Sisters of Misery. Crying for the news cameras that had come from Boston, Kate wiped tears from her freckled cheeks as Bridget clung to her friend, head resting on her shoulder.

"She was our best friend. We miss you, Cordelia. We love you," cried Kate.

"Whoever took her from us is a horrible person and should be punished," Bridget chimed in.

Maddie was overcome by a wave of nausea as she marched alongside Kate and the Sisters of Misery, who led a candlelight vigil that evening. It was an obvious ploy for the media's attention and would no doubt be carried on stations across the country and end up in newspapers across the globe. For a day or two. But no matter how many people were interviewed by the local channels or how many officers were dispatched to search the town, the truth of the matter was this: Cordelia wasn't one of their own. Even though Rebecca Martin LeClaire was originally from Hawthorne, she had left town long ago, and Cordelia was considered a newcomer. The urgency just didn't exist, and it was evident in everyone, from the town officials to the police department to the local volunteers.

When someone goes missing the way Cordelia had, their disappearance leaves echoes and shadows like that of an empty room, stripped of furnishings or inhabitants. Stories swirled around the investigation, everyone in town claiming to have seen Cordelia at one point or another, each tale more unusual than the next. Everyone seemed to have a story about the mysterious teenager who chased fireflies in the evening and danced by the moonlight on Old Burial Hill.

*"Yes, yes, I definitely remember seeing the girl around town at night. Always saw her running around with a different boy. Girls like that should be more careful. They just bring trouble on themselves."*

*"The LeClaire girl? Saw her wandering past our store as she usually does after school. I had just put out some of our clearance racks, and I recall her pulling out one of those multicolored gypsy skirts. She held it up and sort of swirled around with it for a bit. But no, she didn't buy it. Just hung it right back on the rack."*

*"Rebecca LeClaire's child? The flower shop girl? I did see her on that day, now that you mention it. She was waiting in line at the post office ahead of me. The girl was mailing a letter—every inch of the envelope was covered with butterflies and hearts. I remember think- ing she was such an odd girl."*

All of the ordinary actions of a young girl were now offi- cially recorded. Time, place, date, everything taking on a higher significance than if she hadn't gone missing. Ques- tions now left dangling: Who was the letter to? Did she run off with the recipient of the letter? Were the hearts on the envelope the sign of clandestine love? Rumors and stories piled higher by the minute.

But for all the speculation, no clues to Cordelia's disappearance surfaced. It was as if she had simply twirled away, allowing the hem of her skirt to wipe away any tracks she might have left behind.

Everyone—except for Rebecca, Tess, and Maddie—assumed she was a runaway. She had run away once before in California after her father died, and many assumed she'd done it again. She was sixteen, impetuous, rebellious, and free-spirited. She had a chance to take off on her own, and she took it. Case closed.

∞

"I still don't understand what happened out there," Maddie said to the girls after the candlelight vigil when they all met back at Kate's house. It had now been about forty-eight hours since Cordelia's disappearance, and the hope of her ever coming back faded with each minute.

"Shh!" Kate hissed. The girls flipped back and forth between the stations on the wide-screen plasma television, hoping to catch a glimpse of themselves on the news.

During a commercial, Maddie tried again to get answers from her elusive friends. "Why was that night so different from all the other nights? What was the deal with appeasing the gods or whatever? What was in that envelope, Kate?"

All the girls giggled.

"There wasn't *anything* in that envelope," Kate replied smugly. "It was a test, dummy. One that she *obviously* failed. God, Maddie, you really are a baby. What we did out there is no different from any other hazing rituals that sororities or sports teams do all the time."

Confused, Maddie shook her head. "But why would Cordelia go along with it? She didn't care at all about joining our group." She knew there was more to the story.

"She must have been hiding something—something that she didn't want to share with the rest of us. She probably screwed up so bad that she should have been locked up in The Witches' Castle." Bridget sniffed. "You can't trust someone who has secrets like that, if you ask me."

"Plus, Kate wanted to make it extra brutal for her because she heard that Trevor and Cordelia did it."

"That's not true," Maddie insisted. "She didn't even like Trevor. I would have known about it if she did."

Kate gave her a withering look. "I think there are a lot of things that you don't know about your cousin—or your family, for that matter. Screwing my boyfriend is just one of them. She also screwed Mr. Campbell. Doing two brothers? How slutty is that?"

"Yeah," Bridget piped in. "Mr. Campbell's going to be sweating it out for a while since Kate tipped off Sully about their extracurricular activities."

"You did what?" Maddie said in an accusatory tone. "Why would you ever do that? He's our teacher. He's your boyfriend's brother, for God's sake!" Maddie had always known that Kate resented Reed Campbell for rebuffing her advances, but she couldn't believe that Kate would throw him to the wolves and report him to Officer Sullivan. "Anyway, Cordelia wasn't after Trevor or Mr. Campbell or anyone, for that matter."

"Listen," Kate insisted. "Your cousin needed to be taught a lesson not to be such a slut. That's why I made her night on Misery *extra special*. For all I know, she was planning on working her way through all the guys in Hawthorne. I'll bet she's sorry she did it now. Besides, she got off lucky, if you ask me—"

Hannah swatted Kate, cutting her off. Maddie looked back and forth between the two girls. "Got off lucky how?"

Just then the ten o'clock news came on and all the girls shushed each other. "Got off lucky how?" Maddie asked again, impatiently. Maddie felt that Cordelia was slipping further away with every minute, every hour. She tried to imagine her face, but all that was left of Cordelia was a shimmer, a blur, an echo fading to a whisper.

Kate waited until the entire news package had run and then turned back to Maddie. She looked warily at the other girls and then said, "It's a good thing she took off that night because the way I felt after finding out about her and Trevor, I wanted to kill her myself. That witch is lucky that I didn't burn her at the stake."

৪৩

"What's the matter, dear?"

Maddie stopped on her way out of Kate's house that evening and turned to see Mrs. Endicott sitting at the granite-topped island in her whitewashed kitchen. She was dressed impeccably; her fingers glistened, heavy with diamonds, under the halogen track lighting. She was sitting alone, drinking dark liquid from a Waterford crystal glass. Under the lights, it looked like blood.

"I can't . . . it's just my cousin . . . I don't . . ." Maddie stammered.

"Oh, I know, you poor dear. To have your own cousin disappear like that." Mrs. Endicott shook her head in what appeared to be sympathy. "Come sit and have a drink with me."

She patted the plush chair next to her. It appeared that she had been sitting there drinking for quite a while. Maddie could hear the girls still laughing and chattering away in the other room.

Mrs. Endicott pulled another delicate wine glass from the overhead china cabinet and poured the thick red liquid into the glass. It was strange that she was offering Maddie wine, knowing Maddie was only a few months shy of sixteen. But in any case, Maddie accepted it, suddenly feeling grown up, and took a sip. It was port—sickeningly sweet with a thick, coppery aftertaste. It coated her lips, and Maddie imagined it staining her mouth like red berries.

"I think that it's just awful for her to run off the way she did. To make you and your family worry after her," Kiki Endicott said softly, shaking her head. "Such a shame, such a shame."

Maddie took another longer swig of the drink, feeling the wine relax her, hoping it would do something to quell the churning anxiety and anger inside of her. Perhaps if Kate's mother knew about Misery Island, she could help. The idea suddenly seemed plausible.

Maddie drained her glass and said, "But she didn't, Mrs. Endicott. I know she wouldn't run off. I think it may have been my, I mean, our fault."

The older woman looked at her quizzically, cocking her head to the side.

"Why would you say that?"

Pushing her fear of the repercussions aside, Maddie decided that now was the time to come clean. It was now or never. And Cordelia's life might depend on it.

"Mrs. Endicott . . ."

"Darling, call me Kiki," she smiled widely as if she were the real life version of the Cheshire cat.

"Umm . . . okay, Kiki, something awful happened out on Misery—"

"Ah, ah, ah, Madeline darling," Kiki Endicott said as she waved a perfectly manicured finger in front of Maddie's face. It curled slightly at the top like a talon. "Be careful what you say. Kate already told me about what happened out there. Special rituals can only be shared with members of the Sisters of Misery. Do you know why she told me?"

Maddie shook her head, confused.

"I once was a part of the Sisterhood—actually, you never really leave the Sisters of Misery; it's always a part of you—

and I believe that there are some things that are never to be discussed, am I right?"

Confused and taken aback, Maddie nodded dumbly. Mrs. Endicott was once part of the Sisters of Misery? Of course, that made perfect sense because Kate and Carly had both taken their leadership roles so seriously. But it was just a silly girl's group, wasn't it? But Kiki made it seem as though Maddie was about to give up CIA-confidential secrets, as though all of it really mattered in the larger picture.

"It's just that I thought you would know what to do, how to help us," Maddie offered.

Kiki Endicott took another long sip of port, eyeing her over the top of the crystal glass. When she lowered the crystal, the port made her lips glisten blood red.

"I'll give you a little bit of advice from someone older and infinitely wiser," she began. "Never cross the Sisterhood. While your cousin may be blood, your Sisters are your life, your future. Keeping the secrets of the Sisters of Misery is the most important thing you can do to ensure your own safety. Right now, there is nothing that you can do to protect your cousin, wherever she is. You need to be more concerned about yourself. It would be a shame if something were to ever happen to you, your mother, or . . . what is your grandmother's name again? It's Tess, right?"

Maddie dropped the glass suddenly, crystal shards and red wine spread across the granite countertop, spilling onto the marble floor.

Kiki's voice was as sharp as the broken glass. "Dammit, girl! What's the matter with you?" She quickly went to work mopping up the dark red liquid off the bright white floor.

Maddie didn't know what was wrong with her or anyone else in the town, for that matter. She started picking up the broken glass and throwing it into the stainless trash compactor. Kiki went off in a huff, calling for her maid.

Alone in the giant kitchen, Maddie looked down at her hands, noticing blood pooling in her palm. *"Your cousin may be blood, your Sisters are your life."* The words crowded her head dizzyingly as Maddie heard the whooping laughs of the girls in the next room.

The Endicotts controlled all of Hawthorne. Kiki ruled the town with all of her friends, probably all former members of the Sisters of Misery. If Kate and the others had done something to make Cordelia disappear, there was an entire town of women who would do anything to keep it a secret, all in the name of Sisterhood.

# Chapter 10

## ALGIZ REVERSED

## PROTECTION

*A Time of Mental Exhaustion, Emotional Demands; Seek Solace and Self-Protection*

As Maddie walked home that night, she blamed herself for bringing Cordelia to Misery Island in the first place, for letting things go as far as they had. If the situation was reversed, Cordelia never would have allowed any of that to happen to her. But Maddie had been too scared to do anything to stop it.

Despite blacking out that night and somehow ending up back at her mother's house, Maddie knew that she wouldn't have been able to brave the night out on the island alone. Once again, she had allowed the Sisters of Misery to dictate her actions. They had warned her not to interfere with their unusual plans that night, and Maddie had foolishly obeyed. Here she was, once again, following orders despite her better judgment. If any of them broke the pact and told what had happened out on Misery Island, they would go through the same exact ritual as Cordelia had right before she disappeared. Every time Maddie thought about telling someone, about going to the authorities, she envisioned the torturous events of that night and kept her mouth shut tight.

The rumors were already swirling around about Cordelia and Mr. Campbell. Maddie refused to believe any of them. She knew that it was Kate behind that story.

Police had started questioning Mr. Campbell in connection with Cordelia's disappearance. While not officially a suspect, he had been named "a person of interest."

But Maddie didn't believe any of it. If Cordelia had had a boyfriend, Maddie would have known about it earlier. Kate's stories about Cordelia's promiscuity were nothing but jealous lies. True, Cordelia made a habit of taking off in the middle of the night. But sometimes, she invited Maddie along. They would go down to watch the ocean swirl and churn, fantasizing about what existed on the far-off shores.

One night, not long before her disappearance, Cordelia had awakened Maddie by throwing rocks at her window just before dawn. Maddie opened her window and before she could yell down that she would let her cousin in the back door, Cordelia had expertly scaled the oak tree and bounded into her room like a female Peter Pan. When Maddie asked where she'd been, Cordelia simply said that she'd been walking through the sleeping town, peeking in windows and traipsing through gardens. It wasn't far-fetched, considering Cordelia's free spirit.

"You're going to get in trouble if you keep sneaking out at night," Maddie said, regarding her cousin with awe. Even though she'd spent her entire life in this town, she knew she'd never have enough courage to run around the streets of Hawthorne alone at night. But was Cordelia always alone? she wondered.

"Awww, you're like the sister I always wanted, Maddie. Worrying about me like that," Cordelia said, giggling. "But this is our secret, okay? Mom would kill me if she knew that I was running around town at night. She used to get so mad at me when I did it back in Cali. But I just can't be expected to stay inside, especially when the ocean is calling to me!"

Cordelia spun around like a ballerina and then pounced onto Maddie's bed, crawling across the plush quilts and eagerly sharing her nightly adventures: how she had danced on the darkened forest floor in fairy circles and swam through the moonlit waters with mermaids. Maddie knew she was making up the fantastical stories, but she also knew that she and Cordelia were friends, best friends.

And now that Cordelia was gone, Maddie refused to believe that she'd spent her nights running all over town, sleeping with older men and drunken teenage boys.

The days and nights were running together like a nightmare that Maddie couldn't wake up from. She was a zombie at school, and Kate wasn't making it any easier. Kate's nonchalance about Cordelia's disappearance was maddening and turned Maddie's stomach. Deep down, Maddie knew that there was no chance that Kate would ever come clean about that night on Misery Island. And without that crucial piece of information, the odds of Cordelia being found became slimmer and slimmer. Yet Kate insisted they were doing the right thing.

"If they find out that we tied her up out on the island, we'll all be suspects in her disappearance. They could arrest us and charge us with being accomplices!" Kate said one day at their lunch table, directing the last point to Maddie. "We have to make a pact that *no one* is allowed to breathe a word of this to anyone. Understand?"

"But it's our fault!" Maddie insisted, fighting back tears. "If we hadn't left her out there, she'd still be here. We have to tell someone!"

"Shut up, Maddie!" Kate snapped. "So we left her there, so what? She was fine when we left, right, girls?"

"Look," Bridget added, "she probably did one of her

magic tricks and got herself off the island—flew off the island on her broomstick. I think it's all a part of her master plan to get us in trouble, wait until we confess, and then she'll be back in a couple of days, laughing at us all."

The others agreed.

It was easier for them to believe that Cordelia was simply playing a trick on everyone, that she had run away by choice and that it wasn't some evil force at work. Easier, Maddie thought, than admitting they'd done something irrevocably evil to an innocent girl.

೮

No matter how much Maddie argued with the Sisters of Misery over coming forward with new information to help the authorities, it was clear the search for Cordelia was slowly coming to an end. With no concrete leads and airtight alibis all around, the authorities were treating it as a runaway situation, especially since Cordelia was not one of their own. It was painfully obvious to Maddie that the sense of urgency to find Cordelia wasn't really there. And it seemed that Hawthorne and its inhabitants were happy to have the spotlight removed from their quaint town. People peeked through their windows, pleased to see the news vans packing up and looking for the next big story. The K-9 units were dispatched back to Boston, and the searches dwindled in numbers. There were no leads, no witnesses, no motive, no suspects. Just a missing teenager who'd been gone for days. A young girl who had taken off once before and most likely, had done it again.

But Maddie knew differently. Yes, Cordelia would take off like a spirit of the night, but she always came back. In the short time that Maddie had gotten to know her cousin, she knew that the last thing Cordelia would want was for her family to worry about her. But as time went on, it seemed like Maddie was in the minority. Most people believed that Cordelia was simply another runaway. Case closed.

৪৩

Walking alone one afternoon after field hockey practice—despite all of their teachers and parents' insistence that they always travel in pairs at all times—Maddie watched as the sky turned an ashen gray, and the sun prepared for its descent. The darkness came earlier each day, especially since they had turned back the clocks. Nighttime seemed to swallow up the town, leaving Maddie and her family with only a short window of daylight to look for Cordelia. Each day, that window closed a little more, the darkness overcoming them all too quickly. That afternoon, a cool breeze tickled Maddie's spine and sent chills from her fingertips to her toes. *Maaa-a-a-a-d-d-d-d-d-i-i-i-e-e-e-e,* a low wail moaned through the trees of Potter's Grove as the winds started to pick up.

Cordelia had once told her about an old legend warning against ever speaking a name out loud in the woods. The trees, once in possession of the name, would say it over and over, and it would echo and bounce from tree to tree for eternity. And once they had your name, Cordelia informed her, they possessed your soul. You were fated to return to the woods forever.

Maddie had made the mistake of saying Cordelia's name once while they walked past Potter's Grove. Cordelia yelled at her and then sharply called out, *Maddie!,* allowing it to spread and echo throughout the grove. She was furious that Maddie "gave" the forest her name and said that if she were now required to return to these woods eternally, Maddie would have to join her as well.

*It's only fair,* Cordelia had said.

But standing by herself next to Potter's Grove and hearing the winds echoing out her name, Maddie wondered with a chill if Cordelia had been lured into these woods the night she went missing.

Maddie trudged home, stopping at Rebecca's Closet on the way. Tess and Maddie had urged Rebecca to shut the store down, at least until Cordelia was found. But Rebecca staunchly refused. Yet Maddie could see the energy and life fading from Rebecca as the hours turned into days and still Cordelia had not returned.

Maddie peered in and watched Rebecca, now a gaunt shadow of the woman she once had been. Her eyes had the sunken, far-off gaze of someone numbed by great pain. The beautiful red hair that had once flowed down her back like silk was now dirty and knotted. Her arms were scratched from the thorns on the roses she endlessly arranged. They were Cordelia's favorite flower, the Bluebird Rose—a pale lavender-blue rose with the sweetest scent. Cordelia loved that flower because Simon LeClaire had once said they were the exact color of his daughter's hauntingly beautiful eyes.

When she wasn't searching for her daughter, Rebecca spent day and night creating ornate, brilliantly colored arrangements, all of them containing Bluebird Roses.

Word spread throughout Hawthorne about the eerily beautiful floral creations borne from a grieving mother who was waiting for her daughter's return, and crowds gathered daily at the shop window to watch the display. Rebecca hardly noticed—working with the flowers had become a form of therapy for her and replaced the rituals she had foregone since Cordelia had disappeared. Eating, drinking, sleeping, all these habits were a distant memory for Rebecca.

With nimble fingers, she worked those flowers into magnificent constructions—grotesque, exquisite, elegant. The constant wrapping and pruning of the blossoms hardened her skin and stained her fingertips. Watching her aunt through the window, Maddie saw a woman who had lost the will to live and was only surviving through the repetition of arranging the flowers. Again, she puzzled over Cordelia's disappearance. Surely Cordelia wouldn't put her mother through all of this pain by choice.

Maddie entered the store. Rebecca looked up at her niece, but it was as if she was looking right through her. "Rebecca, you need to come home," she said slowly.

"Home," she said, almost a question. She repeated the word home as if she was trying to discern the meaning.

"Y-y-yes," Maddie said, unsure of how to treat the woman that she had idolized for months, the one who had resembled a screen goddess and now looked like an actress in a horror movie, her cheeks hollow, darkened circles beneath her glazed eyes. "Tess wanted me to make sure that you came home. We need to take care of you. It's not doing Cordelia any good with you in this state."

"This state!" Rebecca screeched. "THIS STATE? This God-forsaken STATE! If only we hadn't moved back to this state, Cordelia would be fine. We would be poor, we would be living hand to mouth in California, but we would be together and everything would be as it should be. This state, this town, this horrible place has taken her away from me. And now what do I have? Nothing! I don't have my Simon, my Cordelia, my life! All of it is gone. All that I have left is this." Rebecca lifted her arms and gestured to the store. "This little store, the last place that I saw my little girl. And I'm not leaving this place until she comes home." She stared out through the darkened window and laughed a small, quiet laugh and whispered, "Home."

Realizing that the store was the last place that Rebecca had seen Cordelia, Maddie understood why she refused to leave. It was almost like Rebecca was trying to turn back time, go back a few pages to when Cordelia was with them, brimming with life and a bright future. Maddie wanted to return to those days as well. But all she was left with was the image of Cordelia bruised and battered out on Misery Island.

Maddie backed out of the store into the late afternoon darkness. As the door closed behind her, Rebecca continued talking to herself. Maddie ran back to Mariner's Way, dreading that she had to tell Tess what had happened, that Rebecca was teetering on the edge. It would only be a matter of time before she finally was sent spiraling into the abyss.

∞

When Rebecca hadn't come home by midnight, Tess, Maddie, and Abigail went to the store, determined to bring Rebecca home no matter what. Abigail led the way, and Tess and Maddie tried to steel themselves for what they might find inside the shop. The windows of the tiny store had black, almost funereal curtains to block out the sunlight. When Maddie tried to push the door open, it was heavy as if something was wedged against it. Abigail and Maddie both gave the door a shove, soon realizing that an overturned bookcase was blocking the entrance.

"Oh, my God!" Maddie said when they finally got inside.

Shards of glass covered the floor like a glittering carpet. The old-fashioned glass counter that Rebecca had so earnestly polished in preparation for the store opening had been smashed. The remaining shards of glass that hung from the counter resembled the sharp, jagged teeth of a monster ready to consume them if they got any closer. All of the bottles and flowers and herbs and gift items had been pulled from the shelves and thrown in a heap on the floor. The store was lit by candles that had burned low, leaving huge pools of melted wax around them, and smelled of acrid smoke.

Abigail looked unnerved, a sight that Maddie wasn't used to seeing. "Rebecca, are you alright? Rebecca!!"

Rebecca was nowhere to be found, and no one answered them. It looked like someone had broken into the store and trashed the place. Could it have been the same person who took Cordelia?

Tess said quietly, "We should call the police. Let's just go." Maddie put an arm around her frail grandmother when she noticed that her tiny body had begun to shake visibly.

Abigail yelled out again, "Rebecca?"

The women heard a muffled sound, like a small child laughing . . . or crying.

"Rebecca!" Abigail said quickly, horrified as she picked her way across the glass-strewn floor.

Rebecca crouched in the corner of the store, rocking back and forth on a pile of glass and ash and flowers and debris. Her hair had become a rat's nest, and her clothes were dingy and stained. There were blood stains on her peasant blouse, and her arms were scratched and torn and bloodied. Tess and Maddie looked at each other through their tears. Without having to say anything, they both knew that the wounds were self-inflicted.

"Come on now."Abigail's voice softened a bit as she tried to pull her sister up off the ground, but Rebecca only cried out as if in pain and scuttled closer to the door.

Tess and Abigail looked at each other helplessly, not sure what to do.

Tess pleaded, "Rebecca, who did this? How did this happen?"

Rebecca looked up, her eyes glazed over. When they finally pulled into focus, they landed directly on Maddie. "You," she said softly. Then her voice got louder and more forceful. "YOU!"

Maddie took a deep breath as she stepped backward into Tess's steadying arms.

"YOU YOU YOU YOU YOU YOU YOU YOU YOU

YOU!" Rebecca shrieked so loudly that it seemed that any remaining pieces of unbroken glass would soon shatter from her shrill tone. Her accusatory voice filled the entire store and burrowed into Maddie's brain.

Finally, Abigail took control of the situation, as she often did, and simply said, "Ravenswood."

Tess looked horrified. Maddie began crying openly. But they all realized that despite their best intentions, Rebecca was too far gone for any of them to help. Cordelia's disappearance had sent Rebecca spiraling away from them, away from her own sanity.

"Go on," Abigail instructed Maddie. "Get your grandmother out of here. She doesn't need to be subjected to this. I'll deal with my sister."

Tess and Maddie hurried out of the store. "Why was she screaming at me like that? I swear I had nothing to do with that mess in there, Grams," Maddie pleaded with her grandmother. She wasn't about to go into the events on Misery Island, and she wondered if somehow, Rebecca had used her gift and had seen the horrible events of that night.

"It's the devil in her," Tess said quietly. "The devil is in all of us at times. Some people more than others. Some people can't help letting him in. Rebecca was just too weak to keep him out. Others, well, they are more than happy to let him in whenever he pleases."

As Tess spoke of the devil, Maddie flashed to an image from Halloween night. Kate was standing before the bonfire. Her pale eyes were lit orangey red, reflecting the color of the flames, her hair lifting up and down with the coastal winds. Maddie felt a sickness in her stomach as Kate seemed to revel in Cordelia's pain. "It was the devil in her," Tess said again firmly. And though on the surface, Tess was talking about Rebecca, Maddie had a sinking feeling that underneath, she was talking about someone else entirely.

&

"It's for her own well-being," Abigail said the next morning at breakfast, her expression tight-lipped. Any sympathy she may have shown for Rebecca the previous evening had turned into annoyance. "She hasn't slept or eaten or even bathed in weeks." Her nose wrinkled in slight disgust. "Rebecca needs help to get through this—real psychological help that we can't give her. She's always been an emotional basketcase. And when that spoiled brat of a daughter returns, I'll make sure she pays for this, once and for all!"

Tess sat at the kitchen table rocking back and forth, staring at her bird-like hands. Maddie knew that it must have been a horrible thing for a mother to experience, seeing her daughter on the brink of madness. Almost as terrible as what Rebecca was going through—having a daughter disappear into thin air. And Maddie felt responsible for all of it. Maddie was desperate to tell Tess the truth about Halloween night. Yet the words choked in the back of her throat whenever she tried. Maddie couldn't bear to see the look of disappointment in Tess's eyes, so instead, she remained silent.

She tried to think of who else she could tell—the police, her mother, anyone—about what went on that night on Misery Island. But her confession to Mrs. Endicott made her realize that it wouldn't make a difference. Cordelia was gone, and nobody really cared.

## Chapter 11

### EIHWAZ REVERSED

**Ƶ**

### THE HUNTER

*Nostalgia and Confusion, Weakness and
Dissatisfaction*

Not long after Rebecca was sent to Ravenswood, Mr. Campbell held Maddie after class. "Now, Madeline," Mr. Campbell said tenderly, dragging a chair over to her desk and flipping it around so he could sit on it backwards. His blue eyes were warm, friendly beneath his blond lashes. "I know that this has been a difficult time for you." He paused and took a deep breath. "But I wouldn't be doing my job as your teacher if I didn't discuss this with you and how it is affecting your grades in my class."

Maddie tugged at the ends of her hair, nodding halfheartedly. Cordelia had been missing for weeks, and her sleepless nights were starting to show. Mr. Campbell dropped his head to his arms folded over the back of the chair, looking more like a guy her own age than her twenty-two-year-old teacher. "Looks like Maddie's the new teacher's pet," Kate said. The others laughed as they pushed out the door. If Mr. Campbell heard the comment, he paid it no mind.

"What can I do to make things easier for you? Would tutoring or, I don't know, counseling help?"

Maddie shook her head, staring out the window. *Why is he singling me out now?* she wondered. He never seemed to care this much about her before. She entertained the thought— for just a moment—that maybe he was digging to find out how much she knew about the night of Cordelia's disappearance. Could her cousin have gone to Mr. Campbell's house after getting off the island? Did he know about what went on that night?

"Are you still on the field hockey team?" he asked.

"I don't have time," Maddie said, not wanting to explain that she had nothing *but* time these days. She just didn't want anything to do with Kate and the rest of the Sisters of Misery. Every time she looked at them, the guilt only dug its bloody claws deeper.

"What about friends? It seems like you don't have time for them anymore either," he offered. "Are you going to visit your aunt a lot?"

Maddie shrugged off the question. Since Abigail had Rebecca committed to Ravenswood, her aunt had shut the entire world out—Maddie especially. It was as if she were frozen in time, Sleeping Beauty locked up in her castle, surrounded by thorns and bracken, waiting for Cordelia to return and break the trance. She was so far gone that Maddie wondered if she even recognized herself in the mirror. But Mr. Campbell didn't need to know that.

After the breakdown in the shop, Maddie couldn't face her beloved aunt. Her nights were haunted by Rebecca's accusatory shrieks—*YOU, YOU, YOU!* Maddie didn't have the strength to face her, not until she found Cordelia and made things right again.

Seeing that he was getting nowhere, Mr. Campbell tried another tactic. "I think that you are taking on an awful lot for a girl your age. I know it's hard, but you should let the police do their job of getting Cordelia back, let your aunt recover from all this craziness, and you just worry about taking care of yourself." He patted her gently on the back and moved his hand up to give her shoulder a squeeze. Ticklish tingles traveled up from Maddie's shoulders, along her neck, up to the base of her hairline. His hands were like magic.

"My age?" Maddie laughed, realizing the irony of his comment. Girls her age were responsible for this mess. Girls her age were capable of unspeakable things. "You're not that much older than me—or Cordelia, for that matter. You have no idea—" She stopped herself, afraid that she would say something that she'd regret. Something that Kate would *make* her regret. She dropped her face into her hands. "I just feel like I should be doing something. Something more. Like it's my responsibility to find her."

"Your job is to get good grades, and right now, you're averaging a D in my class. It's my job to step in when there's a reason for concern." He paused. "Should I be concerned, Maddie?" She trembled. What exactly was he asking her? Was he asking her what she knew, what Cordelia may have told her in confidence?

"I'm sorry, Mr. Campbell," Maddie said. "I'll try harder. I really will." She yearned to tell him more, tell him about what happened on Halloween night, but from the rumors that were swirling around about his alleged affair with Cordelia, he was the last person she should trust.

His face was close to hers, his blue eyes searching. When the silence between them became too awkward to bear, Maddie blurted out, "You're Cordelia's favorite teacher. Did she . . . say anything . . . to you?"

"I wish she had come to me, if she needed help," he said, sighing. He shook his head and looked down, a sad smile spread over his face. "She was really something special."

"She *still* is special! I don't know why everyone keeps referring to her in the past tense!" Maddie insisted.

"I'm sorry, Maddie. I never meant to say—to suggest . . . Well, you're right. If she's found, it will be a great relief to all of us . . ."

*"When* she's found," Maddie whispered, lowering her eyes to the floor.

He reached out and covered her slender hands with his. Maddie noticed the blond hair moving as the sinewy muscles in his hands tightened around her own. "Yes, *when* she's found."

He swung his head downward; they were sitting so close that the tips of his soft blond hair gently brushed past her cheek. It smelled like a combination of woods and sand, just how she always imagined it would.

Maddie wanted to tell him that she knew he wasn't involved in Cordelia's disappearance and that if there was a way Maddie could set things straight with the people in town, she would. Maddie wanted to express something, but every word she tried to say got stuck somewhere down in the base of her throat. With the town's rising suspicions regarding his involvement with her cousin, Maddie could see the visible effects of the toll it was taking on him. His eyes were rimmed red, and the circles under them were deep.

A noise made them both look up. Trevor Campbell stood in the doorway with an odd accusatory look on his face. Mr. Campbell's face darkened. He met his brother's gaze and shook his head subtly. Trevor paused for a moment before walking away. Once he was gone, Mr. Campbell smiled, his watery blue eyes crinkling at the corners, and he clapped heartily as if a weight had been lifted. "Good. I'm glad we had this little talk."

But before she left the classroom, Maddie was struck suddenly by the look on Trevor's face. "Mr. Campbell," she asked quietly, "has Trevor said anything about Cordelia?"

Mr. Campbell's smile froze on his face for a moment as

he seemed to carefully choose his response. "Not really. I mean, he's upset by her disappearance. We all are," he paused. "Why do you ask?"

"No reason," she replied, suddenly overcome with the feeling that Trevor seemed unusually pleased that Cordelia wasn't around—almost as happy as Kate. "See you in class tomorrow."

She left Reed Campbell staring after her, his eyes narrowed and head cocked to the side.

∞

As Maddie lingered on the edge of sleep, her mind drifted to a conversation she had with her grandmother years before Cordelia and Rebecca came to town. It was the first time that she had ever suspected Tess had a "gift." That night, the winds rattled the old window panes, and Maddie gathered her grandmother into a long hug, "I'm never going to leave you," Maddie said, deeply inhaling the comforting scent of rose and gardenia. Tess swatted her granddaughter away playfully, accusing her of trying to get a peek at her well-worn Gypsy Witch cards during their game of gin rummy.

She chuckled softly. "Well, I guess it's my own fault. I shouldn't have taken you two in so quickly after your father left town. If I'd had my wits about me, I would have forced you two to move somewhere else. But I guess I was selfish. I wanted to help raise my lovely granddaughter, even if it prevented your escape from Hawthorne."

"Escape, Grams?" Maddie giggled, thinking that her grandmother could be so overly dramatic at times. Looking back now, Maddie could see what Tess meant, though at the time, she'd never felt any danger in her hometown. "What's there to be afraid of in Hawthorne?"

Tess looked Maddie squarely in the eyes as she dropped

her hand to the quilt displaying three Jacks and a run of spades. She plucked the Ace of Diamonds and Ace of Hearts from her granddaughter's hand as if she knew exactly what cards Maddie held and turned them so that she could read the fortunes printed above a slew of birds on a bloodred background and a monstrous-looking fox.

Maddie read the fortunes out loud:

> *"The birds foretell dire misfortune and fierce enemies when near. The fox in close proximity augurs distrust of acquaintances who seek to betray you."*

"Madeline Crane, when the time is right—and trust me, you'll know when that time comes—leave everything, all of us, behind," she whispered as she leaned across the bed and grabbed Maddie by the shoulders, her fingers digging sharply into her skin, "and just run."

Maddie was still not sure what Tess had known at that point—or if she suspected the terrible events to come. It was long before Cordelia and Rebecca moved back, so it couldn't have had anything to do with them. But the look in Tess's eyes at that moment—like she was looking into the future and seeing only horrific events unfolding—haunted her for months.

Now, lying in the darkness, Maddie watched the shadows of tree branches come alive on her wall, moving with the wind. Chances were that someone who was still living in this town was involved with Cordelia's disappearance. And if that person was still out there, Maddie wondered if she was going to be the next target. It made sense. Maddie was the only person convinced that Cordelia hadn't run away. And perhaps the person responsible didn't want her looking too deep. Perhaps that person would do anything to keep the secret of Cordelia's disappearance buried.

But from what Maddie knew of Hawthorne, a dark place

trapped in time that seemed to be straight out of a Grimm's fairy tale, untouched by the rest of the world, secrets didn't stay covered up for very long.

People lived in the houses built by their ancestors, dwellings that remained unchanged despite the decades they had weathered. Townspeople coveted the antique houses with low ceilings and uneven pine floorboards that seemed to grow up out of the sidewalks, jutting into the crooked streets like hollyhocks. They boasted about their gardens filled with jewel-colored flowers that grew lush and wild, fed by a steady diet of salty air and coastal sunshine. The same houses and the same gardens tended to year after year, generation after generation.

There was the Hawthorne that most people talked about: the one with stories as old and weathered as the shingles of the historic houses. The town that's picture postcard perfect, a Currier and Ives landscape filled with scents of apple cider in the fall, pine and woodsmoke in the winter, and honey and jasmine in the summer. The town known for sailing and quaint shops and an enviable coastline.

And then there were the legends.

Stories of ghostly soldiers that still lurked outside the Old Sandy Dog Tavern and the specter of Jack Derby, the tyrannical sheriff who terrorized the town over two hundred years ago. But the most startling of all were townspeople reporting the sensation of a small hand reaching up to grab hold and be helped across the street—the tiny hand of Hester Proctor, who died so many years ago, trampled by a horse and wagon.

Tess claimed that when she was a girl, the thick, heavy scent of the flowers was so overwhelming in Hawthorne that people had to shut their windows during dinnertime or else it overpowered their meals. And at night, many teenage girls were forced to sleep in the stifling heat with windows locked up tight, or else the heavy aroma of the flowers would drive them wanton with ecstasy, causing them to leave the confines of their bedrooms and set off into the night in search of young men.

And then there was the modern-day Hawthorne that Maddie knew all too well: a town made up of small-minded people, people who resisted change, embraced conformity, and despised outsiders. A town filled with men and women who tried to destroy anything unfamiliar or unwelcome. This was the side of Hawthorne that most people tried to hide, the place that had shaped who Maddie had become. The real Hawthorne, the place that had frightened her for all of these years, was something she'd learned to keep to herself.

And what scared her most was this: Maddie was one of them.

∞

Almost a month had passed since Cordelia had vanished. Maddie trudged through the crackling piles of leaves on her way to school each morning, scuffing her knee-high boots through the undergrowth that ran the length of the narrow pathway. Maddie had lost twenty pounds and stopped bathing regularly. Her mother was furious at her appearance, but Maddie had given up caring. She was consumed by guilt and sadness. All other emotions seemed futile.

Life goes on. But Maddie couldn't. Though Tess visited Rebecca every day, Rebecca just stared out the window at the ocean, remaining completely mute. Her doctors said she was in a "state of shock" and was going through PTSD, or Post-Traumatic Stress Disorder.

Maddie typically walked with Tess to Ravenswood, but she would hang back and wait for Tess in Fort Glover, the part that was open to the general public and ran alongside of Ravenswood Asylum. The fort itself consisted of a sloping mound of earth that perched high on top of a cliff above the water. It was rumored to be connected to Ravenswood by narrow underground tunnels. At the center, there stood a dungeon sunken like a pirate's ship. A narrow fence ran along the perimeter of Fort Glover, offering minimal protection from taking one false step and tumbling downward to the jagged rocks below. Maddie had heard stories of teenagers who would drink at the fort at night and dare each other to dive into the churning waters below. The unlucky few who were either too drunk to know any better or too desperate to fit in ended up at Bell Hospital with concussions or broken bones. Some kids managed to steal into the long-abandoned prison—where the Pickering sisters had been held captive—and throw parties or have sex on the dirt floors.

Maddie remembered going to a party at Fort Glover a few months before Cordelia had arrived in Hawthorne. On their way up to the fort, some of the kids from Hawthorne Academy slapped the faces of the Pickering sisters that were carved into the main wall of the original fort. While the rest of the fort area had been turned into a beautiful park overlooking the ocean, the older walls still connected to Ravenswood, adding to the crumbling Gothic allure of the place that once served to protect the town from outsiders and now protected them from those inside the asylum. No one ever knew how the faces of the sisters had gotten there or who kept returning them to their former state after town officials covered them over again and again, not wanting to be reminded of the cruelty their ancestors had inflicted on victims of the witch trials. But the faces of the three sisters always reappeared, each time looking a little more haggard and vengeful. Maddie never looked directly at them, recalling a playground song that warned against doing such a thing:

*Don't look now at the faces three,*
*The Witch Sisters of Misery.*
*Close your eyes and hold your breath*
*Witches of Misery will bring you death.*
*Shut your windows, doors up tight*
*The Witches of Misery come tonight.*

As she walked up and down the path between Fort Glover and Ravenswood that afternoon in November, waiting for Tess to come out and inform her of another uneventful visit with Rebecca, Maddie noticed from the look of the dark sky and ocean that a storm was approaching.

Maddie averted her eyes as usual as she passed the faces of the Pickering sisters, but something caused her to stop suddenly. The tendrils of ivy, too stubborn to die off in the shivery November weather, had been pushed aside as if someone or something had recently been there. The faces of the sisters pushed out of the massive fortress wall as if trying to break free of their stony prison. But there was another face that had joined the three sisters. The color of the mortar was darker, fresher than the other three faces, which were bleached to the color of sand. This face didn't have the harsh features and wicked grimaces of the Pickering girls. This face was softer . . . beautiful . . . haunted.

It was the face of a young girl who was both familiar and horrifying. And it took her breath away when Maddie realized who it was supposed to be.

Someone had added a fourth face.

And this face looked remarkably like the person Maddie most wanted to see.

But not like this. Not here, not now.

It was the face she had seen in her dreams long ago.

It was the face of Cordelia.

# Chapter 12

ANSUZ

## F

MESSAGE

*A Revealing Insight or Signal; Prophecy and Revelation;
Wisdom and Reason*

### DECEMBER

There was a flurry of activity as Hawthorne Academy shut down for the holidays. Kids ran across the hallways slapping each other on the back, girls huddled in tight knots by their lockers. Laughter, shouts, screeching of sneakers.

And then, after a half hour or so, silence.

Maddie waited until everyone had gone to start cleaning out her and Cordelia's lockers. She hadn't told any of the other girls of her plans of taking a semester off. She didn't want a lecture from Kate on how she was throwing away her chance of getting into one of the Ivies. At this point, she didn't know what she wanted to do, but she knew this much: Hawthorne Academy was the last place in the world she wanted to be.

Maddie succeeded in getting the headmaster to let her take the semester off to care for her family and recover from the loss. While it seemed like a kind gesture on the surface, Maddie knew that the school board made that decision not out of goodwill, but as a way of taking the spotlight off of the school. Private schools never liked it when anything bad happened to their students, even if it didn't happen during school hours or on the property. It made parents uneasy. So when Maddie approached Headmaster Collins, he seemed happy to have an excuse to let her leave the premises for a few months—at least until all the news surrounding her cousin's disappearance and her aunt's institutionalization died down. Abigail was thrilled as well, because Tess was displaying clear signs of dementia, obviously brought on by the recent tragic events and was becoming more of a challenge to care for. The dementia was steadily taking over, and it wasn't uncommon to find her grandmother in the strangest of places or situations.

After cleaning out her own locker, Maddie made her way down to Cordelia's locker, her footsteps echoing through the deserted hallway. She stopped short, hearing a shuffling noise behind her. She turned, half expecting to see Cordelia escaping from a classroom, running down the corridor. But the hallway was empty.

She opened Cordelia's locker and started pulling out books and paperwork and school supplies to throw into the trash.

Most of Cordelia's personal belongings had been taken away by the police as evidence. Just as Maddie was about to slam the door closed, she noticed a rune stone stuck way in the back of the locker floor. Reaching down to retrieve the stone, Maddie realized the base of the locker was loose. After making sure no one was watching, Maddie pulled up the locker floor and was shocked to discover a stack of opened letters. Letters that must have been delivered by hand as they were unstamped and without a return address. Maddie flipped through them and then quickly stuck them into her bag, fighting the urge to read them all right there in the middle of Hawthorne Academy. She slammed the locker door closed and continued down the hallway.

Maddie walked into the older section of Hawthorne Academy where the teachers had their offices. She wanted to see if the rumors about Mr. Campbell getting fired were true. The mansion that once served as the original schoolhouse remained virtually unchanged since the school had opened its doors decades earlier. Perhaps the hardwood floor didn't gleam as brightly as it once had, but now with all of the scuff marks and chinks, the thickly varnished planks of pine gave off a warm amber glow. The front door banged open suddenly.

*Maddie!* A raspy, ghostlike voice suddenly filled her ear.

She spun around quickly to see who called out, or rather whispered, her name. But no one was there—only the faint tinkling of laughter, from one of the classrooms, perhaps. Her heartbeat quickened, and her breathing became shallow.

The nameplate had been torn from Mr. Campbell's office door, so it was as though he never existed at the school. The esteemed academy probably felt it important to remove any chance of being implicated by association with the disappearance of Mr. Campbell's favorite—perhaps too much of a favorite—student, Cordelia LeClaire.

Maddie always believed that if anyone was involved with Cordelia's disappearance, it was Trevor, not Mr. Campbell. She wanted to believe that Mr. Campbell with his twinkling blue eyes and obvious concern for her feelings was innocent. But sometimes when you put a person too high up on a pedestal, you no longer see their actions clearly. And Maddie was smart enough to realize that her feelings for Mr. Campbell were deeper than a mere student–teacher relationship, and that those feelings might be clouding her judgment.

Maddie reached into her bag and felt the stack of letters, wondering if they held the answers to her questions. Was Cordelia involved with Mr. Campbell? Were these actually love notes between them, confirming a relationship? Maddie raced out of school, anxious to get home and read the letters that might hold the clue, the missing piece to this puzzle. She was so lost in thought over the letters that she didn't even realize that someone was watching her the entire time. Someone who knew what those letters would ultimately reveal. Someone who would do anything to get them back.

୧୦

Maddie's relief at being out of Hawthorne Academy was short-lived when she caught sight of the note from Abigail scrawled on the kitchen counter, detailing her list of chores. The old family station wagon, complete with fake wood paneling adorning the sides, needed the brakes checked, the oil changed, and various other life-extending procedures. The fact that she was a few months shy of getting her license didn't seem to bother her mother, so why should she care?

"Happy holidays to you, too, Mom," Maddie muttered. As she maneuvered the old car away from Mariner's Way, Maddie wondered how this decrepit ancestor of the SUV had managed to survive all of the brutal winters and actually run despite the salt water mists that ravaged the metal undercarriage. The way it was handling, Maddie wasn't sure if it would even make the short distance to O'Malley's local body shop. Upon entering the old auto shop, Maddie again felt a strange sense of being watched despite the fact that the place seemed empty. She looked around for a security camera, but couldn't spot one. There was a bell on the Formica counter. The smell of oil and grease permeated the place.

"Hello?" Maddie called as she tentatively rang the bell. And then a little louder, *"Hello?"*

A voice came from behind her. "Hey there, Maddie, what's up?"

Maddie turned quickly, surprised by the unfamiliar voice saying her name. A tall, lanky guy stood there, his dark eyes peering from behind long strands of hair.

"Do I know you?" she asked in a clipped tone.

He looked slightly hurt that Maddie didn't recognize him, but then seemed to shrug it off and said in a cool tone. "You go to Hawthorne Academy."

His features were strikingly handsome, in strong contrast to the gritty condition of his longish hair, goatee, and oil-stained clothing. It was almost as if under all that dirt and grime, there was an incredibly hot guy. With his high cheekbones and strong jaw, he definitely didn't fit in with the doughy, baseball-capped guys that Maddie knew from school.

"You go there?" She cringed upon hearing her own voice—just like a typical Hawthorne snob. "I mean—what I meant to say was . . . um . . . are we in any classes together?" *God, I'm such a bitch.*

He shook his head and smiled faintly before lighting a cigarette. "Nah, I work there. I go to the tech school over in Lynn, but I work odd jobs around the Academy. My old man's the groundskeeper there."

"Are you, I mean, you're not O'Malley, are you?"

"Yup, Finnegan O'Malley in the flesh." He eyed her for a moment. "Don't look it, do I? I'm what they call Black Irish."

He had read her mind. His features were too exotic for him to be named O'Malley. His eyes were dark, so black that she could barely see his pupils. He looked at her intensely, making her feel somewhat exposed. He was very different from anyone in Hawthorne. Maddie was surprised she'd never noticed him before.

"You're Cordelia's cousin." He stated this, letting it hang uncomfortably in the space between them. It was weird. Usually, people referred to Cordelia as "Maddie's cousin," not the other way around. It was as if, to Finnegan, she held ownership to this town in the brief time she had spent here, and Maddie was the visitor.

"Did you know her? I mean, I know that everyone knew *about* her," Maddie stopped, wondering how to phrase this tactfully, "but she was here for such a short time." She was confused. Maddie knew everyone that Cordelia knew—she was the one who introduced her around—so how did this total stranger know her? "Were you friends or something?"

For a moment, he seemed guarded, his eyes drifting over her shoulder. Taking a deep drag off his cigarette, he nodded as he exhaled. A smile lingered at the corner of his lips, and his eyes glossed over as if he was lost in thought. It was the look of someone who knew a person intimately.

"I just heard the stories about her. About how she disappeared and all." He moved back behind the counter. "I'd seen her around a few times. I used to think I was the only one crazy enough to walk around the town at night—well, me and the drunks coming outta the Sea Cap, of course." He smiled, his face softening slightly, and then continued. "Yeah, I used to see your cousin in all sorts of crazy places real late at night."

Scratching the back of his head, he continued, "That really sucks that she's gone. Especially after everything she went through. I'm really sorry—I mean, I feel bad for your family . . . and for Cordelia."

"Yeah, well, you know . . ." Maddie wasn't sure how to respond. Talking about Cordelia with this stranger, this very unusual, very cute stranger, was making her extremely nervous for some reason. Maddie couldn't put her finger on it, but his presence, the way he looked at her as if he could see right through her, unnerved her. "It just seems, I mean, the way you talk about her and all . . . how well did you know my cousin?"

He held her gaze for a few beats, almost staring her down. "Like I said before, I've seen her around. I've seen lots of things going on in this town, doesn't mean I'm a part of it."

Maddie nodded, not quite sure what he was getting at. "But, I mean, if you knew—"

"Listen," he said sharply, "I'd love to do this stroll down memory lane, but I've got a lot going on right now." He pointed to the garage, which seemed nearly empty. "Lots of work I need to get back to."

"Oh," she said disappointedly. Why was he so quick to get rid of her? "Okay, Finnegan, I'm sorry. I'll just leave you the keys, if that's alright. My mom needs the whole thing fixed up—oil, brakes, the works. It's barely hanging on, and we'd like to see it through the winter."

He nodded as she slid the keys across the counter into his grease-laden hands. His voice softened a bit. "Call me Finn. I'll see what I can do."

"Thanks, Finn," Maddie sighed and closed her eyes, rubbing vigorously at the pressure point between her eyebrows. "I'll be back later to pick it up."

When she opened her eyes, he had already vanished into the back room, making her feel as though she had been talking all along with an apparition. Maddie shook her head and set out into the bright winter light.

It was only after Maddie had settled into a booth at the coffee shop across the street and spread out the paper that something Finn had mentioned caught her completely off guard. What did he mean when he said, "after everything she went through?" Was it possible that he knew about that night out on Misery Island? And if so, how?

# Chapter 13

## LAGUZ

ᛚ

## WATER

*The Knowing and Healing Power of Renewal;*
*Psychic Intuition and Abilities*

"Just bring her into town," Abigail instructed Maddie a few days before Christmas. "Maybe some fresh air and Christmas festivities will snap her back."

Tess was sitting in her rocking chair, singing to herself as she looked out the window toward the ocean. She was always staring out at the waves, looking out to where her husband—Maddie's grandfather, Jack Martin—died at sea. "The sea gave him life and took it away," Tess once said, often pointing out such examples of the cyclical nature of the world. She encouraged Maddie to become aware of such patterns, to pay attention and be guided by the little signs offered to them, if they knew just where to look.

Tess was always the one who seemed to guide them—she was the rock that Maddie turned to whenever she needed strength and stability. Now Maddie watched as her grandmother became more and more childlike and helpless, unable to fight off the dementia that was quickly taking over her mind. The grief and tragic events were too much for the old woman to bear.

Both Abigail and Maddie felt that Tess's daily visits with Rebecca were doing more harm to Tess than help for Rebecca. Each time Tess returned from Ravenswood, it was as if she had left a piece of her self, her very soul, behind. Abigail had recently put a stop to the visits.

Maddie forced a smile as she said brightly, "Come on, Grams. Let's go check out the Christmas festival. I could use a nice cup of mulled cider, couldn't you?"

Tess stopped rocking and looked past Maddie. She smiled as if she was seeing an old friend. It unnerved Maddie so much that she had to turn to make sure that she was still the only one in the room.

"We'll have fun together, won't we?" Tess asked in a tiny voice. "We always had lots of fun at the festival. It's a pity Rebecca and Cordelia never got the chance to go."

But Tess's positive mood drastically changed once they began their walk into town.

"The people here are evil. Pure evil. Nothing we say or do will bring Cordelia back," Tess hissed as they walked past carolers and women loaded down with shopping bags.

Maddie truly believed that some fresh air and time out-side of the house would do wonders for Tess and help raise both of their spirits. Yet the yearly Christmas festival did nothing to alleviate the pain and anxiety that had become a constant for both of them. Tess clung to Maddie's arm, hiss-ing into her ear about all the different people who were putting hexes on their family. Maddie tried to calm her down to no avail. At one point, Tess pulled her shaking hands from behind the starchy folds of her dress and subtly raised her index and pinky fingers. This hand gesture, according to su-perstitions she had told Maddie since she was a child, warded off the evil eye. She pointed her narrow fingers at whoever she believed was intending them harm or bad luck.

"Look at her," Tess pointed at a well-dressed woman

bossing around a worker tying a Christmas tree to the top of her Mercedes. "She doesn't even care about the O'Malley boy helping her. He's freezing and working his fingers to the bone, and she's too busy and full of herself to even give him a tip."

"How do you know Finn?" Maddie pressed as Finn continued to hoist trees out for potential buyers' inspection with ease. The O'Malley body shop lot had been turned into a forest of Christmas trees overnight. Maddie's stomach did a little flip when she saw Finn spin an eight-foot balsam around for a little girl's inspection, obviously wanting to help the girl pick the perfect tree.

"Oh, the O'Malleys have been around forever," Tess clucked. Her bad mood lifting for a moment as it always did whenever she spoke about Maddie's grandfather. "Your grandfather went way back with the O'Malley boys. They always used to get each other into trouble, but there was never any harm done. It was all in good fun."

As if on cue, Finn turned and locked eyes with Maddie. She quickly looked away, chiding herself for staring. He was dressed in a lightweight flannel shirt, despite the cold winter air, and his hair was tucked back into a knitted cap. She had never noticed how strong and muscular he was until she saw him lifting the huge firs and balsams onto the expensive cars with ease.

"Did Cordelia ever talk about Finn?" Maddie asked in a hushed tone. She knew that he couldn't hear them, but the way that Finn eyed them, she could have sworn that he knew they were talking about him.

"Finn? The young boy? No, I never met him, but he looks just like his grandfather did at that age. Spitting image," Tess chuckled, lost in thought. "If I hadn't already given my heart to your grandfather . . ." Tess's voice trailed off. "Good men, those O'Malleys. Had a bit of a wild streak in 'em, but at least they were real. Not like most of the people in this town."

While the afternoon started off tense, their walk through the Christmas festivities in town, making their way past storefronts wrapped in ribbons and lights, sipping hot cocoa and mulled cider, seemed to ease Tess back into a light-hearted mood. Maddie was delighted.

As they strolled by the festival booths, they reminisced about some of the past Christmas festivals they'd attended together. Carolers, ice sculptures, the smell of wood smoke and pine trees in the air. Carefree times. Times that were filled with happiness, before Cordelia came bursting into their lives like a flame and then, just as quickly, was extinguished.

Tess had always been the comforting presence in Maddie's life, the kind of mother who she always wished for. Tess comforted her as a child when Maddie woke up in the deep, heavy hours of night, pulled from her dreams by the sounds of the pounding surf. As the tide got higher, Maddie feared the waves were somehow reaching out to her, calling and echoing down the crooked cobblestone streets, rising up over the trellises choked with tuberose and clematis, through the shutters of the creaking window, and along the knotted and gnarled floorboards. Finally, they reached their way across her patchwork quilt, whispering, *Come and play.*

When fear of the churning waters finally got the best of her, Maddie would scurry up to Tess's room, the weathered pine floors groaning beneath her naked feet while echoes from the sea drifted in. Tess always welcomed Maddie into her bed, banishing any fear or monster that Maddie had been dreaming of. Back then, Tess had a way of making the bad things go away, but with Cordelia's disappearance, Rebecca's breakdown, and her own battle with dementia, even Tess couldn't make the monsters disappear.

But for now, Maddie was relishing the moment, allowing the Christmas spirit to envelop them both. For a little while, at least, they could pretend that life was normal. They tried to enjoy themselves as they went from store to store, picking out presents for each other and gazing at the window decorations until Tess stopped suddenly. The way that she stopped and the force with which she grabbed Maddie's hand made her fear that her grandmother was suffering a heart attack. Maddie followed her grandmother's gaze over to Rebecca's shop. The plywood used to cover the windows and door until Rebecca's return had been spray painted. The word DIE stretched vertically over the door, and the word WITCH was sprayed in bloodred block letters across the window. Tess squeezed Maddie's hand until her fingers tingled from lack of circulation.

"Let's go home," Tess said firmly. "Now." They walked quickly and in silence. Maddie noticed Tess dabbing at her eyes the entire way home. But they never mentioned what they saw to Abigail—or to each other.

Someone was giving them a message, and it came through loud and clear.

∞

Later that night, Maddie let Tess go on and on with her stories of Hawthorne and the original settlers. It was a good way for both of them to come to terms with what they had seen down at Rebecca's store earlier that day.

Maddie had heard all her grandmother's stories numerous times and never tired of them. And now with Tess facing the prospect of losing her stories and memories forever in a battle with her own mind, Maddie was anxious to hear Tess's stories again and again so that they'd never disappear.

"Doesn't surprise me one bit what they did to that storefront. Not one bit," Tess spoke solemnly. "Back in the days of the early New England settlements, stories traveled quickly of a town occupied by women and children who threw rocks and terrorized any outsiders who dared to enter. And the men were even more brutal and savage, capable of unspeakable acts. Hawthorne never welcomed strangers." She paused for a moment. "I should have known better than to bring Rebecca and Cordelia back to this place. This place has trapped us all."

Maddie knew that when Tess was a young mother and wife, leaving Hawthorne was what she had wanted more than anything in the world. The only thing that kept her going on those long days and nights while Jack was at sea were their plans of traveling around the world once Jack returned. Just Jack, Tess, their daughter Rebecca, and the new baby—the one that even Jack didn't know about yet—growing inside Tess's swollen belly.

But sadly, her dreams of escape quickly turned into a nightmare. On the day that Jack planned to return to Hawthorne, Tess waited by the window, watching for his ship as she packed up and boxed away their belongings. The ocean and the sky shared the same color of slate gray that afternoon.

"The color of death," Tess said knowingly. She heard a moan, a wail, a cry that broke across the horizon, something that was imperceptible to others but that rang out in the deep hollow of her heart.

"You're friend's grandfather, Matthew O'Malley, came to my door that day. He didn't have to say a word. I could see it in his eyes. Jack was dead, his ship lost at sea. It was at that moment that I knew I was to remain in Hawthorne for the rest of my life. And I did."

Maddie had heard that story before, but only now did she

really feel the sorrow and loss—the loss of a man she never knew, but was part of her family, the love of her grandmother's life.

Tess added, "I should have stopped you girls on Halloween night. If only I hadn't been foolish enough to take that nap—but then, I'm not as strong as I once was." She shook her head, the gray braid that ran down her back moving like a silver fish. "I should have told you."

A chill ran down Maddie's spine. "Told us what?"

Tess turned and looked Maddie straight in the eye. "The ocean that day was the same color as it was when your grandfather was lost at sea. But then, you didn't go near the ocean that night, did you?"

Tess held Maddie's gaze for a few beats. *What does she know?* Maddie thought as guilt crept through her body. Before Maddie had a chance to respond, Abigail came bursting into the room.

"Look what Santa brought us! Maddie, you have to come and see."

Maddie left Tess lying in her bed, and she followed her mother into the living room. A beautiful Christmas tree stood in the center of the room. She noticed someone underneath the tree, trying to straighten it and tighten the stand. Finn stood up after the tree was secure.

"What do I owe you?" Abigail asked as she scanned the room for her checkbook.

Finn held his gloved hand up and shook his head. "This is on the house, Mrs. Crane. After the year you all had, this is the least my family can do for you this holiday season."

Maddie felt her cheeks flush. "Well, tell your family I'm very grateful," Abigail said before leaving the room. "And happy holidays!"

"Thank you, Finn," Maddie stammered. "You didn't have to—"

He held his hand up, stopping her from saying any more. "I saw what they did to your aunt's store. I'm going to go over there tonight and put some new boards over the spray-painted ones. I'm just sorry that your grandmother had to see that."

"Do you know who did it?" Maddie asked.

"I have a couple of people in mind that could have done it. Nothing surprises me in this town anymore." Finn sighed. "I just knew that your family could use a good dose of Christmas cheer more than anyone else right now."

Before Maddie could say anything, Finn continued with a crack of a smile, "Besides, my grandpa was a sucker for Tess. He would have kicked my butt if I didn't do something nice for you all this holiday."

Maddie burst forward and hugged Finn. She assumed that he was doing this out of his feelings of loyalty toward Cordelia, but she suddenly was overwhelmed by his kind gesture. He smelled of Christmas trees and woodburning smoke. "Thank you," she whispered, holding back tears.

He held her for a moment, squeezed her tightly to his body, and then let her go.

"Merry Christmas, Maddie," he said softly and turned toward the door.

By the time she returned to Tess's room, Tess had fallen asleep. Maddie covered her grandmother with the bedsheets and turned off the lights, placing a soft kiss on her cheek. It wasn't until later that night, with thoughts of Finn O'Malley crowding her mind, that she remembered her grandmother's words before Finn and the Christmas tree's arrival. *But then, you didn't go near the ocean that night, did you?* Tess knew about Misery Island. But how could she? And why had she waited this long to speak up?

The next day, Maddie checked Rebecca's store. Finn had been true to his word—the plywood had been replaced, and the cruel words were gone. As she made her way home through town, Maddie realized how taken aback she was at her mother's reaction toward Finn O'Malley the previous night.

For as long as Maddie could remember, Abigail Crane would never lower herself to show appreciation for or to speak to someone like Finn O'Malley. Even though she had grown up with a similar background, once Abigail married into the Crane family, one of the most well-known and wealthiest families in Hawthorne, she had become deeply rooted in the lifestyle she had grown up idolizing. Abigail did everything she could to distance herself from her poor upbringing as a sailor's daughter. Immediately, she joined all the exclusive clubs in town—ones that would never have let her in prior to marrying into the Crane family. Abigail became so involved in the community that she overlooked her husband's penchant for late nights at the local taverns. Malcolm Crane was the one who finally ended the marriage. He just picked up and moved to Maine with one of the young barmaids in town, instantly severing all ties with them.

According to Tess, Maddie's mother was more concerned with how the divorce would affect her social position, as opposed to mourning the loss of a marriage, a family, and a home.

And while Maddie had initially grown up in a stately colonial at the end of Crane's Way, formerly known as Crooked Way (which Tess felt was a name far better suited for anything associated with that family), after the divorce, Maddie and her mother were left to fend for themselves. The Cranes were known for having "old money," but Malcolm had squandered away most of his family's legacy gambling and drinking. Maddie had faint memories of her father, and none of them were good.

&

When Maddie returned to the house, something felt different, out of place. Tess was in the living room singing softly to herself about a young girl with "hair as crimson as a rose," and the sound of furniture scraping across the old pine floors came from above.

Maddie walked up the flight of stairs to see that Abigail had rearranged Cordelia and Rebecca's rooms and boxed up their belongings.

"What's going on?" Maddie asked. She looked around the room hesitantly, feeling like she had walked in on something she shouldn't be seeing.

"Oh," Abigail said brightly. "Rebecca is going to need her things when she gets out of Ravenswood, and I figured that I'd just box all of their stuff up so that it would give us some extra room."

*Extra room?* Maddie thought. It was just the three of them wandering around in the big, empty shell of a house, and Tess only went from her bed to her rocking chair in the living room. Why was her mother in such a hurry to remove all traces of Rebecca and Cordelia?

"But . . . when they come back . . ." Maddie said slowly, eyeing her mother and noticing that she seemed far too light-hearted to be doing something as morose as packing up her sister and niece's belongings, not knowing if either one would—or could—ever return to retrieve them.

"Oh, Madeline, don't be silly," Abigail scoffed. "Cordelia has made it pretty clear that she has no intentions of coming back to this house . . . or this town, for that matter. And Rebecca—well, Rebecca won't move back in here without her daughter." She looked Maddie straight in the eye, talking to her like she was a little girl. "You know as well as I do that when this whole thing blows over and Cordelia comes back after her little runaway stunt, they will want to get as far away from Hawthorne as they can. I'll bet that they even go back to California. Probably better suited for it anyway." Abigail continued talking as she turned back to the boxes. "This weather is probably what drove them crazy—not that it takes much for Rebecca to go off the deep end. No, they're not strong enough to withstand these New England winters—long nights, freezing days . . ."

Maddie walked out of the room in the middle of Abigail's sentence. She didn't need to hear any more. Abigail was erasing Rebecca and Cordelia and their time at Hawthorne in the same way that she had erased all memories of Maddie's father when he took off. There wasn't a picture of him to be found in the house. Everything that he'd ever bought or given to them was destroyed the minute he left town. If anyone ever left Abigail, they were simply erased. *Gone.* Maddie wondered what would happen if and when she left her mother behind one day.

Would it be that simple to erase her own daughter?

# Chapter 14

## FEHU

## FORTUNE AND WEALTH

*Feeding and Nourishing Personal Wealth and Greed*

### MARCH

*Sweet darlin',*
*"Beauty walks like the night." I think of that line of poetry every time I see your face. I wonder when I can hold you again. Even just one moment would make a lifetime of happiness. Your eyes are pools of clear blue tranquility. When you look at me, it's an indescribable rush. Like nothing I've ever felt before.*
*Now isn't the time for us.*
*We both know that.*
*But soon, very soon.*
*Forever yours,*
*me*

*Cordelia,*
*You drive me wild when I see you! It's all I can think about—day, night, day, night. When I saw you last night, you were like an apparition at my door. I couldn't believe it was really you. How can this be*

*wrong when everything about you, my sweet darlin',
makes me feel like I'm finally getting my life right?*

*Why did you run off so soon? Don't you know that
you can always trust me? No matter what?*

*Soon, very soon, I will come to you, my sweet
Cordelia.*

*xoxo*
*me*

*Cordelia,*
*You are like a goddess of the night. How can you
even exist in this town? On this earth? Your silly talk of
fairies is all too real because you are one of them.
You're like an angel that has fallen into my life. I
watch you swim in the ocean at night, and you are like
a mermaid—a princess of the sea. I'm just afraid that
one night, you'll just keep on swimming, swimming,
swimming away into the deep black night. Don't ever
leave me. I couldn't go on without you here—my one
bright spot in this ancient town.*

*Eternally yours,*
*me*

Maddie had read and reread the letters so many times she
could practically recite them in her sleep. The paper had become so worn that they were soft as cotton, the ink faded.
No chance of getting any fingerprints off of these, she sul-
lenly realized after the hundredth time she'd read them. Not
the smartest move in the world on her part. They gave her no
clue as to the author, but it was someone clearly infatuated
with her cousin. She became so involved in the letters, trying
to decipher them, trying to figure out the time frame in which
they were written, that the winter months passed in a blur.

The letters were all basically the same—telling Cordelia

of her exquisite beauty, how the author longed for her, thought of her day and night. Sometimes, there were poems from William Blake, Wordsworth, Tennyson, Byron. The letters were almost stalkerish, but it seemed that Cordelia had been a willing participant in whatever affair was taking place, though there was never any direct mention of any physical relationship. It really seemed like a fairytale romance. And like many fairy tales, this one ended with the princess meeting a cruel fate.

Since Maddie wasn't in school, Abigail had her running around with more chores and responsibilities than she'd ever had before. It made Maddie almost wistful for the long, boring classes and hours and hours of homework she was missing.

Meanwhile, Tess, Abigail, and Maddie moved around each other like ghosts in the old Victorian, which felt very empty and cold. Maddie yearned to connect with Tess, to tell her what she knew about that night—and find out what Tess knew—but her grandmother was mentally slipping away from them all more and more each day.

Away from Hawthorne Academy, it was easy to distance herself from the Sisters of Misery. She avoided Kate's phone calls and invitations to parties. It was like she had fallen off the face of the earth and was only now resurfacing as spring was approaching. As winter stretched on and the police gave up the search, Maddie pressed on, doing research and handing out flyers. But now that the bitter cold winter had come to a close, Maddie resolved to find Cordelia by any means and at any cost. If that meant reliving the horrific night on Misery Island and grilling each and every person associated with that night—Kate and the Sisters of Misery, Reed, Trevor, even Finn—she would do it. And as much as she dreaded it, Maddie knew who she had to start with: Kate Endicott.

Cordelia had once referred to Kate and the Sisters of Misery as the Greek mythological creature Hydra, a serpent-like beast with many heads. It was after studying Greek myths in their European culture class that Cordelia made the connection. Maddie remembered her teacher describing how Hercules had tried to kill the beast by cutting off the heads. But every time a head was cut off, two more would grow in its place. Hercules realized that he had to sever the main head, the immortal one, and use that poison to kill each of the other heads. Maddie knew if she could get Kate to fall, the rest of the Sisters would collapse like a house of cards.

Nine Elmwood Lane. The Endicott house perched at the top of a manicured lawn that sloped down to the ocean's edge. Maddie's car tires crunched on the gravel driveway. It was funny how Kate always acted like this was her property, the rest of her family merely tenants.

After a few minutes of knocking at the oversized door, Maddie figured that no one was home. She had started back to her car when she heard the shout, "Damn it, you're going to kill me!"

Maddie found Kate and a very attractive, dark-haired man, both dressed in tennis whites on this unseasonably warm spring day, playing on the Endicott's tennis court, the plunk of tennis balls heralding the coming of warmer weather.

"When I said I wanted a workout today, I didn't think it would be on the court," Kate's raspy laugh carried across the court, making the man visibly blush.

"Sorry, sugar, let's try that serve again," the instructor's voice called out seductively.

"Kate," Maddie called out across the sprawling lawn. Kate turned and shielded her eyes to the sun. A slow smile spread across her face.

"Madeline Crane. Well, what have I done to deserve this

special visit?" Kate was patronizing her, but Maddie didn't care. She wanted answers.

Maddie moved toward her friend and lifted her cheek to receive Kate's customary air kisses, but Kate surprised her by gathering her into a tight hug, enveloping her with the smell of sun, sweat, and apple-scented hair. Up close, the tight expression on Kate's face softened. Her pale eyes were weary.

"Hey, hon," Kate said in an alarming tone of sincerity. And then in a sharper tone, she yelled, "Jeffrey, you can take the rest of the afternoon off. My friend and I have to talk."

They linked arms as Kate led her along the meandering rock path that curved its way around to the house. A lingering feeling of dread suddenly overcame her. It was the sensation that a tiny mouse might feel just before being swallowed whole by a giant reptile. A Lilly Pulitzer-clad snake, but a snake nonetheless.

ဆ

Kate strode across the interior of the immaculate living room that seemed straight out of the pages of *Martha Stewart Living*. The interior of the Nantucket-style house was blindingly white, from the stark beadboard on the walls to the whitewashed furniture to the bleached pine floors. Everything was antiseptically clean.

Maddie tried to make small talk, lulling Kate with flattery before hitting her with some harder questions. "Wow! Is that a promise ring from Trevor? It's beautiful."

Kate extended her arm so that Maddie could get a good look at the thick gold band on her right finger that was swollen with channel-set diamonds. Then she held it up to the light to inspect it herself, a large smile stretched across her face. Then she pulled a cigarette out of a sterling silver holder (most likely from Tiffany's) and tapped it on the engraved, initialed cover for a few beats.

"Is it a promise that we will someday get married? Yes. When will we walk down the aisle? That, I'm not so sure about. I really feel like I need to experience as much of college life as I can before I get married. Or rather, college men. Unfortunately, Trevor is only applying to the same schools as I am. And having Trevor at the same school will make that . . . tricky." She laughed again, twisting the ring around her long fingers. She lit the cigarette and sighed, exhaling a thin curl of smoke. "We'll definitely get married someday. But until then, a girl's got to have her fun, right?" She winked before nodding out to the handsome tennis instructor on the court, gathering his equipment.

At only a few months past her sixteenth birthday, Kate could put any famous, slutty socialite to shame. As far as Maddie knew, there'd been only one man to resist her, and Trevor was the main reason for it. Reed Campbell had made it clear that he wasn't about to betray his own brother for a one-night stand with Kate. And Kate would never forgive him for that. Though there was no way to prove it, Maddie was still convinced that Kate was behind all the rumors of an affair between Reed and Cordelia, ultimately leading to his termination from Hawthorne Academy.

"So, where's Trevor today?" Maddie asked. "Securing an internship at the state house for the summer?" Maddie remembered how the Campbells desperately wanted a Congressman in the family, almost as much as Kate wanted to marry someone powerful.

"Trevor? No, he's off applying to do that silly boat patrol thing this summer. He said it will look good on his college applications, but I know it's just an excuse to go out on the harbor and drink with Reed, who is officially the town drunk now that he's unemployed and living on his boat like some kind of homeless freak." Kate snorted and waved her French-manicured hand in disgust. "I've told Trevor again

and again that it's a bad idea to spend so much time with
Reed—you know, after everything he's put the family
through—but what can I say? They're brothers. Some kind
of unspoken code or some shit like that. But then again, Reed
probably still has a special place in your heart, doesn't he?"

Fighting a blush, Maddie said, "I think we all have fallen
under Mr. Campbell's spell at one time or another. Right,
Kate?"

Kate's face hardened. "Well, the only one who was actually *under* Reed at all was your cousin. And from what I
hear, Cordelia was *under* him a lot before she took off."

Maddie was instantly defensive. Despite all the rumors
that swirled around, Maddie still chose to take her cousin at
her word.

"You don't know what you're talking about, Kate. Cordelia
was never *with* Reed Campbell. He's our teacher, for God's
sake!"

Kate smirked. At least she no longer needed to find a way
to bring up Cordelia. Kate had done it for her.

"Well, he's certainly not teaching now, that's for sure." It
was obvious that she took great pleasure in Reed Campbell's
downfall. Then she added innocently, "But what do I know?
I didn't really keep tabs on your cousin anyway. She wasn't
worth my time. She was so attention-starved. Had to go and
run off and cause all that craziness just to get some attention."

"You still really believe that, Kate?" Maddie asked, shaking her head in disbelief. "After everything that happened
that night?" Maddie was pushing for answers, but if she
pushed too hard, Kate would shut her out completely.

"Hmmm . . ." Kate pursed her lips, fighting back a smile,
and folded her legs beneath her in the oversized chair, nar-
rowing her eyes. "What're you getting at, Crane?"

"I need to know, Kate. None of the Sisters of Misery were

ever straight with me about what happened that night," Maddie leaned forward. "Tell me everything you remember."

Kate looked at her incredulously. "What's with you, Maddie? Why are you even asking me these questions like you weren't even there? You must remember what happened. It was our Sisterhood ritual. You've done it out there on Misery Island with us tons of times. You were lucky, though. I made sure that you never had to stay out there on the island. I looked out for you, you know."

"That night was different. You know it was." Maddie's voice rose and cracked. Try as she might, she could still only remember snippets of that night, short clips playing in her mind: *Cordelia in pain, crying . . . Girls voices chanting . . . laughter . . . round and round in a circle . . . fire!* "You hurt her! It was like you were torturing her! And what was with the 'appeasing the elements' crap? We've never done that before. And then . . . then . . . I-I don't know what happened. Why can't I remember the rest of what happened?"

Kate regarded her for a moment. "You really don't remember? Hmm . . . you were pretty out of it, I guess." Kate bit her bottom lip, carefully choosing her words. "You're right. It was a little more, uh . . . intense than other nights on Misery. But that was because your slut cousin was hitting on Trevor. It's your fault, really. You should have warned Cordelia to back off."

"*My* fault?" Maddie was enraged. She wanted to lash out at that smug, spoiled, evil bitch, but she tried to cool herself down, reminding herself that she needed answers—answers that she could only get if she refrained from alienating the Sisters of Misery. Not yet, at least. "Why did you even let Cordelia come out to Misery with us in the first place? You never would have let her into the Sisterhood—we all knew that."

"Why shouldn't we think that *you* were the one responsible? Everyone could see how jealous you were of your *beautiful* cousin." She dragged out the word beautiful in an exaggerated way and punctuated it with air quotes, rolling her eyes. "You know, we never wanted to say anything at the time because you seemed so upset . . ." She hesitated, "But I always wondered if you had . . . you just disappeared for the whole semester and then, oh well . . . never mind." She sat back, complacent and smug.

Maddie was overcome by a strange mixture of outrage and fear. She couldn't have had anything to do with Cordelia's disappearance. And yet . . . could that be the reason why her memories of that night were so fuzzy? Could she be blocking out that night because *she* was responsible?

Furious and confused, Maddie stood up to leave. Kate had definitely crossed the line, and she seemed to realize it.

"Sweetie, wait. Come on, I'm sorry," she said. "Maddie, I didn't mean that. I'm just teasing. Please sit down."

Slowly, Maddie lowered herself back onto the couch. Kate knew something that she wasn't telling. Maddie could feel it.

"Obviously, you had *nothing* to do with Cordelia disappearing that night, right?" Kate's rhetorical question and singsong tone had Maddie reeling. She tried to will the memories of that night back into her mind. But no matter how hard Maddie tried, the night remained a mystery, like a movie she'd seen a long time ago, but couldn't remember the plot, the dialogue, or the actors. "I mean, we took things too far, that's a given. But, when we left her, she was *fine*. End of story."

Kate's cell phone rang, and she looked at the number that came up and pressed it against her diamond-studded ear. Stretching her legs out on the jacquard-covered chaise lounge, Kate stared out the French doors that led to the flagstone patio overlooking Hawthorne Harbor. "Hey," she said. Maddie followed Kate's gaze out onto the patio and was suddenly reminded of their eighth grade field hockey "orientation." She and Kate, along with ten other girls, were locked out on that patio on an unseasonably cold September night and forced to finish a half-keg of beer. The orientation took place at the Endicott's mansion that year because Kate's older sister, Carly, was captain. But that didn't mean that Kate got off any easier than the rest of the girls. If anything, she got it worse than anyone else.

Once they were thoroughly loaded, the older girls on the team scribbled in indelible marker on their faces and all over their bodies, emblazoning the words *slut, dyke,* and *whore* on their skin like tattoos. A few were even taken to the football orientation party and dropped off in various rooms with randomly chosen boys. Other girls had their hair hacked off with a dull Swiss Army knife.

Some of the girls cried in fear and humiliation on that night, but not Kate. She'd grown up learning to withstand her older sister's torments, whether it was pulling the head off a favorite doll or waking up with a large wad of bubble gum gobbed up in her long hair. When Kate was a girl, Kiki Endicott had berated her for crying, telling her that she needed to grow a thicker skin, toughen up. "Life isn't fair, Kate. The sooner you figure that out, the better." That was the Endicott mantra.

Sitting with Kate that day, Maddie felt as if the mantra was true. Life wasn't fair, and there wasn't anything that Maddie or Rebecca or Tess or even Cordelia could do to change that. Maddie had to keep up this charade of "friendship" with Kate Endicott if she had any hopes of unraveling Cordelia's mysterious disappearance.

After blowing off whoever was on the phone with a "Love ya. Call ya later, hon," Kate gave Maddie an unprecedented look of concern. But Maddie wasn't ready to buy it.

Not now. Not after knowing what she was capable of. "Maddie, I'm sure Cordelia is fine. Isn't it true that she used to run away all the time when she was in California?"

Flustered and angry at her condescending tone, Maddie snapped, "That only happened once. And it was right after her dad died."

"Well," Kate said, sitting back with a self-satisfied look, "my mother told me that your aunt Rebecca was notorious for disappearing when they were teenagers. It must be something that runs in your family."

Just as Maddie was about to respond angrily, a flurry of activity erupted down the corridor.

"What's going on?" Maddie asked. "Is that Carly back from school?"

Kate stretched lazily like a cat. "No, it's not Carly. She's traveling in Europe." She took a long drag of her cigarette, returning her attention to Maddie. "Major war room with investors. I'm going to stay clear of them that's for sure."

Maddie gave her a blank stare, so Kate explained. "My parents are putting together some big real estate deal as usual, but they have some major red tape to cut through." Tapping her cigarette ash into the Waterford crystal ashtray, she smirked. "Actually, you're probably aware of what's going on, what with your aunt being locked up in that loony bin. Too bad she's going to be homeless soon."

Kate eyed her, gauging her reaction. Maddie remembered that when dealing with Kate, you had to steel yourself for any cruel comment she might hurl at you. She kept her face blank. "What are you talking about?" Maddie said.

Kate looked amused. "Ravenswood? It's getting shut down. Don't you read the newspaper? There is a growing group in town—my family is just the driving force—that is rallying to force the state to close it down. And when it does get shut down, a beautiful luxury hotel—The Endicott—will be taking its place. I mean, Ravenswood is right in the middle of town, it's such an eyesore. And all those creepy patients . . ." She paused long enough to take another drag off her cigarette. She exhaled slowly and waved the smoke away. "All it needs is a little TLC, and it will become a destination resort, complete with waterviews, the latest spa and fitness equipment, a gourmet restaurant, and the thrill of being near the ghosts and witches and other spooky legends of New England history." She spoke as though she was a tour guide, reading from a book. "And after I graduate with a degree in hotel management, I get to run the place."

Maddie shook her head, trying to process the absurdity of the situation. Instead of raising money to fix the hospital for people who were actually in need of therapy and counseling, the wealthy elite of Hawthorne were raising money to turn it into a luxury hotel, putting even more money into people's pockets that obviously weren't hurting for it in the first place. Why wasn't she surprised that the Endicott family was leading the charge?

"Good for you, Kate," she sighed.

Kate batted her eyes. "Well, dear, you know that I've always wanted to be a princess. Well, now I'll be a princess with my very own castle." Her laugh filled the airy room.

Disgustedly, Maddie nodded, stood up to leave, then turned back to face her friend once more. "You know, Kate, you may end up the queen of the castle one day, but don't forget, it's always going to be known as 'The Witches' Castle.' So I guess that makes *you* the witch, doesn't it?"

"Trust me, Maddie, *I'm* not the one people are worried about becoming a witch."

# Chapter 15

## EOH

# ᛖ

## THE HORSE - IDEAS & PARTNERSHIPS

*Gradual Development and Steady Progress; Partnership
with Someone Strong-Willed*

Maddie spotted the sails of Reed Campbell's boat as she walked down the narrow, winding road that led to the docks. After her brief visit with Kate Endicott, Maddie knew exactly where to find Reed on any given morning. The sailing vessel gleamed from the seemingly endless hours of hard work, sweat, and elbow grease it must have taken to make the boat the envy of all others in the harbor.

Maddie's heart pounded a little faster when she caught a glimpse of his sand-colored hair from a distance. Despite their age difference, the gap didn't seem to matter as much now that he wasn't officially her teacher.

Luckily, Reed didn't need a steady income, as he lived off the interest of his grandfather's oil company. The one stipulation from his grandfather's trust, however, was that he had to remain in town to collect it, a requirement that irked most of the townspeople, given the scandal that had surrounded him in the last few months.

"Any chance of a storm out there?" Maddie called out to her former teacher. He turned in her direction and squinted into the early morning sun. Lifting the baseball cap off his head, he combed his hands through his longish dirty blond hair and tugged the cap back on again.

"Hope not," he called back. "Weather calls for some bumpy conditions this afternoon, but I'll take my chances."

"Well," Maddie said as she walked down the dock to the side of the boat, drawing on some unknown well of courage that existed somewhere within her, "have you got enough room in there for one of your students?"

*Am I insane?* Maddie thought. She knew that her mother would kill her if she was seen talking to Reed Campbell. He'd never officially been cleared as a suspect, but Maddie wanted desperately to believe that he could never have anything to do with Cordelia's vanishing, even though he did look a little haggard these days. But Maddie let her heart get the better of her head. Reed squinted at her for a moment or two, as if he was trying to decide how to act in front of one of his former students—the cousin of the girl that he had been a suspect in the disappearance of, no less. He said casually, "Hey there, Maddie. It's been a while."

Reed held her gaze for a few beats, his crystal blue eyes glistening in the sunlight. An awkward silence hung between them, and for a moment, Maddie didn't want to be Cordelia's cousin; she didn't want to be a teenager. "Well, don't mind my saying this, but I'm probably the last person that I would think you'd want to talk to right now," he offered tentatively.

"I know that you had nothing to do with her disappearance . . . you couldn't have," Maddie blurted out before she could stop herself. "But I do have some questions. I—I need to know things about her. You were close—" She noticed his jaw tighten. "Not in that way, I mean. I . . . I don't know. I just thought . . ."

His face darkened for a moment, and he looked out toward the horizon. Maddie's confidence fled, and she was ready to turn and run back up the road, away from the marina when he said, "I'll tell you everything I know, Maddie. But honestly, most of what I have to say—and there's really not all that much—is already on police record. You can go look it up for yourself."

Maddie dug her foot into the planks of the salt-worn dock and stared down at her hands. "I want to hear it from you, Mr. Campbell."

"Reed," he smiled, leaning against the handrails. "I'm not your teacher anymore."

Maddie tried not to indulge in her schoolgirl fantasies, but having him look at her that way, like she wasn't just another student, was almost too much for her to handle.

"So how fast does this thing go?" Maddie nodded toward the boat.

Reed hesitated for a moment, eyeing her suspiciously. Then his dimples deepened, and he gave a gruff laugh as he turned away from her, muttering quietly, "What the hell, I've got nothin' else to lose." He reached into a cooler and grabbed a beer.

*What am I getting myself into?* Maddie thought as she stepped into the boat.

He looked at her again and shook his head. "Never mind," he said smiling. "Now, Maddie, as your former teacher, I'm supposed to keep you safe." She wasn't sure what he was talking about until he reached under the bench, grabbed a life vest, and threw it to her.

"I'm a big girl," Maddie laughed uneasily. "I can take care of myself." But could she? They would be heading out toward Misery Island where no one had been able to come to Cordelia's rescue, no one could hear her cries for help.

He eyed her warily, then his square jaw slid easily into a boyish grin. "I'm sure you can, my dear."

Maddie looked around the boat. Sleeping bag, beer cans,

cigarettes, wine bottles. The inside of the boat was a disgusting mess. No wonder Kate had made fun of him. Despite living on a hundred-thousand dollar boat and sleeping in Brooks Brothers clothes, he lived like a homeless person. A very well-dressed, insanely handsome homeless man.

As he guided the boat out of the harbor, he turned back to her, his eyes now hidden behind his wraparound RayBan sunglasses. "Now, what did you want to know about Cordelia?"

"Well, I know that she spent a lot of time with you after classes—er, helping you with tutoring and all." Maddie watched Reed carefully for a reaction. His body language never altered—his posture showed no sign of tension or guardedness. He simply nodded his head, looking out over the bow of the boat. "I'm just trying to retrace her steps. Talk to everyone who was—I don't know—special to her."

"Well," he said. "I hope you find what you're looking for, Maddie." There was no sign of guilt or sadness in his face. Then he added, "I just wouldn't get your hopes up too high. Sometimes, some people just don't want to be found."

Maddie nodded, considering the possibility that he could be right. But she was still determined to get some answers. *No matter what.*

"Why do you—and everyone else—think that she just ran away?" Maddie asked desperately. "Of all people, you should know how devoted she was to her mother. It would kill her to know that Rebecca's lost her mind over all this."

She thought she noticed Reed giving her a sidelong glance when she uttered the word *kill.*

He carefully guided the boat through the harbor, saluting various people who were out on their boats. Most turned their heads and busied themselves with something else, pretending not to see the "fallen son" of Hawthorne.

"Beautiful," Reed said. "Just when people are starting to

get off my case about your cousin, now they see us together."
Then he turned to her and said sharply, "Just don't go falling
off the boat or tripping and hitting your head or anything.
I've got all the grief I can handle right now."

Maddie heard him mutter under his breath, "Teenagers."

They sat in silence until they reached the mouth of the
harbor. Reed's mood seemed to lift as they made their way
out into the open water.

"Where to, Captain?" he asked, smiling as he guided the
boat out of the harbor.

Once they were out on the Atlantic, Reed let her steer the
boat for a little while. Their hands grazed a couple of times,
sending ticklish tingles up her spine. When he stood behind
her, helping her guide the wheel, shouting directions over
the howl of the wind into her ear, Maddie was overcome by
the juxtaposition of his strength and masculinity, and the
gentle way he treated her. His bad mood seemed to disappear the further they got from Hawthorne.

When he looked at her with those piercing blue eyes, she
felt the world around her drop away, yet Cordelia was with
them at all times. Reed's possible involvement with her disappearance stayed in the back of her mind, wriggling in like
a worm.

"Did Cordelia ever say anything about Kate or Trevor or
anyone to you? Did they ever say anything to you about her?"

His face grew dark for a moment. The mention of Kate,
the person responsible for spreading rumors about their il-
licit affair, seemed to send him back to his gruff, prickly
mood.

"Kate says a lot of things. Most of them are lies. You should
know that by now," he said, his jaw twitching in anger. "I
have no idea what my little brother sees in that—that—" He
stopped for a moment and chose his words carefully, "—girl.

And my brother said the type of things about Cordelia that most teenage boys would say about a beautiful girl that wouldn't give 'em the time of day."

Maddie bristled a little when she heard him call Cordelia beautiful.

"So you never thought there was anything going on with Cordelia and your brother?"

Reed turned and stared at her for a moment. "Do *you* think there was anything going on between them?"

"She thought he was a disgusting pig," Maddie said.

"Well," he laughed. "Then there's your answer."

"But I'd bet that she flirted with him to piss Kate off."

"That's not too hard to do—piss off Kate Endicott."

Maddie agreed. "You're telling me."

Later that afternoon, just as the sun was beginning to sink into a wash of pinks and purples over the horizon, they pulled back into the harbor. Reed helped her onto dry land, letting her lean on him as she hoisted herself onto the dock. Her knees felt a little shaky, and Maddie almost toppled back into the boat.

"Easy there," he said, jumping up out of the boat and putting his hands on her sides. "Just wait a minute or two to get your land legs back." Maddie had forgotten what the transition period felt like, going from a boat onto solid ground. It was almost like those first few minutes after coming off of a treadmill—your body feels like it's still moving even when you are perfectly still. Or the heady feeling of a first kiss.

Reed bent down a bit and peered into her eyes. "You okay there, sailor?"

Maddie blushed and nodded. It was then that Maddie felt eyes on her and turned to see a bunch of Hawthorne old-timers milling around the docks. Nothing ever changed in this town—people just waited around to collect any piece of gossip that came their way. Reed must have noticed them as well, because he quickly removed his hands from her hips and shoved them into his pockets, backing away from her a few steps.

"Well, okay then," he stammered. "If you're sure that you're alright, I'm going to go out and moor this boat." He spun on his heels and jumped back into the boat.

Just as he started unraveling the rope from the dock, Maddie called out, "Reed!"

He looked up at her, squinting.

"Thanks. I had fun," she offered.

He nodded his head in agreement. "Anytime, sweet darlin', anytime."

And then they went their separate ways.

As Maddie turned the corner onto Main Street, her legs went weak beneath her again, but not from the sea.

*Sweet darlin'.*

That's what Cordelia's admirer called her in those unsigned love letters that Maddie had found in her locker. Despite his denials, could Reed have been involved—even in love—with Cordelia?

She ran back to the house, determined to find more clues in those letters that would link them to Reed. She could compare the handwriting on the letters to the ones from her English papers. When she got to her room, breathless, she knew right away that something was wrong. Her room felt a bit off, as if someone had been in there recently. She ran to her bedside table and yanked open the drawer.

The letters were gone.

# Chapter 16

## MANNAZ

ᛗ

### THE MAN - JUDGEMENT

*The Man who Watches; Friends and Enemies
Seeking Middle Road*

With everything that was running through her head that night—the boat ride with Reed, the missing letters, the conversation with Kate—Maddie hardly slept. She woke just after daybreak. Craving her daily caffeine fix—one that Abigail firmly disapproved of—Maddie realized she had to get out of the house.

Maddie crept out of the house, careful not to wake anyone. Once down at the waterfront, she was thrilled to see that The Coffee Shack, which catered to all the sailors and fishermen who began their days long before most people reached over to shut off their alarm clock each morning, had already opened its doors and rolled out the tattered striped awning. After grabbing her coffee, Maddie walked outside along the harbor front, gazing out at the boats bobbing and swaying off the glinting waters, scanning the buoys for Reed's boat. It was gone. He must have taken it up the coast to Portsmouth. Maddie recalled him saying that he preferred spending time in the laid-back, artsy community of Portsmouth, New Hampshire, to the rigid social code of Hawthorne.

Maddie pictured him out on the ocean, his boyish face slightly grizzled by a few days of beard growth, the wind tangling his sandy hair. Even though he represented everything she hated about prep school boys—the trust-fund mentality, the irresponsibility, the Peter Pan syndrome—plus the fact that he was her former teacher, Maddie couldn't prevent the return of her old schoolgirl crush on him.

She had turned those letters around in her mind every which way, trying to convince herself that even if they had been from Reed, they were harmless. Just a harmless flirtation. Nothing more. There was nothing sinister in those pages.

But where had the letters gone? Perhaps Tess had gone into her room and thrown away the letters, not realizing that they were of any importance. Tess had been doing more and more odd things lately—roaming the yard in her nightgown, talking to herself late at night, opening and closing the basement door for no reason—so throwing away a stack of letters wouldn't be completely out of character.

Coffee in hand, Maddie made her way up the winding road to Fort Glover and the lookout point. The moss-covered walls were still firmly rooted in the ground and were in surprisingly good condition despite their age. The fort had been used in the Revolutionary War, and the stone walls were erected proudly high up on the rocks, overlooking the churning waters of the Atlantic Ocean. The path leading to the fort was usually filled with joggers and moms with strollers. But on this early morning, the path was deserted, the benches empty.

Maddie sat on one of the benches and took a sip of the steaming hot coffee, the aroma of freshly ground beans mixing pleasantly with the salty air. The fort overlooked the mouth of the harbor, so from this vantage point, Maddie could clearly see all of the boats moored there. She closed her eyes, getting lost in the sound of the waters lapping against the jagged rocks below.

"Beautiful morning, isn't it?" A voice came from behind her.

Her heart hiccupped as Finnegan O'Malley appeared behind her, silent as a ghost. She hadn't spoken to him since Christmas.

"Sorry," Finn said earnestly. "I didn't realize that I would scare you like that."

Maddie relaxed, smiling. "Oh, that's alright. I just didn't think that anyone would be up here this early in the morning. It's too early for the soccer moms and their strollers. So I figured that I'd be safe."

Maddie took another sip of coffee, spilling part of it down her chin. *Smooth, Maddie, very smooth.*

"Careful, or I might call the authorities," he joked. "Park rules, reckless drinking not allowed."

Embarrassed, Maddie smiled and wiped her chin with her sleeve. "I don't like to discuss my drinking problems with strangers." *Ouch, bad joke.*

Finn fought back a grin.

"So, what are you doing out here this morning besides scaring unsuspecting girls?" she asked.

His face grew serious, and he shook a large ring of old keys. "Well, Maddie, I'm here to lock you up." He pointed to the rusted gate of the old fort prison.

Maddie hesitated, nervous fear twitching in the back of her throat. "Ha, ha," she said, desperate to break the lengthy silence.

He raised an eyebrow and said without any hint of emotion. "This property is under my jurisdiction. I make the rules, Maddie."

Furrowing her brow in confusion, Maddie waited for the punch line.

A wide grin broke across his face. "Scared you."

"No, you didn't." She wasn't quite sure what to make of Finn O'Malley and his weird sense of humor.

"Yeah, I did," he said evenly, staring her down with his wide-set dark eyes. "You scare pretty easy. Not like Cordelia. Nothing scared her."

"That's true," Maddie offered, forcing herself to look away from his steady gaze and out toward the ocean. "You sound like you knew Cordelia pretty well."

Finn dropped down on the bench next to her. She could smell the sweet scent of fresh-cut grass mixed with wood smoke on him. The smell reminded her of autumn and pumpkin stands and apple cider. He said nothing in return, but nodded his head as he pulled out a worn pack of Marlboro Reds from his pocket. He jutted the open package in her direction after he'd taken one out for himself.

Maddie shook her head, and he shoved the package back into his jacket pocket.

Maddie asked, "So what are those keys for anyway?"

"Crockett Powder house, Fort Glover," he said, pointing with his cigarette. He swiveled around the bench, looking behind them. Maddie could feel him expel his smoke on her neck. "Old Burial Hill, Ravenswood, Old Potter's Tavern—what's left of it. Pretty much every historical monument and town building in Hawthorne."

"Even the fort prison?"

"Even the prison," said Finn.

"How come?"

"I take care of the town monument grounds. Me and my old man were hired by the Historical Society." He added sheepishly, "I'm actually a volunteer member of the society."

Now Maddie was the one who raised an eyebrow. Town volunteer work seemed quite out of character for him.

"Yeah, I know. What is a guy like me doing in the Historical Society? My dad figured it was a good way to keep us in good standing with the town so the committee wouldn't give the work away to different landscapers."

"Isn't that a little self-serving? There has to be a bylaw or two that you are breaking."

"Yeah, well, if it bothers you that much, you can bring it up at one of the town meetings."

"You go to town meetings, too?" Somehow, Maddie couldn't get a mental image of this teenage guy in dirty jeans and a leather jacket sitting at the town meetings with Mr. Krantz, her old science teacher, and Mrs. Malone from the garden club.

His eyes widened, making him appear childlike. "I'm an upstanding citizen of Hawthorne. Of course I do."

Maddie laughed.

"What? You don't think that they let guys like me in, do you?"

"No, really, I'm—I'm sure you're a very influential member of the committee," she said through her laughter.

"Snob," he said, smiling.

Maddie glanced down at the large brass circle of keys he held, thinking that it resembled a prop straight out of an old Western movie.

"Sorry, Sheriff. Hey, I've never seen the prison before. What's it like?"

"I'll have to take you on a tour sometime," he said in an amused tone. "I took Cordelia there a couple of times. She called it *magical*." He wrinkled his forehead and laughed, remembering. "I don't know. She could be pretty out there, sometimes." He slowly exhaled.

Maddie bit her lip thoughtfully. "I didn't think you knew her that well."

He stiffened. "I know that she didn't deserve what happened to her. I know that she shouldn't have disappeared the way she did."

"Some people think that she ran away," Maddie offered.

"Some people are fuckin' idiots."

"What do you think happened to her?"

Finn looked at her squarely, daring her. "You're her cousin. You tell me."

Maddie was slightly ruffled by his accusatory tone and intense stare. She tried to look casual and shrugged it off, saying, "I have no idea. I mean, my gut feeling tells me that she didn't run away. She couldn't have. She wouldn't have done it to the people that cared about her. And I don't think she was killed. I mean, I know it sounds weird, but if she were dead, I think I'd feel it. I think I'd know it was time to stop looking."

Finn nodded solemnly as Maddie continued, "So that means that she was taken against her will. Who didn't like her in town?" she asked rhetorically. "Well, just about everybody. You know how hard it is to be an outsider here. Well, at least you did before you started campaigning to be the town mayor." Smiling, Maddie hoped that her teasing would lower his guard.

"Please, no comments from my campaign at this time," he said stoically. Maddie choked back a laugh.

"But seriously, it was always hard for Cordelia. And people in this town didn't make it any easier for her. I know that some of *my friends*," Maddie paused, making air quotes with her fingers as she spoke of the Sisters of Misery, "were awful to her, but I didn't think that anyone was capable of actually hurting her or making her disappear."

He raised his eyebrows, cocked his head, and then quickly looked out at the water.

"Why?" Maddie said quickly. "What do you know?"

He shrugged, grabbing his pack of cigarettes again from his pocket. He hunched over to light one and then said, exhaling, "Like I said before, I know about a lot of things that go on in this town. For instance, I know why you are out here this morning."

"Oh, really. Why then, oh knower of all things in Hawthorne, am I out here?"

"Checking to see when your favorite teacher pulls back into the harbor, perhaps?" Finn said with sarcasm, cigarette dangling from the corner of his mouth.

"How did you . . . ? I mean, I wasn't . . . Jesus, I hate how small a town this is," Maddie stammered. "Seriously, doesn't anyone have anything better to do than to check up on each other and get into each other's business?"

"Well, I'm the last person to care about other people's business," Finn said defensively. "If you want to get involved with an asshole like Reed Campbell, then by all means, go for it. I just thought that you should be warned."

"Warned? Warned about what?" Maddie demanded.

"You can't see what's going on here, can't see past the little bubble that you live in. You're too caught up in your own life, your own problems. Cordelia could see it, though. She knew what was going on. She needed you, and you couldn't even be there for her. I was the only one who watched out for her."

Growing more furious with every word, Maddie thought, *Who the hell does he think he is?* "How dare you talk to me about Cordelia! She was—is *my* cousin. *My* family. *My* best friend. If you were so incredibly important to her, why didn't she say a goddamned word about you? She never said one word. And she told me everything. As far as she was concerned, you didn't exist!"

Maddie stood up. Despite how cute he was and how thoughtful he'd been to her family over the holidays, she had quickly lost any desire to continue this conversation with Finn O'Malley.

"Well, now she doesn't exist, so I guess we're even." Maddie must have visibly winced at that comment because his voice softened, "Hey, I'm sorry Maddie. That was a really horrible thing for me to say. I—I don't even know why I said it."

"I do," she said, backing away from him. How much did Maddie even know about him anyway? And why did he just *happen* to show up—practically out of thin air—the minute she came out here by herself?

"You're a self-pitying prick, and you're jealous of people in this town—people who have more, people who want to be more. Well, Finn, that's not someone I need in my life right now. So, I'd appreciate it if we didn't cross paths again."

Hoping that her firm tone masked the sudden fear tightening around her spine, Maddie turned and briskly walked down the hill, away from Finn, away from the feeling that he knew more than he let on.

"It's too small a town for that, my dear," Finn said in a mocking tone. "We'll be seeing each other again real soon. You can count on it."

Once Maddie reached a safe distance from Finn, she turned to catch him taking another long drag from his Marlboro Red, still watching her, still smirking. He gave a two-fingered salute with the hand that held the cigarette and turned to walk in the opposite direction.

Maddie didn't know what angered her more, his callousness about Cordelia's disappearance or that her heart was pounding just as fast as it had when she thought about Reed.

∞

A few days later, Kate left a message for Maddie, instructing her to meet the girls on the expansive deck of the exclusive Crestwood Yacht Club.

The five members of the Sisters of Misery were coming back together again, if only for a few hours. Like five points of a star, one that had shone in a black October sky that fateful night months before, bearing witness to unspeakable, vengeful acts.

Maddie hadn't been to the club since she had attended the Freshman Formal. Despite having grown up swimming at the pool, taking sailing lessons, playing on the tennis courts, and eating dinner with her friends' families in the grand dining room, Maddie always felt like an outsider, like she was masquerading as another young, wealthy child of Hawthorne. Her friends never knew that the amount of money their parents spent on expensive dinners at Crestwood was more money than Maddie's family spent on groceries in a month. But Maddie was a born chameleon, her mother saw to that. She slipped easily into the role that the other girls expected of her and never questioned it. Not until Cordelia and Rebecca came into her life did Maddie begin to see the people she associated with in a different light.

Maddie climbed the wide plank stairs that led up to the main building of the yacht club, suddenly feeling very out of place in the loose-fitting, floral dress that had seemed so appropriate during her days working at Rebecca's store. She felt like she was being appraised by the well-dressed women of the club as she walked through the main room. Moving across the salt-worn, wooden floors, she trailed her fingers along the dark mahogany bookshelves, observing the tall, brass trophies that gleamed in their custom-made cases, the banners and flags that hung limp from the rafters above. The briny smell of salt and sand permeated every object in the building.

From her spot at the front door, Maddie could see the girls waiting for her through the tall windows that wrapped around the building and overlooked the harbor front porch. They were perched on Adirondack chairs waiting for her arrival. Instead of relaxing and stretching out in their chairs, enjoying the unseasonably warm sunshine, they were leaning forward, whispering, the sun gleaming off their various shades of flax-colored hair. It was like a J. Crew photo shoot. All of the girls had that wholesome, just-off-the-yacht look about them. Very New England prep school. And though it had never been this way for Maddie before, very nauseating.

When Maddie approached, their hushed voices halted.

"Maddie, finally!" Hannah jumped from her chair and gathered her into a big hug. Bridget hung behind for a moment and then air-kissed both of her cheeks.

"Bonjour, mon amie!" Bridget exclaimed. The other girls rolled their eyes and laughed.

"Don't pay attention to her," Kate laughed. "She's getting ready for a trip to Paris with the French Club, and she's been driving us all crazy with this French crap." To illustrate, Kate started making some *ohwn . . . ohwn . . . ohwn* sounds, mocking Bridget's terrible French accent.

"Shut up, Kate. You're just jealous 'cause you don't get to spend April in Paris," Bridget shot back. Silently, Maddie was impressed with her ability to give it right back to Kate. Plus, she noticed that Bridget was looking healthy again—almost a normal weight.

"Here, take my seat, Maddie," Darcy offered, perching carefully on the freshly painted white banister that overlooked a dramatic drop down to the jagged slabs of rock jutting out of the blue-gray water. Maddie took the seat at the center of the group.

"Carlos," Kate shouted, waving to get the attention of the cocktail waiter. "Can you get a drink for my friend here? Can we have another round of Cape Codders?" Kate winked at the man in the crisp white uniform. "Just put it on the Endicott tab, thanks."

Carlos nodded and hurried off to retrieve the girls' drinks. Kate's father was the Commodore of the club, so Kate Endicott and her friends always got served despite being underage. Either that, or Kate had probably screwed the handsome waiter at one of the club's many functions.

Kate then turned to her. "So you've finally come out of hiding, I see. I guess Reed Campbell can make any girl come out of the woodwork."

Maddie could physically feel the collective curiosity as it grew around her. Kate was never one to beat around the bush.

"Yeah," Hannah gushed. "What's it like to be with Mr. Campbell? He's so hot."

Kate snickered. "I wouldn't go that far."

Darcy snapped back, "Yes, you would. That is, if he'd let you."

"Bitch," Kate shot back.

"It's really nothing like that," Maddie murmured, but the girls were too busy bitching at each other to hear her.

"Well, I guess Reed is a step up from *the lawn boy*," Kate said as she wrinkled her nose.

"Yeah, since when did you start hanging out with gas station guys and gardeners?" Darcy laughed.

"I'm telling you, it's been a downward slope ever since Maddie became a shop girl," Kate said. "Anyway, that guy gives me the creeps." She visibly shuddered for effect.

They were talking about Finn. Maddie was astonished again at how quickly information traveled around the town.

Hannah added, "Wasn't he the guy that Bronwyn had to yell at to stop staring at us during field hockey practice? I thought the team had some kind of restraining order against him or something."

"You can't get a restraining order for an entire group of people, dumb ass," Kate shot back. "Or else Hawthorne Academy would get one against all the loser townies."

The girls continued their mock fighting and laughing as an endless supply of drinks were at their disposal. Maddie gingerly sipped her strong drink and then whispered to Carlos to make the rest of hers Shirley Temples. She listened to the girls chatter on as they got drunker and louder. If one of them let something slip about that night, Maddie wanted to be sober enough to catch it. Plus, she was curious that the girls knew who Finn was since she had only recently become acquainted with him over the past few months.

"So, Maddie," Kate said, picking up on Maddie's unwillingness to join in on the group conversation, "I must admit that we have some ulterior motives for bringing you out here this afternoon."

The girls all looked at her, wide-eyed and waiting. Maddie knew she should have trusted her gut instinct and blown off this get-together. What was up Kate's sleeve this time?

Darcy piped up, "Yeah, we want to know what this means." She stretched her rail-thin arm out toward Maddie. In her perfectly manicured hand, she held a gray, sea-worn stone a little smaller than a tennis ball. There was a large, blood red H scrawled across it.

"Yeah," Hannah added. "I found one at my doorstep the other day, but I just thought it was someone trying to freak me out. Why would someone put MY initial on it?"

Bridget chimed in, "We all got one. All with an *H* for Hannah? Should she be worried or something?"

"Yeah, is this supposed to be some kind of sick joke?" Hannah asked, glancing at Kate. " 'Cause if it is, it's not funny."

Maddie shook her head, and the girls shot looks at each other as the silence among them grew. *They think it's me,* Maddie realized. She looked at the four girls who had once been her best friends, at the distrust in their eyes, and she knew that she could never forgive them for what had happened out on Misery Island. Even if Kate, Hannah, Bridget, and Darcy weren't directly responsible for Cordelia's vanishing, they set the stage for whatever terrible unknown events unfolded on Halloween night. How dare they act as if *she* was the guilty one? Maddie could barely live with herself for her part of that night, regardless of whatever scraps of memory she could piece together.

"I don't know anything about those rocks or who would have put them at your door."

"Did you get one, too?" Hannah asked, her voice raised an octave. She sounded like a scared little girl.

Maddie shook her head again. "I don't think so. But even if I did, my mom could have thrown it away without telling me." It was plausible that Abigail, known for rising at dawn each day, could have come across the stone and heaved it into the bushes or gotten rid of it somehow without telling Maddie.

Kate stood up and dropped hers in Maddie's lap. "Here you go, Merry Christmas. Now you won't feel left out."

Maddie turned the stone around in her hand. She ran her finger over it and then tried to scratch at it to see if paint would flick off. The crimson color looked like it had actually seeped down into the stone itself. She wasn't sure if it was marker or spray paint, but she knew what it was intended to look like—blood.

"So with your aunt stuck in the loony bin and your cousin

on the run, you're the closest thing we have to a fortune teller," Kate said snidely as she took her seat again, lighting up a cigarette. "What's the story, Crane? What is this supposed to mean?"

Maddie had learned the rune stone meanings by heart in the months that Cordelia had been away. She kept finding rune stones around the house, and as she collected them, she'd consult Rebecca's old book, memorizing the meanings. The symbol "H" was one of the most powerful and dangerous of all the stones. Someone was sending them a message.

"H is the rune stone that means Hagal or hailstorms," Maddie said quietly.

"Oh, right, hailstorms," Kate mocked, her voice thick with sarcasm, "that explains everything, doesn't it?" Then her voice sharpened. "We don't need a weather forecast, Crane; we want to know what it means."

Maddie closed her eyes trying to remember the description from Rebecca's book. "Hailstorms represent . . . um . . . destruction . . . setbacks . . . upheaval . . ."

And then she opened her eyes to meet Kate's and said forcefully, "It means war."

# Chapter 17

## THURISAZ

## THE GIANT - BOUNDARIES

*Shape Changers, Demons, and Negative Energy;*
*A Force of Destruction, Conflict*

"*A*re you in?"
I look around at the insistent faces surrounding me. *There's no escape. I weigh my options. I could go along with them, betraying my closest and dearest friend. Or I could share her pain.*

"*Maddie, are you in?*" *The words hiss at me this time. I look at her lips curling over her gritted teeth. She knows that somehow, I hold her fate in my hands.*

*Slowly, I nod. And, just like that, my fate is sealed.*

&

Maddie flopped backwards into bed after hurling her alarm clock against the wall, pulling the covers up over her face. Still reeling from her encounter with the Sisters of Misery, she was frustrated that the only bit of information she had gotten out of them was who was cheating on their girlfriends-boyfriends, who had come out of the closet, what were the new must-have bags and shoes that they all desperately needed as if their lives depended on it. Nothing about

Cordelia. Even when Maddie had brought it up, the subject was quickly and expertly changed.

Her most recent nightmare—now a common occurrence—gave her a little insight into what *could* have happened. As Maddie went back and reread her entries in her dream journal over the past few months, it read like something out of a Stephen King novel, not something that could actually occur in real life. But Maddie was grateful to finally have a few pieces, even if it was only an image or two, to grasp hold of and roll around in her mind so that they could grow larger and larger until she had something substantial enough to fill the gaps.

And not only did she have a terrible night's sleep, but Maddie also dreaded the upcoming agenda for the day: seeing Rebecca. Once the word got out that Ravenswood was being shut down, her mother had needed help moving Rebecca to a new facility. Abigail also wanted to put an end to Maddie's free time that, according to her mother, was being wasted on Reed Campbell. Abigail gave Maddie the job of overseeing the transfer, doing the paperwork, and making sure that the relocation of her aunt Rebecca was seamless.

৪৩

The red monster jutted out against the backdrop of the Atlantic Ocean at the edge of Hawthorne, as it had for the past century. Trees dotted the perimeter of the insane asylum, the reach of their arm-like branches beckoning, *Come closer. Don't be scared*. The menacing face of the crumbling Gothic hospital erected on the site of Fort Glover appeared to stare at her as Maddie drove along the winding path sheltered by a canopy of trees. Rebecca had been held prisoner there for months. She was one of the last residents of Ravenswood, and now, thanks in part to the Endicotts, the state was officially shutting the place down. Abigail wanted Maddie to check on Rebecca before she was moved to a new facility. Typically, Tess would have done it, but it seemed like each day she was losing more of her grip on reality.

So Maddie was determined to use this as an opportunity to communicate with Rebecca, something that hospital workers hadn't been able to do throughout her time spent there. She was desperate to find the Rebecca she knew and loved. The one who seemed to have disappeared months ago and who had left this hollow shell, this changeling, in her place. But at the same time, Maddie was terrified that she would be on the receiving end of another one of Rebecca's tirades.

The asylum was intended to be an idyllic, soothing environment for the mentally ill when it was originally conceived. The doctor who was responsible for Ravenswood, or as it was called back then, Hawthorne Lunatic Asylum, envisioned a place filled with light and music, surrounded by the calming sounds of the Atlantic Ocean—a haven from the harsh, cruel world. The Gothic spires, turrets, and cupolas served as a picturesque tribute to this vision. But years of overcrowding and underfunding had collapsed this romanticized vision of helping the mentally ill. Many of the most dangerous patients were forced to inhabit the rooms built in the labyrinth of tunnels that ran beneath the massive brick and granite structure. The tunnels were filled with the groans and stench and misery of people trapped in total darkness, who sometimes never saw daylight for weeks or perhaps, even years.

And now the asylum was finally being closed. Maddie noticed some windows, cracked and jagged like teeth, behind the rusted bars. Ivy had grown up like tentacles trying to drag the Gothic fortress back down through the gates of hell from which it was born.

Maddie parked the car and entered the building. Overcoming a sudden urge to run, she resolved to make Rebecca's arrangements for the transfer to the new facility as quickly as possible. It was hard enough for her to wait outside during Tess's visits, but actually going inside and seeing the place that had haunted her throughout her entire childhood was almost too much to bear.

Maddie entered the mouth of the asylum and allowed the monstrous beast to swallow her whole. The negative energy there was gruesomely palpable. The musty air was thick and close. Sounds seemed to come from all around her—a cacophony of groans and cries. Lost souls peered out from sunken eyes suspended in grim, ghastly faces.

Maddie tried to get a good look at the people in the common room to see if she could recognize Rebecca among them. One woman stood in front of the blank television screen and pushed the buttons incessantly. Another man dressed in only a ratty bathrobe and soiled boxer shorts sat next to the peeling, pockmarked walls; he was deep in conversation with an unseen companion. The dilapidated equipment and decrepit wheelchairs littered the hallways. Corridors teeming with shadows appeared to stretch out to infinity.

A stocky nurse turned and looked over at Maddie and sighed as she made her way across the grimy floor.

"Can I help you?" The woman asked. Her upturned nose could almost pass for a snout.

"Yes, I'm Madeline Crane. I'm here to see Rebecca Le-Claire. I'm her niece." Maddie smiled. *Nurse Ratched, I presume?*

"Well, my name is Dot," the woman snapped. "And I'm your aunt's nurse. You'd know that if you had ever come to visit your aunt, but I guess you and your mother were too busy."

Maddie wasn't prepared for this woman's harsh criticism, but she was determined to do the paperwork and see Rebecca, despite this woman's obnoxious attitude.

"Can you just show me to Rebecca's room, please?" Maddie was quickly losing patience. She wanted to get this over with and get out.

Dot stopped suddenly in front of a tremendous spiral staircase completely shrouded in high walls of mesh wire, most likely to keep inmates from jumping to their deaths.

"Are you sure you aren't one of those nosy reporters?" Dot frowned, grabbing her by the arm. "Ya know, we don't need any more reporters digging around here. We're closing down. Isn't that enough for you people? No, the place isn't haunted. No, we don't mistreat our patients. And no, you can't quote me. Got it?"

There was a time when Maddie would have stammered and apologized. But she was a different person now. "Excuse me!" Maddie snapped, wriggling out of the stout woman's viselike grip. "I'm sorry if you've had a problem with over-zealous reporters prying into the back story of what caused the demise of this *impeccably* maintained facility," she said sarcastically, gesturing to the chunks of peeling plaster, gnaw marks in the mahogany banister, and apparently toxic mold visible through the holes in the plaster walls. "But I don't really care to know what went on here or what forced the state to shut you down. Right now, my only concern is signing the paperwork for her transfer and seeing Rebecca."

Dot narrowed her eyes for a moment, then pulled her chapped lips back into an awkward smile, something that didn't seem to come naturally to her. Maddie was pleased with herself for standing her ground. Dot motioned for her to follow as she unlocked the rusted metal door. The large woman started up the staircase, pulling her heavy body up the stairs by hanging on to the metal handrail bolted to the wall, stopping to catch her breath on each landing.

"Well, don't let me stand in the way of your once-in-a-blue-moon visit with your aunt. Now that would just be cruel and indifferent of me, wouldn't it?" Her sarcasm was as thick as the dusty air that surrounded them.

෯

Maddie managed to avoid eye contact with the people on Rebecca's floor, people who were kept in what basically amounted to cages and cells.

*Please don't let her be in one of those*, Maddie silently prayed. Following behind Dot, Maddie kept her eyes on her feet as they shuffled heavily across the chipped checkerboard linoleum. The colors of the various rooms drifted from pale blue to institutional green to soft pink, as if they were experimenting to find the least agitating color for the patients.

Even though she didn't want to see the pallid faces and hollow stares—prisoners of their own minds as well as The Witches' Castle—curiosity overcame her, forcing her to take in the surroundings. The antiquated furniture, the crude artwork scrawled across the walls, the constant hum and buzz of fluorescent lighting, and the smell—a musty, dank scent of sweat, urine, and something indefinable . . . fear, perhaps? And added to that the all-consuming negative energy that seemed to feed on everyone who passed through.

Dot led her down to the end of the J Wing until they finally reached Rebecca's room. The door was ajar, and Dot knocked out of respect for Rebecca's privacy. While she appreciated it, Maddie wondered if the gesture was only for her benefit.

Rebecca sat in a strange contraption that Maddie could only assume was a primitive ancestor of the wheelchair. What surprised her more than Rebecca's haggard appearance was the room itself. Dot had explained as they made their way across the J Wing that the juvenile artwork scribbled across the peeling walls was from Ravenswood's current patients.

Since they were closing down the facilities, the nurses allowed the patients to express themselves on the walls that imprisoned them.

Some drawings were childlike and innocent—happy suns, trees, and flowers, a family. But some were darker and grotesquely disturbing. Many chose to depict the buildings that made up the hospital. However, the pictures were not representative of the idyllic community that the founding doctors had envisioned decades ago. No, these pictures showed Ravenswood Asylum as an evil beast with windows like the eyes of a devil and doors shown as screaming, gaping mouths, which was just how Maddie saw this place when she entered. Others presented visions that equaled the horrors that lay at the deepest levels of Dante's *Inferno*, with turrets and gables as horns and trees with craggy claws reaching out to devour and destroy.

Rebecca's drawings were not like any Maddie had seen up to that point.

Her room was completely filled with flowers. Not real ones, but painted creations that rivaled the beauty of what was found in nature. She had painted them in every imaginable color, every floral and plant species Maddie had ever seen. They were delicately detailed, crowding each other for space to unfurl their trailing leaves, tendrils, and petals. The room was alive with color in every square inch. Even the pine floorboards hadn't escaped Rebecca's paintbrush. She had even ventured outside of the confines of her room and painted the bars on the window varying shades of blue so that on a clear day, the bars blended with the expansive sky.

It seemed unimaginable that a woman who could no longer communicate intelligently through speech, someone who was barely clinging to the edges of sanity, could have created such intricate and complex artwork. How a person who couldn't handle the simple actions of everyday life—

eating, grooming, bathing, talking—was able to capture the smallest details within her artistic creations. Maddie was awed by the display.

And there sat Rebecca in the center of this Garden of Eden she had created. It occurred to Maddie that the snake wouldn't be entering this garden. Instead, the snake had swallowed it whole, and now Rebecca and her garden were trapped for eternity inside the belly of the beast.

ᖫ

"Rebecca, you have a visitor. Do you remember your niece, Madeline?" Dot spoke loudly into Rebecca's ear. "Maddie Crane? Your sister Abigail's daughter."

Rebecca stiffened at the sound of Abigail's name.

At that moment, Maddie remembered walking in on her mother and Rebecca when they were in the middle of one of their fights. It seemed like a lifetime ago. It was after a field hockey practice had been cancelled due to rain. She peeked into the shop and saw her mother and Rebecca yelling and screaming over each other to the point where their words blended and became so muddled that she could barely distinguish one insult from another.

> ". . . never should have come back . . ."
> ". . . just stirring things up again . . ."
> ". . . jealous . . . not my fault . . . what can I do?"
> ". . . stay in California! . . . my life, my town . . .".
> ". . . slut! . . . in my face . . . not here, not now . . ."
> ". . . why don't you . . . because of him . . ."

Maddie slowly entered the shop, wind chimes announcing her arrival. They both turned to look at her, the heat and anger in their faces still present. Her mother turned away from Maddie, her hands fluttered up to her hair, pressing loose tendrils back into her stark bun. Rebecca smiled at her, though she was visibly shaken.

"Hi there, sweetie." She opened her arms wide for a hug. "Where's my little troublemaker today?" she said, referring to Cordelia.

"She had some things to do. Field hockey was cancelled, so I came over here," Maddie said.

Her mother snorted and said something under her breath— too quiet for Maddie to hear, but Rebecca obviously caught it. She turned and looked angrily at Abigail with tears brimming in her sea-blue eyes. "We can finish this later, Abby."

Her mother nodded, turned, and brushed past her. Without even a look in her daughter's direction, Abigail said sternly. "Dinner will be at six o'clock sharp." And with that, she exited the building, taking the heaviness with her like a dark cloud uncovering the bright sun.

Maddie ran over to Rebecca and gave her a big hug. She didn't have that strict "mom" feeling about her, more like a fun older sister.

"What was that all about?" Maddie asked her, looking behind her, suddenly afraid that her mother had witnessed this outburst of affection between them.

Rebecca looked her squarely in the eye. "Some things are better left unsaid, y'know? Anyway, I have a bunch of things that I need help with today, and since the elusive Cordelia is nowhere to be found, I elect you to be my apprentice for the day."

Maddie was excited to spend the afternoon alone with Rebecca. Maddie always felt like a third wheel when Cordelia was around. Now she would have the chance to make some "potions," as they jokingly called them, and maybe learn a little more about divination, tarot, or reading tea leaves.

As Maddie was crushing dried herbs with the mortar and pestle, mixing in just the right amount of foxglove and ginger root, Rebecca came over and gave her a quick kiss on the top of her head. "You remind me of me at your age," she said.

"Really?" Rebecca didn't realize what a huge compliment that was.

"Mm-hmm," she said, hoisting herself up onto the wooden countertop and crossing her legs beneath her. She played with the ends of her long crimson braids and then smoothed out the wrinkles in her tapestry skirt. "Just make sure you listen to Tess. Your mom was always at odds with her, but that old lady is one smart cookie." She laughed as if she were thinking of an old joke.

"Tess really missed you when you were gone," Maddie offered. "But she was happy for you at the same time. She wanted you to get out of this town, wants all of us to get out, actually."

Rebecca nodded slowly, started to say something, paused, and then said, " Just be careful that—" and before she could finish, Cordelia burst through the door, her arms filled with fresh flowers, completely drenched from the rainstorm that had kicked up outside.

"Can I get some help here?" She said laughing, shaking her head like a dog, with strands of red hair sticking across her cheeks and mouth.

Rebecca jumped off the counter and ran over to help her daughter. "You didn't have to pick these up today! I would have helped you once it stopped raining."

"S'okay," she said, looking back and forth between them. "Did I miss anything?"

Rebecca and Maddie looked at each other for a moment. Maddie could tell from the arch of Rebecca's eyebrow that she wasn't to mention the fight she had walked in on earlier.

"Not a thing," Maddie said. And for the rest of the afternoon, they mixed various infusions and unpacked big crates of crystals and amulets in anticipation of the spillover crowds from Salem's October Haunted Happenings. The entire city of Salem was flooded with tourists, and many were anxious to venture into the smaller quaint town of Hawthorne. Rebecca's Closet was the perfect place for them to get their fix of authentic witchcraft and Wiccan items, ones that didn't have the tacky "Witch City" stamp all over them.

As Maddie stood in front of Rebecca for the first time in months, she realized her aunt never finished her warning to her. "Just be careful that . . ." she had said, but she'd forgotten to ask her, *Of what?*

Dot quickly excused herself to tend to a disruption at the far end of the hallway, leaving Maddie alone with her aunt— a woman who seemed like a complete stranger. Rebecca sat at the far end of the room, gazing at the ivy-choked windows. Her blue eyes seemed paler than Maddie remembered, as though the life had been siphoned out of them. She had the look of someone who had accepted her ever-present grief as inevitable. Rebecca seemed to have chosen the peace of mind that cutting all ties with reality afforded her.

Rebecca's once vibrant sheath of red hair had faded to a dull rust color, cut short and ragged. It was as though Rebecca's image had faded and bleached from the sun that soaked through the dirt-streaked windows.

"Rebecca, I'm here to help you get ready for your move. We're going to be taking you to a new place. You're going to like it much better, I promise."

"She don't talk to strangers," a voice came from the doorway. A spindly woman was closely inspecting the wood paneling around the doorframe, carefully avoiding eye contact with Maddie. "You're not her friend. I am. I'm her friend, and she can't leave. We have to be together. She likes it if she talks to me, but she's not gonna talk to you. No way."

The small woman rambled on and on incoherently in a little girl's singsong voice.

"I'm her niece, Madeline," she offered hesitantly. "I'm happy to hear that Rebecca has some friends here."

The woman shot her a harsh look before quickly returning her attention to chipping plaster off the wall. "She don't got no family no more. They're all gone, you know. They're down in the ground and in the sky. She's got nobody but me, Rosie."

"Well, Rosie, it's nice to meet you," Maddie said, noticing that Rebecca hadn't acknowledged anyone in the room, but instead, she had started playing with something in her frail hands. *Click clack click clack.* "Are you going to be moving to the new hospital, as well?"

"Oh no," she said, vigorously shaking her white hair. "Becca and I are staying right here. Becca has to stay in her garden. How will her little girl know where to find her if she leaves? No, we have to stay here until Cordelia comes home."

Maddie felt a spark of hope. Maybe Rebecca *could* actually communicate. "Did Rebecca tell you about what happened to her daughter?" Maddie asked Rosie, noticing that the clacking sound got louder. Turning her attention back to Rebecca, she saw a few small, smooth stones in her hands. She flicked them around and around quickly like meditation balls.

"Oh, yes." Rosie had come all the way into the room at this point and flopped down on Rebecca's bed. "We love spending time with Cordelia, don't we, Becca? We like to go outside and sit under the trees and have tea parties. I always wanted my own little girl, but now I have Cordelia. Rebecca lets me share."

The clicking grew faster and more furious. At that point, Maddie wasn't entirely sure what felt more disturbing: Rosie's tale of spending time with her missing cousin, or the constant clacking of the stones in Rebecca's hands.

"Rosie!" Dot scolded, suddenly reappearing in the doorway. "You know that we only visit with friends at certain times of the day. You can't just sneak out of your room like that. We've all been going crazy looking for you."

"Don't let this lady take my friend away! She's my friend and I don't want her to go away." Rosie pouted, and then she hissed, "You're a bad girl. I know about you. You don't think anyone knows, but I know. I know what you did. *I know!*"

"Rosie!" Dot scolded, sharp as a blade. The large woman cleared her throat when she realized that she had everyone's attention—everyone but Rebecca. "Now it's time to say goodbye, Rosie." Dot grabbed Rosie's arm, hauling her from the room.

As if out of a comedy routine, Rosie yelped, "Good-bye, Rosie!"

"Excuse me, Dot?" Maddie managed to catch the nurse's attention before the two women exited the room. "Does my aunt spend a lot of time with Rosie?"

Dot sighed. "Well, yes, I suppose they do spend a good amount of time together. But I think that's due to Miss Rosie, the social butterfly here. Rebecca keeps to herself. I haven't heard a word out of your aunt in all the time I've worked at Ravenswood. She hasn't made a peep in front of anyone else on the staff either, as far as I know."

Rosie pushed back into the room. "She talks to me all the time, don't you, Becca? All the time we talk and talk, talk and talk. I know everything that happened. All about her little girl. She tells me everything."

Dot snorted. "I'll bet she talks your ear off, Rosie," she said to Rosie, but then she turned to Maddie, shaking her head and mouthing the word, *No.* "Come on, *Really Rosie.* Let's get moving."

The women then moved back down the corridor, Rosie's incessant chattering becoming fainter and fainter until silence fell upon the room once again—even the clacking had ceased.

Maddie edged closer to Rebecca and gently pulled one of the stones from her hand. The smooth, dark stone had a symbol carved into it. A Celtic rune stone just like the ones Cordelia and Rebecca used to sell in the store.

"Rebecca," Maddie said, falling to her knees in front of her aunt, searching her vacant eyes for signs of life, of recognition. Rebecca never took her eyes away from the window. She had that distant, wistful gaze that Tess got at times when  staring out at the ocean. Rebecca looked like she was waiting, watching for Cordelia's return. "Please talk to me, tell me something, anything."

Her hands were cold; her eyes, glazed over. It was like talking to one of the wax figures in the Salem Witch Museum. "I'm sorry," Maddie whispered. "I wish I knew where to find Cordelia. I wish I could have stopped . . ." She let that last word hang between them.

Rebecca had no idea about their night out on Misery, and Maddie wasn't about to tell her and risk making her retreat further into herself. She continued, "I wish I could bring her home. But I don't know where to look. Everyone thinks she's run away, but I just don't believe it. I can't believe she would do that to us—to you. If only . . ."

Maddie looked down at the rune stone in her hand to hide her tears, not that Rebecca had even acknowledged her presence. She thought of Rebecca's stories of being able to see the future with these stones.

*Bet you never saw any of this coming.*

"I'm going to visit you more often at Fairview, Rebecca. I promise," she murmured, touching her aunt's arm and placing the rune back into her upturned hand. Maddie headed for the door and then turned to add, "Maybe I'll even bring my mother with me."

Maddie waited a moment for some kind of response, but Rebecca sat as if cast in stone, facing the window. She turned toward the exit, and just as Maddie was about to step through the doorframe, the rune stone whizzed past like a comet, coming within inches of her head before slamming hard against the wall, leaving an angry gash where it struck. The sound ricocheted and echoed down the corridor. Maddie spun quickly around, but Rebecca's position hadn't changed in the slightest bit. She sat facing the window, spinning the remaining stones in her hand.

*Click clack click clack.*

৪৩

"I am so sorry about that, Ms. Crane. She's never done anything even remotely like that before," Dot said, leading her back to the entrance of Ravenswood. "We only let her have those stones because we thought they would relax her. We never dreamed she'd throw them or try to hurt anyone."

"Relax her?" Maddie asked. "Why does she need relaxing?"

"Well, you saw that room," Dot laughed nervously. "The woman never sleeps! All she ever does is add to the paintings on her walls. When we decided to let the patients express themselves artistically, we thought it would be a nice peaceful activity for them. Boy, were we wrong when it came to Rebecca. Night and day she'd be painting and drawing and creating that jungle of flowers in there."

"Rebecca owned a flower shop when my cousin disappeared. She threw herself into flower arranging as a way to keep herself occupied during that whole ordeal."

"Well, it's important for our patients to rest," explained Dot. "Sometimes we have to restrain her at night so she'll get some sleep. Other times, we use hydrotherapy and put her in one of our continuous baths. Not the freezing cold baths that hospitals got in trouble for in the fifties, mind you. We fix up nice, warm spalike baths for her. Well, your aunt is a regular Houdini. She finds ways out of her restraints at night, and she escapes the baths."

"Runs in the family," Maddie added dryly under her breath. Her hands were still shaking as she filled out the paperwork to have Rebecca transferred to the new facility outside of town. Then she said to Dot, "Well, now that everything is squared away, I hope that the move will be smooth."

"Don't worry, Ms. Crane," Dot squeezed her arm gently, a feeble attempt at kindness. "We'll take care of everything. Your aunt is in good hands."

As Maddie drove away from Ravenswood, a sudden lightness and release came over her. The air within those rooms, corridors, and hallways was so heavy and everywhere Maddie looked she sensed such despair that she promised never to take anything for granted again. For the first time in a long while, Maddie felt like one of the lucky ones.

As she maneuvered the car away from Ravenswood, driving along the road that ran between the ocean and Potter's Grove, Maddie wondered if she could pick out the tree that Rosie and Rebecca had supposedly picnicked under with Cordelia. The place was so darkly Gothic—like something straight out of medieval times—that Maddie could picture Cordelia sitting under one of the massive pines, a wreath of wildflowers on her head like a fairy crown, her long red hair ablaze under the slants of light streaking across the early evening sky. If she let her imagination take over, Maddie could envision Cordelia waving to her as she drove past.

*See you soon, Maddie. I'll be waiting . . .*

# Chapter 18

## TIWAZ

↑

BRAVERY AND COMMITMENT

*Bravery, Honor, and Steadfastness in the Face of Adversity;*
*Justice, Fair Law*

### APRIL

The ocean swirled dark and cool around her ankles as Maddie waded deeper into the water. The sand back on shore still retained some of its warmth from the unseasonably warm early April afternoon. On this particular night, the stars seemed brighter in the inky sky than they usually were during humid summer nights.

Maddie walked barefoot down to the beach at the end of Mariner's Way after Tess and Abigail had gone to bed. Although it wasn't quite ten o'clock, all of the neighboring houses were dark, and Maddie was engulfed by the blackness. A hush lay like a thick quilt over Hawthorne that evening.

Maddie sat for a long time, looking out at the black water, watching the moonlight stream and slip among the waves. Finally, she walked down to the water's edge and slipped her feet into the surf. The night was unusually warm, but the ocean was still frigid. After looking around to make sure she was completely alone, Maddie stripped down to her underwear, plunging headfirst into the chilly, moonlit waves. Tess had once told her that swimming in the ocean at this time of year brought clarity, something she definitely needed. The shock of the cold water on her bare skin sucked the breath from deep inside of her.

She broke the surface, hair slicked back like a seal. As her body trembled from the cold, Maddie thought of how she and Cordelia used to sneak down to Crescent Hollow Cove in the middle of the night the summer before Cordelia started Hawthorne Academy. Maddie never would have done it on her own, but Cordelia convinced her that the sense of complete freedom and release would be worth any punishment if they got caught. They never did.

Maddie stretched her legs out behind her, kicking strongly in order to warm her body before flipping underwater like a dolphin and heading back to shore. She rode the waves into the sandy beach and ran over to the blanket she had brought with her to the beach. Maddie flopped backward, sending droplets of water flying, her body shivering as she quickly pulled on her fleece top and sweatpants. The stars blinked down at her; she caught a glimpse of a falling star. *Make a wish*, Maddie thought. Usually, her wishes involved health and happiness, her family, falling in love—a truly, madly, head-over-heels romance. But tonight, her wish was different.

*To know the truth.*

*To remember.*

A sound to her left made her jump. Maddie looked over her shoulder, but couldn't see anyone. She half-expected Cordelia to come bounding down the beach in an attempt to frighten her. But that would have been too good to be true. Maddie scanned the dark, deserted beach for any sign of life. Quickly, she rose to her feet and gathered her belongings. What was she *thinking* going out there by herself?

Her heart started pounding so loudly in her chest that it drowned out the surf. It was then that Maddie saw the dark outline of a man standing on top of the large rocks that jutted out into the Atlantic, causing her to have an overwhelming sense of déjà vu. Someone had been watching her the whole time. She sprinted away from the water, sure that she heard movement behind her. Maddie ran and ran and didn't stop until she was safely in her house, the front door locked behind her. What was happening? Had she become a target? Was she next?

After catching her breath and allowing her heart to return to its normal pace, Maddie peeked out the window, but the street was deserted. She was safe for now. *But for how long?*

಄

Maddie woke up crying. In her dream, she saw Cordelia tied to a tree. They were running around her in circles.

Sitting straight up in bed, her hair stiff from her late night swim, Maddie felt compelled to write down her dream, trying to recapture the fragmented vision in detail, before it slipped away. Grabbing her dream journal from her bedside, she scratched out a few fragments of her latest nightmare.

> *Bloodied and blindfolded*
> *Red hair in clumps on the sand*
> *Cordelia's body, limp, lifeless*
> *Laughter*
> *Wine as red as blood*
> *Wind whipping through hair*
> *Scratches and burns*
> *Witch!*

Maddie heard a shuffling outside her bedroom door, and shook the last tendrils of the dream from her mind. It was followed by an odd sound. Not quite a whisper but more like a strangled hush. Maddie willed her fears away, convincing herself that it was just the groans of the old house or the loud sleeping sounds coming from her mother or grandmother. Maddie tried not to think about the incident at the beach, banishing the nagging questions that were racing through her mind: *Did he follow me home? Is he in the house?*

Maddie forced herself to take a deep breath and calm down. She was safe at home. She replayed the scene in her mind from earlier down at the water's edge. The feeling of being watched, the sense of déjà vu, visions and dreams of that night on Misery Island. All of it seemed to lead her to the same conclusion: she was finally coming into her gift. The one that everyone in her family except for Abigail seemed to welcome. The ability to know certain things. It wasn't anything concrete like an actual vision, a movie reel playing in one's head. Instead, it was more of a . . . a feeling. A kind of knowing.

Rebecca and Cordelia embraced this gift, allowing it to become a natural part of their lives, whereas Abigail denied it. If it was, in fact, a type of witchcraft, it was the benign, beautiful form of the craft—the way it was intended to be. It included the herbal remedies concocted in Rebecca's Closet, a respect and relationship with natural elements. It consisted of the rituals of swimming in the night sea, bathed in moonlight, searching for fairy circles, or listening to the whisperings in the trees. It was having your decisions guided by crystals and tea leaves and rune stones. If this meant she was a witch, then Maddie would no longer resist.

Maybe somewhere deep down inside, on some unconscious level, Maddie really did know what happened to Cordelia. If she only knew how to channel that energy, focus her thoughts, force structure into the bits and pieces, then maybe she could remember more of that night.

Or perhaps, it was just too horrible to remember.

Maddie looked over the snippets of dreams she'd recorded over the past month.

> *Running. In my dream, I'm running. The cold earth hard beneath my pounding bare feet. The viney arms of the undergrowth are trying to slow me down, pulling me backwards. Sweat pours from my torn and scraped skin. Where am I going? Who am I running from? I fall. The ground grabs hold of me. Screams are all around. Fire. Laughter.*
>
> *Quiet, I tell myself. Don't let them hear. You don't want them to turn on you. They want me to escape, to run away so that they can begin. They're waiting for me to leave.*
>
> *Who's waiting? I wonder.*
>
> *They are.*
>
> *The boys will be here soon, they giggle and whisper.*
>
> *Now she'll pay. Now she'll be sorry.*
>
> *Slut.*
>
> *Running round and round.*
>
> *Fire.*
>
> *Let the witch burn!*
>
> *Shaking leaves and moss from my hair, I stand and walk down toward the water's edge. The edges are blurry and quivering.*
>
> *It's time for water . . .*
>
> *Where am I going? Why am I running away?*
>
> *They'll kill me, too. I don't want to die.*

Do what thou wilt!

Maddie was just about to close the journal when, paralyzed with fear, she noticed that one of the pages near the back of the book was dog-eared. She would never dog-ear the pristine pages of her journal. That was something that Cordelia constantly did that drove Maddie crazy—it was why she never lent her cousin any of her favorite books. Maddie flipped forward and became puzzled as she read an unfamiliar quote:

*"We sometimes congratulate ourselves at the moment of waking from a troubled dream; it may be so the moment after death."*—*Nathaniel Hawthorne*

A shiver went through her as Maddie read the words that she did not recall writing down and that were written in a handwriting other than her own.

# Chapter 19

### EOH - REVERSED

**ᛖ**

### THE HORSE - IDEAS

*Restlessness; Lack of Partnership, Trust, or Help;*
*A Desire to Escape*

*I* can see the outline of your body behind your window shades; I'm curious why you girls seem to come alive at night. You and I are the only ones awake at this late hour. Just like Cordelia. I wonder what you know, what you will discover. It's only a matter of time before the truth comes out. Would you confront me if you knew?

Why must I continue to suffer? Things will never go back to the way they used to be. Back when I had some control in my life. I see you digging, digging, constantly digging for information.

You go to the town library, the police station, the town hall, pawing through archived newspapers and police documents while I hide in the shadows, watching you collect names, concocting possible scenarios of what made Cordelia disappear. It's only a matter of time before you learn the secret. Cordelia's secret. Something that should have been taken care of long ago.

*This is one secret that has to remain buried, even if
I have to bury you along with it:*

> Uncover the secrets
> If you dare
> Cordelia's Fate
> You will share.
> One more face
> Upon the wall
> Down again, down again
> Maddie will fall.

Maddie read the letter twice to convince herself that it
was real. By the time she finished, her hands were shaking.

Could this actually be coming from the same person who
took Cordelia? Or was this just one of Kate's horribly morbid and cruel jokes? She looked at the writing closely to see
if it resembled any of the letters in Cordelia's locker, but she
couldn't be sure. Most guys she knew all had the same
chicken-scratch handwriting anyway, making it nearly impossible to narrow it down to just one person.

Maddie crumpled up the scrawled note that had arrived in
an unmarked envelope and been shoved under their front
door. Then, thinking better of it, she smoothed out the paper,
deciding to bring it down to the police station to make a formal report.

As she jumped into Abigail's clunker of a car to head over
to the police station, Maddie wondered who knew that she
was looking into Cordelia's disappearance. She considered
the other people who might have seen her strolling through
the tall, cool stacks in the town library or noticed her reading
town documents in the Old Town Hall. Maddie hadn't really
made a secret of her intentions. And now there was someone

in town who wasn't keeping his or her unhappiness about her investigation a secret either.

"What does this mean, Sully?" Maddie demanded. Officer Garrett Sullivan's towering body recoiled as she shoved the paper toward him. He smirked, shaking his head. Even in his crisp uniform and closely cropped hair, he still couldn't alter the party boy image that remained crystal clear in Maddie's memory. Despite being a good four years ahead of her, Maddie could still picture him passed out on the floor in a drunken stupor at every party during his time at Hawthorne. Unless, of course, he was hooking up with one of the many girls that followed him like lovesick puppy dogs.

He read the note and then smiled down at her.

"Awww. Come on, Maddie. You don't take this stuff seriously, do you?"

"Hmmm. Let me think. A direct threat to me if I stay in town? Um, yeah, Sully, I take things like this pretty seriously."

"Maddie, this was probably written by some jerk-off kid trying to scare you. Maybe someone who used to have a crush on you wants to get your attention again. Or maybe some girl's jealous of you going off sailing with Reed Campbell. Heck, I don't know. I just wouldn't spend too much time worrying about this if I were you," he said.

"Well, Sully," Maddie said, anger rising, "you're not me. Because if you were, then you would realize that this is the first lead to come out of Cordelia's case in months. If you were me, you would be running fingerprint scans, handwriting analyses, and questioning my neighbors to see if anyone happened to see the person who slipped this note under my door. But you're not me, and maybe that's why this case has never been solved."

Garrett Sullivan's face turned a deep shade of crimson. "Listen here, Madeline Crane," he spat. "I know you're upset by this note, but that doesn't give you the right to come down here and criticize me and the rest of the force. I'm a damn good cop. I keep these streets safe at night—every night. We haven't had a crime here in a long time. And to be perfectly honest, there are a lot of folks here who believe that there never *was* a crime to solve when it came to your cousin's disappearance. Most people think that she just up and took off with some guy. Probably got herself knocked up and was too embarrassed to stick around."

"How dare you say that to me?" Maddie shrieked, holding back tears. "She's my cousin, my family. She's . . . she was my best friend."

"Friends don't always know everything 'bout each other."

"But I know my cousin—she wouldn't . . . she . . . she couldn't . . ."

"Well now, Maddie, I didn't say that was what I believed." He had calmed down a bit. "I'm just saying that no one knows *what* happened to Cordelia. And since they never found a body—and a body *always* turns up especially in a small town like this—a lot of people believe that she was never the victim of a crime."

"But she *was* a victim—" Maddie stopped herself suddenly, fighting the urge to spill everything to Sully right there, right then, not caring about the consequences from the Sisters of Misery. In that instant, the image from her dream flashed into her mind. Cordelia strapped to the tree out on Misery Island. The terrified look in her eyes. Maddie's feelings of utter helplessness. She suddenly felt like she was going to throw up all over Officer Sullivan's shoes.

"We don't typically consider teenaged runaways victims, Maddie, you gotta know that," he said. "We don't have enough time and manpower to drag home every teenager who takes off on a whim."

"Sully," Maddie said, regaining composure, "we all know

Cordelia was a little crazy and wild, but she wouldn't hurt us like that. That's why I'm not giving up on her. Not now, not ever. Not if I get a million threatening letters."

"Good for you, Maddie," he said in a semicondescending tone. "But I wouldn't ruffle too many feathers here in town, if you know what I mean. Go ahead and do what you need to do, but it's always best to let sleeping dogs lie. You don't want to bring any unwanted attention to you and your family." Sully's voice took on a more serious and deliberate tone.

"Are you warning me about digging too deep on this?" Maddie shot back.

"I'm not warning you. But think of it this way: this *is* a small town. Everyone knows everyone else's business. If people catch wind that you're looking for one of their own for this crime—if there even was a crime—well . . . let's just say that you'll probably be receiving more than just letters."

Maddie held herself back from tearing into him. "I'll be careful not to step on any toes as long as I know that I'll have protection from the police for me and my family."

"Listen, I'll do what I can. You or your family feel threatened, you call me, and I'll be there in a flash, you understand?" he said in a puffed-up manner.

"I may want to look at some of the archived police records on this case, if that's alright?"

"Not a problem. Dunno if there's anything useful in those old files, though."

"Thank you," Maddie said, turning to leave. Then just as she got to the door, she turned back to him. "Hey, Sully? How did you know about me and Reed?"

He straightened up and smiled widely. "Small town, Maddie. Real small town."

# Chapter 20

## SOWELO

**ϟ**

## SUN

*Spiritual Energy Reveals Hidden Secrets; Clear Vision,*
*Hope, and Justice*

Maddie searched the stacks at the stately Eldridge Library, reading newspapers and police logs. Someone was watching her every action, keeping tabs on her investigation. So if she didn't let the letter disrupt her routine, perhaps Maddie would learn the identity of her letter-writing stalker. Maddie walked slowly through the aisles, pretending to browse, taking notice of everyone around her. Was anyone watching her? After an hour or so of her "pretend" research, she decided to settle into one of the cubicles and do some real online research. Cordelia came up under a few local articles about missing teenagers, but most of the pieces seemed to focus on the runaway angle. Maddie pulled her notebook out of her leather messenger bag and flipped furiously through the pages, trying to find a quote she'd written down that was in one of her dreams. She typed the phrase, *Do what thou wilt*—something that had been stuck in her head since her dream the other night—into Google. What could it mean? Just before she hit the ENTER button, strong hands gripped her shoulders, and she jumped.

"If you're looking for something good to read, I can make some suggestions," a voice came from above her. "And I promise it's not on the required summer reading list."

Maddie turned to see Reed smiling at her. He was dressed in a blue button-down Oxford and khaki pants. His wire-rimmed glasses finished off the look of high school English teacher. But the stubble and longish hair made him appear more male model than former Hawthorne Academy faculty member.

She watched as he disappeared quickly into the stacks. His presence at the library didn't surprise her. Reed's enthusiasm over books and his students' reading habits were legendary; Maddie remembered how worked up he used to get in their English classes. The subject didn't seem to bore him in the way that it appeared to bore the other teachers she'd had through the years. He became passionate about everything they read, whether it was Shakespeare, Tennyson, Faulkner, Hemingway, and even writers of today, like Jonathan Franzen, Joyce Carol Oates, and Toni Morrison.

At the close of every class, he would write a quote on the blackboard from a famous piece of literature, and whoever figured out where it came from (without the help of the Internet, which almost everyone used and then lied about) would get extra points. When he finally caught on that most of his class was going online to find the quotes, he would only award extra credit if the person had actually read the book or play from which the quote originated.

One Friday afternoon in early fall, he sat on the corner of his desk, facing the class, his shirt slightly wrinkled, his tie crooked, and his pants covered in white chalk. He looked like he could be any one of them. He was so young and full of energy that the only thing that separated him from the rest of them was the desk, which was why he rarely sat behind it. The girls in the class hung on every word. The guys idolized him. He was the perfect embodiment of the favorite teacher.

His quote for that week was on the board.

"Any takers on the person who wrote this?" he asked.

"Reed, is this really necessary? I mean, it's Friday, and some of us have plans," Kate said smugly. She loved calling him by his first name, as if dating his brother gave her top priority over the rest of them.

Mr. Campbell was not impressed. "Kate, I don't care about your plans. And as long as we are in the classroom, it's Mr. Campbell, remember?"

The girls in the class giggled. He rolled his eyes and tapped a long piece of chalk on the board, the elbow patches of his sport coat covered in chalk dust, "Anyone?" he asked again.

*Love is life. All, everything that I understand, I understand only because I love. Everything is, everything exists, only because I love.*

Only one hand raised. And not surprisingly, it was Cordelia's.

"Tolstoy," she said offhandedly. She started gathering her things because the bell was about to ring.

"Okay," he smiled. "So what Web site did you pull that from?"

She shook her head, not understanding. "I don't have a computer."

Everyone laughed. Kate and the rest of the girls made exaggerated sighing sounds.

"Listen, I know that everyone looks up my quotes, and I'm fine with that, but to get the extra credit, you will be assigned the book."

"I don't need extra credit," she said, sounding annoyed. She waited until the laughter and the hoots died down, cleared her throat, and then said loudly, "'*Everything is united by it alone. Love is God, and to die means that I, a particle of love, shall return to the general and eternal source.'* It was said by Prince Andrew in *War and Peace*. I've already read it, have a copy of it at my house, and if you would like me to write a book report on it, I will gladly do it."

As soon as the bell rang, everyone grabbed their books and backpacks and filed out of the room. Kate blew Mr. Campbell a kiss and said, "See you later, Reed."

"Cordelia, can you hold back a minute?"

Cordelia held up a finger to Maddie, indicating that she'd only be a minute. Maddie hung around outside the door, and when she peeked in, she noticed Mr. Campbell looking at Cordelia with such admiration that to this day, it made her ache with jealousy. If Cordelia noticed, she didn't let on. Cordelia dealt with the attention of men as if it was a given that they would fall all over themselves around her. Maddie never thought that anything would happen between Reed and Cordelia, but if she could have read Reed Campbell's mind at that very moment, somehow she knew that she wouldn't have been happy with what she'd found.

Reed returned with a big stack of books and plopped them down next to her. She scanned some of the titles: *The Electric Kool-Aid Acid Test, On the Road, Catch-22.* "This is your reading mission, Ms. Crane, if you should choose to accept it."

Maddie eyed the pile, recognizing the exact books in Cordelia's room. It seemed as though Reed wanted all of his "girlfriends" to take an interest in his reading habits. Even without Cordelia around, Maddie still felt like she was competing for Reed's attention. "What, no Tolstoy? I thought that was required reading for all your favorite students," she said, hating the snaking, jealous "pick me" feeling that came over her, but helpless to stop it. Maddie packed up her belongings, suddenly wanting to be anywhere other than with Reed Campbell.

*"Hypocrisy in anything whatever may deceive the cleverest and most penetrating man, but the least wide-awake of children recognizes it, and is revolted by it, however ingeniously it may be disguised."*

He stood there watching her.

*"Anna Karenina,"* Maddie tossed over her shoulder, leaving him standing there, completely taken aback and speechless.

Maddie was halfway down the stairs leading out of the library when she realized she'd left her reading glasses at the computer terminal. When she got up to the reading room, Reed was gone. She returned to the cubicle where she'd left her reading glasses and realized that she had never finished her search on that phrase. Luckily, her search terms were still up on the screen. *Do what thou wilt*, blinked in the Search box. With one click, Maddie discovered the origin of the quote. It came from The Law of Thelema, an ancient British magic order similar to the black magic witchcraft that the women of Salem were accused of so many years ago. The organization was headed up by an Aleister Crowley. The name seemed familiar, so Maddie did a quick search for him online. A strangled sound came from Maddie's throat as she read about the man whose words were used that night out on Misery Island. Aleister Crowley, known as the "wickedest man in the world," was widely regarded as a Satanist.

Who had called that phrase out into the black night? Maddie just prayed it wasn't Cordelia's voice that was ringing in her ears.

"I thought you left." Reed's voice snapped her out of her daze. She was still staring at the computer in the library, not quite sure how long she'd been sitting there. "You okay? You look like you saw a ghost or something."

Maddie looked up at Reed and shook her head slightly, a frown still firmly in place.

"I'm just stressed right now, Reed," Maddie said, quickly closing the browser before he could see what she was reading.

"Is that why you stormed out of here before?" he asked.

Maddie shrugged.

"Let me take you to the Willows then. It'll be fun," he insisted. "I'll buy you some cotton candy. It'll cheer you up. Come on." Salem Willows was a relatively run-down place filled with carnival rides and games, a giant old-fashioned carousel, penny candy, and coin-operated fortune-telling machines. Maddie remembered thinking it was great fun when she was younger—larger than life. Now she saw it for what it was, just an ancient amusement area by the ocean. A place that was very much like Hawthorne—untouched by time.

Maddie was reluctant, but at least it gave her a good excuse to stay out of the house for a little while longer, a place that was becoming more tension filled by the day. Reed drove them into Salem, past the shade of the weeping willow trees, and parked in front of the old-fashioned attractions. She wandered through the arcade while Reed went off to find them something to eat. She plunked her quarter into the Ski Ball game and held the small wooden ball to her eye, aiming for the center hole at the Ski Ball lane. Just before she rolled the ball, Reed whispered in her ear, "You're off center," causing her to jump forward and slam her shin on the metal bar of the Ski Ball lane.

"Jesus!" Maddie yelled as she turned to face him. "That's the second time today! Do you always sneak up on people like this?"

Reed grinned an apology, then offered her a choice of cotton candy or a corn dog. Maddie relaxed a bit. She and Reed played all the old coin-operated carnival games—all still in perfect working order—like Ski Ball, Kiss-A-Meter, and the coin press. Maddie enjoyed the nickel and dime machines where you could make the puppets dance and the monkeys play instruments and especially enjoyed kicking Reed's butt at air hockey. It was the first time she had felt relaxed and completely at ease in months, and yet she still pulled away every time Reed gave her an affectionate touch or squeeze.

But as the afternoon went on, she couldn't deny how much she enjoyed his company. He even made futile attempts at knocking down milk cans with a baseball in an attempt to win her a god-awful stuffed animal, the kind that was so stiff and ugly, you could just tell it had been sitting there for years, the felt mouth and googly eyes barely hanging on.

While Reed finished up his game, Maddie wandered over to Madame Zelda's Mysterious Crystal Ball and plunked a quarter in to see what the future had in store for her. Secretly, she was hoping it would say something about the object of her affection returning her love twofold, but when she read the fortune card, her happy mood changed:

*"While strongly disposed to have your own way, you will sacrifice that desire for your family's welfare.*

*You have some psychic powers, and unseen influences play strongly on you. Be prepared for betrayal by those you hold close."*

Maddie pushed the uncomfortable feelings from her mind, shoved the fortune into her jeans pocket, and went to find Reed. He had given up on the milk bottle toss and had returned to Ski Ball, racking up a large number of orange tickets, which were curling out of the machine.

"I think I'm ready to call it," he said in a mock defeated tone. "You want to cash these babies in for something?" He reached down and pulled the line of tickets and handed them over to her.

"Gee, thanks," Maddie said sarcastically. "I bet I have enough here to get a spider ring or maybe even a whistle." He playfully shoved his shoulder against hers and then tickled her side. She yelped and jumped out of his reach. "Excuse me while I go collect my winnings."

Maddie turned away from him, flushed from the attention. She could have sworn that several times that day, he'd let his fingers linger a bit longer on her own, she could feel his eyes on her when she wasn't looking, and she even sensed that he was intentionally holding back and playing up the older brother act. At that moment, he came up behind her and swung his arm up around her shoulder, giving her an obvious "buddy" squeeze.

"So, what are we picking out today?" he asked the bored, acne-faced kid behind the counter. There wasn't much she could get with fifteen tickets, so she decided on a small package of Candy Cigarettes, Bit-O-Honey, and Jaw Breakers (the place was so old-fashioned that even the candy was from another decade). As she was collecting her booty, Reed plopped an adorable stuffed frog prince on the counter.

"What . . . when . . . how did you get this?" Maddie was dumbfounded. She tried to internally rationalize his attentions. He was only twenty-two, not *that* much older. And he did seem to be having a good time, didn't he?

She just stood there, smiling awkwardly, until Reed broke the silence.

> *"He had kind eyes and hands, and was a friend of sorrow.*
> *Thus they were married. After all he had compromised her."*

Maddie wracked her brain, trying to think of where she'd heard that poem before.

"Sylvia Plath?" she asked.

"Close," he said, smiling. "Anne Sexton."

" 'The Frog Prince', of course!" Maddie laughed, clutching her prize. "Very clever, Reed, very clever."

Maddie felt her resolve crumbling. What was going on between them?

When Reed dropped her off at home that evening, she had a warm feeling in the pit of her stomach. After leaving the Willows, she replayed the day in her mind—how they had strolled the boardwalk, eating ice cream cones and feeding the seagulls—and for a little while, Maddie was able to leave the craziness of the past few months behind her. Then she noticed another envelope crammed into the mailbox, and reality came crashing back. Maddie hoped that Sully was right—it was just a stupid prank. The envelope had the same block printing as the first letter—and no return address or stamp. This was a hand delivery.

> *You were not wise. You were not prudent.*
> *You have become Reed's favorite student.*

*But everyone knows that the teacher's pet,*
*Has many lost loved ones to regret.*
*You had your life. You had your fun.*
*But now the real party's just begun.*
*Don't think it's over. Don't think I'm gone.*
*I'm back, dear Madeline, where I belong.*
                              *Love and Butterflies,*
                              *Cordelia*

The note inside was drastically different from the stark black letters on the envelope. It was written in purple ink, and the handwriting was delicate—all swirls and loops, as if written by a teenage girl. Her hands trembled as she read the words over and over again. *Love and butterflies.* That was how Cordelia signed all of her cards and letters. Who else would have known that? Maddie edged over to the hallway bench and collapsed onto its wooden frame.

ଓ

Maddie was humming to herself as she did the dishes later that night. She'd decided to focus on the fun she'd had earlier in the day and not on the threatening note she'd received. Her cheeks felt hot and flushed, and her stomach was tied in knots, but she wasn't sure if it was because of her growing feelings toward Reed or the fact that her face was simply a bit wind-burned from her afternoon at Salem Willows. In any case, Abigail noticed and wasn't pleased.

"You know, you can run all over town with that boy, and it just makes people talk more," Abigail fumed.

"I'm not running all over town," Maddie insisted. "Plus, people can talk all they want. I don't care."

"Cordelia didn't care either, and you see what happened to her."

Maddie slammed a pan in the sink. "No, I don't *see* what

happened to her. I don't think *anyone* knows what happened to her. But it does seem like I'm the only one who cares anymore. It seems like I'm the only one that doesn't think she just ran away."

"Well, if you do think something happened to her, why are you spending time with the one person that everyone thinks is responsible for her disappearance?" Abigail asked.

"Oh, please, Mom, Reed had nothing to do with it."

"How can you be so sure?" Abigail asked.

The truth was that she wasn't sure. Was it just a coincidence that he had shown up at the library that afternoon, pulling her away from her research? Keeping her occupied all afternoon so that she couldn't do any additional digging on Cordelia's disappearance? Maddie tried to keep her voice down, aware that Tess was in bed. Sleep was something that didn't come easily for any of them these days. Maddie didn't want to add any unnecessary tension, given Tess's condition.

"What happened to all the candlelight vigils, Mom?" Maddie snapped, steering her mother away from a lecture about Reed Campbell. It was a sore subject, one that she could barely understand herself, so she didn't want to try explaining it to her mother. "What happened to the strong community support that every reporter from here to Boston commented on? Who helped us pull our lives back together? No one seems to care that a member of our family disappeared into thin air. Cordelia's been gone only a few months, and they act like she never even existed."

"These are good people, Madeline Crane," Abigail said quietly, resolved. "They may not be the best, but I can tell you that they are definitely not the worst. They did their best to find that girl. But some people just don't want to be found. And I believe with all of my heart that Cordelia was one of them."

Abigail motioned for Maddie to follow her into the living

room. She paced over to her desk and retrieved a leather journal. "I found this in Cordelia's room when I was boxing up their things. It was shoved up into the crawl space at the top of her closet."

She paused as if contemplating how much she should tell Maddie. Then she continued, "It belongs to Cordelia. I decided that the right thing to do would be to take it down to the police and let them put it with the evidence in her file. Maybe it would have helped with her case, I wasn't quite sure."

Abigail moved over to the antique chaise longue, and Maddie obediently followed, sitting across from her on the sofa. Overcome with curiosity, Maddie stared at the worn journal and then asked, "If you gave it to the police, why wouldn't it still be in her file?"

"Well, I said that giving it to the police would have been the right thing to do. But it's my house and I found it," she said defiantly. "So I read it, the whole book, cover to cover." She stared straight at Maddie, almost daring her to show disapproval. "I felt that if she had disappeared, this would give some clue as to what happened to her. And if she had just decided to take off on her own, well, she would have taken with her what she wanted to keep private."

"What does it say?" Maddie was too concerned with what the journal said to be angry with Abigail at that point. She spoke evenly, hoping to restrain herself from tearing the book from her mother's hands.

"Well, it seems that the rumors were true about your cousin. She was . . . having relations with some boy—or boys, for that matter. Anyway, in one of the last entries, she was worried about being pregnant. Didn't say who the father might be, although with the number of nights she used to sneak out of here, I wouldn't be surprised if there was more than one contender." Abigail shook her head in disgust and wrinkled her nose, her fair hands fluttering up to her neck. "And I wouldn't be the *least* bit surprised if it was your new best friend there, Reed Campbell. Shame on him, taking up with a teenaged girl. And now that she's run off, he's taking up with you."

Maddie wasn't sure why she felt slighted by her mother's insinuation that Reed was only spending time with her because Cordelia was out of the picture.

Abigail continued, "The journal never said whether or not she really was pregnant. I don't even think she knew for sure. But I imagine that it was a good enough reason for her to run away, if that's what did end up happening."

Maddie let the weight of Abigail's words sink in, trying to comprehend it all. Cordelia pregnant? How could that be? They told each other everything. Maddie wasn't even aware that Cordelia had been seeing anyone. She thought about what Kate had said after her cousin's disappearance, how Cordelia had slept with Trevor, Reed, and a number of others. Maybe even Finn. But Kate couldn't be telling the truth, could she?

"I want to read it," Maddie said firmly.

"I figured that you would. Not a word of this leaves this house, mind you. I don't want to get in any trouble with the law for concealing evidence. I wasn't even going to show you this, but I think you'll see that there really isn't any mystery in the first place. Cordelia wasn't kidnapped or killed or anything like that. She was scared. A scared, stupid girl. She got herself in trouble, and she took off. Just like Rebecca did. She's probably back in California right now, pregnant, living in a trailer park. I'd just let the whole thing go. Just leave this family and this town in peace."

Maddie sat there bewildered, shaking her head.

Abigail handed the journal to Maddie. "So there you have it. Here, take it. I don't ever want to see it again. Just don't show it to the police. Or anyone else, for that matter. It's none of their damn business."

"Mother, you're right. It's not their business," Maddie said staunchly. "It's ours."

# Chapter 21

## OTHILA REVERSED

## ANCESTRAL PROPERTY AND AUTHORITY

*Family Disputes and Break-ups; Bad Karma
and Prejudice*

Maddie was almost afraid to see Reed's name mentioned in Cordelia's journal. She didn't want to know about his involvement with Cordelia, not only because of her growing feelings for him, but also because any mention could link him more securely to Cordelia's disappearance. Despite all of her sleepless nights and questions, she just couldn't bear to know that Reed was at all responsible.

But now she had a solid clue into what was going on with Cordelia prior to her disappearance. Maybe there was a name or a hint as to what happened. But if there were any leads, wouldn't Abigail have mentioned them before now? Maddie also was desperate to compare the penmanship between the diary entries and the letters to see if Cordelia really was writing them. Maddie pulled the latest note from her pocket and carried it to her bedroom desk. Switching the desk light on and opening the top drawer, she smoothed the note along the worn grain of the oak desk and cracked open the journal. Mixed in among the scent of mildew was a slight hint of flowers and herbs. It was as though the pages of the journal not only possessed Cordelia's thoughts, memories, and dreams, but also her essence. The curly, flowery script was startlingly similar to that of the second note she received, but Maddie couldn't be absolutely certain that it came from the same hand.

Maddie set the threatening letter aside and skimmed through the pages of the journal crammed with Cordelia's treasured moments and secret thoughts.

*Somewhere in these pages lies the answer,* Maddie thought.

Maddie flipped to the entry written right after Cordelia started at Hawthorne Academy. Cordelia had obviously done her homework on the town's infamous history. It was obvious that Cordelia wasn't very happy with her new home.

*September 5th*

*Only a very thin line separates the people who live in Hawthorne today and the ones who persecuted all those innocent women accused of witchcraft centuries ago.*

*Salem got the infamy, but the surrounding smaller towns like Hawthorne were just as guilty, if not more, for the horrific witch trials. Over the years, the people of Hawthorne have done their best to cut all ties with the witch trial hysteria.*

*Tess told me that back in the 1600s, Salem County extended throughout most of the North Shore. After the witch trials ended, many towns changed their names and broke away from Salem out of shame. In the late 1800s, town officials of Hawthorne decided to take the name of Hawthorne, wishing to be associated instead with the famed writer Nathaniel Hawthorne (who himself chose to add the w to his name out of tremendous guilt over the vile deeds committed by his ances-*

*tors), as opposed to the original namesake of the town, Justice John Hathorne, the bloodthirsty judge whose overzealous nature flamed the witch trial hysteria. And although many in Hawthorne continue to downplay their ancestors' involvement in the infamous witch hunts, I think that the tendency to persecute still comes naturally to some, especially to girls like Kate Endicott. It doesn't surprise me one bit that she is descended from the original ancestors of this horrid town. All of those girls are so proud of their heritage, their esteemed lineage. If I knew that my ancestors were monsters who tortured, persecuted, and killed innocent people, I'd guard it like a sore. A big, painful, wretched sore.*

Maddie flipped through a few pages of simple observations of the town. Daily recordings of getting the store ready, stories of Cordelia and Rebecca getting acquainted with the town. It wasn't until Maddie flipped to the October entries that the writing became more telling.

*October 14th*
*He knows—of course he knows. How could he not? He can read me better than Rebecca can at times. Scary. I'll have to do something about all this. Just not now. Now I just want to be young and in love and happy. Why is that so hard? I've never betrayed anyone in my life. I'm not to blame for this. I refuse to take the blame. I am not going to take it anymore!*

*October 18th*
*Does he know what happened? Is he trying to make amends? I don't know who to trust anymore. Mom told*

*me that we wouldn't fit in here. Who would want to?
Except, of course, Abigail. Poor Maddie, she doesn't
see the snake pit she's grown up in.*

*Tess has known all along. Tried to shield us all. But
I can see it. I have her gift, and it's growing stronger
every day.*

*Sometimes, when I'm sitting by moonlight at the
water's edge, I can hear and know things that I
shouldn't. That night I heard the woman screaming on
the beach was when I knew for sure. Tess told me that
only those with "the gift" can hear the screams of the
Spanish princess who ran ashore at Hawthorne Cove
to escape a pirate ship in the 1700s. She told me only
a select few can hear her pleading, wailing cries. I
heard her plain as day.*

*I guess that means I'm touched. So why didn't I
know better than to head into Potter's Grove alone
that night? Could I have prevented it? Did I unknowingly think I deserved it?*

*I know I'm not the girl I was once in California—
carefree, filled with love, running off into the night
with cute boys. I promised myself things would be different here. I promised Rebecca that I would be pure
and sweet and "virginal" like Maddie.*

*I would make Mom proud.*

*Looks like I screwed that up once again. Even if I
told anyone about what happened, who would believe
me? My word against his. Hardly a fair fight.*

*Sadly,*
*Cordelia*


*October 22nd*

*Everything is wrong wrong wrong. How do I get
myself into these things? Rebecca suspects that some-*

*thing is up. It's like she can see right through me, right down into my belly and see it growing, forming. How??? I'm not even sure, but I think that she knows. SHE KNOWS. And if Rebecca knows, it must be true— I don't need some stupid test in a box to tell me the truth. Now I have no choice but to tell him . . . my dear, sweet, beautiful boy. It will destroy him—destroy us.*

*God, why does this always happen to me? Why do I always screw things up??? Just when things were settling down, becoming normal again. Normal—ha! Like I could ever be lucky enough to be normal.*

*I wish I could just disappear. Just float away into the forest or across the ocean to a place that is warm and magical and free. I want to be free!!! I don't want a baby to be growing inside of me. It will just suck all of my energy. I just wish I could be like Maddie. Sweet, innocent little Maddie. She has no idea what she's up against. She can't see that they're out to get her. The same way they're out to get me. But I'm above it all. I'm untouchable. They'll be sorry. All of them. I won't let them get away with any of it. **Ever.***

Maddie lifted her eyes up from the pages filled with swirling letters and quick sketches of flowers and ivy vines. Sixteen-year-old Cordelia—pregnant! She just couldn't believe it. Maddie collapsed onto her bed, completely exhausted and emotionally overwhelmed. Who was the "beautiful boy"? Was it someone Maddie knew? An image of Reed's face floated into her mind, and she quickly pushed it away. But if not Reed, who? Trevor Campbell? Finnegan O'Malley?

How could anyone have hurt her so much if they knew she was pregnant? And the thought that Cordelia had to withstand all of that pain out on Misery Island while pregnant haunted Maddie to her core. Or . . . maybe that's the reason why she was taken, so that no one would ever know the truth. The truth that Maddie had right in front of her, scrawled hastily among pink and purple flowers.

When she flipped through the rest of the journal, a torn piece of paper fell onto her lap. It looked like an e-mail or a hastily typed text message that had been printed out. The part that would have given the sender's information was gone, but the cruel message was right there in bold letters.

C.
I NEED TO SEE U AND TALK ABOUT WHT HPPND. DON'T SAY U DIDN'T WANT IT, CUZ I NO U DID. KEEP YOUR MOUTH SHUT OR I'LL SHUT IT 4 U.

It occurred to her, then, that maybe the person sending the notes knew that Cordelia kept this journal, the love letters, and now this threatening note, that it would only be a matter of time before he was exposed.

Considering this, Maddie flipped through the journal, desperately looking for a name, a clue, anything that would point to someone. But Cordelia had covered her tracks well—there was nothing. Maddie came across a passage scribbled on the last few pages of the journal. The writing appeared different from the large, balloonlike letters scrawled in assorted colored inks throughout most of the journal. These words, scratched haphazardly in black ink, seemed angry, forced, as if Cordelia had written them in a fury.

*October 30th*
    *The thousand injuries of Hawthorne I had borne as I best could, but when she ventured upon insult, I vowed revenge. You, who so well know the nature of*

*my soul, will not suppose, however, that I gave utter-
ance to a threat. AT LENGTH I would be avenged; this
was a point definitively settled — but the very defini-
tiveness with which it was resolved precluded the idea
of risk. I must not only punish, but punish with impunity. A wrong is unredressed when retribution over-
takes its redresser. It is equally unredressed when the
avenger fails to make himself felt as such to him who
has done the wrong.* Nemo me impune lacessit! *"No
one assails me with impunity!"*

Scrunching up her forehead, Maddie stared down at the
words. *What the hell does this mean?* Cordelia must have
copied it down from a required reading for English class.
But why would she change the name to Hawthorne in the
passage? It sent a chill down her spine when she realized
how fitting that excerpt was—it was as though Cordelia knew
what was coming, what the Sisters of Misery had in store for
her.

Maybe Cordelia had Tess's gift of knowing what was
coming next. Maddie reread the text, wondering if she was
included in the group that Cordelia intended to avenge. The
worst part was that Maddie felt like she deserved it.

Later that night in bed, Maddie felt as if her body was
being sucked downward, sinking deep into the rusted coils
and suffocating in the starchy foam. Maddie thought about
Cordelia's longing to be free. To just take off and leave
everything—all the responsibility, all the guilt, all the questions—to just abandon it all and start fresh.

That's what her father did when he took off, left them all
behind. And maybe Cordelia really did follow through with
the plans scribbled into her journal, escaping from her problems. Maybe Cordelia really *was* the only one responsible
for her disappearance.

Maddie closed her eyes, pressing the heels of her palms against the sockets until she saw little fireflies of light. The pressure felt good against her throbbing temples.

It only occurred to her after she turned out the light, hanging in that limbo stage right before sleep, that one of the last entries in Cordelia's diary—the one that told of her desire to disappear forever—was written on October 22. Maddie knew the significance of that date from living so close to Salem, Massachusetts. October 22, 1692 was when the last hanging of the Salem Witch Trials occurred. And all these years later, Cordelia was being persecuted in the very same way. She had written this passage in her journal exactly nine days before Halloween, the night that they had all gone out to Misery Island.

ॐ

The next day, Sully reluctantly gave her access to the evidence storage room. She was now more convinced than ever that Cordelia had been raped and had continued to be tormented by her attacker. She wondered if her cousin had ever made a formal complaint and if it was one of those loose ends that made the police originally turn to Reed as a "person of interest." She had wondered all along if there was a missing piece, and Maddie suddenly had a feeling of what it might be. Cordelia was pregnant—or at least thought she was—and perhaps her rapist wanted to keep her quiet. Or, at the very least, scare her out of town. Now all Maddie needed was some concrete evidence.

Maddie knew very little about operational procedures when it came to collecting and preserving evidence, but one look at the ramshackle storage facility and she understood why so many cases remained unsolved in small towns. There had obviously been a leak at some point in the decrepit storage room, and many of the corrugated cardboard boxes were water stained and moldy.

Maddie turned to him and asked, "So you guys are real high tech here. Good thing no one needs any DNA samples or evidence out of these disgusting boxes."

He sighed and shrugged his shoulders. "I know, Maddie. There's nothing we can do. It's all the tax cuts."

Her thoughts flashed over to the fleet of new SUV police cruisers parked in front of the station. Maddie assumed that the police department had decided to use their minimal funds to improve their rides, as opposed to building up the aging police facility and dilapidated holding cells. Obviously, prisoners and unsolved case evidence storage took a backseat to allowing the Hawthorne police force to travel in style.

Maddie brought the box into an empty interrogation room, flicked on the fluorescent lights overhead, and began sifting through what little evidence there was on Cordelia's case. The newspaper clippings were yellowing and stuck together from moisture. There were stacks of papers documenting testimonies and witness statements—all had been taken from sightings of Cordelia in the days and weeks before her disappearance. In the transcripts, Maddie finally found the break she was looking for: only one person was known to have seen Cordelia on the morning of November first. As Maddie ran her fingers over his name, she felt simultaneous shock and relief. It wasn't Reed Campbell.

It was Finnegan O'Malley.

∞

Maddie walked home in a daze, his name repeating in her head like a mantra: *Finnegan O'Malley. Finnegan O'Malley.* Could he be the one responsible for raping Cordelia? For sending those threatening notes to Maddie? For sending that horrible message to Cordelia right before she disappeared? After the time she spent in the musty police station, Maddie felt the need to clear her head as well as her lungs. Once home, she pulled on her sneakers and decided to take a quick jog. Running always allowed her mind to regain focus. While her body worked out its kinks as she plodded along, her mind was lulled by the rhythm of her Reeboks slapping against the ground. She decided to run through Potter's Grove in order to retrace the steps of Cordelia on that fateful night she wrote about in her journal. The night she was raped. Maddie could feel her gift growing, but she needed to put herself in emotionally charged places where Cordelia had been. Potter's Grove was first on her list. Rebecca's Closet was next.

Everyone Maddie had come in contact with, including her own mother, was convinced that Cordelia had disappeared by choice. Her grandmother, God bless the poor woman, was becoming more delusional by the hour. And her friends, if you could even call them that, were offering up no new information about that Halloween night. The trail was growing colder by the second, and Maddie didn't know where to turn—or who to turn to—next.

Maddie entered Potter's Grove, stopped for a moment, and bent down over her knees, trying to catch her breath. A searing cramp reached up her torso. She curved away from the cramp, trying to stretch it out, and was instantly aware of the feeling of being watched. Maddie heard what sounded like footsteps ahead of her in the stand of trees.

"Hello?" she called out. There was no answer. Hair stood up on her arms and on the back of her neck. Someone was watching. She could feel the weight of his eyes.

Maddie pulled up each leg behind her, quickly stretching

out her quads before continuing her jog, and then decided to cut past the pond so that she could get to the road quicker.

Footsteps came out of nowhere and thudded up behind her. Before she could turn, Maddie was toppled to the ground by someone.

"What the hell?" Maddie screamed, struggling to pull free from her attacker.

"Hold on, hold on," came the guy's voice. "Jesus, Crane. Where's the love?"

He had her firmly pinned down on her stomach, but Maddie angled her neck so she could look back to see the face attached to the familiar voice. It was Trevor Campbell.

"Trevor!" Maddie elbowed him hard in the side, causing him to roll off of her in pain. "What the hell are you doing? Trying to scare me to death?"

He started laughing. "So, you have no time for me, but you've got all the time in the world for my brother?" He stayed on the ground, opening his arms wide. "Like I said, 'Where's the love?'"

Trevor Campbell was the last person Maddie wanted to run into while she was in the middle of nowhere. She stood up, brushing herself off. "Nice seeing you, Trevor. Say hi to Kate for me."

Maddie started jogging again, and within a minute, Trevor was jogging along by her side. "So, you and my brother seem to be getting along well," he said again, only this time the friendliness had left his voice.

"None of your business, Trevor." She ran a little faster. To Maddie, Trevor Campbell would always be the boy who used to hide under the bleachers to see the girls' underwear, the one who'd find a young girl's weakness or insecurity and then tease her mercilessly, the boy who never had a nice thing to say to anyone, but always expected the world to fall at his feet.

He grabbed her by the arm, hard. "Oh, I think it *is* my business."

Maddie turned to face him, not wanting to show any weakness or fear. "Is that so?"

"You hanging around with Reed just brings up the whole Cordelia business again, and that's not good for me or my family, understand? It just makes him look guilty. He doesn't even know about what went on out on Misery." The look of shock on her face must have clued him in that he'd said too much. *How could he possibly know about Misery Island? Could Kate have told him after she'd sworn them all to secrecy?*

He let go of her arm and put his hands up in the air. "I'm not trying to be the bad guy, okay? I'm just looking out for my brother."

"Trevor, you've never looked out for anyone but yourself."

"I'd look out for you if you'd let me," he said huskily, pulling her body fully against his. Maddie could tell that he wasn't just being playful. His whole body was at attention. He tried to kiss her then, his tongue roving over her lips, his hands everywhere on her body, pulling, prodding.

*Where the hell did this come from? Is this what happened to Cordelia?*

"Get off me, you pig!" She pushed him away from her, coming just short of having to knee him in the groin. He pulled back, laughing. He ran his hand through his closely cropped blond hair. He resembled his brother in so many ways, yet Maddie could see evil and a sense of entitlement when she looked into his eyes, something that she didn't sense from Reed.

"Hey, come on," he said. "Don't save it all for my brother."

"You're disgusting," Maddie snapped. She turned and sprinted away from him, lengthening the space between them with every stride.

Maddie heard him call out after her, "You really are nothing like your cousin, are you?" And then quieter, "Stupid bitch."

All she could think of as she made her way back to the road and out of Potter's Grove was two things.

One, he definitely was involved in Cordelia's disappearance

And two, Kate, more than anyone, deserved to end up with that bastard.

# Chapter 22

## RAIDO REVERSED

## THE WHEEL

*Disassociation from Those around You, A Journey
Backwards; Confusion*

MAY

Tess wandered into the kitchen before bed, her hair all in
disarray and her eyes showing that she had gone beyond
exhaustion but wasn't ready to give up the fight.

Abigail expected Maddie to keep track of her grandmother, which was becoming more and more of a challenge.
When Maddie came home from grocery shopping the other
afternoon, arms overflowing with paper bags, she stopped in
shock at the sight of Tess in her floral nightgown wandering
down the street, heading to the beach.

The other night, Maddie heard a loud banging coming
from Tess's room. After pushing the door open and discover-
ing a chair had been wedged in front of it, she noticed her
grandmother's window open. There sat Tess, perched on the
roof like a white cat, staring up at the moon. She was fright-
eningly close to falling off. Her white hair, normally flat-
tened into even plaits, was wild and splayed around her head
like a halo. Her eyes were distant, and she was singing quietly to herself. Then she mumbled about someone in the

basement. Maddie assured her that there was no one in the basement and convinced her to come back inside to the safety of her own room.

Now in the warm glow of the kitchen, Tess turned to her, whining, "Momma, I'm hungry."

Maddie turned to look at Tess, trying to discern if she was joking or if she really saw Maddie as her own mother.

"Grams," Maddie said sharply, hoping it would snap the woman out of her trance. When she realized that Tess was still staring blankly, Maddie mentally added another item to her to do list. *Call Dr. Stevens.* "If you eat anything right now, it will just give you bad dreams."

"I don't have bad dreams, Momma. Only happy ones. I promise," her grandmother insisted in a child's voice.

"Grams, I've heard you crying out for the past few nights," Maddie said hesitantly, not sure if she should encourage this regression. "It sounded like you were having nightmares. Plus, I found you out on the rooftop. Do you know how dangerous that is? You could have killed yourself out there."

"That's not me, that's the girl. I hear her crying, too. Can't sleep 'cause of all that crying." Tess shuffled over to the kitchen table, looking out the window at the inky sky, and continued, "I keep telling her to leave me alone. Don't bother me. Keep me out of it."

A weight fell across Maddie's shoulders, the same gnawing feeling that she felt when she visited Rebecca.

"What girl are you talking about, Tess?"

"The one who lives in the basement," she replied flatly.

Maddie could feel herself getting slightly annoyed, perhaps to cover her growing uneasiness.

Forcing a laugh, Maddie said, "Well, Miss Tess, you have quite an imagination, don't you? I'd think that you of all people would be used to the sounds that come out of this old house at night—the ocean, the wind, the creaking of the old floors—all these things are making your dreams seem like they're real. But that's all they are, just dreams. There's no girl in the basement. There's nothing here for you to be afraid of." Maddie heard her own voice rising a few octaves, the way it did when she was nervous.

"Oh, I'm not scared. I'm too old to get scared of the dead. It's the living that I'm worried about." She clucked her tongue and gave out a whoop of laughter, chattering to herself as she pushed away from the table and moved out of the kitchen. Maddie could hear her giggling to herself all the way up the stairs, mumbling to herself that "the dead can't hurt ya, but the living sure can" before slamming her bedroom door.

∽

Maddie had settled into bed with a book when she first heard the crying.

"Tess," Maddie murmured, shoving the covers away. "I'm coming."

She quickly moved up the steps toward Tess's room. The sounds became louder and clearer. Upon reaching the door, the crying stopped as she raised her fist to knock.

Silence. "Are you okay, Tess? I'm coming in now."

There was no answer.

Maddie turned the glass doorknob, pushing her way into her grandmother's room. The only sound was the night breeze blowing through an open window and the rise and fall of Tess's sleep-heavy breath. Confused, Maddie made her way across the room and closed the window. Tess stirred. Maddie stood still for a moment, not wanting to startle her grandmother.

"Who's there? Leave me alone!" Tess shouted, squinting up at her, confused.

"It's just me, Grams," Maddie assured her. "I'm closing your window. You're going to catch a terrible cold if you sleep with it open like that."

"I didn't open it. That girl did. She's always doing things like that."

"Tess, there is no girl, okay?" Maddie said firmly, her voice rising. Her eyes darted around the darkened room, taking in every corner. Maddie moved over to the window and peered out at the spindly arms of the oak tree. No one would be able to climb it without being noticed by a neighbor. Not taking any chances, she swung the heavy latch on the old window and pulled the shades down tight.

"Tess, I want you to keep these windows locked from now on. Call me if you hear anything else or if you need me, understand?" Maddie whispered, trying to calm the pounding in her chest. She bent down closer to Tess, listening for her answer, but her grandmother had already drifted back to sleep.

Maddie was making her way out of the room when something sharp dug into the arch of her foot. "Damn!" Maddie cried out. Tess mumbled unintelligibly and then rolled back onto her side. Reaching down to the floor, Maddie's fingers caught on something jagged attached to a cord. She brought it over to the window to get a better look at it.

It was Cordelia's quartz crystal necklace. Where had it come from? Maddie held it up so it hung directly in her line of vision; the moonlight streamed through making it shimmer. She slipped it into her pocket and silently exited the room.

It wasn't until she was back in her room that she remembered her reason for going upstairs in the first place. She'd been so startled by finding Cordelia's necklace that she had forgotten all about the crying.

Perhaps it was Tess in her sleep. Or maybe a stray cat was

prowling outside the window—the lonely cries of cats in heat can almost sound like a child wailing in the night. But the cries seemed too close, too real for any of those explanations. As she got into bed and pulled the covers up tight, she thought of the scary stories that Cordelia used to tell her—about the lonely wails of banshees that crouched beneath windowsills foretelling a death in the family.

And then at that weightless moment right before sleep, a time when the mind is unfettered and often has the most brilliant and true thoughts, only to have them slip away once the shape-shifting light of daybreak creeps in, causing the memories from the night before to scatter and hide—at that moment, Cordelia's quote sunk in.

*For the love of God,* the words came back to her from Reed Campbell's literature class. *In pace requiescat.* As Maddie tossed and turned that night, the gruesome Edgar Allan Poe short story, "Cask of Amontillado," played out in her mind. Only, in her dream, Cordelia was the victim who had been suffocated and buried alive, stone by stone by stone. A chill shot through her as she remembered Tess's dream about stones. Could they have been prophetic once again?

> *Down again, down again*
> *Maddie will fall*

In a cold sweat, Maddie woke up to the sound of knocking. In those first few moments of being roused from a fitful sleep, she realized that something terrified her even more than finding out what had happened out on Misery Island on Halloween. Deep down, what chilled her to the bone was this:

Cordelia would soon be back. And she'd want revenge.

# Chapter 23

## PERTHO

ᛈ

### CHANCE

*Secrets, Mystery, and Revelation; Things Are Not What
They Seem; A Game of Chance*

Maddie checked the clock. It was past midnight. Haunted
by her earlier conversation with Tess about the girl in
the basement, she was almost afraid to go downstairs and
find out who was knocking. Then Maddie worried that Tess
had gone downstairs for a glass of water and had fallen. And
there she was, cowering like a child under the covers, scared
of a monster in the basement.

Maddie pulled on her faded flannel robe, slipped her feet
into her scuff slippers, and moved carefully down the staircase. The knocking was low and steady, insistent.

*Knock knock knock . . . tap . . . tap.*

Maddie stopped at the basement door, which had swung
slightly open again. She pushed it closed.

The knocking continued.

Who would be here at this hour? No one in Hawthorne
would ever think of dropping in at this time. Not in a town
that shuts down and rolls up the sidewalk at sundown.

Maddie peeked out through the stained glass windows

that framed the door. She could see the outline of a man, but couldn't make out his face.

"Who is it?" Maddie whispered through the crack in the door.

Reed Campbell moved his face over to the window, smiling his boyish grin.

"The Boogeyman," he laughed, making a clawlike movement with his hand.

Maddie opened the door, flustered but smiling.

"Anyone interested in a moonlight cruise?"

"Sailing? Now? I can't," she stammered. "Are you insane, Reed?"

He walked past her into the living room, lifting up knick-knacks and poking around like a kid. He peered at framed pictures that Abigail had scattered around the room: Tess and Jack down at the docks; Abigail and Rebecca holding hands as young girls in their matching coats, hair neatly styled with wide, matching ribbons.

Maddie followed behind Reed, straightening frames and putting things back into place, praying that her mother or grandmother wouldn't wake up from all the noise.

"Come on, Maddie. I've missed you. Can't you come out and play?"

"Reed, it's too late," she said, attempting a stern tone but not quite achieving it. She could smell alcohol on his breath, and yet he seemed as harmless as an overgrown puppy. As much as she tried to resist him, his boyish charm and model-perfect looks always won her over, and he knew it. At the top of the stairs, Abigail loudly cleared her throat and slammed her bedroom door.

Reed whispered in the darkened room. "Are we in trouble?"

"No, I am," Maddie said, swatting Reed.

"Well, since you're already in trouble, you might as well

come with me before you get grounded," he whispered into her ear. "Come on, just one little trip around the harbor. I'll have you back before they get up. Promise."

She hesitated, knowing it was the wrong thing to do, but suddenly, she wanted to do something bad. She wasn't that innocent little girl that Cordelia wrote about in her diary. She could take risks and be bold and go off into the night with an older guy. Cordelia could do it. Why shouldn't she?

Even though Reed was turning out to be drastically different from the golden boy teacher she'd admired from afar, she was flattered by his attention. With other guys, she'd always felt secondbest—like there was always someone cuter or sexier just waiting in the wings. But, the look in Reed's eyes tonight told her that he wasn't looking at her like a former student or as a buddy to hang out with—he looked at her with desire. And it felt really nice.

"Okay," she whispered. "But you have to promise to have me back at a reasonable hour, or else I'll really be in trouble."

Reed winked, pulling her close and overpowering her with the scents of salt, honey, pine, and the slightest hint of whisky, making her feel like she was in the cool, damp woods. Maddie's body tensed as she anticipated a kiss, but instead, he whispered in a gravelly voice, "You have my word."

∞

The harbor was deserted, eerily similar to the night Cordelia disappeared. When Reed guided the boat past Misery Island, Maddie surprised herself by asking him to dock there for a little while. She'd just about finished the bottle of beer he'd handed her once they first got on the boat, and the alcohol made her braver than normal. She hadn't been back to the island since that night, and while she feared being confronted with all of those images and memories, her desire to figure out what had happened won out.

So many emotions flooded her mind once she set foot on the island. Maddie walked over the sandbar, past the dunes, toward the grove at the center of the island, holding Reed's faltering flashlight in her shaking hands.

"So," he said clapping his hands together and looking around the island, "you've got me out here in the middle of nowhere." Reed cracked a devilish smile. "What exactly do you have up your sleeve, young lady?"

Maddie threw the flashlight beam back at him. "I want to look around here for a little bit. Lead the way."

He narrowed his eyes suspiciously. "What exactly are we looking for?"

"I don't really know," Maddie said truthfully. "But I'll let you know when we find it."

Maddie pushed Reed toward the trailhead that led up through the bracken to the center of the island. The full moon provided plenty of light, which helped to ease Maddie's nerves. Soon they stood at the Sacred Birch. Maddie expected some rush of feeling, but there was only the sound of the sea and Reed's breathing. All evidence of Halloween night seemed to have been scrubbed away by the coastal winds and tides.

"We used to party out here when I was your age," Reed laughed. "Looks like things haven't changed much." He pointed to some beer cans and bottles.

Maddie walked over to the tree that haunted her dreams and ran her fingers down the slender curve of the birch. *I'm so sorry I left you here*, she thought.

The wind picked up suddenly, swirling sand all around them.

"Storm's coming," Reed said knowingly. "Sorry to cut this trip short, but unless you want to get stuck out here, we'd better get back to the boat."

Maddie reluctantly took one last look around. She willed herself to remember, but the island refused to give up its secrets. Sadly, she headed back to the cove. She stumbled over some brush, and Reed was quick to steady her, the warmth of his skin melting away her fears. Even though she knew she'd catch hell from Abigail in the morning, she wasn't ready for the night to end.

Hours later, they watched the sunrise from the deck of Reed's boat. The storm stayed out at sea, so they were able to remain on his boat for the rest of the night, talking. The sun turned the water the same shade of blue as Reed's eyes. Maddie looked over at him, impossibly handsome in the early morning light, even with the sandy stubble across his jaw and upper lip. Despite his playful advances, she was a little disappointed that nothing had happened between them on the boat.

Maddie was also frustrated by the trip out to Misery Island. What had she expected to find out there? A large X-Marks-The-Spot to show where the crime took place? Or maybe an envelope with information about the guilty parties, just like in the game of *Clue*. It was Kate Endicott in the Parlor with the Rope.

"So, what's on your mind?" Reed asked, his voice rough as the salty air, snapping her out of her thoughts. He sat up halfway and rubbed his eyes. "Looks like you're carrying the weight of the world on those shoulders." He reached over and rubbed her shoulders and neck, kneading his thick fingers into the muscles tightened by the night on the boat. It was the most he'd touched her all night, and the feel of his hands on her shoulders sent shivers up her neck and feathered around the base of her hairline.

"What's worrying that pretty little head of yours?" Reed's raspy voice felt hot on her ear.

"It's your brother—he paid me a visit during my run the other day."

"He didn't hurt you, did he?" Reed growled, his brow furrowed with true concern. Her heart fluttered a bit.

"No," Maddie said, shaking her head. "No, I'm fine. I just—I don't know what I thought. Why don't we just forget it?"

"Hey, hey, hey," he said, reaching for her hand and pulling her close. "I would never do anything to hurt you, you gotta believe that." He tenderly brushed her hair back from her face. "And my brother," he said as his face hardened and then fell into a sexy half-smile. "Well, just in case you didn't know, my brother's a bit of an asshole."

Maddie laughed, burying her face in her hands.

"Don't tell anyone, but he's really the black sheep of our family. Everyone thinks it's me, but we've got 'em all fooled. Hey," he said, tipping her chin up with his finger so that she could meet his warm gaze. "You let me handle my brother, okay?"

"Okay," she said reluctantly.

"Okay," he said brightly. "Anything else on your mind?"

"Well," Maddie said hesitantly, not wanting to ruin the moment. "I still can't figure out what could have possibly happened to Cordelia. I keep trying to put myself in her position. Trying to understand what she was capable of doing." She desperately wanted to tell him about what really happened out on Misery—the parts of the night that she'd been able to piece together so far—but she was still ashamed, still afraid of what would happen if she ever spoke of that night.

"That must be hard for you to do. You're nothing like your cousin," Reed said softly. He'd stopped massaging, but his hands remained on her shoulders, warm and strong. "She was a ball of fire, that's for sure. Definitely stuck out in this town. Then again, I'm not one to talk."

"You think she was wild?" Maddie asked.

He hesitated briefly. "Well, I figure she had to be. Taking off like that, leaving everyone and everything safe behind her. I don't know if I'd be strong enough to do that. Hell, the whole town hates me, and I *still* haven't left." He laughed.

"So you think she ran off. That she chose to leave. To make us all worry and think she's been killed or kidnapped or God knows what. You honestly believe that she was capable of that?" Her voice rose above the morning harbor sounds. Gulls screeched overhead; boats clanged in off-key tones as they rocked against salt-worn moorings; a foghorn bleated off in the distance as the mists scattered.

Reed grasped her by the shoulders and turned her around to face him. He seemed weary, tired of having to explain himself, but all Maddie could focus on was how close they were. She looked back and forth from his lips to his eyes as he spoke. "First of all, no one ever found her. This town is too small to have no leads turn up, no suspects, no witnesses, no evidence of foul play, nothing. Second, Cordelia was too strong and tough to ever be abducted, and third, she told me she was tired of this town. She wanted out, Maddie. She wanted to see the world. Hawthorne was holding her back. Man, she was a smart girl, so filled with curiosity and a thirst for knowledge . . ." He stopped himself. He was gushing, and they both knew it. "She's out there somewhere, honey. Who knows? Maybe someday, she'll come back."

Maddie fought back the jealousy now so familiar to her. There was so much Cordelia hadn't told her. Why? And even if she never returned, would her presence always be between Maddie and Reed? Would Cordelia always be his favorite?

Maddie took a deep breath and asked the question she'd been holding inside for months. "Did you care about her? Did you . . . was there . . . I mean, was there more to your relationship than just friendship?" She let out a shaky sigh.

She had to know if Reed was the "beautiful boy" from Cordelia's journal.

"What? No, hell no, Maddie!" Reed answered quickly. Almost too quickly. "I was her teacher, that's it! No way would I cross that line." He stood up, sticking his hands in his pockets uncomfortably.

"I've just lost my job, a lot of my friends, and the respect of my family over half-truths and speculation. I just want to know when I get it all back, you know? People can say whatever they want. They can try to destroy my life again and again, and I'm supposed to . . . what . . . just sit back and take it? Dammit, when does the persecution end for me?"

Maddie was speechless. She was just as guilty as everyone else, assuming that something inappropriate had happened between Reed and Cordelia. That he was the reason she had disappeared.

"Listen, Maddie, I've made mistakes in my life, there's no doubt about that. Bringing you out on my boat last night could have been a disastrous one. It's just, I don't know, there's something about you—like you don't judge me or blame me the way the rest of the town does. Cordelia's cousin, of all people." He laughed, shaking his head. "But I'm not one to risk everything just to follow my heart."

It was the most open Reed had ever been about his feelings toward her. Knowing she would regret it if it never happened, Maddie stood, placed a soft kiss on Reed's lips, and then gathered her things, preparing to leave the boat.

Before she walked back up the dock, Maddie turned to him once again. His face held a mixture of emotions.

"My God, you're gonna get me in trouble if you stick around here," he said, pulling his baseball hat over his face. "Go!" he yelled, pointing toward land.

"Will you wait a few years for me?" Maddie asked playfully.

He slid his hat back on his head and walked over toward her, looking very serious now. He leaned in for another kiss. It started gently, hardly a flutter against her lips, but then a surge of passion rose between them, and the kiss filled with the urgency of unfulfilled desires, unspoken thoughts. Maddie pressed herself against him, never wanting it to end.

Reed was the one to finally break it off. "Sweetheart, you're worth the wait," he whispered. "Now get lost before I do something I regret."

Maddie practically floated back to Mariner's Way. Could she really have a future with Reed? Possibly. But as she walked away, she knew she couldn't ignore her obligations to her family, to the past. Nothing would keep her from looking for Cordelia. Not a new crush. Not a threatening letter. Not even a spirit who cries in the night. At this point, nothing but a force of God could stop her.

# Chapter 24

## DAGAZ

ᛞ

### DAWN

*Daylight Clarity Breaks Through Nighttime Uncertainty;*
*Growth and Release*

Maddie was halfway home when it hit her. Spinning around, she looked back at the harbor. From that distance, Maddie could still make out Reed's boat bobbing at its mooring, surrounded by slivers of sunlight glinting off the choppy waters.

*Water.*

Something clicked into place. Maddie had been present for all of the element rituals on Halloween night, except one.

*The element of water.*

They had sent her back to the shore to retrieve buckets of water for the ritual, but she got knocked out at the boat. But what if . . . ? What if the girls just sent her away in order to get rid of her so that Maddie couldn't stop what they had planned for Cordelia? It all made sense. Maddie had obviously been drugged. Why else would she have had such a difficult time remembering what happened to Cordelia? And Maddie knew that the girls had access to their drugs of choice. And they'd drugged her before with that Ecstasy at Trevor's party—what would stop them from doing it again?

As she walked, anger fired up inside of her. The element of Water had to be appeased, and the ritual took place right in the middle of an island. Images of school field trips Maddie had taken as a little girl flooded back: the Salem Witch Museum with all the various ways that the townspeople tortured people accused of witchcraft. They were burned at the stake . . . Fire . . . pressed to death . . . Earth . . . hanged at the Gallows . . . Air . . . and finally drowned . . . Water.

They tried to drown her.

Everything was finally making sense. A body was never found because everyone was looking in the wrong place. Because no one knew that the last place Cordelia LeClaire had been was fifteen miles off shore. But then how had Finn O'Malley seen Cordelia on November first? Could he have been in on the whole thing as well?

Too wired to go home, Maddie spun on her heels and walked back down to the waterfront. Rather than returning to the docks, she veered off in the direction of the stately waterfront row houses where Darcy Willet lived. Someone was finally going to give her some answers.

෨

"Maddie, hi? Um, it's pretty early. Is everything okay?" Darcy squinted at her in the early morning light, wrapping her robe tightly around her.

"What was *Water*?" Maddie asked hurriedly, suddenly realizing that she must look frightful to Darcy after her night out on Reed's boat.

"Maddie, honey," Darcy said, eyeing her like she was one of the inmates at Ravenswood. "I have no idea what you are talking about. Do you want to come inside? Is everything alright?"

She squeezed her arm tightly—a little too tightly—and led her into the foyer. There was a shuffling sound coming from above them. Darcy's parents were probably going to come down any minute, so Maddie didn't have much time to get answers.

"What happened after I passed out?" Maddie demanded, spinning around and facing her. "What did you do to Cordelia to appease the element of water?"

"Appease the . . . ? Madeline, what is this all about? Kate and Trevor told me about all your questions . . . but you can't be serious in thinking that we had anything to do with your cousin disappearing," Darcy scolded, nervously looking over her shoulder. "We were just being bitchy. You know, putting her through some hazing. Sororities do it all the time, for God's sake. I mean, I'm not proud of the way we treated Cordelia, but that doesn't mean that we killed . . ."

"Who said anything about killing?" Maddie demanded. Darcy blinked rapidly and looked away, so Maddie continued to grill her, watching her squirm. "I just want to know what you guys did for the water ritual. Although, it's funny that I don't remember any of us having to go through that type of torturous hazing to get into the Sisterhood. I guess you guys saved that especially for Cordelia."

Darcy paced the living room as if collecting her thoughts. Finally, she abandoned the confused little girl act and hissed, "Listen, Maddie, I don't know what you think you're going to achieve ·by harassing everyone about that night. But I don't have to remind you that you were there, too. So before you go around town crying that we made your freaky cousin disappear, you should remember that *you were just as much a part of it as we were!*"

"I wasn't given a choice. I didn't know what you had in store for Cordelia. I still don't know the whole story. But I'm not leaving without answers, Darcy, real answers."

"I'm warning you to leave it alone, Maddie," said Darcy

firmly. There was more noise upstairs, but Maddie paid it no mind.

"Is that a threat?" she demanded.

"It's not a threat. It's just a piece of good advice. None of us are proud about what we did to Cordelia. But I swear to you, when we went back that night, she was gone. I really don't want to talk about this now, Maddie." Darcy glanced at the staircase. "This isn't the time or the place. I think you should leave," she said, pushing Maddie toward the front door.

"Wait, wait, wait. That night? I thought you went back in the morning? Didn't you make her stay the night on the island? Wasn't that part of the whole ritual?"

Annoyed, Darcy shook her head. "The ritual went too far. We didn't think she could handle the whole night after everything that happened. So after we dropped you at your mother's house, Kate, Hannah, Bridget, and I went back to the island, and she was gone."

"Why didn't you ever tell me this?"

"You were so worked up about everything that night. That's why I slipped that pill into your drink. I thought you were going to get us all in trouble with your screaming. Kate had some pills on her that she was going to give to Cordelia, in case, well, in case she fought back."

"So, it *was* all planned in advance. Kate had chosen Cordelia before we even got out there."

Darcy nodded nervously. "Like I said before, I'm not proud of it, Maddie. But it's in the past, and there's nothing we can do to change it. But I swear this to you: we didn't kill your cousin. I don't know what happened to her, but I swear it had nothing to do with any of us. Now, let's talk about this later, okay?"

At that moment, Trevor Campbell thundered down the

staircase in boxer shorts and just-rolled-out-of-bed hair. "Oh, wow, uh . . . hey, Maddie, what's going on?" He brushed his hand through his hair and tried to act like nothing out of the ordinary was going on.

"Trevor?" Maddie asked incredulously. Darcy looked like she wanted to sink through the cracks in the wide plank floors. Kate would absolutely crucify her—completely destroy both of them—if she knew about this.

"Why am I not surprised? Cordelia went through hell for something—or someone—she didn't do," she said disgustedly at Trevor. "And all along, you were the one who was sleeping with Trevor. You're the one who deserved that night out on Misery. Not Cordelia!"

"Maddie, wait—" Darcy pleaded. Trevor moved uneasily from one foot to the other.

Maddie cut her off with a laugh. "Now it makes perfect sense. Now I know why you allowed Kate to think there was something going on between Cordelia and Trevor—so that you two could continue your little affair. Cordelia took the fall for your indiscretions."

"I don't need this shit," Trevor said under his breath before wandering into the kitchen.

"Nice seeing you, too, Trevor. I'll be sure to give Kate your love when I see her," Maddie said coyly as she turned to leave.

"Just another bit of advice from a friend," Darcy told her icily as she came up behind her. "I'm a firm believer that you should live your life the way you want to. But I wouldn't want your family to get any backlash from all of this finger-pointing you've been doing lately, especially given your grandmother's poor health." She lowered her voice to a whisper. "So don't go around talking about *things* that are none of your business, okay?"

Facing Darcy, Maddie could feel her face getting red as

she said, "Are you threatening my family? Because if you are, I can guarantee that it would be the biggest mistake of your life. Especially since Kate would be very interested to know where her boyfriend has been spending all of his free time."

Darcy forced an innocent smile. "No, Madeline, don't be silly. I'm not threatening anyone," she insisted, choosing her words carefully before continuing. "Cordelia's gone, Maddie. You need to accept that and move on. And you should also stop nosing around in other people's business. That's what gets people in trouble around here."

"So, is that it? Is that why you made Cordelia disappear? Because she found out about you and Trevor? Or is there some other nasty little secret that you all didn't want her to tell anyone about?"

"I have no idea what you are talking about, Maddie. You need to put your tired little mind to rest; focus on other things for a while. Trevor said that Reed would keep you busy, keep your mind off of those troubling thoughts. I guess he's not doing his job very well, is he?" Darcy said in a mock innocent tone.

Maddie felt like she'd been punched in the stomach. But the look on Darcy's face told her the truth. Trevor and Darcy had used Reed to keep Maddie from looking too deeply into Cordelia's disappearance. Or to keep her from finding out about their torrid affair. No matter what the reason behind his attentiveness, it was all just a big, fat lie.

She wanted to run away—away from this evil town and these evil girls. But she'd come too far to do that. Instead, Maddie choked back her tears, squared her shoulders, and said, "Darcy, I'm not going anywhere until you tell me what you did for Water."

"We all took part in the second part of the ritual, Maddie. Just because you weren't there the whole time—or, or, because it's convenient for you to forget these things, doesn't mean you weren't a part of it, too."

*The second ritual?* Maddie thought helplessly. *Why can't I remember any of that?*

Darcy stared at her and then looked down, swallowing hard. Maddie didn't want to let Darcy in on her own confusion and the holes in her memory, so she continued to stare her down. Maddie knew Darcy would do anything to keep her from telling Kate about the secret affair with Trevor.

"We made her drink something."

"What did you make her drink?" Maddie demanded. Darcy looked around the room, anywhere but at her face. "Did she have the drugged wine that you gave me?"

Darcy shook her head. She reached up, straightening her wheat-blond hair with trembling fingers.

"Darcy, I'm only going to ask you one last time. After you drugged me and I passed out, WHAT DID YOU MAKE HER DRINK?"

Finally, Darcy spat her answer out, as if the words were too vile to hold inside any longer.

"Urine. We made her drink our urine."

# Chapter 25

## MANNAZ - REVERSED

## ISOLATION

*Blindness, Self-Delusion, Manipulation; Expect
No Help Now*

Maddie crawled into bed after coming home from Darcy's, and stayed there all day. She was sick, sick with the thought that she'd been played and humiliated by Reed, Trevor, and everyone else in this town. Sick with the knowledge that she'd played some part in that horrible night that she couldn't even remember. How could she have blocked out all that had happened that night? And why wasn't anyone filling her in on the details? How much of a role had she really played in Cordelia's initiation ritual?

Maddie turned to look at the clock. It felt like she'd been running every possible scenario through her mind for hours. Midnight. It was at this time that Maddie became most haunted by Cordelia's disappearance. It hurt to imagine her out there, lingering in the shadows, just waiting to be found. She pictured the whole mystery surrounding Cordelia unraveling like a loosely knit shawl. Maddie just needed to figure out which string to pull.

When Cordelia and Maddie had made their way down to the docks that Halloween night, neither of them had realized what was in store for them on Misery Island. As Tess would say, they didn't watch for the signs that were all around them.

Despite her doubts over the past months, Maddie knew there was something no one wanted her to find out. She could sense it in her conversations with Kate and the other Sisters of Misery. The way they glossed over the events of that night, as if it were something they had watched in movies like *Carrie* or *Heathers*, and not something that they had been a part of. It had always been between her and Reed, no matter how much she'd tried to deny it. And it was in Finn O'Malley's eyes. It hovered over her house, floated into her bedroom at night, and curled up next to her like a shape-shifting specter.

Something was coming. Like a low wail calling out to her from across the water, rising like mist and slowly taking its dark form. Maddie had noticed that lately, the ocean, despite the warmth of early spring, appeared icy and black and brought only one word into her mind: DEATH.

∞

The ringing phone shook the house to life. Maddie fumbled across her bedsheets and grasped the receiver.

"Hullo," Maddie mumbled into the mouthpiece, squinting her eyes to get a better read on the clock.

3:33 AM.

Only bad news could come at this hour.

"Ms. Crane? May I speak with Madeline Crane?"

"This is Madeline."

"I'm sorry to disturb you at this late hour, but you were listed as the contact person for Ms. Rebecca LeClaire. Is that correct?"

"Um, yeah. We just moved her to your facility earlier this month," Maddie replied. "Is there a problem?" Maddie shifted into a sitting position, brushing her hair out of her face.

"I'm sorry, Ms. Crane. But your aunt is missing."

"Missing?" It was like going back in time to when Cordelia disappeared. Maddie could almost hear Rebecca's voice again. *Cordelia's gone.* **Gone!** *She never came home last night. Something's not right. This can't be happening. Maddie, what are we going to do?* "I'm sorry," Maddie snapped. "How can that be? Don't you have security at your facility?"

"Yes, we do, ma'am. But we have recently admitted patients from all over the Commonwealth, and we are severely shorthanded. We are extremely sorry about this situation. And we are doing everything in our power to rectify it."

"Well, that's reassuring," Maddie said, her voice thick with sarcasm. "When was the last time anyone saw her?"

"We're not sure exactly, Ms. Crane." The woman sounded embarrassed and flustered. "She was reported missing right after the midnight bed check. We've been combing the property for the last few hours. Often, when new patients are unaccounted for, they simply get lost in one of our facilities—the library, the dining hall. But your aunt is nowhere on the premises. We are notifying you because patients will usually return to their homes or to the houses of family members."

"No, she hasn't come back here," Maddie said uneasily. "Please keep me posted. I'm going to start looking for her as well. I assume you have already contacted the authorities."

"Yes, ma'am. We called the police, and we have our people on it. We'll get her back safely."

Replacing the receiver, she listened for a moment to the silence that slipped around her.

Fairview was a palace compared to the dilapidated monstrosity of Ravenswood. While Maddie had hoped that the new place would help Rebecca to open up, there still wasn't a hint of any emotion within her—no animosity, anger, sadness . . . nothing.

Maddie hadn't forgotten Rebecca's unwarranted attack during her visit at Ravenswood. It was as if an unseen force had ripped the rune stone from the woman's hands and whipped it at Maddie's head.

And this is what frightened Maddie as she pulled on a few layers of warm clothing, preparing to set out in search of Rebecca. As she passed Tess's room, Maddie was instantly overcome by a sudden chill. Was her window open again? Maddie pushed the door open, and her heart skipped a beat.

Tess was sitting straight up in bed, looking out the window toward the ocean.

"Tess, you scared me to death," Maddie whispered. "What's wrong?" When Tess didn't answer, Maddie said, "Go back to sleep, Tess. Everything's okay. You're just having another bad dream."

The look in Tess's eyes chilled her. She held her arms out briefly as if motioning for Maddie to hug her, but then turned her attention back to the window.

"Get some rest," Maddie said, backing out of the room. Tess burrowed back under the quilts on her bed.

As she pulled the door closed, Maddie heard her grandmother whisper, "She's in her garden again, isn't she?"

*Ravenswood.*

The thought of it made Maddie physically shake, but at least she knew where to start.

ॐ

Maddie eased her way into her mother's room. "Mom, I need the car keys. Rebecca's gone. They can't find her anywhere at Fairview. I don't know what to do."

Abigail sat up in her bed, nodding, not at all surprised.

"I knew something like this would happen again," Abigail said knowingly.

"Something like what? Why would she come . . . ?"

Maddie's voice trailed off. Suddenly, something clicked in her mind. "What do you mean *again?* Mother, has Rebecca been here before?"

It was all making sense—Tess's dreams of a red-haired girl, the crying in the night, the rune stones that popped up all over the place. It wasn't Cordelia haunting them. It was Rebecca.

Abigail shut her mouth in a grim line and turned her head away from Maddie.

"I have no idea what you're talking about. Things are getting too difficult, too crazy around here for all of us."

"But why? What's going on?" Maddie said, growing more and more anxious by the minute.

"I wasn't surprised when she slipped through the cracks at Ravenswood with the place being shut down and all. But Fairview," she continued, shaking her head, "I was convinced they'd keep her away from us. Now she's coming for me, and probably you, too. I knew this would happen. I just prayed it wouldn't happen like this."

Maddie was reeling from her mother's words. Since when was Rebecca such a huge threat? She knew that her aunt was unstable, that she had been mentally destroyed by Cordelia's disappearance, that she most likely held some anger against her family, the town, the world, for that matter. But dangerous? A threat? It was hard to imagine, despite the stone-throwing episode at Ravenswood.

"Why couldn't you just tell me that you were afraid of Rebecca? Couldn't you have at least warned me? That she resented us so much? That she *blamed* us?" Maddie screamed the words at her mother, but she was really only shouting out of fear. Then she composed herself.

"Get up, Mother. We're going to Ravenswood to find Rebecca. Where can I find a flashlight?"

Abigail climbed out of bed and went to the closet for her clothes.

"Rebecca's been here before, hasn't she? And you tried to keep it from me. You knew that she could get out of Ravenswood, but you were too afraid to say anything. But why? You never cared about her before. Why protect her now?"

"She had her reasons for taking out her anger on me, and I had mine for keeping it a secret. That's all you need to know," Abigail said firmly, jutting her chin out in defiance.

"No, Mother," Maddie shouted as she grabbed hold of her mother's rail-thin arm. "You are going to tell me everything that I need to know, starting this minute. After everything you've put me through, it's time for you to start talking. I need to know *now*. And if you don't tell me, I'm going to call the police and get to the bottom of it that way."

Abigail took a deep breath.

"No police, they wouldn't be any help to us anyway. Garrett Sullivan doesn't know his ass from his elbow." Abigail shook her head. "I'll fill you in on our way to Ravenswood. Let's just go."

Maddie left Abigail to get dressed while she ran down to the kitchen in search of a phone book. There was only one way to get into Ravenswood.

Finnegan O'Malley.

He was the only person who could get her inside and help her navigate that maze of a building.

O'Connor . . . O'Donnell . . . O'Leary . . . O'Malley, Finnegan . . . 781-555-4343.

Her nail-bitten fingers flew over the telephone buttons. *Come on, come on, pick up, dammit!*

"It's three in the fuckin' morning," growled Finn. "This'd better be important."

"Finn, it's Maddie Crane. I need your help. Rebecca is missing. You have to get me into Ravenswood right now."

"Whoa . . . whoa . . . whoa . . ." Finn countered. "What the hell is going on, Maddie? Why haven't you called the police? Why're you calling me? You don't want to be trekking around in that place in the middle of the night by yourself. It's suicide."

*Suicide* . . . The word hit her like a weight. That's what her mother was worried about.

"Please, Finn, I need your help!" Maddie screamed into the phone. "Just meet me at Ravenswood. I don't have time to explain." Grabbing the keys, Maddie ran out to the car. Abigail was already waiting in the passenger seat.

"There's no turning back now," Abigail said calmly, almost to herself. "I knew it was going to come to this. I just didn't know it would happen so soon."

# Chapter 26

## NAUTHIZ REVERSED

### NEED

*Hasty Decisions That Lead to Destruction;*
*A Difficult Time is Ahead*

They sped along the winding road carved through the passage of trees to Ravenswood Asylum. Out of the corner of her eye, Maddie detected movement in the darkness, but told herself it was only the shiver of low-hanging tree branches. She scanned the asylum grounds for any sign of life as her mother spoke in slow, even tones.

"They called her Houdini, she escaped so much," her mother said wryly. "She resented me for putting her into Ravenswood. Thought her time would be better spent out looking for Cordelia." Her mother laughed a dry, tinny laugh. "Rebecca quickly discovered the tunnel system beneath the hospital. That's when she started paying us visits, always at night. She hid in the basement."

Maddie tried to imagine Rebecca, the stranger she'd visited briefly at Ravenswood, a shell of her former self, returning to Mariner's Way again and again. But she seemed so far gone mentally, and so frail, that Maddie couldn't imagine her having the strength to actually go through with it.

Maddie looked at her mother in the glow of the pale moonlight. Her face, usually angular and stiff, looked softer, almost remorseful.

"But why would she do these things to you, Mom? Why blame you? If she wanted to blame anyone, she'd blame Kate and all the rest of the girls from the Academy. They were the ones who made Cordelia's life hell. Or me, for that matter, for not sticking up for her when I had the chance."

"I don't know. You'd think that she'd go after the bastard who got her pregnant. Your new best friend there. Reed Campbell."

"What are you talking about?" Maddie pulled the car to a stop in front of the monstrous building. "Reed had nothing to do with Cordelia's disappearance. They were never involved. End of story," she said furiously, slamming the car door.

"Then why did he give her money for an abortion?" Abigail's voice was muffled behind the car window as Maddie walked over to the weed-covered stairs of concrete.

Spinning back to face the car, Maddie blurted out, "How could you possibly know that?"

Abigail thrust her jaw to the side as if she realized she'd gone too far.

"I have my ways," she said firmly as she got out of the car.

Just as Maddie was about to grill her for her sources of information, a woman's scream pierced the silence.

Maddie pivoted, trying to see where the sound came from. Shadows danced along the boarded up doors and windows. There had to be a way inside.

"Mother, you stay here. I'm going to find a way in. Get back into the car and wait for Finn. If he shows up, tell him to try to find me in there."

"I don't want to stay out here by myself. I'll come with you."

"No, Mother," she instructed. "I'm sorry, but you'll just slow me down. I need to find Rebecca before she does anything to hurt herself. I owe at least that much to Cordelia."

Thrusting her cell phone into her mother's hands, Maddie turned toward the vacant building. Maddie had to find Rebecca before she did something to hurt herself. She wasn't the same woman who had moved back to Hawthorne months ago. Her aunt had been drastically psychologically altered. And in this huge monster of a hospital, anything was possible.

"If I don't come out in twenty minutes or so or if you hear or see anything unusual, call the police," she ordered. As Abigail started to object, Maddie said, "Listen, I don't know what reasons you have for not wanting to get the police involved. But right now, I really don't care. You will do as I say, understand?"

Abigail nodded meekly for the first time ever.

Maddie turned on her flashlight and circled around the perimeter of the building, trying to find a way in. In the moonlight, Maddie could see tattered window shades blowing in and out of broken windows like ghosts. It looked like the monstrous building was breathing. As she crept around the building, the first thing Maddie came upon was the faces of the Pickering sisters and Cordelia carved into the wall. They took on an unearthly glow when her flashlight illuminated their hollow eyes and cavernous grins, as if they were daring her to enter, daring her to join them.

⁂

Maddie stumbled her way around the building. Guided by instinct, she groped the walls as brick and mortar came loose in her hands. She smelled dank, mossy decay mixed with something more pungent.

She fell to her knees when she noticed a loose board covering a basement window. Maddie pulled at the board, cursing as splinters wedged their way under her fingernails. Finally, she pried the board loose and kicked the glass out of the window. Yanking off her jacket, she placed it along the bottom of the window, hoping that it would protect her from any remaining shards of glass. Maddie then lowered herself down, trying to ignore the scurrying sounds. Clinging to the flashlight, she dropped down to the cement floor. Once on level ground, she directed the flashlight's beam around the room and tried to get her bearings. The subterranean room was freezing.

This had to be the creepiest thing she'd ever done in her life. There she was—someone who couldn't even watch a moderately scary film—right in the middle of a real-life horror movie.

Maddie had to mentally bark orders at herself to stay motivated and not crumble with fear. *One foot in front of the other . . . just move forward . . . push on . . . keep moving . . . you can't stop now . . .*

She was in some type of medical storage room with metal gurneys haphazardly lined up next to each other. Maddie knocked into one, and the cool metal clanged, announcing her entrance, as it slid into the others. Maddie tried to hold the flashlight steady to find the door. Running her hands across some metal file cabinets that lined the walls, Maddie edged her way across the dank room. It wasn't until she saw one of the drawers fully open that Maddie realized where she was; her stomach began involuntarily heaving when she realized that she hadn't been clinging to file cabinets after all.

Maddie was in the asylum's morgue. She charged for the door, which was, mercifully, unlocked.

*Don't lose it, Maddie. You can't freak out now. Keep it together.*

Who knew what was waiting for her? Maddie simply

wanted to find Rebecca and be done with this place, this family, and this town once and for all. With every step deeper into the asylum, Maddie wondered if she would live to regret coming here, as she regretted going to Misery Island on Halloween night, for the rest of her life.

Here she was in the middle of the night in a deserted insane asylum looking for a woman with a death wish. *And who said that small towns were boring?* Maddie thought as she brushed cobwebs and God knows what else from her clothing.

Maddie crept through the tunnel, searching for a door or a staircase, anything that led up to the main level of the building. She desperately hoped that her terrible sense of direction wasn't leading her away from the main building, off into one of the many corridors that stretched out away from the heart of the hospital like a spider's web.

Echoes reached down to her from above. Maddie heard heavy footsteps just above her head. Was that Rebecca? And then, silence.

Maddie raced ahead blindly, praying for a staircase, a ladder, an elevator shaft, anything that would help her climb up out of the depths of this evil place.

As she finally reached a staircase that led up to the main floor, Maddie began to wonder what would bring Rebecca back again and again to their basement.

*What happened in that basement?*

Maddie could only think of one logical reason for her aunt to return: Cordelia.

# Chapter 27

## ANSUZ REVERSED

ᚨ

### WARNING

*A Misunderstanding or Delusion; Manipulation through*
*Trickery and Pranks*

Maddie ran up the stairs, desperate to find where the footsteps were coming from. Reaching the top of the staircase, she slowly turned the knob and pushed the door open, stepping into the hallway right off the admittance area. There was a shuffling sound to her right. Creeping across the room, Maddie headed in the direction of the footsteps, stepping gingerly, not wanting to startle Rebecca.

*Who am I kidding?* Maddie asked herself. *Rebecca knows I'm here. She planned this. She knows this place better than I ever could. She wants me to pay for whatever happened to Cordelia.*

Maddie heard different, heavier steps—slow, steady, methodical—heading in her direction. Maddie prayed it was Finn, but she didn't want to take any chances. She sucked her breath in, squeezing her body against the damp, mildewed wall, wishing for invisibility. It would be one thing if it was daytime, and she could at least see her surroundings. Suddenly, everything quieted down. The footsteps were gone. She tried to quiet the sound of her own breathing, but was convinced that the sound of her heart was loud enough to fill the entire room with pounding, unrelenting noise. A hand reached out and covered her mouth. Maddie swallowed her scream and bit down hard on the hand, pulling away with every ounce of strength left in her body.

"Jesus!" Finn yelped, shaking his hand wildly. "What the hell did you do that for?"

"Oh, my God, Finn," Maddie yelled, adrenaline pumping in her chest, her body shaking. "What are you doing? Why did you cover my mouth?"

"Well, I didn't want you to yell and attract any attention to us. But I guess we need to move on to Plan B. Come on, let's head up this way. I heard some footsteps right before you decided to make a meal outta my hand."

Maddie obediently fell into step behind Finn, feeling a little more secure. At least she had company.

"Thanks for coming," she said sheepishly.

"Now, tell me what's going on. Why didn't you go to the police?" Finn whispered as they crept through the corridor.

"My mother didn't want us to go to the police. Not yet. I guess she was afraid that we'd get Rebecca in trouble," Maddie said weakly. She was making excuses for Abigail, though she didn't really understand her mother's reasoning. "Besides, everyone's looking for her over at Fairview. This was just a hunch."

"So you drag me out of bed in the middle of the night to go on a wild goose chase in the creepiest place on the planet, all because of a hunch?" He reached behind and grasped her hand, pulling her forward in order to speed her along.

"I don't really know. My mother isn't one for airing our family's dirty laundry. She probably was afraid that it would get around town and embarrass her."

"So she'd rather read 'Teenagers Arrested for Breaking

and Entering Ravenswood' in the paper tomorrow?" Finn offered sarcastically.

"Well, if you had gotten here earlier, it wouldn't have been breaking and entering. It would have been entering with a key. That's not a crime."

"This is definitely out of my jurisdiction right now. I could get into all kinds of shit for doing this. You'd better be right about your aunt being here."

"I am, Finn," Maddie said, her voice quivering. "I have to be. If I'm wrong . . . I . . . I don't know where else to look."

Finn stopped and turned, unexpectedly pulling her into his chest. He smelled of laundry soap and cedar, not at all what she had expected.

"We'll find her," Finn whispered. "I won't let you lose any more of your family, I promise."

Then, as if on cue, a woman's wail echoed off in the distance.

"Let's go," Maddie said.

They raced down the hallway, carefully avoiding the stray wheelchairs and piles of loose plaster and debris that cluttered the floor. They were in a part of the hospital that had been shut down over a decade ago, and it was already in a severe state of deterioration. Passing from room to room felt like being in a neverending maze in a rundown funhouse. Still in the distance, Rebecca's cries propelled them further and further into the core of Ravenswood. "I don't know why she's doing this," Maddie said, gulping down air as they ran, the muscles in her legs burning. Finn confidently navigated them through the long corridors, never faltering.

"Maybe she blames you for what happened on the island," Finn called over his shoulder. She came to an abrupt halt. Maddie had never told him about that night on Misery Island. And she was sure that no one else had either.

"How could you know about that?" Maddie asked, becoming all too aware of what a vulnerable position she was in. Finn stopped and slowly paced back a few steps toward her.

"I was there, Madeline," he said quietly. "I know what you girls did to Cordelia."

&#8734;

Maddie never realized how dark Finn's eyes were until that moment.

"You . . . ? But how?" Maddie stammered as she backed up slightly, realizing she had gotten herself into a place of horror with someone she barely knew, someone who knew his way through the belly of this beast all too well. How could Maddie even be sure that Finn wasn't involved in Cordelia's disappearance?

Finn turned and walked slowly toward her, shining the light into her face so that he became a darkened shape behind the blinding glare, ignoring the screams and shouts coming from up ahead of them. Finn didn't seem to be in any rush to find Rebecca. Not yet, anyway.

"I overheard what was planned for Halloween night. All the Hawthorne Academy assholes talk about all sorts of stuff around me because in your minds, I don't matter. I'm just the handyman's kid. Some poor, working-class schmuck who didn't deserve any attention," he growled. "But Cordelia paid attention to me. She was the only one. To all the rest of you, it's like I don't even exist."

Maddie's breath came in ragged gasps. The water-stained walls felt like they were closing in on her, and Finn continued his story, his voice hard.

"So," he flashed the light directly in her eyes, "I heard about this hazing ritual you girls had planned for her. Kate was the one who came up with it, but she wanted to get the guys from school in on it, too. She told them to boat out to Misery sometime after midnight, that they would all get a chance to join in on the fun. Now, I didn't know exactly what was going to happen, but I knew that it couldn't be good. Not the way they were laughing and carrying on about it, like it was friggin' hysterical."

"You don't know what you're talking about," Maddie stammered, trying to squint and avoid the bright light glaring into her eyes. "There weren't any boys. It was just us girls out on the island, the Sis . . ."

"Yeah, I know, the Sisters of Misery. I know all about your little sorority," Finn snapped. "And I know what kind of savage crap you did to her . . . all that bullshit about fire and earth and whatever. It was just an excuse to beat the shit out of her. And you just stood there and let it happen. She was your cousin, for Christ's sake." He shook his head in disgust. "Yeah, I saw it. I saw everything."

Maddie's emotions were out of control, swirling like the madhouse that had engulfed them. She was overcome by guilt, elation, fear, hope, and finally relief that there was someone who could finally give her the answers she'd been looking for all along. As she tried to absorb what Finn was telling her, tears started falling down her cheeks as she slowly backed away from him.

"Finn, I . . . I never knew what they had planned. You *have* to believe that," Maddie cried, her voice rising up and filling the space between them. "I never would have hurt Cordelia on purpose. And . . . and, I know that you'd never hurt her either, at least not on purpose."

"But *they* did. And they weren't satisfied by just humiliating and degrading her." His voice grew angrier and louder, echoing off the walls. "No, they wanted a bunch of Academy boys to come out to the island to hurt her even more. I heard them talking about it out on the sports fields. Your rich bitch friend Kate promised them 'a night of fun' with your cousin if they came out that night. 'You can all have a shot at that slut, Cordelia,' was what she said. All your old Hawthorne buddies planned on taking a boat out to Misery. But I beat 'em out there. I watched and I waited for the guys to show up. But while I was waiting, I saw what you girls did to her. And I'll tell ya, I've seen a lot of shitty things in my life, but I'd never seen anything like that."

His voice grew thick with disappointment and disgust, even sadness.

"So I guess the guys from the Academy never showed up then." Maddie said. Finn allowed the flashlight to drift down from her face so that her eyes were able to adjust to the darkness again.

"Are you kidding? Turn down a sure thing with the hottest girl to ever come through Hawthorne? Of course they showed up. But they never got close to you girls. I caught them as they were pulling their boats up to shore. Met Trevor and his football buddies at the beach when they showed up, ready for their big conquest. But I was able to change their plans for the night when I showed them my dad's nine millimeter," Finn laughed, remembering. "You should have seen those guys scatter. They were practically shitting in their Brooks Brothers pants, trying to get back into their boats."

His laughter subsided, and he grew more serious. "Anyway, by the time I got back to the center of the island, Cordelia had been knocked out and was bleeding. She was soaking wet and freezing, I'm sure, even though there was a fire built around her. I don't know what happened to her jacket, but it had disappeared. You were passed out at that point. Took a big hit to the head by one of your *Sisters*." He spat the word out like it was equivalent to a murderer or criminal. He probably wasn't so far off from the truth.

Maddie stumbled back a bit, shocked at this new information. All this time Maddie had doubted herself. The dreams she'd had about tearing at Cordelia's skin, Kate's insinuations that Maddie had somehow hurt her own cousin. All of it was untrue, and for that, Maddie was overcome by relief. Kate had taken advantage of her memory loss to plant a seed of doubt in her mind, fully aware that it would grow like a horrible, strangling weed.

"So you were the last person to see Cordelia that night," Maddie said, recalling the police report, and yet another piece of the puzzle clicked into place.

Finn nodded. "Now you know why I couldn't tell anyone. Those kids would never admit to what they had done to her, what they were planning on doing. They'd all stick together and pin it on me. And I was the last person seen with her before she disappeared. Imagine how that would've looked. I could've gone to jail. I'm eighteen. The worst that coulda happened to those guys was that they'd get sent to juvey—and that would never happen 'cause their parents wouldn't let it. Plus, Cordelia swore me to secrecy."

"What did she say to you?" Maddie asked, her curiosity growing with every word he uttered.

"Well," he said, scratching the side of his face. "I gave her my coat—man, she was freezing—and helped clean her up a bit. Luckily, I had some blankets and a first aid kit in my dad's boat. She was beat up bad. We took the boat back to the mainland. She was still bleeding pretty bad, so I wanted to walk her home or take her to Bell Hospital. I told her to go to the police, and she said that she had other plans for the kids that did this to her. She never told me what she wanted to do. Cordelia was probably right about not going to the police because they wouldn't have listened to her. Hell, those Hawthorne Academy kids have parents that practically own this town. They're not going to care about a girl like Cordelia."

Maddie nodded and waited for him to continue.

"I asked her why she went along with the whole ritual thing in the first place. She told me that they gave her an ultimatum at the start. It was either gonna be you or her going down that night."

Maddie inhaled painfully.

*She saved me*, Maddie realized, tears streaming down her face. *Cordelia sacrificed herself for me.* An intense rainstorm kicked up outside. A streak of lightning lit the darkness, followed closely by an earthshaking boom of thunder.

"Maddie," Finn said, his voice rising to be heard over the heavy rains that echoed off the roof, "she knew that you weren't strong enough to take whatever crap they had in store. Plus, she didn't want to be responsible for you getting hurt. She couldn't live with that. And she figured that whatever they had planned, she could take it."

Maddie nodded, tears spilling down her face. "And that was the last time you saw her?"

"I was going to walk her home. But she said she had some unfinished business to attend to. She had someone she needed to talk to." Finn stopped talking and swallowed hard, his Adam's apple bobbing sharply. "Now, this is something I have regretted until this day. Probably gonna regret it the rest of my goddamned life. I never should have let her walk home alone. But I was an idiot. I was scared of a guy like me walking a girl home looking the way Cordelia did—like she'd been to hell and back. Plus, I was still carrying the gun I'd stolen from my dad. How do you think that would look if we were stopped by anyone? A punk kid like me with a beautiful girl like Cordelia, all cut up and shit. I mean, what if Cordelia tried to pin the blame on me for some reason?"

"She wouldn't have done that," Maddie offered quietly.

"I know," he said in a strained voice, almost quivering. "And that's what gets me. That maybe she'd be here if I'd only . . ." Finn's voice trailed off. He shook his head as if willing the surge of emotions away. His voice cracked when he said softly, "I really loved her. And instead of protecting her, I spent my time writing her sappy letters like some love sick puppy. I should have known better. I should have watched out for her. I-I," he said with growing anger as he punched the wall, cursing loudly.

Maddie wanted to tell him that she was sorry for suspecting him and that she shared his overwhelming sense of loss. But words just didn't seem like enough. Finn was the one who wrote all those beautiful letters to Cordelia. It was all making sense. Maddie suddenly wondered if he knew about the pregnancy. Was the baby his?

"How close were you exactly? I mean, did you know—did she say anything about . . . ?" Maddie's voice trailed off. What exactly was the etiquette for asking a guy if he's the father of an unborn child that may or may not still be alive?

Finn abruptly turned and punched the wall, "Dammit!" he shouted, his voice echoing through the barren hallways. He regained his composure and turned to Maddie, tears flooding his eyes, "Tell me that I might be a dad? Yeah, she mentioned that. She wasn't sure. If she had told me before that night out on Misery Island, there's no way I would have let her go out there at all." He shook his head emphatically, "No way, man. No way would I have let her go through that shit." He was silent for a moment.

Maddie was confused. If Finn was the father of the child, why did Reed give Cordelia money for the abortion? And how could Abigail possibly even know about that?

"Anyway, she told me if there were ever consequences from that night . . . that I should get you out of town fast. That's why I wrote all those notes to you. When Cordelia disappeared, I figured that whoever took her would be coming for you next. Cordelia had this weird way of knowing that something bad was going to happen. I just wish . . . I wish I had known at the time—then I . . . I . . . well," he choked on his words with sobs coming from deep within his chest.

Maddie lunged forward and clasped Finn tightly in her arms. Both of their faces were wet with tears. He squeezed her into his chest, and she listened to the strong beat of his heart mixed with the sound of his ragged breath.

She pulled back and said gently, "Finn, you know you were a suspect. You were put down in the police reports as the last person to see her. Why didn't you tell them any of this?"

He looked at her fiercely. "I never talked to any of the police—I was never questioned. How do they know I was the last person to see her? Who could have known that?"

She shook her head, not knowing what to say to him.

He laughed a short, curt laugh. "I'll bet one of those asshole Hawthorne guys set me up. They wanted to cover their own asses if Cordelia ever came forward. They're probably the ones who made sure that she couldn't report anything on her own." He punched the wall. "If they hurt her—if I could have protected her . . . if only I hadn't been such an idiot and made sure that she got home okay. Damn it!"

"You saved her, Finn. No matter what happened to her that night, you were her savior. You have to remember that always," Maddie said, placing a hand on his damp cheek.

"And YOU KILLED HER!" shrieked a voice from above where they were standing.

They both looked up, and there inside the steel cage of the staircase was Rebecca, illuminated briefly by a flash of lightning from the storm outside. Her hair was wild and ragged, and a dirty nightdress clung to her thin frame.

Maddie wasn't sure how long Rebecca had been listening to them, but her face appeared shiny and slick with tears.

Maddie grabbed the flashlight out of Finn's hands and aimed it at Rebecca. "You killed my baby! You all did!" Rebecca screamed, digging her fingers into the steel mesh that caged the stairwell and shaking it so hard that debris and dust took flight into the musty air around them. "I knew that those girls were evil! I warned you!!"

Then she turned and ran up the staircase, her footsteps echoing as she fled away from them down the hallway. Finn and Maddie raced toward the steel cage. Finn fumbled with his keys.

"Hurry up," Maddie yelled. "We're going to lose her."

"I'm trying, hold on!"

He spun the key in the lock, and the door screeched open. They ran up the stairs, following the demonic sounds of Rebecca's screams.

# Chapter 28

## WUNJO REVERSED

## SORROW

*A Time of Sorrow, Strife, and Raging Frenzy*

Finn and Maddie raced, climbed, and stumbled through the decrepit maze of Ravenswood. The rumors of it being haunted seemed more real than ever—it was alive with a buzzing electricity she'd never experienced. The walls seemed to be moving, breathing, churning with energy. Instead of fearing it, however, Maddie was channeling it to propel her forward.

They finally caught up with Rebecca in one of the turrets of the sprawling madhouse. The rain-soaked winds swarmed into the cavernous room through the smashed blue-black glass of the window frames.

"Rebecca, please," Maddie begged her aunt, "don't do anything dangerous. We're here to help you. We want to bring you home."

Rebecca stared at her, her eyes flat and lifeless.

"Home? I don't have a *home* anymore. Cordelia was my home, and now that she's gone, I have nothing!" Tears streamed down her face as she hissed, "Do you have any idea of the evil that was unleashed on that island? You've cursed us all. Cordelia is gone, and now I have to go to her."

"What do you mean cursed? How are you going to go to her? Rebecca, do you know where Cordelia is?" Maddie wanted to keep her aunt talking until she could figure out how to get them all safely out of Ravenswood.

Rebecca's mouth gaped open, and she let out a maniacal laugh. "Do I know? DO I KNOW? What do you think, Maddie?? I knew all along that those girls were somehow responsible, but I just couldn't believe that you were a part of it. I didn't know about the island and the black magic that took place out there. I warned you! I warned Cordelia! And she did it all to save you—to take care of you! How could you let this happen to her?"

"I swear I didn't know that any of this would happen," Maddie cried. Finn backed slowly out of the room, Maddie kept her eyes on Rebecca, trying to keep her talking. And considering that no one had heard the woman speak in months, she was certainly making up for lost time. *Please, Finn, go get help*, she silently willed. "Rebecca, I had nothing to do with Cordelia's disappearance—or that black magic or whatever you call it. I promise you."

"LIAR!" Rebecca wailed. "I found these, and they told me the truth. These belonged to Cordelia. She never went anywhere without them. They kept her safe. Safe from people like you!" Rebecca held up the same rune stones that she had hurled at Maddie during her visit to Ravenswood.

"Those aren't Cordelia's. You sold them in the store, remember? You had lots of them. It doesn't mean anything," Maddie explained. "And the things that happened on the island . . . I thought it was just a silly ritual. But it got out of hand. Yes, those girls were horrible to Cordelia—and I'm ashamed that I did nothing to stop it—but they didn't make her disappear."

Maddie stepped closer to Rebecca.

"Rebecca, you need to listen to me."

"No!" screamed Rebecca and in a flash she was perched at the edge of the open window. "You all must pay for this. I need to find Cordelia, bring her home. She was cursed on that island. Our family has been cursed. She had no choice but to leave, and now she'll never return. Never! And it is all your fault!"

"Madeline had nothing to do with it, Rebecca," a voice said from behind them.

Maddie spun around quickly, shocked to see her mother standing in the doorway. Abigail stepped slowly into the room, careful not to excite Rebecca any further.

"Maddie had nothing to do with Cordelia's disappearance. It was all my doing."

"Mother, what are you saying?" Maddie hissed incredulously.

"I'm saying that it is my fault that Cordelia's gone," Abigail said stoicly. "There is no one to blame but me."

৯০

Maddie looked back and forth between the two sisters, her mentally disturbed aunt and her secretive mother. She noticed Finn edging back into the room from one of the arched corners, entering through a hidden passageway. Maddie noticed him shoving his cell phone into his jacket pocket, but didn't want to call any attention to him.

"I knew it," growled Rebecca. "I knew that you were the reason for Cordelia's disappearance. I'll make you all pay for this."

"Rebecca," her mother snapped, "keep Maddie out of this. She doesn't know anything about what happened. She never did. It's all my fault. I'm the one who should be punished, not Madeline."

"Why?" Rebecca shrieked. "Why did you do it?"

Maddie was becoming more and more confused.

*My mother killed Cordelia?* Madeline thought incredulously.

"How? I—I don't understand," Maddie whispered, afraid of her mother aggravating the situation any further, terrified of what Rebecca would do if she became more agitated.

"I'm saying," Abigail said as she strode past Maddie toward her sister, "that it's my fault that Cordelia's gone. It wasn't intentional. At least that's what I've told myself again and again. I made a mistake, but then again, we all are guilty of making mistakes, aren't we, Rebecca?" She paused for a moment. "I've had to live with my actions. If you are looking for someone to punish, to blame, to hate, then hate me, Rebecca."

Rebecca fell down off the window frame to the floor in a mass of sobs and howls. "Why?" she cried again and again. "How?"

Maddie watched her mother in horror. It just couldn't be possible.

"I think you should start explaining, Mrs. Crane," Finn said, moving out from the shadows and over to Maddie's side. "Not only to us, but to the police as well. I called them earlier. It's only a matter of time before they arrive."

Abigail no longer paid any attention to Finn or Maddie; she was confessing her sins to her older sister, seeking forgiveness by finally speaking about her actions.

"There were so many reasons, Rebecca. You knew that I didn't want you back here. Hawthorne is *my* home. You left it behind and created a life far from here. But, you see, I never wanted anything but this town, this life. And then, all of a sudden, you're back—you and Cordelia. Don't you think I heard what the people in town said about you, how they looked at you? Didn't you *ever* once think about how you and your wild daughter's actions would reflect on me, on *my* life, *my* reputation?"

Abigail's voice trembled in growing anger and frustration.

"I worked so hard to be accepted. Again and again, my position threatened. First, when Malcolm took off with some slut. And then the money—ha! Never enough!" Then Abigail turned quickly to her daughter, as if begging for her forgiveness as well.

"I did it for both of us, Maddie. It was so important for you to befriend those girls. You didn't think I knew about the Sisters of Misery, but I did. They've been around for a long time—generations. I could never be a part of that group because we didn't have the money or the family name. You had the opportunities that I never had," she reasoned. "Those families are powerful. Being accepted by them opens doors that will never open any other way. I did that for you. But you turned your back on them and chose to spend your time with Cordelia and Rebecca."

Rebecca's sobs had subsided, and she watched intently as Abigail paced back and forth between them.

"And then that Halloween night, I waited up for the girls to return. When I found Madeline passed out on the front stoop, I was livid! Cordelia didn't even have the decency to see my daughter home safely. Got her drunk or drugged and just left her on the front stoop for the whole world to see. I was angry with Maddie, but even more furious with Cordelia for letting this happen to my daughter. I never could have imagined what would happen, what I was capable of, when she returned."

The tension in the room was overwhelming. The world seemed to drop away. Even the rainstorm that raged through the broken windows seemed to die down a bit. Everything awaited the outcome of Abigail's story.

"And so I waited. And when she snuck into the basement, stinking of booze and cigarettes and Lord knows what else, I confronted her. She had money on her, a lot of it. I asked who she stole it from. She tried to push past me, said it was none of my business. I was so angry that I yelled. 'Answer me! This is my house!' She ignored me and said that she needed to sleep, needed her mother, needed a shower. And so I told her that what she really *needed* to do was leave. And that if she didn't, I would throw both of you out on the street for good," Abigail rambled on.

Finn squeezed Maddie's back closer to his chest as he inhaled sharply. She could feel his racing heart beating against her. They stood there listening, barely breathing, waiting for the inevitable.

"Cordelia swore at me, saying awful, dirty things. She told me that I'd be sorry if I tried to force you out. That she'd make me pay, just like she'd make the others pay. I slapped her hard across the face. And then, I don't know, something just exploded inside her. She tore at me like a wild animal. I grabbed her by the hair and shoved her backwards. She fell against the wall and then down to the dirt floor. I told her to get up and get the hell out of my house. Now, I didn't think I pushed her that hard, that I swear to you. But I must not have known my own strength because that's when I saw the blood on her. It looked black in the dim light of the basement, and it smelled of old pennies as it dripped down from her hair into her face. She got up off the floor and spit at me.

"And so that's when I told her the truth—the truth about who she really was."

Rebecca held her head regally like she was the queen of this fallen castle. Her face slick with tears, her voice was calm, resigned as she asked firmly, "How could you have told her? That's why she's gone. Don't you see? She hates me now. She'll hate me forever!"

Maddie searched her mother's tired face, almost afraid to hear what was coming next. Abigail turned to her and simply said, "Maddie, Cordelia's not your cousin. She's your half-sister."

It was at that moment that Maddie finally understood the animosity between her mother and Rebecca. Her father had an affair with Rebecca. When she left town as a pregnant, unwed mother, everyone assumed that Simon LeClaire was the father. Simon had raised Cordelia as his daughter, even though he knew that she wasn't biologically his own.

Cordelia and Maddie were sisters.

Maddie finally spoke. "Mom, where is Cordelia?"

Abigail shook her head. "I honestly don't know. She left the house in a rage, screamed at me that we'd all pay for what we've done. I thought she was just playing a game—punishing us for everything that happened. I never reported it. I couldn't. It would have—I just didn't want—"

"You didn't care about Cordelia, Mother. You just didn't want anyone to know the truth," Maddie said flatly. "And all this time, it was more important to keep up appearances than to help us find her. What kind of person are you? How can you be so cruel? How—how could you!?"

Abigail looked like she had been physically struck by her daughter's words. She hung her head and started weeping. It was the first time Maddie ever remembered seeing her mother cry.

"All those nights that I escaped from here, from this prison, watching, waiting, listening, returning to Mariner's Way, trying to discover who had taken Cordelia from me—I never dreamed it would have been you, Abigail," Rebecca cried, bringing her hands to the sides of her head and shaking it as if she was trying to comprehend it all. "I thought it was those girls, so I left them a warning. I gave them each a stone. Then, I thought it was a boy, so I stole her love letters to try to learn the truth. I even wrote in Maddie's journal, trying to scare her into coming clean about what happened to Cordelia. But nothing worked. All of those nights, all of that wasted energy, all of my carefully planned escapes, all of it, only to discover it was you all along, Abigail." She looked at her sister incredulously. "I know you hated me for what happened with Malcolm, but I never thought that you'd punish me by taking away the only thing I have in this world to live for. That you would make Cordelia leave me forever!"

All of the questions that had plagued Maddie for months— the red-haired girl in the basement, the missing letters, the rune stones, the scribbling in the journals—all of it could be explained with one word: Rebecca.

When Rebecca finally stood, she was trembling, her body was drenched from rain, sweat, tears. Maddie could see the pale skin of her arms glistening. She reached her arms out toward them, palms out, fingers pointed to the ground. In front of her lay a shard of glass that had come from one of the broken windows. At that moment, Maddie noticed it was stained with blood.

Grabbing the flashlight from Finn's hands, Maddie pointed it directly at Rebecca, who recoiled from the bright light. At this point, they all noticed for the first time that Rebecca was not drenched from the rainstorm—her veins were split open from wrist to elbow, and her body was covered in blood. The entire time Abigail had been telling her story, life was slowly draining from Rebecca's body.

Abigail sprung across the room and grabbed her sister. Tearing the scarf from her neck, Abigail made a feeble attempt to stop the flow of blood.

"Call an ambulance!" Abigail shrieked. "Do something!" Rebecca tried to pull away from her; the women struggled back and forth. Through Maddie's tears and in the shadowy room, it almost looked like they were dancing.

Finn ran over to Rebecca, pulling off his belt, and used it as a tourniquet on one of her arms. He ripped the scarf from

Abigail's hands and pulled it tight around the other arm. He spoke in a calm voice. "Hold on, Rebecca. It doesn't have to end like this. You've got to look at me. Do it for Cordelia. If she's still out there, she's gonna need her mother. You gotta hold on for me, okay?"

Abigail was sobbing and cradling her sister's head as Rebecca seemed to drift away. It occurred to Maddie then, in a moment of morbid absurdity, that it was the first time she had ever seen them embrace.

In the distance, the sirens of police cruisers grew louder. Tires crunched up the gravel path to Ravenswood. Hopefully, it wasn't too late. If they got Rebecca to the hospital quickly, she could be taken care of. Everything could be taken care of, Maddie was sure of it.

Minutes later, Sully stepped through the door with his gun drawn. "Alright, everyone stay right where you are. Jesus H. Christ, what the hell is going on in here? Is everyone okay? Someone had better start talking right now."

Maddie said in loud, panting sobs, "My aunt Rebecca . . . she . . . she . . . You have to help her. She needs an ambulance."

Maddie looked over at Finn for help, dizzy with confusion. When he stood up, he was covered in blood.

"Finnegan O'Malley, you have the right to remain silent," Garrett Sullivan barked as he wrenched Finn's arms behind his back. "I knew I should have listened to Kate Endicott when she told me you were nothin' but trouble. First, you go after the daughter, now the mother. I shoulda put you away when I had the chance."

"Sully, no!" Maddie screamed. "He's trying to help us. He's saving my aunt. She . . . she did this to herself. We need to get her to a hospital now!" Sully reluctantly released his grasp on Finn.

Just then, a team of men entered the room: EMTs, firemen, and policemen. After they removed Rebecca from the room, Finn filled the authorities in on the details.

Maddie went to her mother, who was slumped on the floor, sobbing uncontrollably. She put her arms around her and helped her to her feet.

"My sister . . . please . . . I didn't mean to—don't let anything happen to her. She's my sister," she cried to the EMTs as they placed warm blankets around both her and Maddie's shoulders.

Emotions surged through Maddie's body—at one moment, nausea, and the next, crippling sadness. She walked over to the shattered window, gripping the blanket tightly around her, shaking more from the events that had just taken place than the chill of the night. Headlights swirled below her, creating a sense of vertigo. Maddie braced herself against the rotting sill to keep from falling. Then Finn was at her side, his warm hand on the small of her back. His touch felt familiar somehow. Right. He whispered something about the EMTs taking her mother outside to make sure that she was okay. Maddie nodded, finding it difficult to absorb what had just occurred, still focusing on the mosaic of lights below her.

Maddie stayed at the window a few moments more, and behind all of the swarms of activity, the flashing lights, the sirens, the commotion, and the sea of uniforms, she saw movement in the shadows. There in the blue, white, and red flashes of emergency lights, Maddie thought she saw the twirl of a skirt and then a glimpse of long red hair. Perhaps it was the flashing lights reflected off the raindrops, playing tricks on her eyes, but as she watched, she was sure she saw Cordelia and Rebecca, mother and daughter, reunited, dancing. And then just as suddenly as they had appeared, their images disappeared into the shivering trees.

Maddie smiled.

# Chapter 29

## INGUZ

### EARTH - POTENTIAL

*A Time When All Loose Strings Are Tied; Freedom
to Move in New Direction*

### JUNE

"Everything comes full circle. Life is lived in a series of cycles," Tess once told Maddie when she was a little girl, curled up like a cat on Tess's large quilted bed. Now those words rang loudly in her ears, as Maddie realized that through all of her running around Hawthorne, fighting with her mother, looking into Cordelia's disappearance, spending time with Reed, Tess had been slipping away from them all. The morning after that horrible night in Ravenswood, Maddie shuffled into the kitchen, still in a fog of sleep, and saw fresh grief streaked across her mother's face. Though not a word passed between them, Maddie knew that the worst had happened: Tess was finally granted her life's wish—to leave Hawthorne forever. While Rebecca began her recovery, Tess had passed away.

When the will was read, Tess had left money for Maddie to go away to school. It was her dying wish for Maddie to leave Hawthorne and start a new cycle far from this town. How could she possibly object? Besides, leaving this town and going away to boarding school would give her the time and space to deal with everything she'd been through over the past year. It would give her a chance to heal.

It was a pale, unseasonably cool day in early June that Tess Martin was put into the earth, laid to rest for all eternity.

Maddie stood at the gravesite, welcoming words of support and acknowledging the kindness of people who had come to pay their respects. She tightly clasped her mother's hand, giving her support and deriving her own comfort from her steady presence.

Maddie tried to be cordial as Kate and the rest of the Sisters of Misery pressed their cool cheeks to hers, all showing the appropriate amount of sorrow.

She accepted their condolences, for what else could one do at a time like this? But in her heart, she was unwilling to forgive them for their part in Cordelia's final days in Hawthorne. They may not have been directly involved with Cordelia's disappearance, but in her mind, they were still guilty. Cordelia and Rebecca's blood was on their hands. What they did to Cordelia may not have ended her life, but it did, in fact, set in motion a chain of events that destroyed the bond between mother and daughter, between sister and sister.

*She was my sister.*

Kate pressed her lips to Maddie's cheek and whispered, "If there's anything . . ."

Maddie nodded. Kate hesitated for a moment and looked into her eyes, searching for something.

"Maddie," she said as she leaned in closely, a faint smile tugging at the corners of her mouth like a cat watching a mouse squirm right before it pounced. "Maybe you can't remember that night because you don't want to. But I remember." She looked over her shoulder at the girls. "We all do. So you can run off to boarding school and try to start over, put this all behind you. But deep down, you know that you're a part of us—a part of Hawthorne and the Sisters of Misery. You always will be. The choice is up to you, Crane. Do what thou wilt."

Maddie resisted the urge to slap Kate across the face. "*Do what thou wilt*, Kate? Have you decided to lead the Sisterhood into black magic?"

Kate held Maddie's gaze for a long time. She reached up and brushed a strand of Maddie's hair back from her forehead, eyeing the spot where Maddie had been struck by the rock. Maddie knew instantly that Kate was the one who had struck her that night out on Misery Island "Fine, Maddie. Run away, run away from all of us. Just like your . . ."—she leaned in closely and hissed the last word into Maddie's ear—"*sister*."

Maddie's eyes went wide with shock. *How does she know?*

Kate gave a saccharine smile and said smugly, "What can I say, Maddie? Payback's a witch."

With that, Kate turned and joined the rest of the girls. Maddie hated that even after everything that had happened, Kate was still able to get under her skin and ultimately, get the last word. Did Kate really know that Maddie and Cordelia were sisters? Or was she referring to Cordelia finally being initiated into the Sisters of Misery? It was just one more piece of the puzzle that Maddie didn't have the strength or desire to put together.

Looking around at the memorial service, Maddie understood why Abigail hadn't wanted to get the police involved. Their family saga became the big news of the moment. There were people present at the memorial services who Maddie had never seen before—people more curious about the rumors of the tragedy that had occurred at The Witches' Castle than concerned about Maddie's family. It was sure to become part of the local lore: months after a teenager goes missing, the crazy mother of the missing girl slits her wrists in The Witches' Castle just before the demolition of the asylum. The only witnesses were the sister, the niece, and one of the main suspects in her daughter's disappearance. Meanwhile, the grandmother dies alone at home.

It had all the makings of one of the many legends of Hawthorne. Was it a crime of passion? Did Rebecca try to kill herself out of guilt? Was she responsible for her daughter's disappearance? Was Cordelia a runaway or a murder victim? All were good questions—great questions, in fact. Questions that would probably remain unsolved.

Both Reed and Finn attended the service. Maddie stole a glance at them during the service, such a contrast to each other. Blondhaired Reed, with his sexy stubble and broad shoulders, appeared rattled and sleep-deprived. And then there was Finn, dark-haired, handsome, troubled. His hands clasped respectfully in front of his crisp suit, his face unreadable, eyes downcast. She was bonded to both of them by a force greater than she ever could have imagined.

"Maddie," said Reed as he finally made his way over to her. "How are you doing?"

"I'm fine, Reed," she said in a clipped tone.

"I don't—I can't really think of anything to say, except that I'm sorry. I'm so incredibly sorry for your loss," he said softly. Despite the moment they'd shared on the boat, Maddie didn't feel the same warmth and affection she'd felt—or imagined she'd felt—for him a few weeks ago. His feelings for her had never been real—they'd been a favor to the Sisters of Misery.

"I'm sorry for yours as well," Maddie said coldly.

"I don't . . . wait, what are you talking about?" Reed asked hesitantly, the pupils of his deep blue eyes grew slightly wider.

"Your loss. Your baby," Maddie snapped. "The one you fathered with Cordelia. The one you gave her money to get rid of. Or maybe you just gave her the cash to disappear so she wouldn't cause you any more embarrassment than she already had. I'm sorry for *that*, Reed. Oh, and I'm sorry that you failed to do your job and keep me occupied so that I wouldn't find out what happened to my cousin. I'm sorry about so many things, Reed, that I can't decide which one I'm *most* sorry about."

"N-No, no, you don't—you don't understand . . ."

"No, Reed, *you* don't understand," Maddie continued. "I put my trust in you. Cordelia put her trust in you. I don't understand how you could take advantage of my cousin like that and then turn around and lie to me about it."

Reed looked around uncomfortably. "I know how it looks, but I swear, Maddie. I—I've made mistakes before, but not like this. It's not what you think."

"What I think, Reed, is that you're pathetic. I'm sorry that my cousin had anything to do with you, and I'm sorry," Maddie spat, "that I made the same mistake as Cordelia. Luckily, I know how to learn from my mistakes. Unfortunately, Cordelia wasn't as lucky."

Maddie didn't wait for a response. She walked away, ending the conversation on her terms for a change.

৪১

Maddie walked down the slope of the hill, away from the burial ground. She had to pass right by the crimson brick monster of Ravenswood on her way back home. It no longer scared her—it seemed to be smiling at her, pleased that its mysteries were finally made known and that it possessed new secrets, secrets about her own family. But Maddie didn't care anymore. It was all behind her. It was time to move on.

Maddie saw Finn standing in front of the faces in the wall, his hand resting on the fourth face, the one that had an uncanny resemblance to Cordelia.

"Don't you know that it's bad luck to touch them?" Maddie said, smiling at him.

He shrugged. "It'd be pretty hard not to touch them when I'm carving them out."

"You? You're the one who's been carving the faces in the wall for all of these years?" Maddie said, unbelieving.

"How old do you think I am, Maddie? Two hundred? These faces have been here a long time, my dear. And I'm not that old."

"So then . . . ? I mean . . . why?" she asked.

"I took over doing this for my dad. And he took over for his dad, and so on and so on. You see, my great, great, great grandmother's maiden name was Pickering." He paused, waiting for the look of surprise to cross her face. "Yes, *that* Pickering. So, you see, I'm a descendent of the Pickering sisters, the so-called witches of Misery Island.

"My ancestors have been taking care of the town properties since the town was settled, so we've had access to all parts of Hawthorne. That's how we've been able to carve their faces without being caught for all of these years. We didn't do it for a curse or any of that garbage going around town. It was just a way to honor them. To make people in this town remember how badly they were treated. And it was my decision to add Cordelia's face because I think she was treated the same way that the Pickering sisters were treated. And well, I guess partly because I was hoping that one day, she would have become a part of my family. A part of my own history."

Stepping closer to Finn, Maddie gently kissed him on the cheek. "Thank you," she whispered. "Cordelia was very lucky to have someone care about her the way that you did."

"The way I still do." He corrected her and then looked away, not wanting her to see his eyes fill up with tears. "You don't stop loving someone after they're gone."

Maddie thought of Tess and of Cordelia and nodded her head. "You're right. You never stop."

"So, Stanton Prep, huh?" Finn said with a wink. "You really going away to school, or is this just an excuse to look for Cordelia?"

Maddie laughed. "Maybe I can do both."

She turned back to the faces because she knew that it would be a long time before she'd see them again. Hopefully, the next time she'd be looking at them would be with Cordelia at her side. "So it looks like you can stop feeling guilty about not walking Cordelia home. Turns out she got home safe and sound. There's nothing you could have done any differently. You can finally move on . . . without the guilt."

"Maybe," he said tentatively. "But I'm still responsible. I'm the one who gave her that money."

"You gave her the money?" Maddie was in shock. Maybe Reed *was* telling the truth after all, she thought suddenly, painfully.

"All I knew was that she needed the money, and I gave it to her. It was her decision. I told her I'd support her no matter what she wanted to do. But if I really was a father, I would have heard from her by now, don't you think? Maybe she was just playing me to get some cash to get out of town. Who knows? With that cousin of yours, everything's a mystery," he said, eyes brimming with tears. "I really did—still do—love her. And I don't think she's gone for good. I think she's going to come back. One of these days."

Maddie nodded solemnly. It seemed that with every answer, there were many more questions raised.

Finn put his arm around her and walked them down the path away from the hospital.

"Take care of her for me," Maddie said then about the carving of Cordelia.

"I will," he said. "Take care of yourself. It's a dangerous world out there."

"Not as dangerous as it is in a small town like this," she replied.

A wide grin spread across Finn's face. "I guess you're right about that. Oh, and don't tell anyone about the carvings—or the money, for that matter. I figured I'd let you in on some of my secrets since I know so many of yours. Are we even?"

"I'll take 'em to my grave."

Finn shook his head sadly. "There's no reason anyone needs to know about these things. It won't do anyone any good. Not anymore."

"Well," she said, "I don't think I'm going to be coming back to Hawthorne any time soon, so I guess this is good-bye."

"Good-bye, Madeline."

"And, thank you for everything, Finn," Maddie said. "For watching out for Cordelia and, I guess, for me, too."

"You don't have to thank me, Madeline. I always liked watching out for you girls. Even if it was only for a midnight swim," he said with a wink.

Maddie's eyes widened, and a smile spread across her face. *He* was their mysterious midnight watcher. He was always there . . . watching, protecting. "What about the rumors of avenging your ancestors? Is there any truth to *that* legend?"

Finn smiled and seemed to roll the idea around in his mind for a moment. "*In war, personal revenge maintains silence*," he said, smiling, and then added, "Nietzsche."

She laughed, realizing how much he knew about her and Cordelia and the games they played. "Ah, very impressive, Mr. O'Malley." He took a mock bow. "But you know

Mr. Shakespeare once said, 'Kindness, ever nobler than revenge.' "

"Yes, but Shakespeare never had the pleasure of meeting Kate Endicott," Finn deadpanned.

Maddie laughed again, then Finn nodded, signaling goodbye. Without another word, he turned and continued down the path.

She watched Finn until he turned the corner and then said under her breath, partly to herself, partly to Tess, and partly to Cordelia, wherever she was, "And as Hamlet said in his final speech, 'The rest is silence.' "

# Chapter 30

## BERKANA

## BIRTH

*Promise of Rebirth and New Beginnings*

Maddie entered the house on Mariner's Way for the last time. She walked over to her mother, who was sitting at Tess's place at the kitchen table, staring out the bay window into the backyard. Maddie covered her mother's hand with her own and squeezed. Abigail refused to look at her—perhaps she was angry at Maddie for leaving her, abandoning her to contend with this town alone. Allowing her to live with her memories, her ghosts.

Now that Tess was gone and Rebecca was back at Fairview, it was time for Maddie to leave Hawthorne and to finally move on. She had been accepted at Stanton Prep, a boarding school in Maine that was far away from all of the craziness of Hawthorne and the Sisters of Misery. She was planning on moving there for the summer to work and make some extra money for books and living expenses, though most of her tuition had already been set aside for her in Tess's will.

The house was too quiet without the endless, usually nonsensical chatter that came from Tess. Without her there as a distraction, it was just Maddie and her mother, face to face with all the unanswered questions, all the words that needed to be said, but were not. Maybe they could start over from a fresh place—they had all the time in the world to work things out.

"I found this in the basement," Abigail said quietly. She pulled a smooth stone out of her pocket and handed it over to Maddie. *Another rune stone. Where do they keep coming from?*

The stone was marked with a large **B**.

Maddie took it from her mother's hand and started turning the cool stone over and over and then slipped it into her pocket. "I wonder what it means," Abigail said without meeting her daughter's eyes. "I know how you and Cordelia and Rebecca used to play with those things even Tess used to see meaning in those silly rocks. Then again, Tess saw meaning in everything."

They both laughed.

"Mom," she said. "I feel guilty that we weren't here when Tess passed away. I mean, if we were here, maybe there was a chance we could have done something. It just breaks my heart that she was all by herself. No one should have to die alone."

"Oh, honey," she said softly, draping her arm around her daughter. "She wasn't alone. We were here when she passed. The coroner said the time of death was 10:30 PM. We were just across the hall from her. She wasn't alone."

Maddie felt a strange tingling sensation come over her body, and it must have registered on her face. Could she have imagined seeing Tess sitting up in bed that night, talking to her on the night that Rebecca escaped to Ravenswood? When Tess told Maddie that Rebecca had returned to her "garden"? Could Maddie have imagined it all?

"What's wrong, Maddie? What is it?" Abigail looked concerned.

Maddie shook her head. "Nothing." Maybe when more time had passed, Maddie would tell her mother about her last conversation with Tess. She held up the stone. "I think that if this is a sign from Rebecca, Cordelia, or Tess, I'll bet it means forgiveness."

Abigail's eyes met Maddie's, and she grasped her hands.

"I never meant to hurt her—or you, for that matter. Honestly, Maddie, you have to believe me."

"I know, Mom, I know." And Maddie did believe her.

"If I could take that night back, I would in a minute," she said. But she was asking forgiveness of the wrong person. Forgiveness was something that only one person could give her. And right now, that seemed impossible. "And you! To learn that Cordelia was really your half-sister . . ." her voice trailed off.

"It explains a lot, Mom," Maddie said, smiling weakly. "At least I understand why it was so hard for you to have them back here with us. I just wish you could have told me."

"There are a lot of things I wish I had done differently, Maddie," she said, tears now appearing. "You have no idea." And with that, Abigail pushed herself away from the table, stopped to embrace Maddie quickly, giving her a quick kiss on top of her head, and then turned toward the staircase.

"Mom," Maddie said. Abigail stopped and looked back at her. They held each other's gaze for a moment, then Maddie nodded her head. Abigail nodded hers slowly in return and continued up to her bedroom, quietly closing the door behind her.

That was their good-bye.

∞

Pacing from room to room, unsure of what she was looking for, Maddie decided to go down to the basement, to see the last place anyone had seen Cordelia alive.

Maddie walked down the steep, narrow staircase. The air grew colder. Dust and dirt filled her nostrils. A single-strand light bulb suspended from the low ceiling strained wearily against the darkness of the cellar.

Moving forward into the subterranean room, the sounds of the house and street were muffled. Maddie picked her way around old furniture and trunks. The room was cluttered with leftover inventory from Rebecca's shop. Crates overflowed with gardening paraphernalia and tools. She spotted an open bag of rune stones and crystals. Tess must have come down here and grabbed them, hiding them around the house like they were Easter eggs. The thought of Tess down here made her cringe. An old woman like Tess shouldn't have been wandering around a cold, dank basement amidst the assortment of tools and sharp objects.

Maddie made her way over to the darkest corner of the basement where the stones of the wall were mottled and darkly stained. She brushed her fingertips along the jagged crevices, trying to imagine that night. It was still hard for her to understand it all. Abigail's years of hatred and resentment toward Cordelia and Rebecca; finding out that Cordelia was really her half-sister, the product of an affair her father had with Abigail's own sister. All of these things had built up within her mother's mind and mixed with her intense desire to fit into Hawthorne's elite society—all of it had caused her to snap.

Shoving Cordelia against the wall was unforgivable. But Maddie knew that the minute Abigail realized what she had done, saw the blood on her cousin's face, and gotten her senses back, she regretted ever hurting Cordelia, both physically and mentally.

If Cordelia really did run away—angry at Rebecca for lying to her all these years, angry at Maddie for Misery Island, angry at Abigail for lashing out at her, angry at Reed or

Finn (or whoever the "beautiful boy" was) for the baby that may or may not have been growing inside of her—perhaps, one day, she would forgive and come back to them, give them the answers that they all so desperately needed.

Maddie turned to go back upstairs to finish packing for her transfer to Stanton Prep. Placing her foot on the first stair of the basement steps, something caught her eye. Maddie turned, half expecting to see Cordelia sitting there cross-legged, smiling. But it was only another stone, this one marked with the letter *M*. Surprised that she hadn't tripped over the oddly placed stone, Maddie picked it up and ran her finger along the etched letter before shoving it into her pocket along with the other one that Abigail had given her earlier and continuing up to the foyer.

Then, there came a soft tapping at the door. Maddie turned to see a familiar shadow in the pane of glass that ran alongside the door.

Reed.

She opened the door angrily. What could he possibly have to say to her now?

Before she could open her mouth, Reed said quickly, "I never slept with her, with Cordelia. But yes, I did give her money."

"Why?" Maddie was in shock. Had Cordelia been lying to both Reed and Finn as an excuse to get money to leave town? Was she ever really pregnant?

"You could say I was cleaning up after my asshole little brother's mistake. He—they—well, she said that the baby was his. Trevor needed help making the situation go away. And I wanted to help Cordelia get a fresh start."

"She told you about all this? When?" Maddie was so confused. *Why would Cordelia ever sleep with Trevor? Why didn't she tell Maddie?*

"Right before Halloween during one of our tutoring prep

sessions. I made the mistake of not reporting the incident because I was trying to protect my brother."

"Incident? What do you mean, incident? Protect Trevor from what?"

Reed sighed heavily, running his hand through his hair. "Rape charges. He forced himself on Cordelia. It's happened before, and he's gone to juvenile detention, but if it ever got out that he'd done it again, they'd press full charges. He could go to jail."

She turned, trying to piece all of it together, and walked into the living room, collapsing on the sofa, willing herself not to cry.

Reed followed her and sat down next to her on the loveseat, covering her hands with his own. "I really cared about Cordelia, and I wanted to help her in any way that I could. But even though Trevor is a spoiled asshole, he's still my brother. But I care about you in a different way, Maddie. And I can't act on those feelings. If I was a few years younger or you were a few years older, things would be different."

Maddie tried to control all the emotions that swirled through her body. Everything was falling into place and finally making sense, and instead of relief, she felt completely overwhelmed, as if she were floundering in the ocean, being hit by wave after wave after wave. Trying to tread water and not get pulled down by the undertow.

Cordelia and Finn were together. Finn thought that he was the father of the baby. She couldn't tell Finn the truth because she was afraid of what he'd think of her or what he'd do to Trevor after he learned about the rape. Reed was trying to help her through the whole situation while protecting his brother.

And he'd kept her secret—as well as the evil truth about his younger brother—even though it led to his own downfall.

Was this the "secret information" Kate had in the envelope that night out on Misery? Maddie knew that Kate would never tell. Even though she said it was empty, perhaps only she and Cordelia knew the contents of that envelope. It was just one of those things that she had on people—her way of making everyone do what she wanted.

"Why are you telling me this now?" Maddie asked.

"Because I know that you're leaving Hawthorne, and I couldn't stand having you think those horrible things about me. I knew it was a risk—that you might go to the police and that you might never speak to me again. But I had to take it. I couldn't let you leave without knowing the truth."

"Why didn't Cordelia go to the police?"

"That," Reed sighed, "is a good question for Cordelia when you find her."

"You think she's out there somewhere?" Maddie asked hopefully.

"I'd bet my life on it," he said, smiling. "And I have a feeling that she'll find us when she's ready to come home."

Reed reached over and gathered Maddie into a long hug. She held back the urge to cry into his shoulder, to let him hold her. Her emotions were all over the place. She had so many things to resolve internally. But for now, she had to get ready to leave.

They stood and walked to the door.

"I hope you'll keep in touch," Reed said softly. "You know, I hear that Stanton Prep's English program is pretty intense."

Maddie smiled up at him. "Of course I will. Someone needs to help me with my writing assignments." He ruffled her hair and then turned to leave.

"Reed, wait," Maddie said quickly. As he turned, she reached up and kissed him gently. She pulled back for a moment and looked into his eyes, and when he didn't move away, she kissed him again passionately.

He gently pushed her back, trying to restrain his surging emotions. "I *will* wait for you. I can promise you that." He smiled down at her. "Be good."

Reed turned and walked out the door. He stopped at the end of the pathway and turned back to smile and wave at Maddie. She smiled and closed the door, breathless and lost in the incredible feeling of kissing Reed Campbell one last time.

&#8723;

Just as she was taking one last run through the house to make sure she had everything, Maddie heard something scurry up above her head. She crept up the staircase, hesitating on the first landing, and then continued up to the third level of the house, taking care not to interrupt her mother's nap. Tess's door was shut tightly. Maddie didn't remember closing the door earlier when she'd made a final sweep of all the rooms. As she turned the handle of the door, Tess's faint voice echoed in her ears.

*She likes the window open. The girl in the basement is gonna be so sad when we leave her. Why does she cry all night long?*

Maddie pressed forward into the room and was met with a rush of cold air. The window overlooking the ocean was open, lace curtains snapping and flaring in the breeze. She strode across the room and tugged the window shut.

The taxi wasn't scheduled to pick her up for another few hours. Maddie collapsed onto Tess's bed and stared out at the ocean as her grandmother had day after day, night after night. Maddie felt so close to her, the scent of her Tea Rose perfume still lingering, as if her grandmother were standing above her, her frail hand lowering to smooth her hair back. Maddie tried to recall one of the last coherent conversations she'd had with her grandmother before she fell victim to dementia. They were sitting downstairs, and Tess had been telling her again that she'd been dreaming of stones.

*Stones*, Maddie thought, her eyes drifting closed. Soon, Maddie had that sinking, almost falling sensation as she drifted into sleep, only to be pulled quickly upward as if yanked by an unseen force. She looked around to see what had interrupted her midday nap and then sank back into fitful sleep.

∞

*The rock hit her squarely on the forehead. Maddie stumbled backwards in shock and felt herself fall into the soft sand. When she finally opened her eyes, she saw a figure standing above her, holding a large jagged rock. It was Kate Endicott.*

*"I hope you weren't planning on leaving us," Kate snapped. "The fun is just starting. Come on!" She yanked Maddie to a standing position. They made their way back to the bonfire, Kate dragging Maddie with one hand and a large bucket of water in the other. Maddie saw Cordelia's lanky shape through the flames, which appeared to lap at her arms and legs.*

*"Girls, now that Cordelia has appeased the elements, it is time for us to do the same," Kate ordered.*

*Maddie looked at the other girls quizzically. This had never been part of the ceremony. Were they all going to spend the night on the island?*

*Kate walked over to Darcy and placed the bucket of ocean water in front of her. "You are Water." Kate reached down into the bucket, and Darcy cringed, bracing herself for whatever Kate had planned. With a soaked hand, she anointed Darcy as if with holy water.*

"*Hannah, you are Air.*" Kate whispered something into Hannah's ear. She looked at Kate and nodded.

"*Bridget, you are Fire.*" She whispered something to Bridget and handed her a long, slender piece of driftwood.

"*And Maddie, you are Earth.*" She walked over to Maddie with a large, sharp stone. Maddie shook when she saw the stone, preparing herself for another blow, but relaxed when Kate simply slipped it into her hand.

Behind the flames, Cordelia's eyes grew wide.

Kate smiled. "*Let the* second *part of our Sisterhood ceremony begin.*"

She yelled out, "AIR!"

Hannah quickly tore Cordelia's jacket off her, leaving her exposed to the elements with just a thin peasant blouse on, and threw it high up into the air so that it was carried off into the night by the gusty island wind.

Kate then yelled, "FIRE and WATER!"

Bridget set her stick into the bonfire in front of Cordelia until it caught and then raised it in front of Cordelia's face. Cordelia shook in horror and started screaming. Darcy hoisted up the bucket of water and stood next to Bridget. Maddie watched, confused, but couldn't make herself move from the spot. It was happening so quickly and methodically, it seemed almost choreographed.

Bridget brought the flame closer and closer to Cordelia, and suddenly, the blouse and part of her hair caught on fire. She began shrieking and crying, but before the flames licked her skin, Darcy doused them with the bucket of water.

Maddie watched helplessly as Cordelia shivered uncontrollably from fear as much as the frigid water and whipping winds. Then suddenly, it was her turn.

"Earth!" Kate shouted. Maddie looked down at her hand and realized that she'd been gripping the heavy stone so hard that it had almost pierced the skin.

*Everyone looked at Maddie expectantly. In a moment of pure disgust and horror, Maddie realized what Kate wanted her to do. She was supposed to hurl the stone at Cordelia.*

*"NO!" she shouted, backing away from them, crying. "No no no no no no."*

*Kate flew over to her side. "Maddie, the ceremony won't end until you finish it."*

*"I won't," Maddie cried. "I can't!"*

*"Maddie, you can do this the easy way or the hard way. Don't be a coward! Why are you protecting her? You know you hate her just as much as we do, or else you wouldn't be here. Do it! NOW! DO WHAT THOU WILT!" She spat her hot words into Maddie's face, their breath mixing in the cold darkness. "If you don't do it, you are gone, you are nothing. You and your pathetic mother will have no place in Hawthorne."*

*Maddie looked at Kate. Her pale blue eyes appeared almost red, demonic in the reflection of the fire as she waited for Maddie to respond.*

*"Then I guess we'll just have to let Cordelia go. I know that Mr. Campbell is probably expecting her. Tell me, it must be hard to have such a beautiful cousin, such a perfectly beautiful face. Flawless, really. You know, if she stays here, you'll start being referred to as 'the ugly one.' That will be hard for you, won't it?"*

*Maddie looked past Kate at Cordelia. Despite the brutal night, she still looked beautiful, haunted. Rage pulsed through Maddie, though she wasn't sure where to direct it.*

*"Maddie," Kate hissed. "You* do *know that we can start this entire night over and* you *can be the guest of honor. All I have to do is say the word, and you can take your cousin's place. Is that what you want?" Maddie continued to avoid her gaze, then Kate suddenly lowered her voice to a growl. "Cordelia even suggested it to me on our way out here. She*

*knew that she was the one who was going to end up on the is-land, and she practically begged me to pick you. 'Pick Maddie,' she said. 'She doesn't even like you girls. And she hates you especially, Kate.' Now, is that the type of slut that you are willing to sacrifice everything for?"*

Maddie walked toward Cordelia. Her cousin's eyes widened in confusion and fear. She would throw the stone at her cousin, and that would be the end of it. She knew Kate was lying, but she just wanted all of it to be over. To put the night behind them. Cordelia would be a part of the Sisters of Misery, and they would go on like none of this had ever happened.

Maddie looked at Cordelia's shoulder and knew if she aimed it there, it wouldn't hurt as much, even though she knew that Kate wanted her to hit Cordelia squarely in the face. Maddie drew back her arm and threw the rock at Cordelia's shoulder as hard as she could. But as soon as the stone left her hand, Maddie could see—almost in slow motion—Cordelia cringe and turn her head in the direction of the stone. Before Maddie could yell out for her to move, it smashed into Cordelia's forehead, and she slumped forward, blood flowing from the gash.

Kate yelled in mock surprise. "What the hell *did you do, Maddie?"*

Maddie backed up as the other girls looked at her with a mixture of awe and disgust.

"I did what you told me to do, Kate! You . . . you . . . I didn't . . . I only . . . you—you said," Maddie stammered incoherently.

Cordelia was bleeding heavily, and Darcy went over and put a towel over the angry gash on her forehead.

Kate said to the other girls, "I never said anything like that. God, Maddie, you really do have issues."

She turned, afraid of what she did, afraid of what she was

*capable of, afraid that she had killed her own cousin. And
then the night swallowed her up into its blackness. Maddie
screamed loud, louder than the pounding surf, "NO!"*

∞

"No!!!" Waking suddenly, Maddie looked around, trying
to get her bearings, desperately trying to catch her breath.
Had all of this really happened? Maddie was the one who
betrayed Cordelia? She was worse than everyone else because she was Cordelia's sister. Lying there for a few moments, Maddie knew it wasn't only a dream. Tears streamed
down the sides of her face as the weight of what really happened that night finally hit her. Abigail hadn't been responsible for the gash on Cordelia's head. It was Maddie's doing.
Even if Cordelia hadn't been told the truth about her real father, Maddie knew deep down that Cordelia would never return to Hawthorne, to a family that betrayed her at every
turn. That is why Maddie had to find Cordelia on her own,
and bring back her sister.

They had each hurt Cordelia in their own way—Abigail,
with words; Rebecca, with lies; and Madeline, with jealousy
and fear. Tess's dreams of stones were true after all, and
Maddie prayed that Tess never knew the horrible truth behind them, that she never connected her dreams with what
happened out on Misery Island.

All of the pieces of the puzzle had finally come together.
It was time for her to leave Hawthorne—only this time, it
would be for good. It was, as they say in fairy tales, the end.

# Epilogue

"Crane, you've got mail," the RA said, knocking at Maddie's door, and slipped the letters underneath. She'd been sitting and staring at the blank screen of her computer. It blinked back at her, taunting, yearning for black characters to march across the screen like ants. Her first writing assignment was an article on dealing with the loss of a loved one, as if the overwhelming emotions she had experienced recently could be tied up neatly in two thousand words or less.

Maddie leaned back in her chair, closed her eyes, and listened to the sounds and chattering that filled the dormitory. Suddenly, she heard something tumble onto the hardwood floor. She looked down and saw two onyx rune stones lying at her feet. *This must have been the jacket I was wearing the day I left Hawthorne,* she thought. She picked them off the floor, running her fingers over the etched letters. She clicked over to a Web browser page of Nordic rune markings and their meanings.

Maddie scanned down the page to the letter *B*. It meant

*Birkano, the symbol of the birch goddess.* She suddenly had an image of Cordelia tied to the tree on Misery Island. The Sacred Birch in the grove on Misery. She continued to read, *rebirth . . . new beginnings . . . renewal . . . freedom.*

Her eyes then traveled down the page to the letter *M— Ehwal, the horse . . . travel . . . movement . . . forgiveness.*

It couldn't have been a coincidence that these stones somehow found their way to her just as she was embarking on an essay about the many tragedies she'd endured over the past year. Maddie believed they were a message from Tess. She smiled, realizing that if ever there was a way for spirits to communicate from beyond, then Tess would be the one to find it. It was the first time in many months that Maddie felt a sense of peace—the weight of her guilt was lifting off her each day, stone by stone by stone.

Maddie squeezed her eyes shut and tried to get a strong visual image of Cordelia. Not the girl tied to a tree, lifeless and broken—the person who haunted Maddie's dreams— but the old Cordelia, the one who came to Hawthorne filled with light and happiness and a generous spirit. She had a half smile, and her eyes shone with amusement. Her red hair fell in thick tangles down her back. Maddie clung to these details, this clearly defined picture of Cordelia, because she feared she might never have it again.

Maddie's eyes fluttered open, swelling with tears as she placed the rune stones next to her keyboard. This assignment will have to wait, she thought.

She got up and grabbed the mail that had been shoved under her door. Maddie smiled when she saw the return address on the first envelope. It was a letter from home.

*Dear Maddie,*
   *I hope that you are well. Your aunt Rebecca is making great strides in her recovery. I think that the im-*

*pact of the horrific events that occurred at Ravens-
wood actually helped snap her back into reality. She's
been talking with grief counselors and psychologists
on a daily basis, and they have been helping her with
various types of medication. I've even gone to visit her
a few times. I know that is what Tess would have
wanted me to do.*

*It seems that the plans for The Endicott Hotel have
been halted. I didn't realize that your friend Finn and
his father were so involved in Hawthorne's Historical
Society. It seems that they've pushed for the Ravenswood Asylum and Fort Glover to be declared historic
properties and have stopped any future plans for the
luxury hotel to be erected on that site. It's just about
destroyed the Endicotts since they've put millions into
plans and contractors for the hotel. Plus, their investors are dropping like flies. There are whisperings
of illegal money transactions as well. I wouldn't be
surprised if they get indicted. It's like Tess always used
to say, "What goes around . . ."*

*Next time I see Finn, I'll have to thank him myself.
That'll put those Endicotts in their place.*

*In any case, I hope you decide to come home for
Thanksgiving. I've enclosed a letter that was left for you
(probably from someone who doesn't have your address up at school). I had half a mind to open it and
make sure it's not from that Reed Campbell, though
that's not my decision to make. In any case, I miss you
very much, and I hope that all is going well for you up
at Stanton.*

*Love,*
*Mom*

Just as Rebecca had predicted, Kate tried to send evil out

into the world, but it came back to her threefold. *Karma's a bitch*.

Opening up the second letter, Maddie wondered if it was from Reed, who kept in touch as often as he could. Or maybe it was from Finn, gloating over the fact that he was able to stop Kate's family from building the hotel, costing them millions. Maddie couldn't believe how he had managed to single-handedly bring down the Endicott family. And it was all in Cordelia's honor. She would be thrilled.

The letter was written in block letters, definitely a guy's handwriting. It was similar to the letters she'd received before from Finn, but there was no signature. Was that intentional? The hairs on the back of her neck stood on end as she scanned the brief note. It read:

> *MADDIE,*
> *CORDELIA IS ALIVE.*
> *SHE'S COMING FOR YOU.*
> *BE CAREFUL.*

After reading it several times, trying to discern the handwriting and the tone of the message, Maddie folded the paper and put it into her pocket. She walked back over to the computer screen and scrolled down to the reversed meanings of the stones. Chills went down her spine when she read the reversed meaning: *Your desire to escape is thwarted by many problems, obstacles, and false starts. Expect disturbing family news, especially involving a sibling . . .*

If Cordelia was alive, it would only be a matter of time until Maddie found her.

*Or*, Maddie thought with a shudder, *she finds me*.

Please turn the page for a sneak peak of
THE LOST SISTER,
available in Mass Market in September 2010
from Kensington.

# Chapter 1

## JUDGMENT

*The card signals great transformation, renewal,
change, rebirth, resurrection, making a final decision.
You cannot hide any longer, face what you have to
face, make that decision. Change. Time to summon
the past, forgive it, and let it go, begin to heal.*

Dear Diary,
  If it weren't for the little baby boy with the Coke-
bottle glasses, I would have killed my father by now.
The poison would be seeping into his veins effortlessly
with every sip of the herbal tea concoction that I made
especially for him. But the moment I saw that little
boy, my stepbrother . . . half brother . . . whatever—I
couldn't do it. It's not because I want Malcolm Crane
to live, not after what he's done to me and the lives of
all the women in my family, but because he has another life dependent on him: the life of an innocent little boy. And so, for that reason, I'll let him live.
  For now.
  No one knows me here. Even those I've left behind
in Hawthorne couldn't recognize me now. Besides, no
one would ever think to look for me up in the boon-

*docks of Maine. My hair, once a brilliant shade of red,
my most striking feature, has been dulled to a mousy
brown, courtesy of a sable-brown henna.*

*I often wonder if anyone has even noticed that I'm
gone, not that I really care. Everyone I trusted, everyone I loved has lied to me or let me down. I've always
felt like I was on my own. Now I know that to be true.*

*All I know is that I have to get back home to Cali-
fornia where I belong, and find some way to make it
back there by myself. But first things first. Someone
needs to be taught a lesson. And I'm not leaving until
everything—and everyone—has been taken care of.*

"One cup of passion fruit-lime green tea," Cordelia said
softly to the man behind the newspaper. She poured the tea
carefully, watching the leaves swirl in the bottom of the cup.
Rebecca had taught her to read the messages in the leaves,
not only once the cup was finished, but also as they swirled
into the delicate teacup. She tried not to read the warning in
the leaves. Once you knew where to look for certain signs, it
was hard not to see them in everything. And she could read
this message as clear as day: *Kill him.*

She looked at the little boy sitting across from his father.
He peered up at her face, which was half hidden behind her
long sheath of brown hair. She winked at him, causing him
to erupt into giggles. He couldn't be more than three or four.
Cordelia wondered where his mother was, who his mother
was. What would become of this little boy if she went ahead
with her plan: to pay Malcolm Crane back for all of his wrong-
doings? For deserting Maddie and Abigail, for impregnating
her mother and never taking responsibility for any of his
children back in Hawthorne, Massachusetts, and then simply
running off to Maine to start all over again. Cordelia wondered if he would desert this little boy as well. Maybe she

would be doing him a favor by stopping Malcolm Crane—the father she'd only known of for a very short time—from hurting anyone ever again.

"And for the little man?" she asked quietly. She waited for a glance from the man she now knew to be her father. The man that up until only a few minutes ago she had planned on killing in cold blood.

After leaving Hawthorne, she quickly made her way up to Maine where she knew that Malcolm had been living for more than a decade. Once she found him—which wasn't the hardest thing to do, since he was known for being not only the town drunk, but also one of the professors in the tiny community college—she shadowed his every move. She knew about all of the girls that he was sleeping with—students, assistant professors, barmaids. This was something that she was able to figure out very quickly. She crept into the back of his lectures, studying the man that was her biological father.

She noticed some similarities in their appearance. Although everyone always said that she was an exact replica of her mother—the fair, porcelain skin, the copper hair, the delicate features—she detected some traits that she inherited from her father. The husky, butterscotch voice, the intense, lavender-blue eyes, the lean, athletic build. These were all things that she—as well as many of the dreamy-eyed girls in his classroom—noticed right away. The only two places that he frequented besides his lecture halls and his home were the town pub and the coffee and tea shop across from the college.

She had watched Malcolm Crane in between his classes. She'd managed to get a job at the Maine Tea and Coffee Bean—the only place he frequented during the week—and served him almost daily, but he never showed any sign of recognition. He was flirtatious and friendly, but it was all on the surface. She truly believed that if there was anything good in him, he would recognize his own daughter. But then, sadly, he probably wouldn't even recognize Maddie and he had watched his little girl grow up and knew her to be his own. But even that didn't give him reason enough to stick around in Hawthorne, to stay with his wife and young daughter.

Everything that Cordelia had done up until this point had been meticulously planned. She had taken the rat poison from the storage room—there were so many boxes, she was sure that no one would miss it. By the time anyone realized that Malcolm Crane had been murdered, she would be long gone. They didn't even know her real name. Over the past few months, she'd made sure not to leave a mark. She lived like a ghost among mortals. She felt like she had died that night out on Misery Island and could only be brought back to life once she'd exacted her revenge. And the first one on her list was Malcolm Crane. But then this little boy had to come along and change everything.

"Danny, you heard the lady, did you want something to drink?" The little boy looked up and smiled at her and the toothy grin broke her heart.

"Milk, please," he lisped.

"Sure, right . . . milk," she stammered, backing away from the counter, feeling the rat poison burning in her apron pocket. She couldn't do it. Not with this little boy. No matter how much she blamed Malcolm Crane for everything that had gone wrong in her life up until this point—the lies from Rebecca, the return to Hawthorne, even the death of the man she believed to be her real father up until a few months ago, even though deep down she knew he had nothing to do with Simon LeClaire's death—she couldn't make this little boy, Daniel Crane, go through the pain of losing a parent. It was still too real and raw for her—too hard for someone her own age to deal with, let alone a little boy.

She backed up into another table and practically knocked over another waitress. "Hey, watch it, CeeCee." Cordelia steadied herself and turned to apologize to her coworker. She'd gone by CeeCee, a nickname given to her by the man she grew up thinking to be her father—the man that up until his untimely death from cancer was her true father. The man who cared for her as if she were his own flesh and blood, and who, a few horrible months ago, she discovered was not her real father. Her biological father was this man sitting in front of her. This waste of a human being. This horrible, selfish narcissist. He finally looked up at her. After months of her serving him his morning coffee and his afternoon tea, he actually made eye contact with her.

"Are you all right, darlin'?" A look of concern crossed Malcolm Crane's face, the lines around his eyebrows deepened. Despite his weather-beaten face, she could see why some girls in his classes hung on his every word and the waitresses at Maine Tea and Coffee Bean cooed about him looking like Robert Redford. Yet instead of the lusty feelings that his gaze seemed to evoke with everyone around her, she only felt nausea.

"I'm fine," she clipped. "I'll be back with the milk for your son."

He winked, rolled his newspaper up, and lightly bonked the little boy's head. "Say thank you to the pretty lady, Daniel."

"Thanks, pretty lady," the little boy whispered, and then giggled.

Cordelia knew in her heart that she couldn't go through with it. She couldn't take away this little boy's father. But that didn't mean she couldn't stick around long enough to make Malcolm Crane wish he was dead.

From behind the Formica counter, she saw a look of concern wash over Malcolm Crane's face. He scrunched up his forehead and peered more closely at the newspaper. Then he sat back and stared straight ahead for a few moments, looking as though he were very far away, while little Daniel busily colored the paper place mat with the café's crayons. Cordelia walked hesitantly back to the table, curious to learn what had caused this sudden shift in his mood. She placed the plastic cup in front of the young boy and tried to see what paper Malcolm had been reading.

It was the *Hawthorne Gazette*. Odd that he was still receiving news from home all the way up here in the boondocks. She prayed that it wasn't another article about her disappearance. By now she had managed to avoid the second glances and the quick looks of recognition, people trying to place her face, knowing that she looked familiar, but not quite sure from where. When she first left Hawthorne, she had chopped what was left of her hair and dyed it brown so that she could slip away easily. Redheads often commanded more attention than brunettes. But she couldn't change her features. People often called her beautiful, ethereal, even exquisite. She wondered how they'd describe her after she'd become a murderer.

Cordelia watched as Malcolm gathered up his son and left the coffee shop in a hurry. She rushed over to the empty table and grabbed the newspaper that was left behind in haste. Her eyes flicked down the page and a jolt of shock went through her body. There was an article about an ongoing fight between the Endicott family and the historical society of Hawthorne. Other neighboring towns of Salem, Marblehead, Beverly, and Swampscott were weighing in on the historical importance of the building. But that wasn't what caught Cordelia's attention. The article was written about all of the tragedies that occurred at Ravenswood Asylum throughout the years, especially the most recent one that took place only months ago.

Cordelia's fingers trembled as she read the story entitled

"Bloody Night at Ravenswood Remembered." She skimmed the story, picking out the most disturbing phrases.

> Rebecca LeClaire, one of the last inmates before the closing of the asylum, apprehended after apparent suicide attempt . . . Witnesses at the site were sister, Abigail Crane, niece, Maddie Crane, and local teen Finnegan O'Malley. Tess Martin, 82, passed away in her sleep that same night, unaware of the tragedy that had overtaken her family.

Cordelia inhaled deeply as she continued reading about what had happened in the wake of her disappearance. Since that night, there had been an ongoing fight over the property—how the Endicotts wanted to turn it into a luxury resort, capitalizing on the fright factor of its proximity to Salem, Massachusetts, and the witch trials, as well as all of the tragic legends that surround the place. The historical society had tied up any future projects with enough red tape until they could declare it a historic property.

Cordelia was hit by a wave of vertigo. The world spun around her, almost knocking her from her feet.

*I have to go back,* she thought. Something she thought she would never do.

"Easy there, CeeCee. Take a load off. You look like you're going to be sick." Her manager, Chris Markson, had come up behind her and noticed the color drained from her face. "Sit down, I'll get you some water."

Cordelia was used to getting this attention from the guys in her life. She knew that the girls were probably in the back gossiping about how she was being a drama queen and how unfair it was that she got a break in the middle of her shift. But Cordelia didn't care. All she could think about was what her family had gone through—all of the pain that she had brought upon them by running away—and all that she had missed while she was gone. How long had it been? How many months had she made them suffer in her absence? Could it really be almost a year? A year of hiding her past, her true identity, her intentions. Keeping everyone at an arm's length, not letting anyone in and trying desperately not to think of all the people she'd left behind.

In her attempt at starting a new life and seeking vengeance on the one person who, in her mind, was responsible for destroying all of their lives, she had done even more damage by leaving than she could ever have thought possible.

In her attempt to cut herself off from everyone and everything in Hawthorne and create this new life, she never realized all of the destruction she caused in her wake. Why would she do that to herself and her family?

"Water?" the voice called out. And then again, "Water?"

Cordelia looked up and saw her coworker holding a glass of water in front of her.

"Yes, water," Cordelia said in a daze, remembering the ritual hazing events that took place on Misery Island—Fire, Water, Air, and Earth—the degrading and painful events that forced her to leave it all behind. The pain and humiliation she endured. The betrayal. The lies.

"Thank you, Chris," she said, taking the glass from his hand, ignoring his perplexed expression.

As she gulped down the water, she allowed herself to think about what had happened that night. Since she'd moved to Maine, she had managed to put those memories aside, choosing not to think of that night, but instead to channel her anger and energy toward the man she believed was at the root of all of her suffering: Malcolm Crane.

"Uh . . . CeeCee?" Chris hesitated. "You need to lie down

or something? Do you need a break?" She could hear her female coworkers snickering behind the coffee bar. Cordelia was uncomfortable with this kind of attention. She had managed to fly under the radar for so long, she wasn't about to let anyone get too close to her. Not even a handsome and sweet college student like Chris Markson. When she looked at him and his perfectly sculpted features, all it did was make her miss Finn and his crooked smile even more. She couldn't imagine facing Finn again. For all he knew she had taken off carrying his child. He must hate her for not letting him know if he was a father or not. The truth was that even though she might have been pregnant, she couldn't even be sure that the baby was his. It could just as easily have been Trevor's. A bastard child from a bastard rapist.

"Yeah, I just need some fresh air," she managed. Standing up, she tucked the newspaper under her arm and rushed past him and out into the crisp autumn air. She walked across the street to a bench and sat for a few minutes staring at the paper folded on her lap.

*What's happening? Everything was falling into place and then that little boy came out of nowhere, and then this newspaper shows up with the article about Tess and my mother's attempt to kill herself. What have I done?* she thought miserably. She knew what Tess and her mother would say, that she should pay attention to these signs, that they were pointing her in a new direction. Maybe killing her father wasn't the answer. Maybe she had unfinished business to deal with in Hawthorne instead. True, she had been betrayed and lied to and hurt and deceived, but her family needed her. Finn and Reed needed her. Rebecca needed her. And Maddie . . . she didn't know what she felt about Maddie.

*My sister, my cousin?* she thought. It didn't matter what relationship they had—Maddie had had the chance to save her when she needed her most, and she didn't. She was too weak and scared. But Cordelia really couldn't blame her. Hawthorne and those girls were all she ever knew. She aimlessly thumbed through the pages until she noticed something fall out of the paper onto her lap.

She looked at the glossy tarot card that had fallen out of the paper. It looked brand-new, right out of the pack. Suddenly she felt like someone had known all along where she was and what she was planning. Someone was trying to scare her by letting her know that there was unfinished business. Someone was out to get her.

A man on a horse marched triumphantly over fallen bodies. He was holding a large black flag. But instead of a face, there was only a skull. And the eyes of the horse were bloodred.

It was the Death tarot card.

∞

Reed Campbell lifted the brown glass bottle to his lips, letting the liquid fill and burn the back of his throat. The cool salty air rubbed his throat raw, forcing him to indulge in his preferred medication. He caught a glimpse of himself in the glass window of his boat—the only place he felt at home these days.

He was the bastard son, all right.

While his baby brother, Trevor, had somehow become the golden child of Hawthorne, Massachusetts—the fair-haired prodigal son who could do no wrong—Reed occupied the role of town drunk, screwup, alleged murderer, and pedophile. On his sober days, he realized how the drinking was becoming a problem, which was why he'd made sure that those days were few and far between. It had already cost him his job, his dignity, and countless friends.

But thanks to Great-grandfather Campbell and the little oil company he started decades ago, Reed no longer felt the need to be gainfully employed. His bank account remained healthy thanks to the thousands of people who needed to stay warm on shivering New England nights. Reed often reminded himself of that fact on nights when he careened down to the waterfront after last call at one of the local taverns. Even though he was personally a failure and unable to support himself, the oil company that bore his family name kept everyone in town warm, and by default, lined his own deep, albeit threadbare, pockets.

He drowned out his sorrows in bottles and bars. He knew that his feelings for Cordelia and Maddie could be seen as inappropriate—that his actions could be called into question. Cordelia just blew him away with her love of literature and her free spirit. He knew that her time in Hawthorne would be short-lived, but he just couldn't understand why people would think he had anything to do with her disappearance. If anything, he was more enthralled and enchanted by her than anyone else in town. Perhaps that was his downfall.

And Maddie. Ever since she left for boarding school, he realized how deep his feelings ran for her. There were hundreds of reasons why he should stay away from her and keep her out of his mind. But he couldn't get over the way that she looked at him—like he was a knight in shining armor. She saw past all the flaws that his family and the town of Hawthorne held over him. She made him feel like a man. And even though he was in a relationship with someone new—someone his own age, someone more appropriate—he couldn't get Maddie out of his head. Which was why he kept the liquor flowing and the nights endless so he was never faced with the harsh light of the dawn.

Finnegan O'Malley didn't believe in ghosts, but he swore on his great-grandmother's grave that he saw one. And not just any ghost. Not the random specters known to wander through the historical properties he took care of, the ones who seemed to have no awareness of their ghostly state, but just continued their daily activities in the same manner that they had done centuries before. Not Deacon Knott, who was believed to still take up residence on the top floor of the Knott Cove Inn, his heavy boots famously echoing throughout the Victorian bed-and-breakfast. Curls of smoke from his pipe hovered in the air of the grand parlor, his shadow loomed over the pretty women who dared to stay overnight as guests. Some even claimed to have been pinched rather viciously in their sleep, the purplish bruising on their backsides or upper thighs the only physical proof.

No, this ghost was a familiar one to Finn, or at least, she had been in life. This was a girl who continued to haunt Finn equally in his dreaming and wakeful states. A girl whose voice still rang out as clear and lyrical as it had when she first swept into town. She was a misfit and an outsider, not unlike himself. Someone whom he'd admired and even loved (though he'd never admit it to anyone—hardly even to himself), and ultimately had lost. But Cordelia LeClaire hadn't slipped away easily. He couldn't let her go—his heart wouldn't allow for it.

He'd loved her from the first moment he'd laid eyes on her. He loved her even more when he observed her midnight swims and watched as she danced through gardens in the early morning hours. He didn't know why he felt the need to watch over her. It just came instinctually. It was like watching over a beautiful rainbow fish in a sea of sharks. He still remembered their first kiss. It was just as important—if not more—than the night that they first made love. He'd secretly watched her midnight swims with Maddie, and he knew that she would return on certain nights alone. He knew she would need protection, even if she didn't believe it herself. And knowing the rough treatment she'd received upon her arrival in town, that there would be some people who would take advantage of her solitary swims if they ever found out. Which was why he was determined to never let her out of his sight on those hot, humid nights when the ocean beckoned to her like a siren's song to a sailor.

One stifling night at the end of August, he watched from behind a rock as she dipped in and out of the ocean like a mermaid. He was afraid to take his eyes off her for fear that she'd slip beneath the water and swim away forever—taking his heart with her.

He watched as she cocked her head to the side and spun around in the water. She looked right over to where he was crouched and he slunk backward, afraid that he'd been caught as a sort of Peeping Tom.

She came right out of the water—letting the heat of the night burn the water droplets off her skin, her long red hair clinging to her wet skin—and instinctively moved over to his hiding spot.

Before he could come up with a plausible excuse, she smiled widely and put her hand on his cheek.

"My own personal bodyguard," she said brightly. "My valiant knight, I know that you've been keeping watch over me. I can feel your eyes on me."

He stuttered, trying to come up with an explanation. Wanting her to believe that he wasn't some kind of a stalker. Before he could say anything more, she quieted him with a kiss. At first it was tentative and sweet. And then he reciprocated with a longer kiss, embracing her and not minding that her wet body was soaking his clothes. It was a kiss that he'd remember until his dying day.

He knew her intimately and he knew her secrets. He'd

once heard his grandfather say that if two people shared a secret—one that nobody else knew about—it bound them together until the secret was finally revealed. He swore on his life that he'd never reveal it, not when she went missing, and not even when he'd been suspected of being involved in her vanishing. He gave his word—and his heart—to Cordelia.

And now, with no warning, in the bright light of day, he saw her. She'd come back to him. It was only for a moment and could be blamed on the dehydrated and overtired state he was in after doing the landscaping in the Old Town Hall's courtyard. He knew it was Cordelia because he caught her familiar scent of apples and lavender. He knew it was her from the look in her eyes. It was the same look he saw in her pale, watery blue eyes that she had the last time he saw her. Those eyes were forever etched in his memory. They were wide-set, haunted, shimmering, and most memorably, they were filled with fear.

ॐ

Kate Endicott didn't believe in coincidences.

She was not superstitious, and wasn't really concerned with improving her luck, which was why Kate still wasn't sure what had compelled to her ask her mother, Kiki, to bring in a feng shui expert to enhance the flow of their house, and ultimately, their lives.

Maybe it was due to the Ravenswood debacle. The fact that Finn had royally screwed over Kiki Endicott's plans to turn Ravenswood Asylum into the luxury hotel, the Endicott. Well, it wasn't just him; it was that entire historical society.

Whatever.

They had screwed everything up big time and now millions of dollars were at stake. Investors were getting angry.

And Kate saw the look of pity in her friends' eyes. Nobody pitied Kate Endicott. No one!

Kate and her mother were always on top of new trends. Always the first in line for the new yoga club or Pilates classes that had sprung up around Hawthorne. And when the topic of feng shui cluttered the pages of Kate's favorite magazines and lifestyle journals, she knew that she would have to improve her family's chi by renovating their house.

Perhaps she was just restless.

She could feel the change in the tide that was upsetting the smooth sailing of her life. Something had floated into the harbor of her perfect life and was threatening to capsize her carefully guarded vessel. Kate Endicott wouldn't let that happen; she refused to go down with the sinking ship. That was something that Kiki had taught her long ago, and she wasn't about to let it happen to them now. Not now, not ever.

∞

Abigail Crane pinned her hair up carefully as she looked at her reflection in the low light of her bedroom. She tried wrapping her mind around what the doctors had told her—chemo was the only course of action to stop the spread of cancer in her body. Toxins placed in her body to seek out and destroy other deadly toxins. It was like sending in a black widow spider to take care of a venomous snake. The goal was for them to destroy each other—her body would end up as the ravaged battlefield.

She had just placed the call to Maddie at Stanton, asking her to come back to Hawthorne for winter break. It wasn't too much for a mother to ask of her own daughter, but there were plenty of reasons that Maddie would want to refuse. True, most children would want to take care of their sick mothers, but most children hadn't been betrayed in the same way that

Abigail had betrayed Maddie. She realized that not telling Maddie the truth about Cordelia—that they weren't cousins, but really half sisters—was the wrong thing to do, but she couldn't take it back now. What else could she do to make it up to her? When Maddie left Hawthorne, she left with her own baggage—guilt about her treatment of Cordelia and over Rebecca's mental state that had nothing to do with Abigail. She had her own demons to fight.

Abigail had been visiting Rebecca for months—trying to make up for own failings—for causing Cordelia to run away, for not telling Rebecca about their confrontation. If she'd told the truth sooner, perhaps that night at Ravenswood and Rebecca's attempted suicide could have been avoided. She had her own ghosts to put to rest. But she needed her daughter now; perhaps tough times would help to mend their broken family. She didn't think her request of Maddie was too much to ask.

But the horrified reaction from Maddie made her think otherwise. Madeline had made it clear that she didn't want to return to Hawthorne until she had successfully tracked down Cordelia—a means of assuaging her own guilt. But it was too late for that. Abigail's cancer wouldn't wait for a flighty teenager who could be anywhere in the country to be tracked down. She had made her amends with Rebecca—or was at least trying to. Now it was Maddie's turn to come home and put things to rest. No matter how painful or uncomfortable it would be—for all of them.